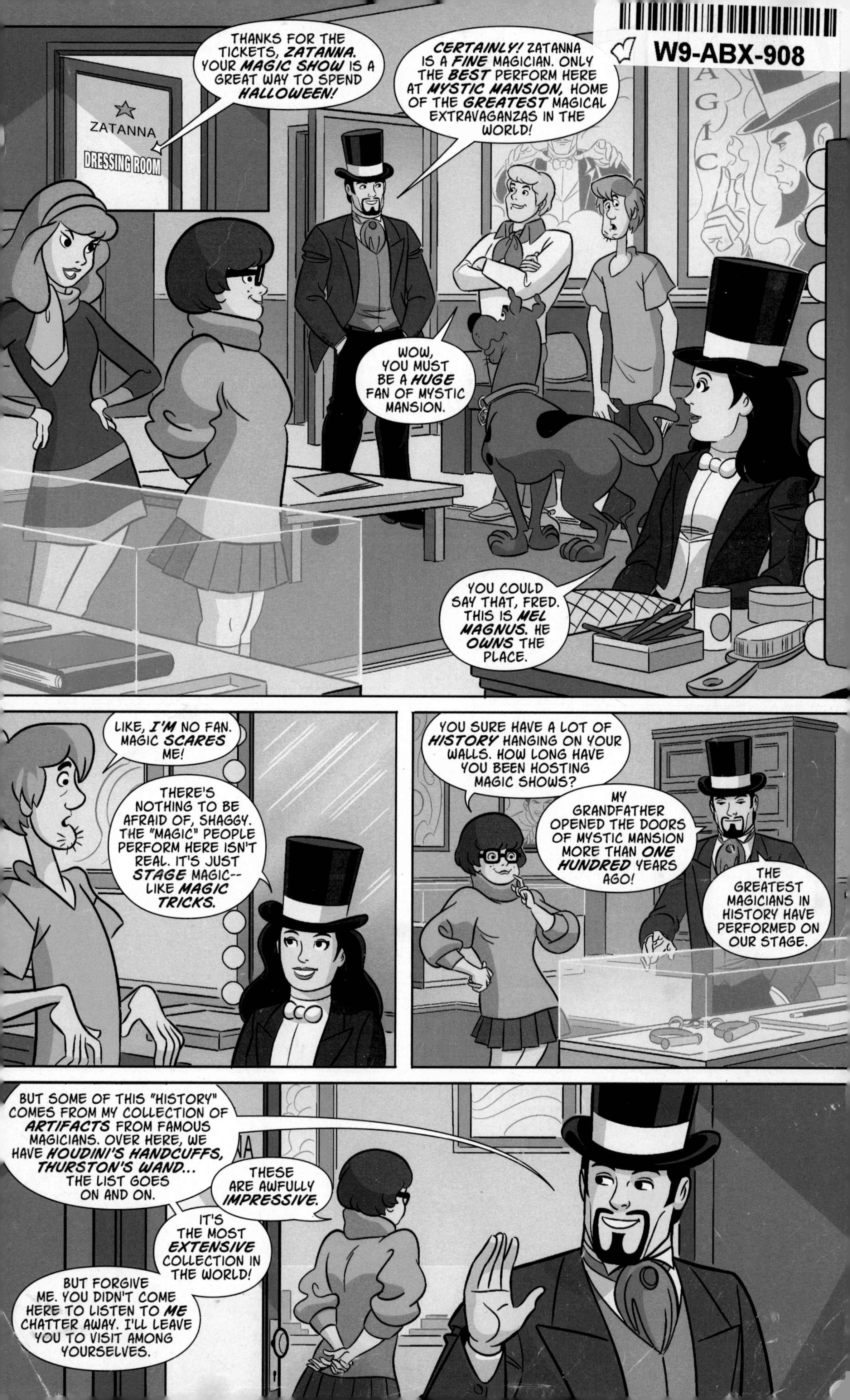
ZATANNA
DRESSING ROOM
THANKS FOR THE TICKETS, ZATANNA. YOUR MAGIC SHOW IS A GREAT WAY TO SPEND HALLOWEEN!
CERTAINLY! ZATANNA IS A FINE MAGICIAN. ONLY THE BEST PERFORM HERE AT MYSTIC MANSION, HOME OF THE GREATEST MAGICAL EXTRAVAGANZAS IN THE WORLD!
WOW, YOU MUST BE A HUGE FAN OF MYSTIC MANSION.
YOU COULD SAY THAT, FRED. THIS IS MEL MAGNUS. HE OWNS THE PLACE.
LIKE, I'M NO FAN. MAGIC SCARES ME!
THERE'S NOTHING TO BE AFRAID OF, SHAGGY. THE "MAGIC" PEOPLE PERFORM HERE ISN'T REAL. IT'S JUST STAGE MAGIC-- LIKE MAGIC TRICKS.
YOU SURE HAVE A LOT OF HISTORY HANGING ON YOUR WALLS. HOW LONG HAVE YOU BEEN HOSTING MAGIC SHOWS?
MY GRANDFATHER OPENED THE DOORS OF MYSTIC MANSION MORE THAN ONE HUNDRED YEARS AGO!
THE GREATEST MAGICIANS IN HISTORY HAVE PERFORMED ON OUR STAGE.
BUT SOME OF THIS "HISTORY" COMES FROM MY COLLECTION OF ARTIFACTS FROM FAMOUS MAGICIANS. OVER HERE, WE HAVE HOUDINI'S HANDCUFFS, THURSTON'S WAND... THE LIST GOES ON AND ON.
THESE ARE AWFULLY IMPRESSIVE.
IT'S THE MOST EXTENSIVE COLLECTION IN THE WORLD!
BUT FORGIVE ME. YOU DIDN'T COME HERE TO LISTEN TO ME CHATTER AWAY. I'LL LEAVE YOU TO VISIT AMONG YOURSELVES.

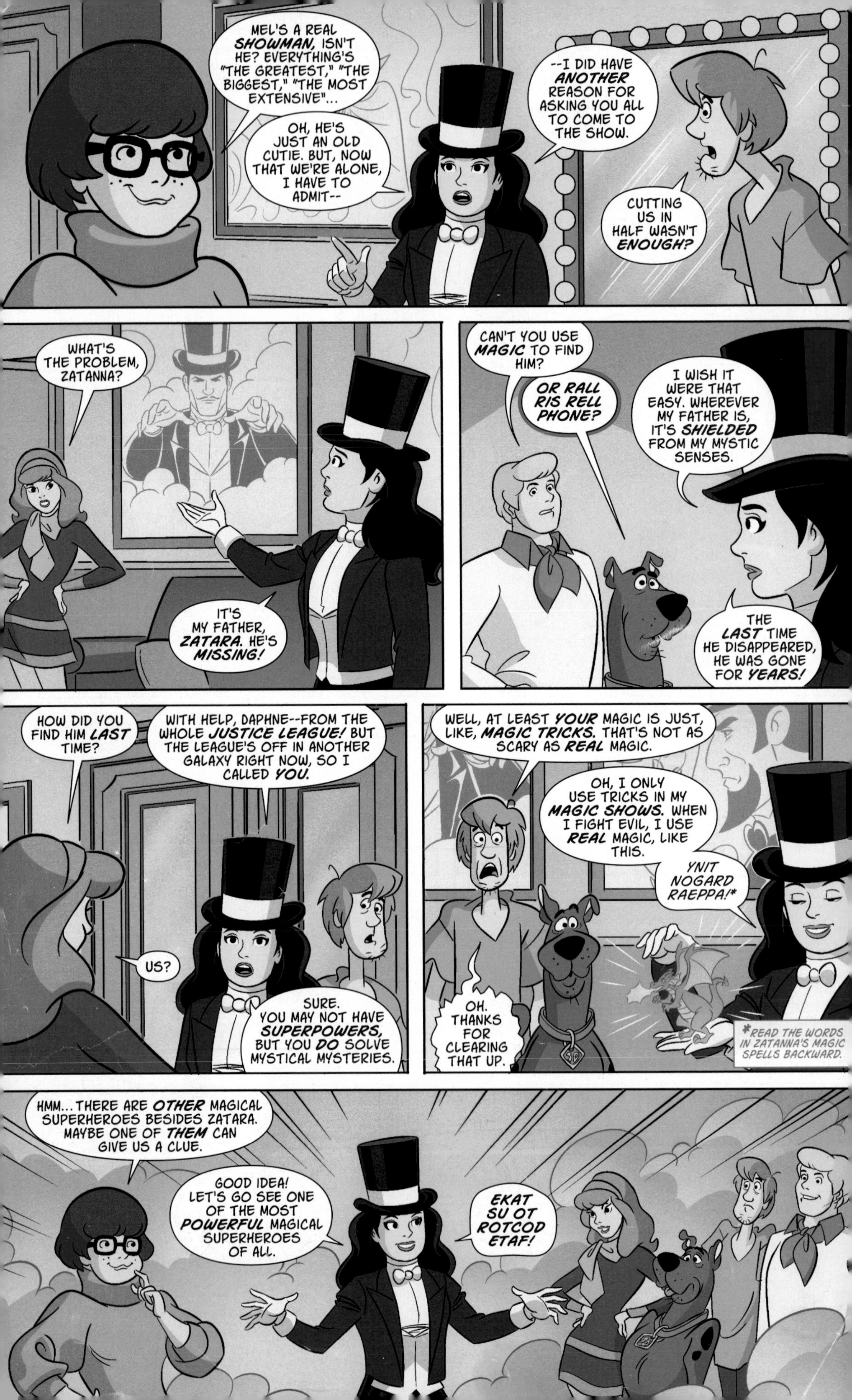
MEL'S A REAL SHOWMAN, ISN'T HE? EVERYTHING'S "THE GREATEST," "THE BIGGEST," "THE MOST EXTENSIVE"...
OH, HE'S JUST AN OLD CUTIE. BUT, NOW THAT WE'RE ALONE, I HAVE TO ADMIT--
--I DID HAVE ANOTHER REASON FOR ASKING YOU ALL TO COME TO THE SHOW.
CUTTING US IN HALF WASN'T ENOUGH?
WHAT'S THE PROBLEM, ZATANNA?
IT'S MY FATHER, ZATARA. HE'S MISSING!
CAN'T YOU USE MAGIC TO FIND HIM?
OR RALL RIS RELL PHONE?
I WISH IT WERE THAT EASY. WHEREVER MY FATHER IS, IT'S SHIELDED FROM MY MYSTIC SENSES.
THE LAST TIME HE DISAPPEARED, HE WAS GONE FOR YEARS!
HOW DID YOU FIND HIM LAST TIME?
WITH HELP, DAPHNE--FROM THE WHOLE JUSTICE LEAGUE! BUT THE LEAGUE'S OFF IN ANOTHER GALAXY RIGHT NOW, SO I CALLED YOU.
US?
SURE. YOU MAY NOT HAVE SUPERPOWERS, BUT YOU DO SOLVE MYSTICAL MYSTERIES.
WELL, AT LEAST YOUR MAGIC IS JUST, LIKE, MAGIC TRICKS. THAT'S NOT AS SCARY AS REAL MAGIC.
OH, I ONLY USE TRICKS IN MY MAGIC SHOWS. WHEN I FIGHT EVIL, I USE REAL MAGIC, LIKE THIS.
YNIT NOGARD RAEPPA!*
OH. THANKS FOR CLEARING THAT UP.
*READ THE WORDS IN ZATANNA'S MAGIC SPELLS BACKWARD.
HMM... THERE ARE OTHER MAGICAL SUPERHEROES BESIDES ZATARA. MAYBE ONE OF THEM CAN GIVE US A CLUE.
GOOD IDEA! LET'S GO SEE ONE OF THE MOST POWERFUL MAGICAL SUPERHEROES OF ALL.
EKAT SU OT ROTCOD ETAF!

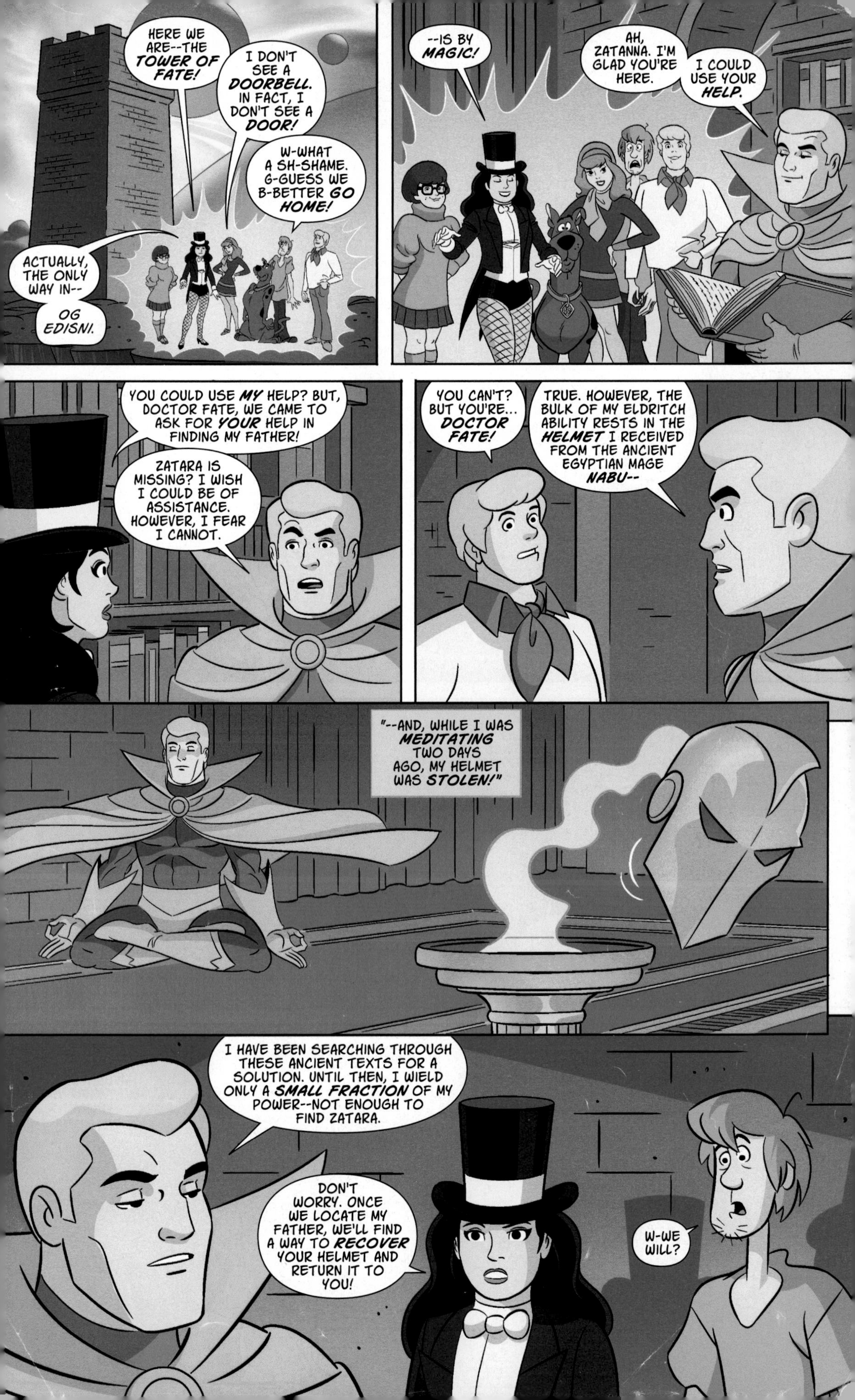
HERE WE ARE--THE TOWER OF FATE!
I DON'T SEE A DOORBELL. IN FACT, I DON'T SEE A DOOR!
W-WHAT A SH-SHAME. G-GUESS WE B-BETTER GO HOME!
ACTUALLY, THE ONLY WAY IN--
OG EDISNI.
--IS BY MAGIC!
AH, ZATANNA. I'M GLAD YOU'RE HERE.
I COULD USE YOUR HELP.
YOU COULD USE MY HELP? BUT, DOCTOR FATE, WE CAME TO ASK FOR YOUR HELP IN FINDING MY FATHER!
ZATARA IS MISSING? I WISH I COULD BE OF ASSISTANCE. HOWEVER, I FEAR I CANNOT.
YOU CAN'T? BUT YOU'RE... DOCTOR FATE!
TRUE. HOWEVER, THE BULK OF MY ELDRITCH ABILITY RESTS IN THE HELMET I RECEIVED FROM THE ANCIENT EGYPTIAN MAGE NABU--
"--AND, WHILE I WAS MEDITATING TWO DAYS AGO, MY HELMET WAS STOLEN!"
I HAVE BEEN SEARCHING THROUGH THESE ANCIENT TEXTS FOR A SOLUTION. UNTIL THEN, I WIELD ONLY A SMALL FRACTION OF MY POWER--NOT ENOUGH TO FIND ZATARA.
DON'T WORRY. ONCE WE LOCATE MY FATHER, WE'LL FIND A WAY TO RECOVER YOUR HELMET AND RETURN IT TO YOU!
W-WE WILL?

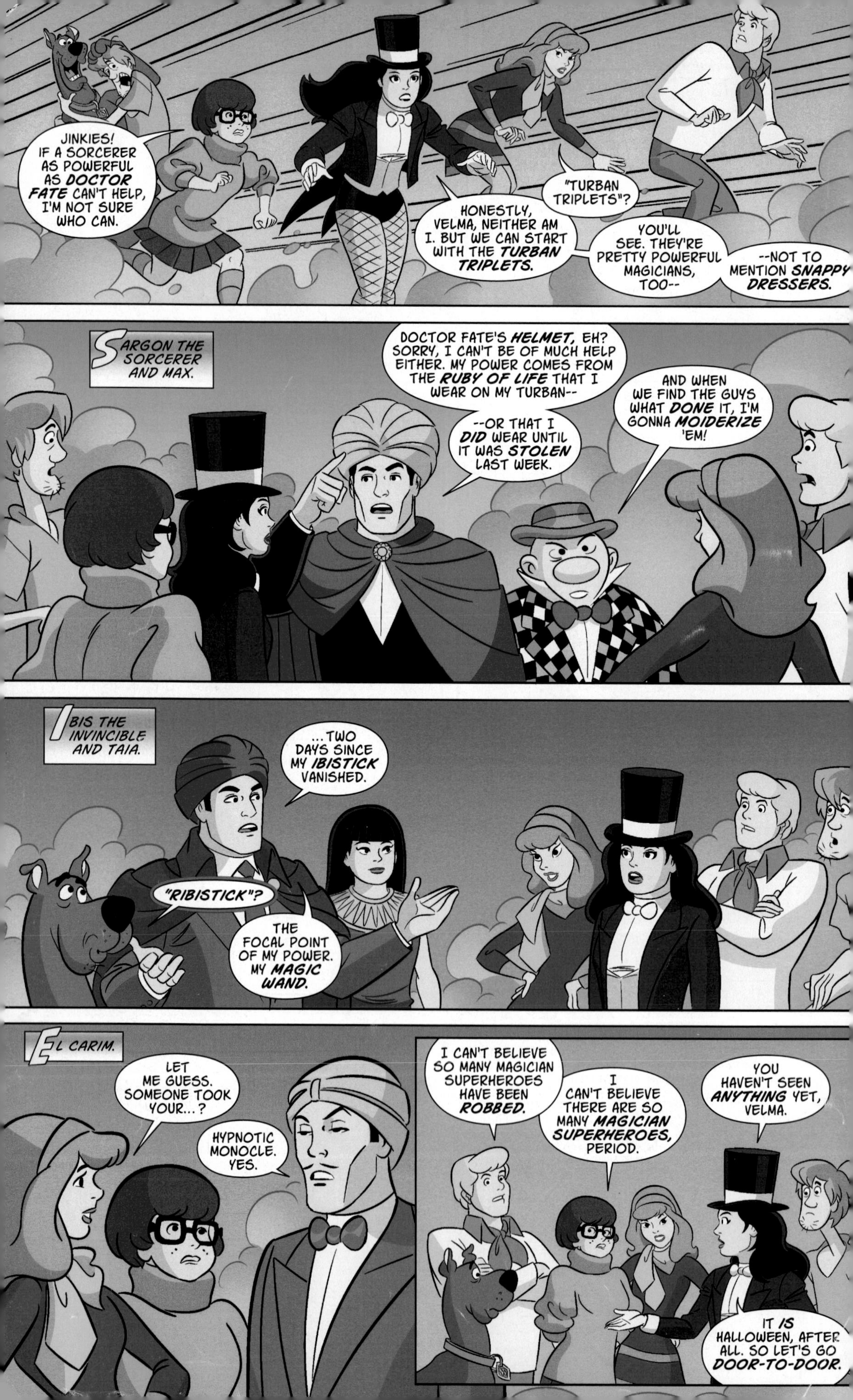
JINKIES! IF A SORCERER AS POWERFUL AS DOCTOR FATE CAN'T HELP, I'M NOT SURE WHO CAN.
HONESTLY, VELMA, NEITHER AM I. BUT WE CAN START WITH THE TURBAN TRIPLETS.
"TURBAN TRIPLETS"?
YOU'LL SEE. THEY'RE PRETTY POWERFUL MAGICIANS, TOO--
--NOT TO MENTION SNAPPY DRESSERS.
SARGON THE SORCERER AND MAX.
DOCTOR FATE'S HELMET, EH? SORRY, I CAN'T BE OF MUCH HELP EITHER. MY POWER COMES FROM THE RUBY OF LIFE THAT I WEAR ON MY TURBAN--
--OR THAT I DID WEAR UNTIL IT WAS STOLEN LAST WEEK.
AND WHEN WE FIND THE GUYS WHAT DONE IT, I'M GONNA MOIDERIZE 'EM!
IBIS THE INVINCIBLE AND TAIA.
...TWO DAYS SINCE MY IBISTICK VANISHED.
"RIBISTICK"?
THE FOCAL POINT OF MY POWER. MY MAGIC WAND.
EL CARIM.
LET ME GUESS. SOMEONE TOOK YOUR...?
HYPNOTIC MONOCLE. YES.
I CAN'T BELIEVE SO MANY MAGICIAN SUPERHEROES HAVE BEEN ROBBED.
I CAN'T BELIEVE THERE ARE SO MANY MAGICIAN SUPERHEROES, PERIOD.
YOU HAVEN'T SEEN ANYTHING YET, VELMA.
IT IS HALLOWEEN, AFTER ALL. SO LET'S GO DOOR-TO-DOOR.

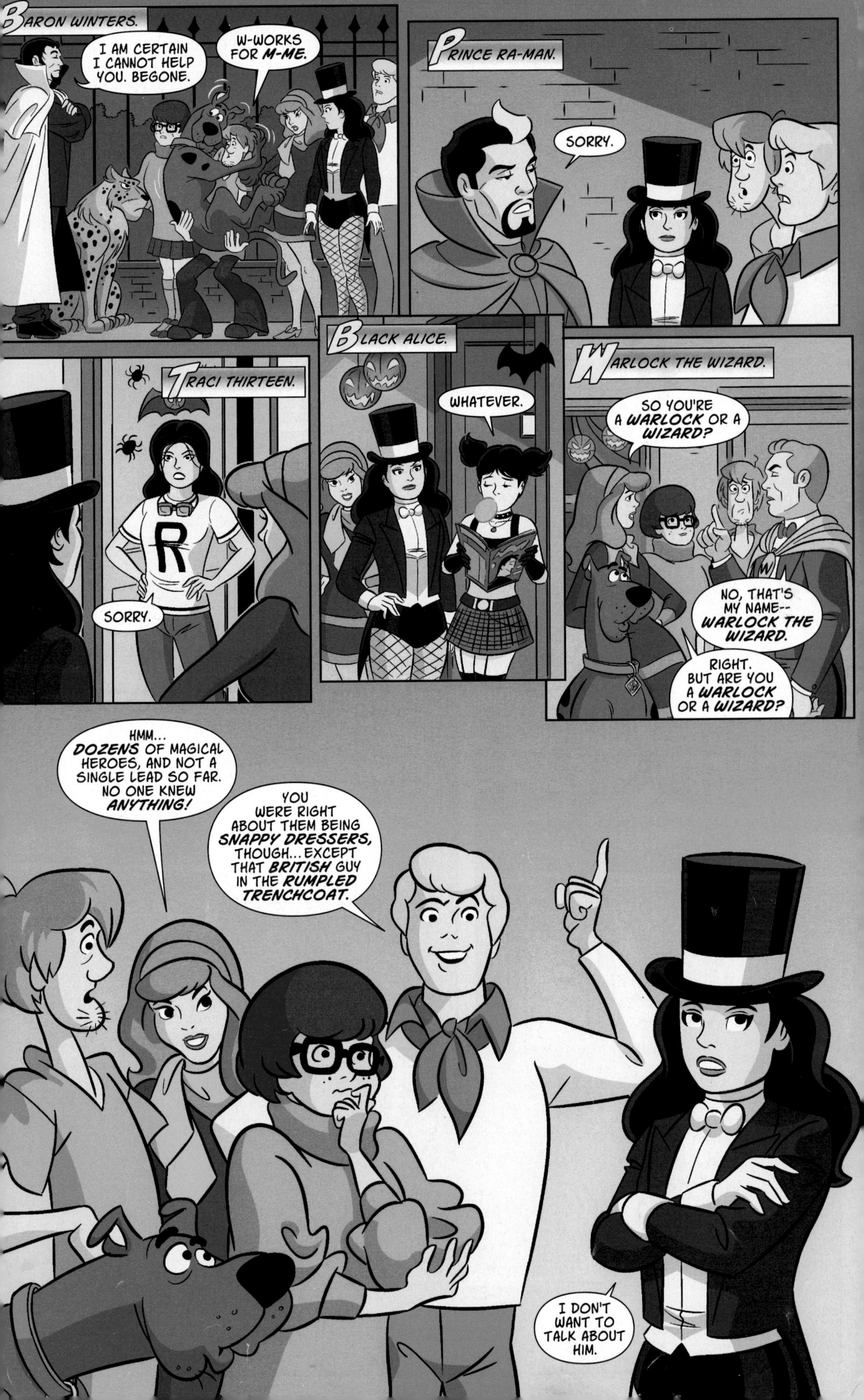
BARON WINTERS.
I AM CERTAIN I CANNOT HELP YOU. BEGONE.
W-WORKS FOR M-ME.
PRINCE RA-MAN.
SORRY.
TRACI THIRTEEN.
SORRY.
BLACK ALICE.
WHATEVER.
WARLOCK THE WIZARD.
SO YOU'RE A WARLOCK OR A WIZARD?
NO, THAT'S MY NAME-- WARLOCK THE WIZARD.
RIGHT. BUT ARE YOU A WARLOCK OR A WIZARD?
HMM... DOZENS OF MAGICAL HEROES, AND NOT A SINGLE LEAD SO FAR. NO ONE KNEW ANYTHING!
YOU WERE RIGHT ABOUT THEM BEING SNAPPY DRESSERS, THOUGH... EXCEPT THAT BRITISH GUY IN THE RUMPLED TRENCHCOAT.
I DON'T WANT TO TALK ABOUT HIM.

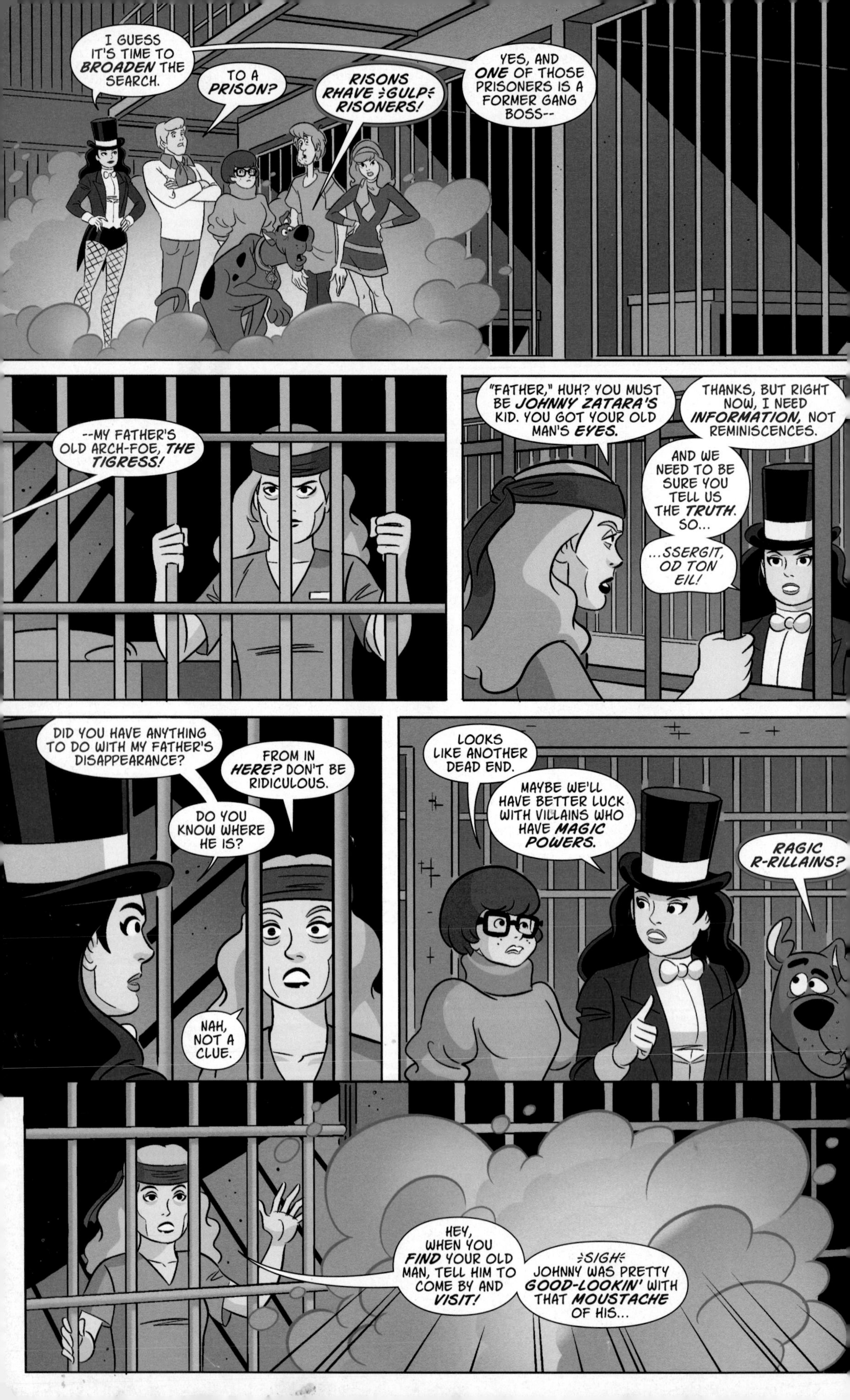
I GUESS IT'S TIME TO BROADEN THE SEARCH.
TO A PRISON?
RISONS RHAVE ⁑GULP⁑ RISONERS!
YES, AND ONE OF THOSE PRISONERS IS A FORMER GANG BOSS--
--MY FATHER'S OLD ARCH-FOE, THE TIGRESS!
"FATHER," HUH? YOU MUST BE JOHNNY ZATARA'S KID. YOU GOT YOUR OLD MAN'S EYES.
THANKS, BUT RIGHT NOW, I NEED INFORMATION, NOT REMINISCENCES.
AND WE NEED TO BE SURE YOU TELL US THE TRUTH. SO...
...SSERGIT, OD TON EIL!
DID YOU HAVE ANYTHING TO DO WITH MY FATHER'S DISAPPEARANCE?
FROM IN HERE? DON'T BE RIDICULOUS.
DO YOU KNOW WHERE HE IS?
NAH, NOT A CLUE.
LOOKS LIKE ANOTHER DEAD END.
MAYBE WE'LL HAVE BETTER LUCK WITH VILLAINS WHO HAVE MAGIC POWERS.
RAGIC R-RILLAINS?
HEY, WHEN YOU FIND YOUR OLD MAN, TELL HIM TO COME BY AND VISIT!
⁑SIGH⁑ JOHNNY WAS PRETTY GOOD-LOOKIN' WITH THAT MOUSTACHE OF HIS...

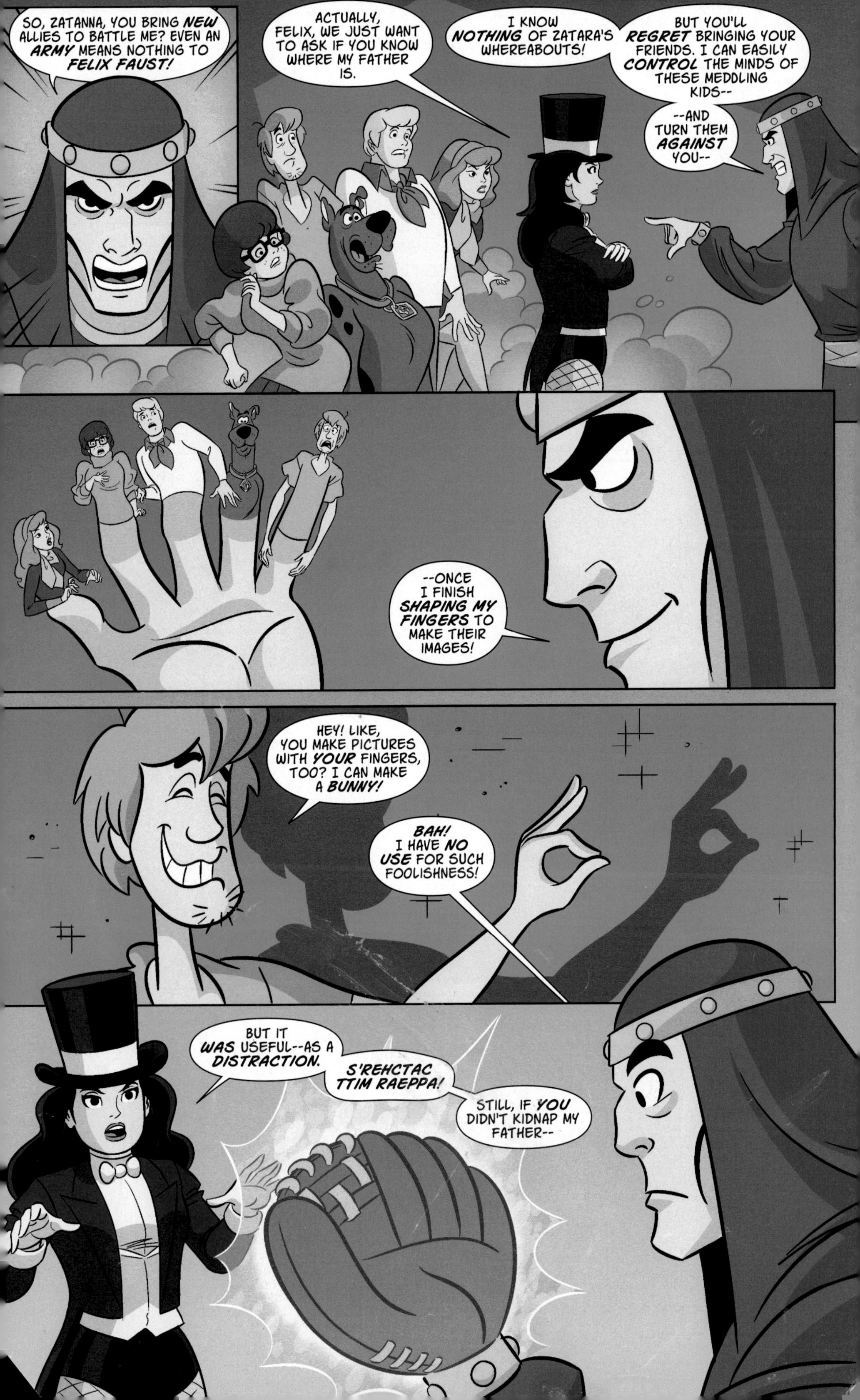

SO, ZATANNA, YOU BRING NEW ALLIES TO BATTLE ME? EVEN AN ARMY MEANS NOTHING TO FELIX FAUST!
ACTUALLY, FELIX, WE JUST WANT TO ASK IF YOU KNOW WHERE MY FATHER IS.
I KNOW NOTHING OF ZATARA'S WHEREABOUTS!
BUT YOU'LL REGRET BRINGING YOUR FRIENDS. I CAN EASILY CONTROL THE MINDS OF THESE MEDDLING KIDS--
--AND TURN THEM AGAINST YOU--
--ONCE I FINISH SHAPING MY FINGERS TO MAKE THEIR IMAGES!
HEY! LIKE, YOU MAKE PICTURES WITH YOUR FINGERS, TOO? I CAN MAKE A BUNNY!
BAH! I HAVE NO USE FOR SUCH FOOLISHNESS!
BUT IT WAS USEFUL--AS A DISTRACTION.
S'REHCTAC TTIM RAEPPA!
STILL, IF YOU DIDN'T KIDNAP MY FATHER--

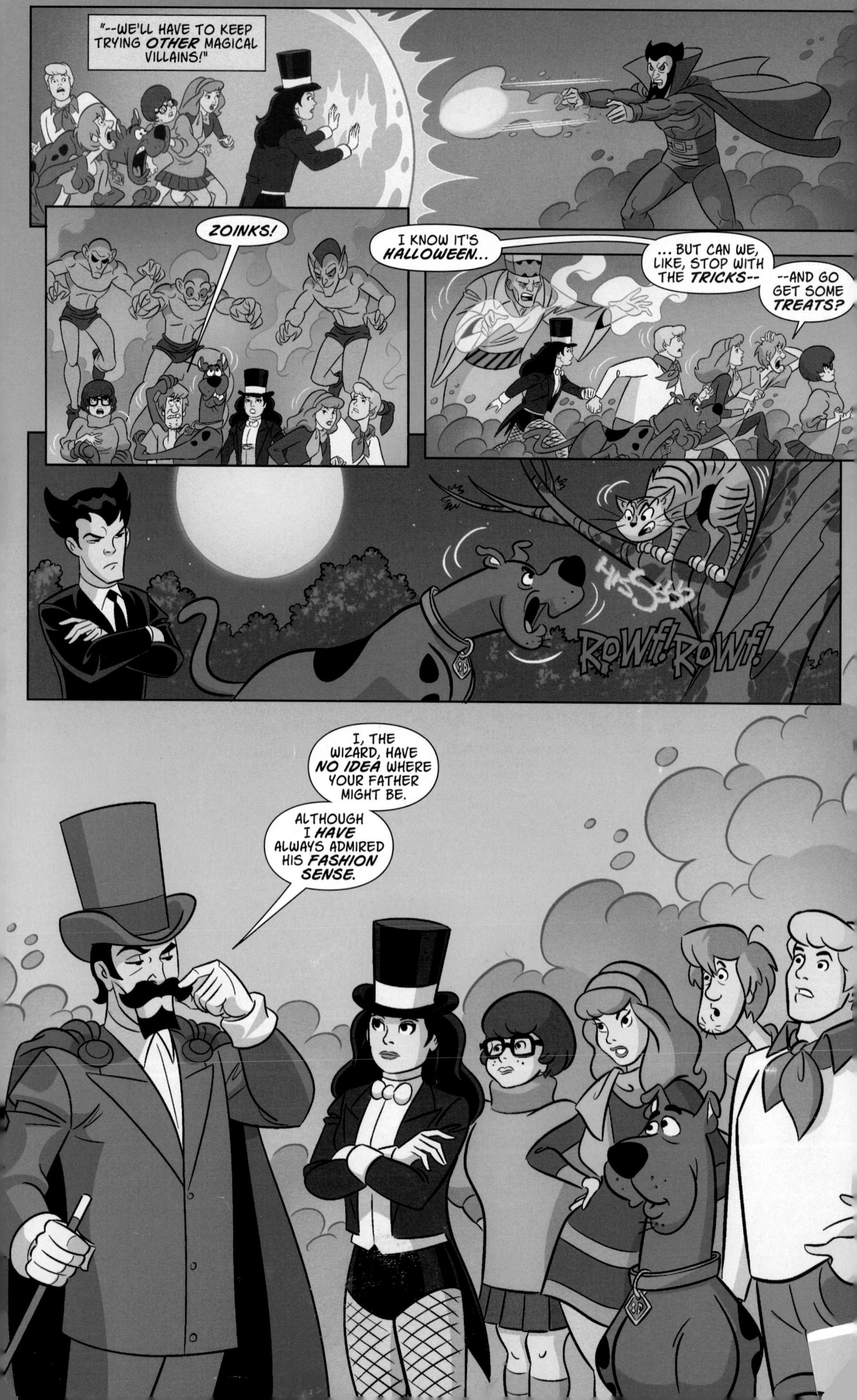

"--WE'LL HAVE TO KEEP TRYING *OTHER* MAGICAL VILLAINS!"
ZOINKS!
I KNOW IT'S *HALLOWEEN*...
... BUT CAN WE, LIKE, STOP WITH THE *TRICKS*--
--AND GO GET SOME *TREATS?*
HISSSSS
ROWF! ROWF!
I, THE WIZARD, HAVE *NO IDEA* WHERE YOUR FATHER MIGHT BE.
ALTHOUGH I *HAVE* ALWAYS ADMIRED HIS *FASHION SENSE*.

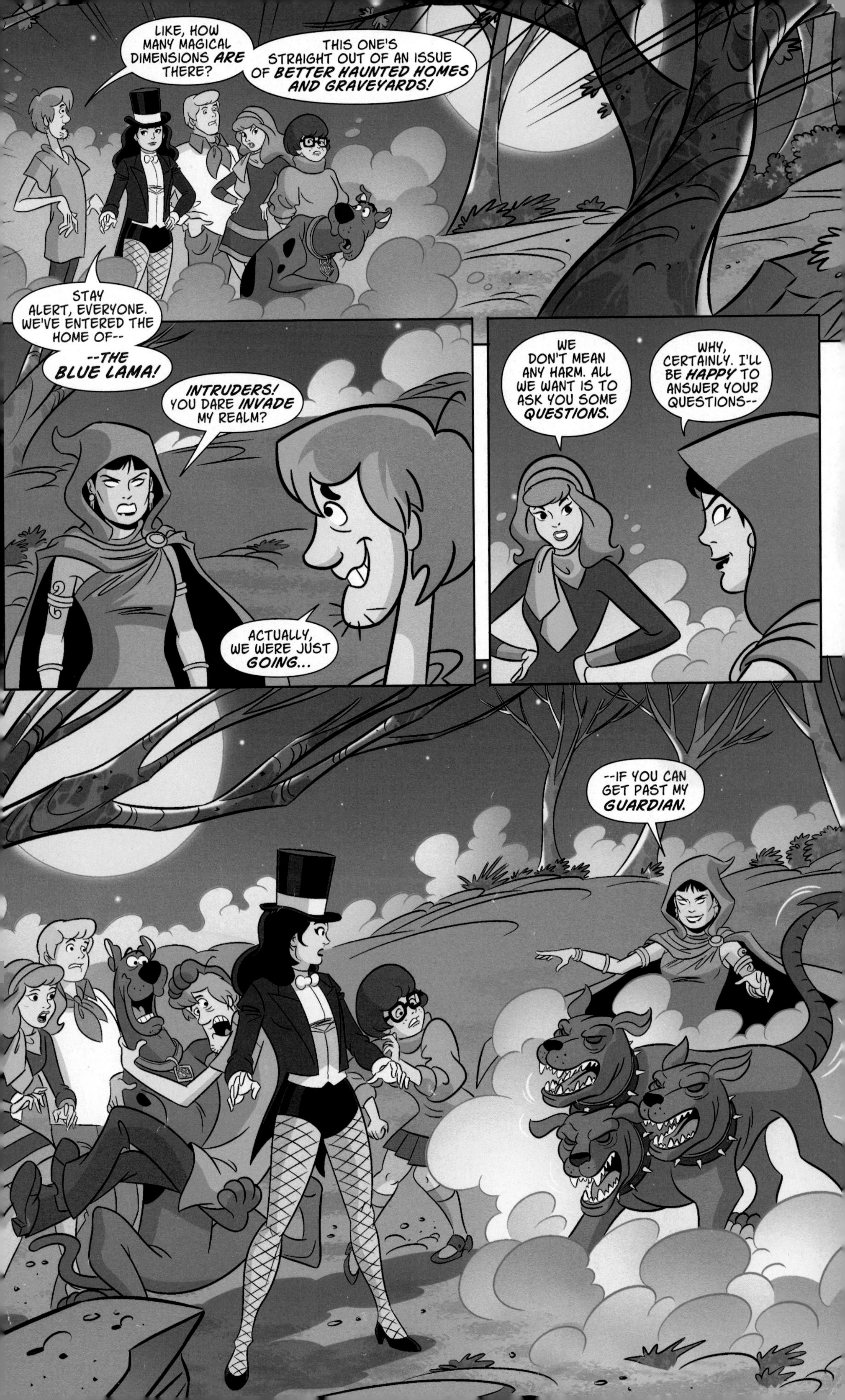
LIKE, HOW MANY MAGICAL DIMENSIONS *ARE* THERE?
THIS ONE'S STRAIGHT OUT OF AN ISSUE OF ***BETTER HAUNTED HOMES AND GRAVEYARDS!***
STAY ALERT, EVERYONE. WE'VE ENTERED THE HOME OF--
--THE BLUE LAMA!
INTRUDERS! YOU DARE ***INVADE*** MY REALM?
ACTUALLY, WE WERE JUST ***GOING...***
WE DON'T MEAN ANY HARM. ALL WE WANT IS TO ASK YOU SOME ***QUESTIONS.***
WHY, CERTAINLY. I'LL BE ***HAPPY*** TO ANSWER YOUR QUESTIONS--
--IF YOU CAN GET PAST MY ***GUARDIAN.***

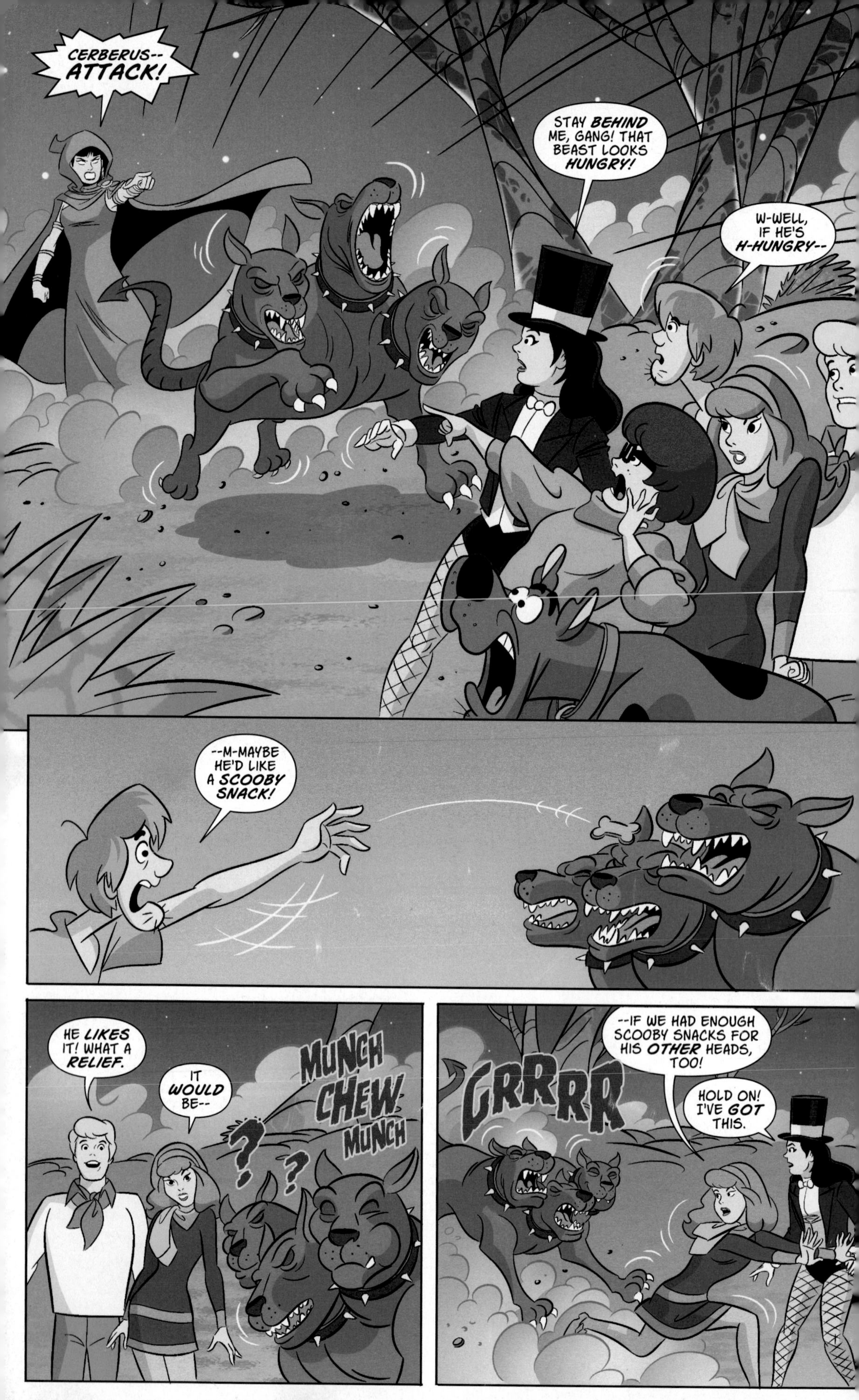
CERBERUS-- ATTACK!
STAY BEHIND ME, GANG! THAT BEAST LOOKS HUNGRY!
W-WELL, IF HE'S H-HUNGRY--
--M-MAYBE HE'D LIKE A SCOOBY SNACK!
HE LIKES IT! WHAT A RELIEF.
IT WOULD BE--
MUNCH
CHEW
MUNCH
??
--IF WE HAD ENOUGH SCOOBY SNACKS FOR HIS OTHER HEADS, TOO!
GRRRR
HOLD ON! I'VE GOT THIS.

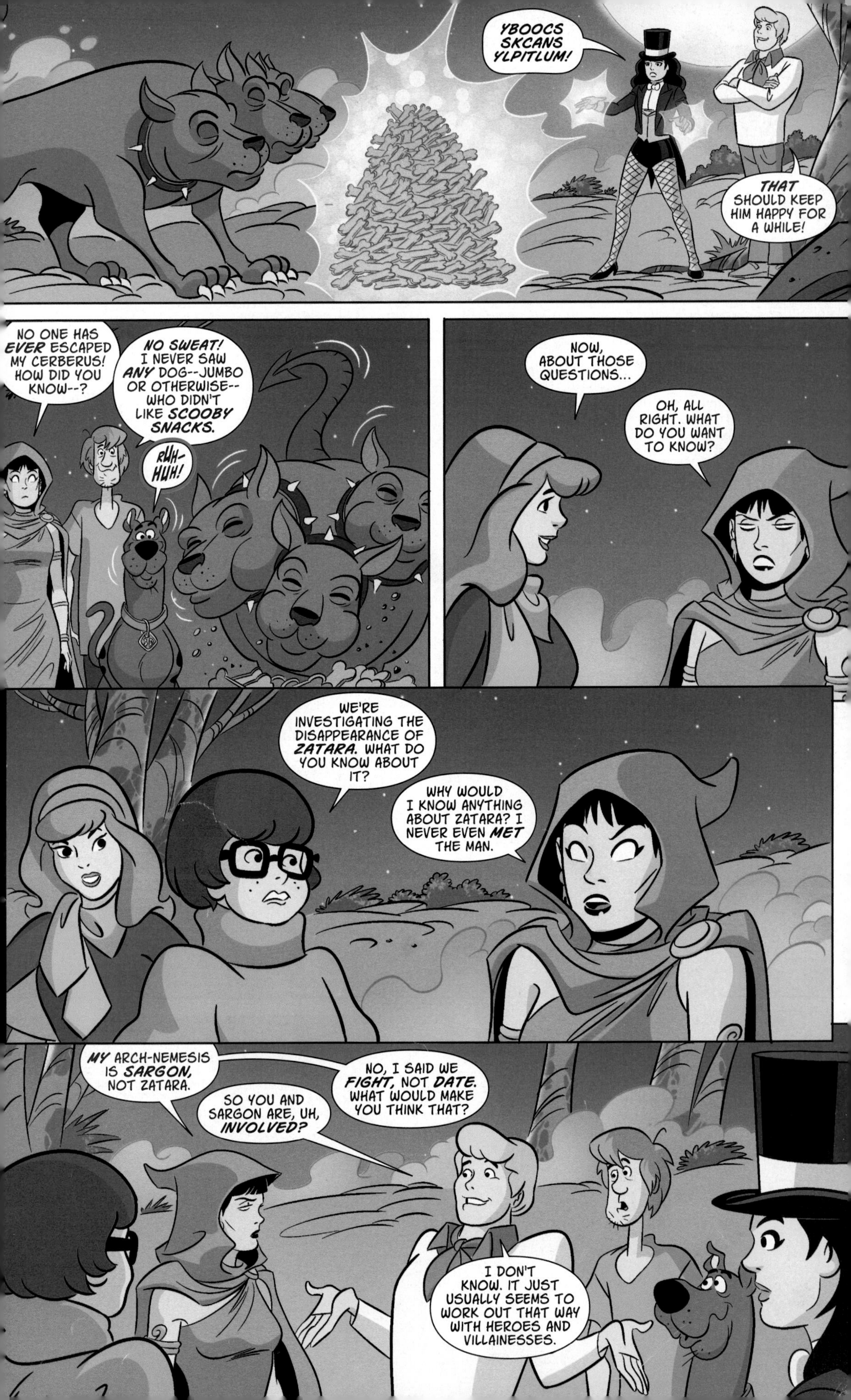
YBOOCS SKCANS YLPITLUM!
THAT SHOULD KEEP HIM HAPPY FOR A WHILE!
NO ONE HAS EVER ESCAPED MY CERBERUS! HOW DID YOU KNOW--?
NO SWEAT! I NEVER SAW ANY DOG--JUMBO OR OTHERWISE--WHO DIDN'T LIKE SCOOBY SNACKS.
RUH-HUH!
NOW, ABOUT THOSE QUESTIONS...
OH, ALL RIGHT. WHAT DO YOU WANT TO KNOW?
WE'RE INVESTIGATING THE DISAPPEARANCE OF ZATARA. WHAT DO YOU KNOW ABOUT IT?
WHY WOULD I KNOW ANYTHING ABOUT ZATARA? I NEVER EVEN MET THE MAN.
MY ARCH-NEMESIS IS SARGON, NOT ZATARA.
SO YOU AND SARGON ARE, UH, INVOLVED?
NO, I SAID WE FIGHT, NOT DATE. WHAT WOULD MAKE YOU THINK THAT?
I DON'T KNOW. IT JUST USUALLY SEEMS TO WORK OUT THAT WAY WITH HEROES AND VILLAINESSES.

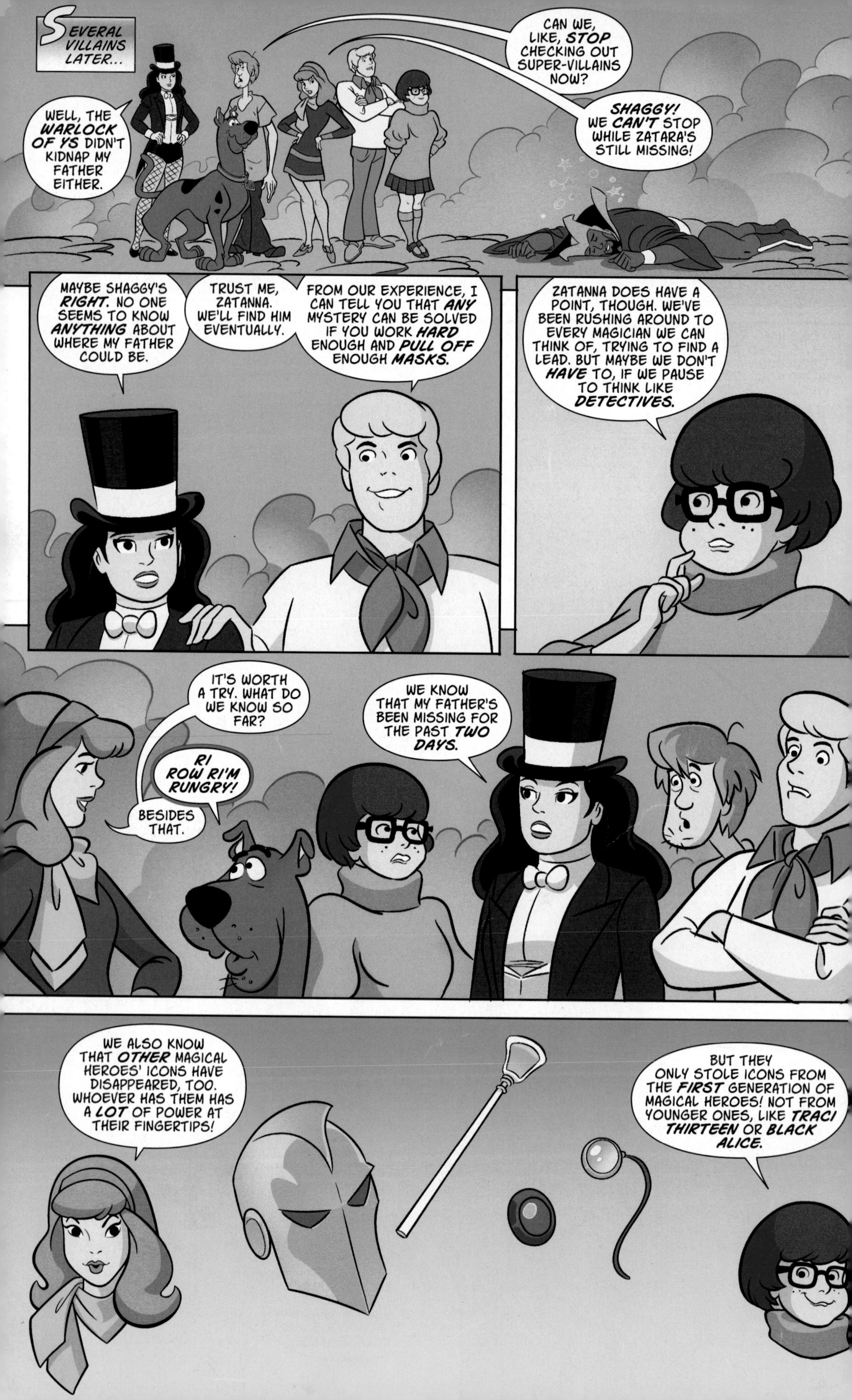
SEVERAL VILLAINS LATER...
CAN WE, LIKE, STOP CHECKING OUT SUPER-VILLAINS NOW?
WELL, THE WARLOCK OF YS DIDN'T KIDNAP MY FATHER EITHER.
SHAGGY! WE CAN'T STOP WHILE ZATARA'S STILL MISSING!
MAYBE SHAGGY'S RIGHT. NO ONE SEEMS TO KNOW ANYTHING ABOUT WHERE MY FATHER COULD BE.
TRUST ME, ZATANNA. WE'LL FIND HIM EVENTUALLY.
FROM OUR EXPERIENCE, I CAN TELL YOU THAT ANY MYSTERY CAN BE SOLVED IF YOU WORK HARD ENOUGH AND PULL OFF ENOUGH MASKS.
ZATANNA DOES HAVE A POINT, THOUGH. WE'VE BEEN RUSHING AROUND TO EVERY MAGICIAN WE CAN THINK OF, TRYING TO FIND A LEAD. BUT MAYBE WE DON'T HAVE TO, IF WE PAUSE TO THINK LIKE DETECTIVES.
IT'S WORTH A TRY. WHAT DO WE KNOW SO FAR?
RI ROW RI'M RUNGRY!
BESIDES THAT.
WE KNOW THAT MY FATHER'S BEEN MISSING FOR THE PAST TWO DAYS.
WE ALSO KNOW THAT OTHER MAGICAL HEROES' ICONS HAVE DISAPPEARED, TOO. WHOEVER HAS THEM HAS A LOT OF POWER AT THEIR FINGERTIPS!
BUT THEY ONLY STOLE ICONS FROM THE FIRST GENERATION OF MAGICAL HEROES! NOT FROM YOUNGER ONES, LIKE TRACI THIRTEEN OR BLACK ALICE.

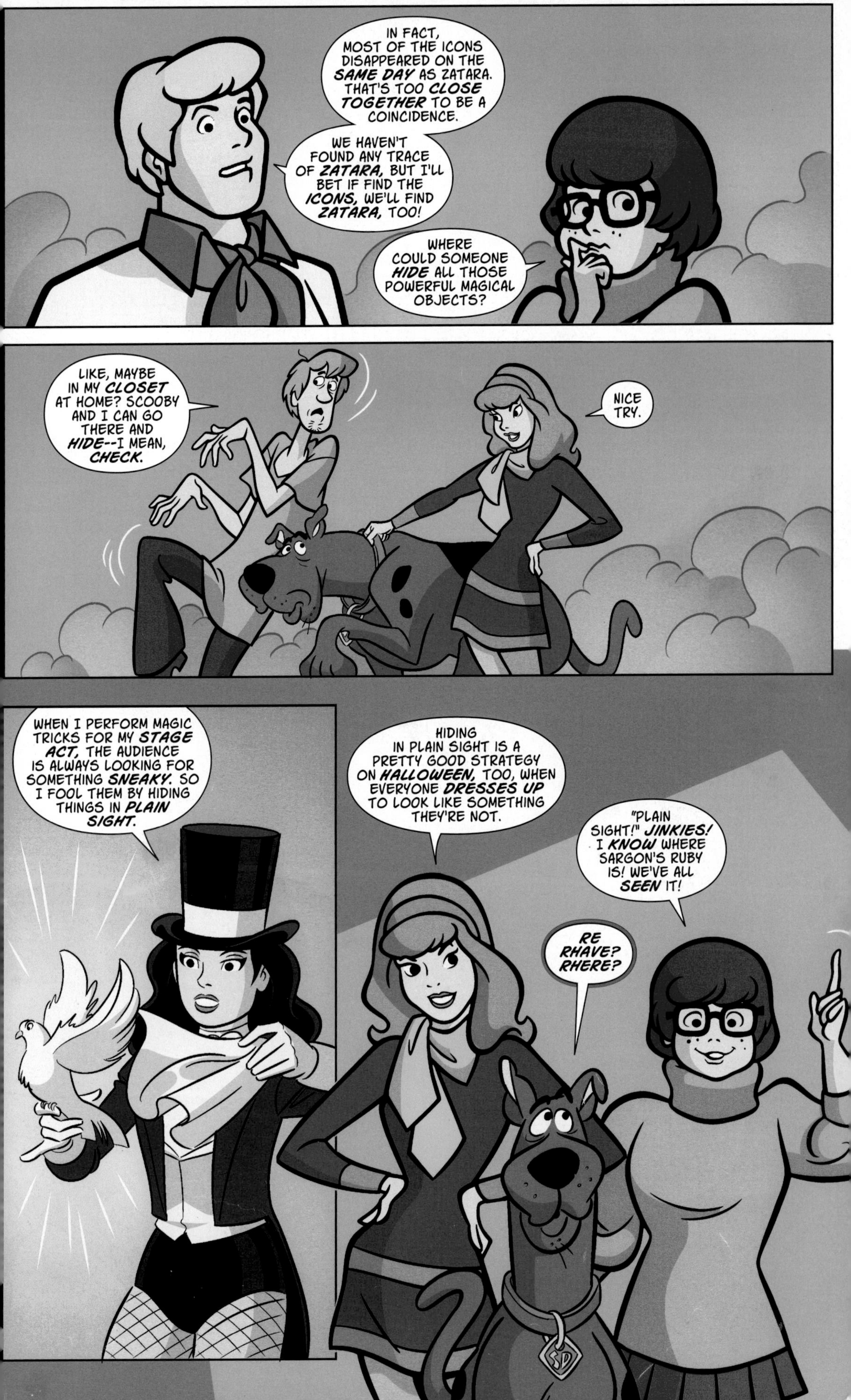
IN FACT, MOST OF THE ICONS DISAPPEARED ON THE SAME DAY AS ZATARA. THAT'S TOO CLOSE TOGETHER TO BE A COINCIDENCE.
WE HAVEN'T FOUND ANY TRACE OF ZATARA, BUT I'LL BET IF FIND THE ICONS, WE'LL FIND ZATARA, TOO!
WHERE COULD SOMEONE HIDE ALL THOSE POWERFUL MAGICAL OBJECTS?
LIKE, MAYBE IN MY CLOSET AT HOME? SCOOBY AND I CAN GO THERE AND HIDE--I MEAN, CHECK.
NICE TRY.
WHEN I PERFORM MAGIC TRICKS FOR MY STAGE ACT, THE AUDIENCE IS ALWAYS LOOKING FOR SOMETHING SNEAKY. SO I FOOL THEM BY HIDING THINGS IN PLAIN SIGHT.
HIDING IN PLAIN SIGHT IS A PRETTY GOOD STRATEGY ON HALLOWEEN, TOO, WHEN EVERYONE DRESSES UP TO LOOK LIKE SOMETHING THEY'RE NOT.
"PLAIN SIGHT!" JINKIES! I KNOW WHERE SARGON'S RUBY IS! WE'VE ALL SEEN IT!
RE RHAVE? RHERE?

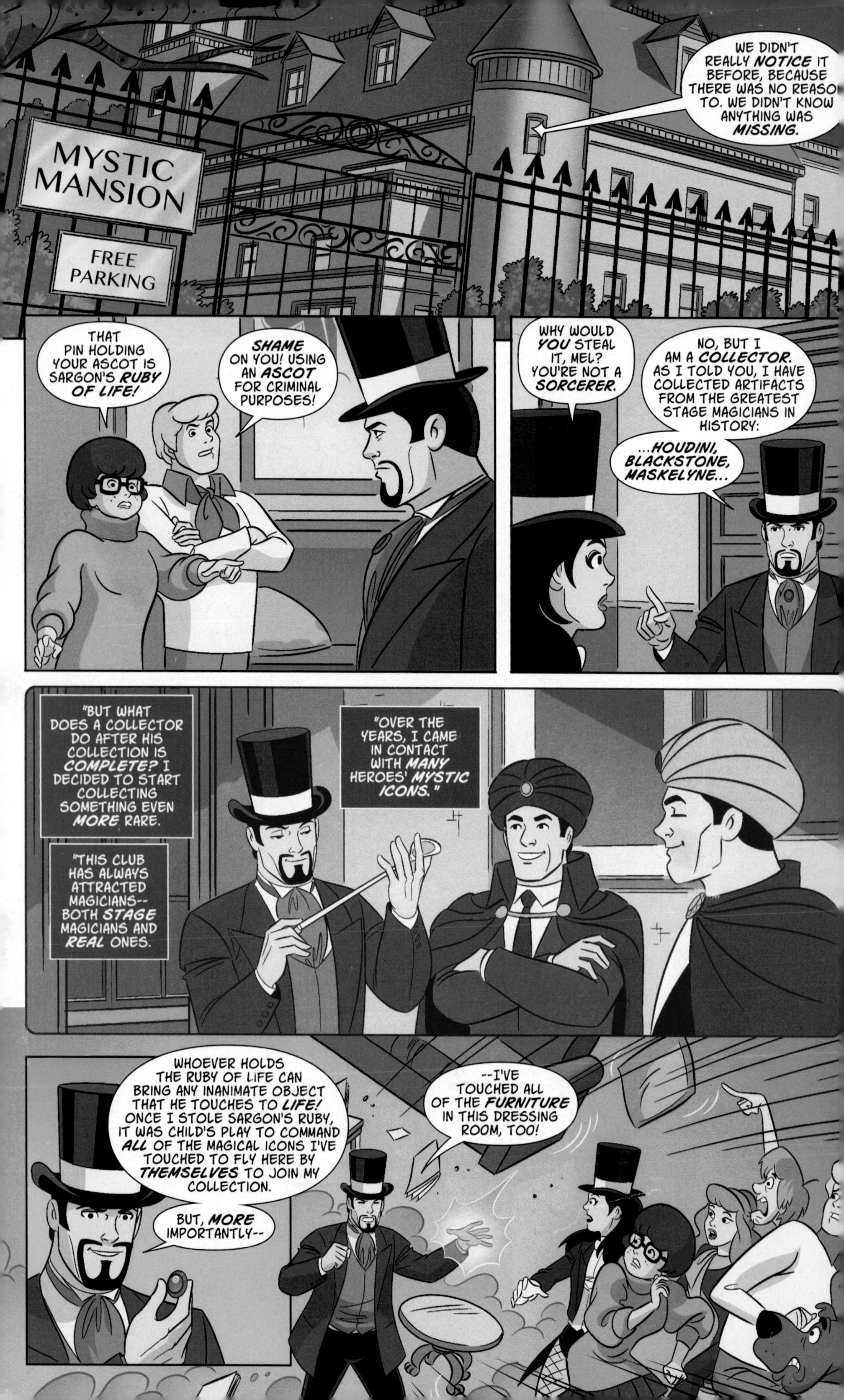
MYSTIC MANSION
FREE PARKING
WE DIDN'T REALLY NOTICE IT BEFORE, BECAUSE THERE WAS NO REASO TO. WE DIDN'T KNOW ANYTHING WAS MISSING.
THAT PIN HOLDING YOUR ASCOT IS SARGON'S RUBY OF LIFE!
SHAME ON YOU! USING AN ASCOT FOR CRIMINAL PURPOSES!
WHY WOULD YOU STEAL IT, MEL? YOU'RE NOT A SORCERER.
NO, BUT I AM A COLLECTOR. AS I TOLD YOU, I HAVE COLLECTED ARTIFACTS FROM THE GREATEST STAGE MAGICIANS IN HISTORY:
...HOUDINI, BLACKSTONE, MASKELYNE...
"BUT WHAT DOES A COLLECTOR DO AFTER HIS COLLECTION IS COMPLETE? I DECIDED TO START COLLECTING SOMETHING EVEN MORE RARE.
"THIS CLUB HAS ALWAYS ATTRACTED MAGICIANS-- BOTH STAGE MAGICIANS AND REAL ONES.
"OVER THE YEARS, I CAME IN CONTACT WITH MANY HEROES' MYSTIC ICONS."
WHOEVER HOLDS THE RUBY OF LIFE CAN BRING ANY INANIMATE OBJECT THAT HE TOUCHES TO LIFE! ONCE I STOLE SARGON'S RUBY, IT WAS CHILD'S PLAY TO COMMAND ALL OF THE MAGICAL ICONS I'VE TOUCHED TO FLY HERE BY THEMSELVES TO JOIN MY COLLECTION.
BUT, MORE IMPORTANTLY--
--I'VE TOUCHED ALL OF THE FURNITURE IN THIS DRESSING ROOM, TOO!

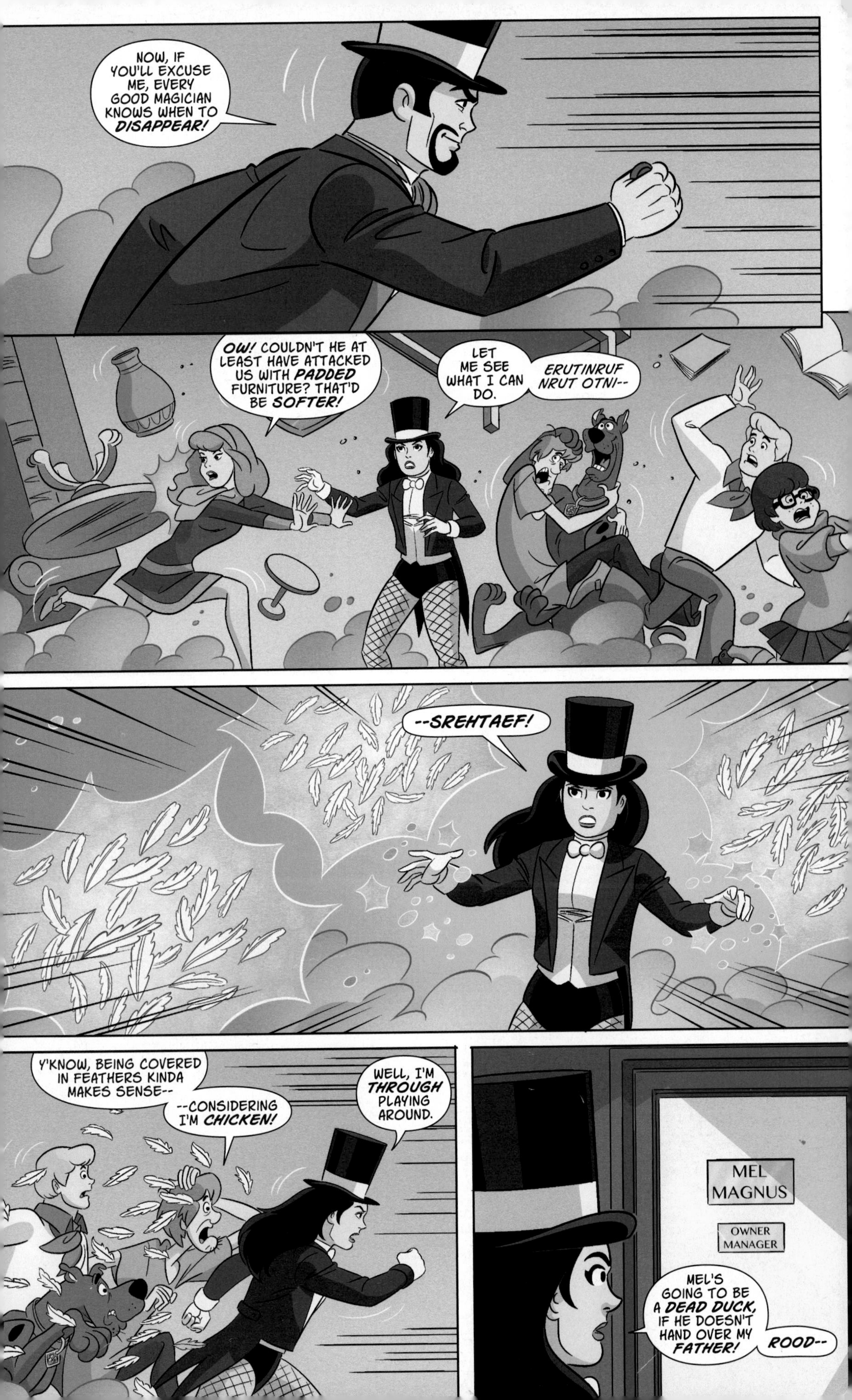
NOW, IF YOU'LL EXCUSE ME, EVERY GOOD MAGICIAN KNOWS WHEN TO DISAPPEAR!
OW! COULDN'T HE AT LEAST HAVE ATTACKED US WITH PADDED FURNITURE? THAT'D BE SOFTER!
LET ME SEE WHAT I CAN DO.
ERUTINRUF NRUT OTNI--
--SREHTAEF!
Y'KNOW, BEING COVERED IN FEATHERS KINDA MAKES SENSE--
--CONSIDERING I'M CHICKEN!
WELL, I'M THROUGH PLAYING AROUND.
MEL MAGNUS
OWNER MANAGER
MEL'S GOING TO BE A DEAD DUCK, IF HE DOESN'T HAND OVER MY FATHER!
ROOD--

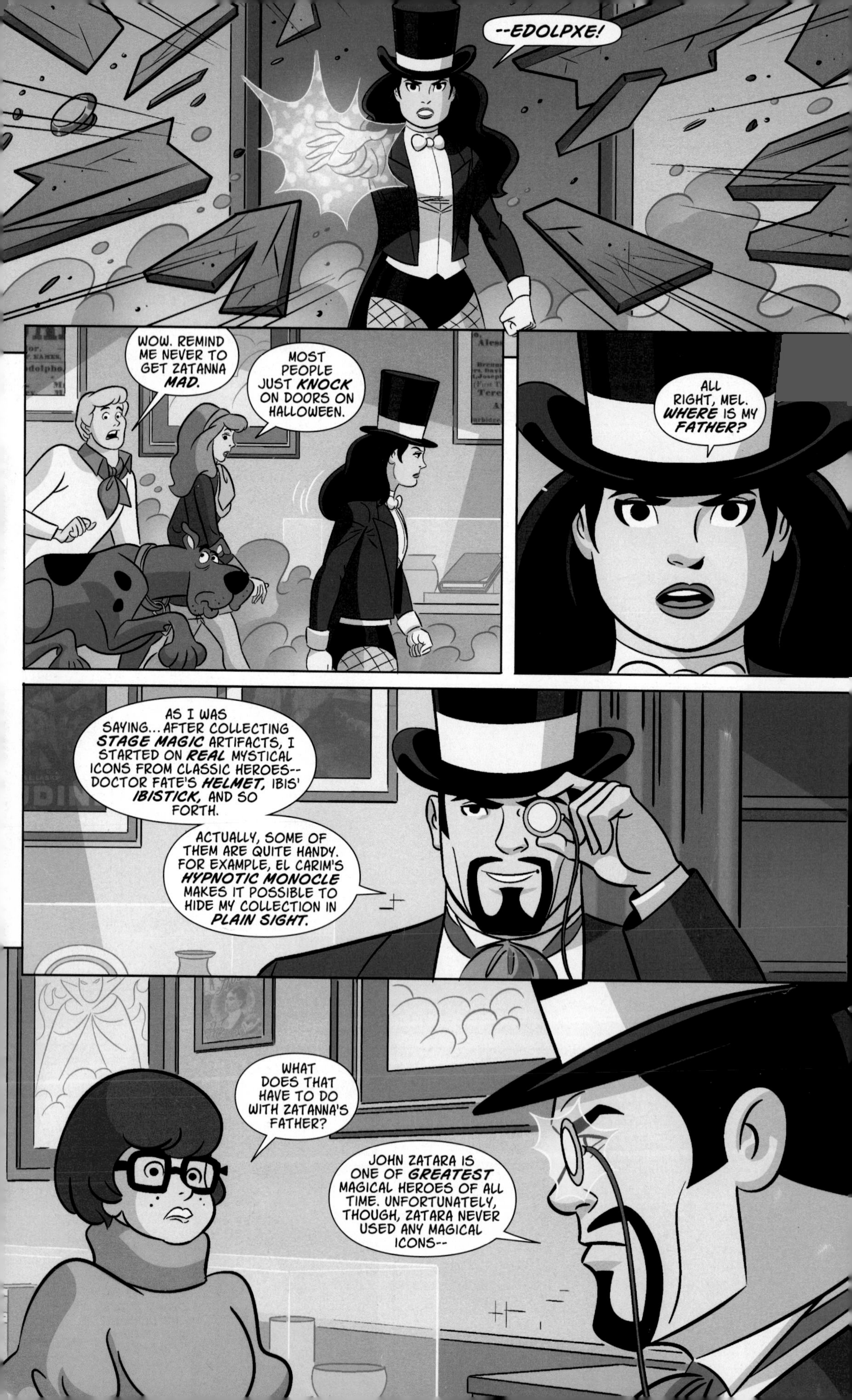
--EDOLPXE!
WOW. REMIND ME NEVER TO GET ZATANNA MAD.
MOST PEOPLE JUST KNOCK ON DOORS ON HALLOWEEN.
ALL RIGHT, MEL. WHERE IS MY FATHER?
AS I WAS SAYING... AFTER COLLECTING STAGE MAGIC ARTIFACTS, I STARTED ON REAL MYSTICAL ICONS FROM CLASSIC HEROES-- DOCTOR FATE'S HELMET, IBIS' IBISTICK, AND SO FORTH.
ACTUALLY, SOME OF THEM ARE QUITE HANDY. FOR EXAMPLE, EL CARIM'S HYPNOTIC MONOCLE MAKES IT POSSIBLE TO HIDE MY COLLECTION IN PLAIN SIGHT.
WHAT DOES THAT HAVE TO DO WITH ZATANNA'S FATHER?
JOHN ZATARA IS ONE OF GREATEST MAGICAL HEROES OF ALL TIME. UNFORTUNATELY, THOUGH, ZATARA NEVER USED ANY MAGICAL ICONS--

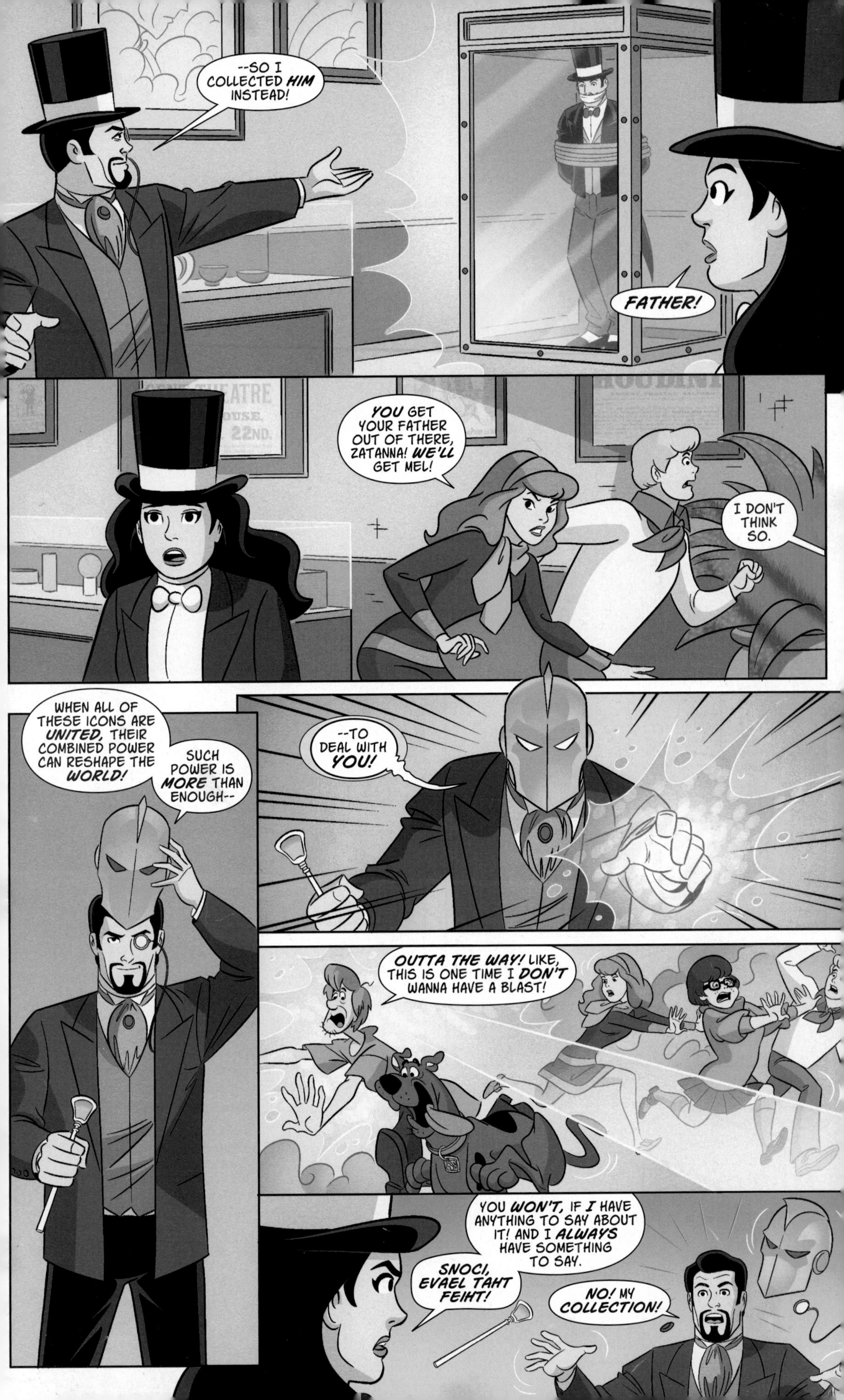
--SO I COLLECTED HIM INSTEAD!
FATHER!
YOU GET YOUR FATHER OUT OF THERE, ZATANNA! WE'LL GET MEL!
I DON'T THINK SO.
WHEN ALL OF THESE ICONS ARE UNITED, THEIR COMBINED POWER CAN RESHAPE THE WORLD!
SUCH POWER IS MORE THAN ENOUGH--
--TO DEAL WITH YOU!
OUTTA THE WAY! LIKE, THIS IS ONE TIME I DON'T WANNA HAVE A BLAST!
YOU WON'T, IF I HAVE ANYTHING TO SAY ABOUT IT! AND I ALWAYS HAVE SOMETHING TO SAY.
SNOCI, EVAEL TAHT FEIHT!
NO! MY COLLECTION!

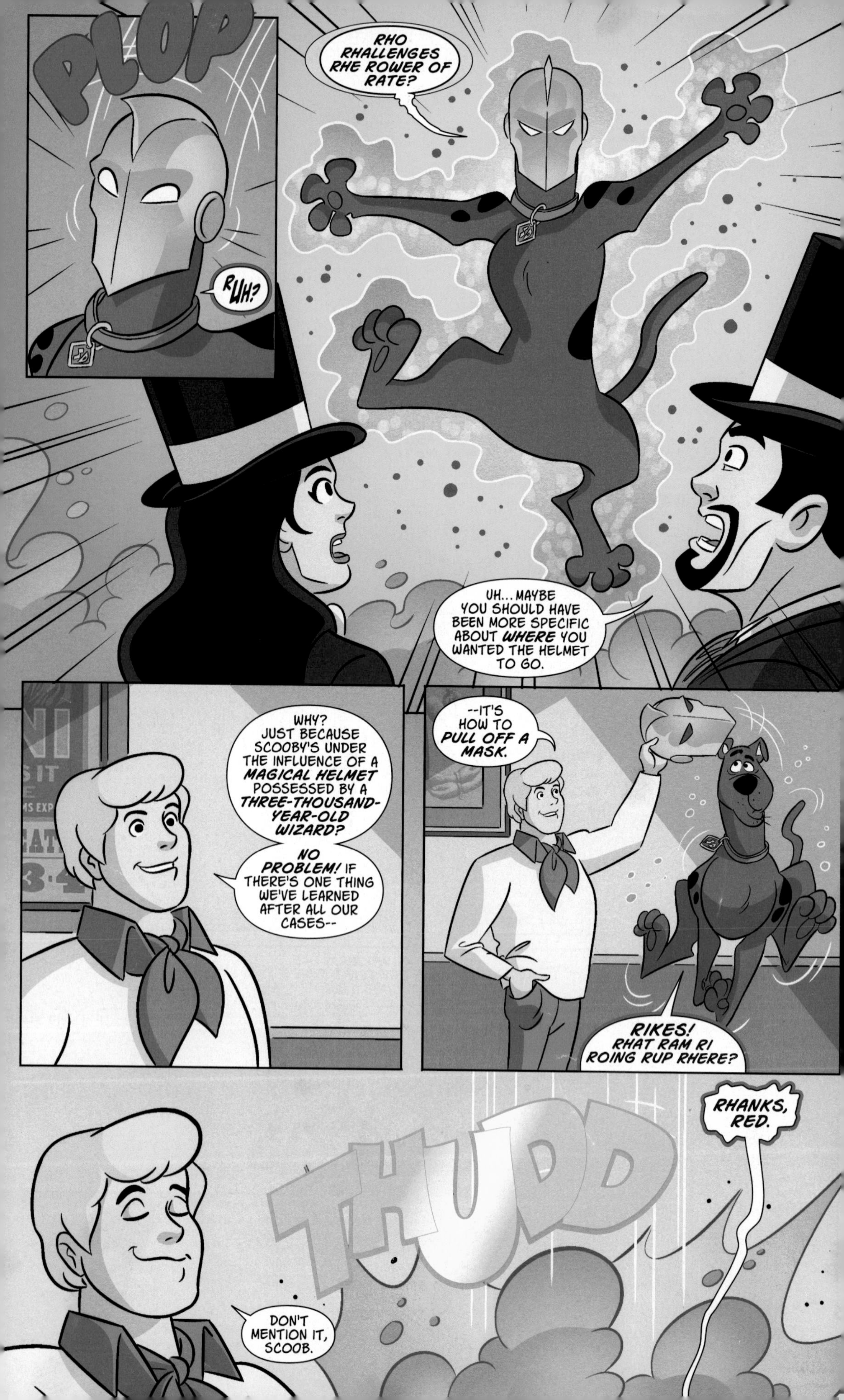
PLOP
RHO RHALLENGES RHE ROWER OF RATE?
RUH?
UH... MAYBE YOU SHOULD HAVE BEEN MORE SPECIFIC ABOUT WHERE YOU WANTED THE HELMET TO GO.
WHY? JUST BECAUSE SCOOBY'S UNDER THE INFLUENCE OF A MAGICAL HELMET POSSESSED BY A THREE-THOUSAND-YEAR-OLD WIZARD?
NO PROBLEM! IF THERE'S ONE THING WE'VE LEARNED AFTER ALL OUR CASES--
--IT'S HOW TO PULL OFF A MASK.
RIKES! RHAT RAM RI ROING RUP RHERE?
THUDD
RHANKS, RED.
DON'T MENTION IT, SCOOB.

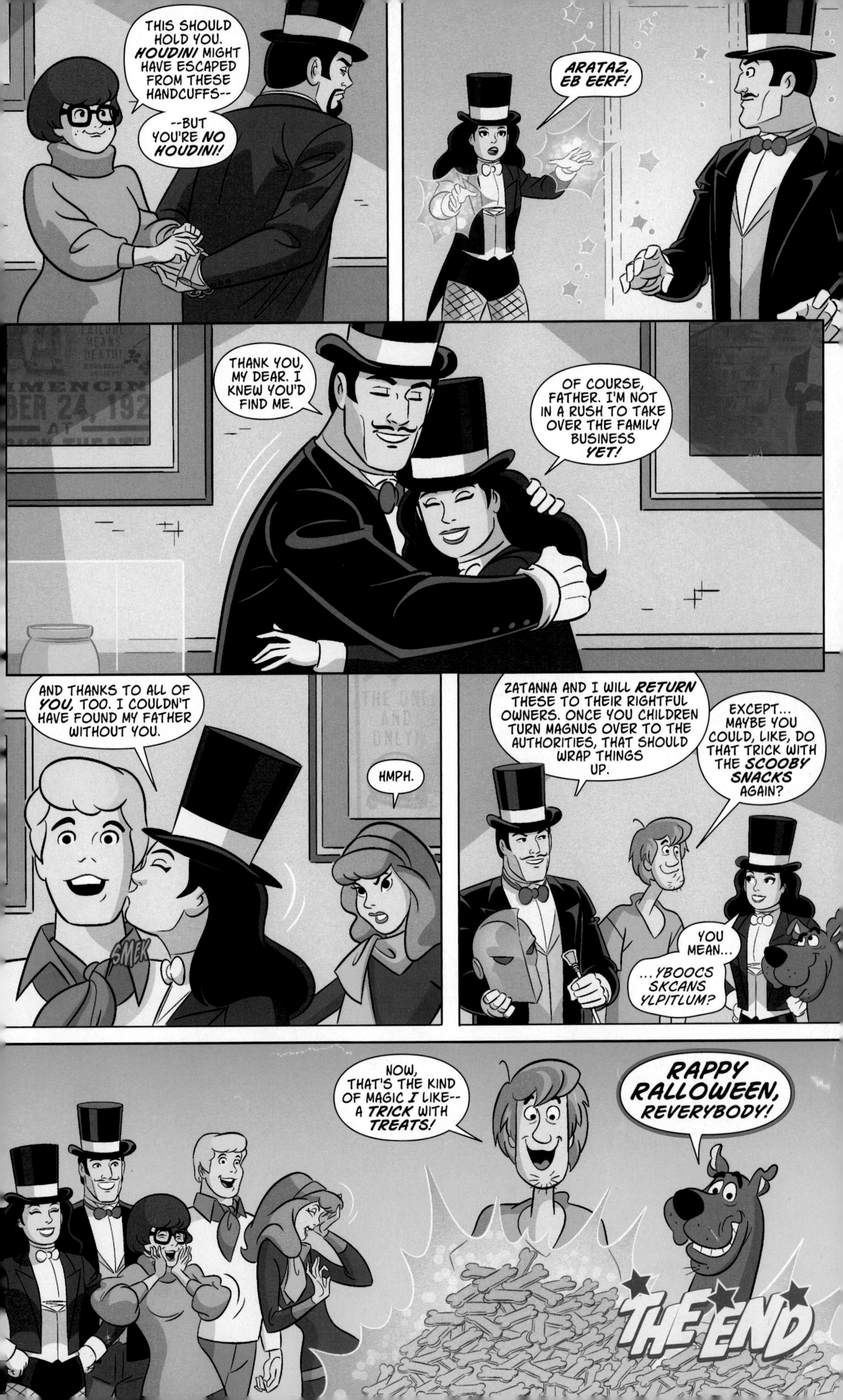

THIS SHOULD HOLD YOU. HOUDINI MIGHT HAVE ESCAPED FROM THESE HANDCUFFS--
--BUT YOU'RE NO HOUDINI!
ARATAZ, EB EERF!
THANK YOU, MY DEAR. I KNEW YOU'D FIND ME.
OF COURSE, FATHER. I'M NOT IN A RUSH TO TAKE OVER THE FAMILY BUSINESS YET!
AND THANKS TO ALL OF YOU, TOO. I COULDN'T HAVE FOUND MY FATHER WITHOUT YOU.
SMEK
HMPH.
ZATANNA AND I WILL RETURN THESE TO THEIR RIGHTFUL OWNERS. ONCE YOU CHILDREN TURN MAGNUS OVER TO THE AUTHORITIES, THAT SHOULD WRAP THINGS UP.
EXCEPT... MAYBE YOU COULD, LIKE, DO THAT TRICK WITH THE SCOOBY SNACKS AGAIN?
YOU MEAN...
...YBOOCS SKCANS YLPITLUM?
NOW, THAT'S THE KIND OF MAGIC I LIKE-- A TRICK WITH TREATS!
RAPPY RALLOWEEN, REVERYBODY!
THE END

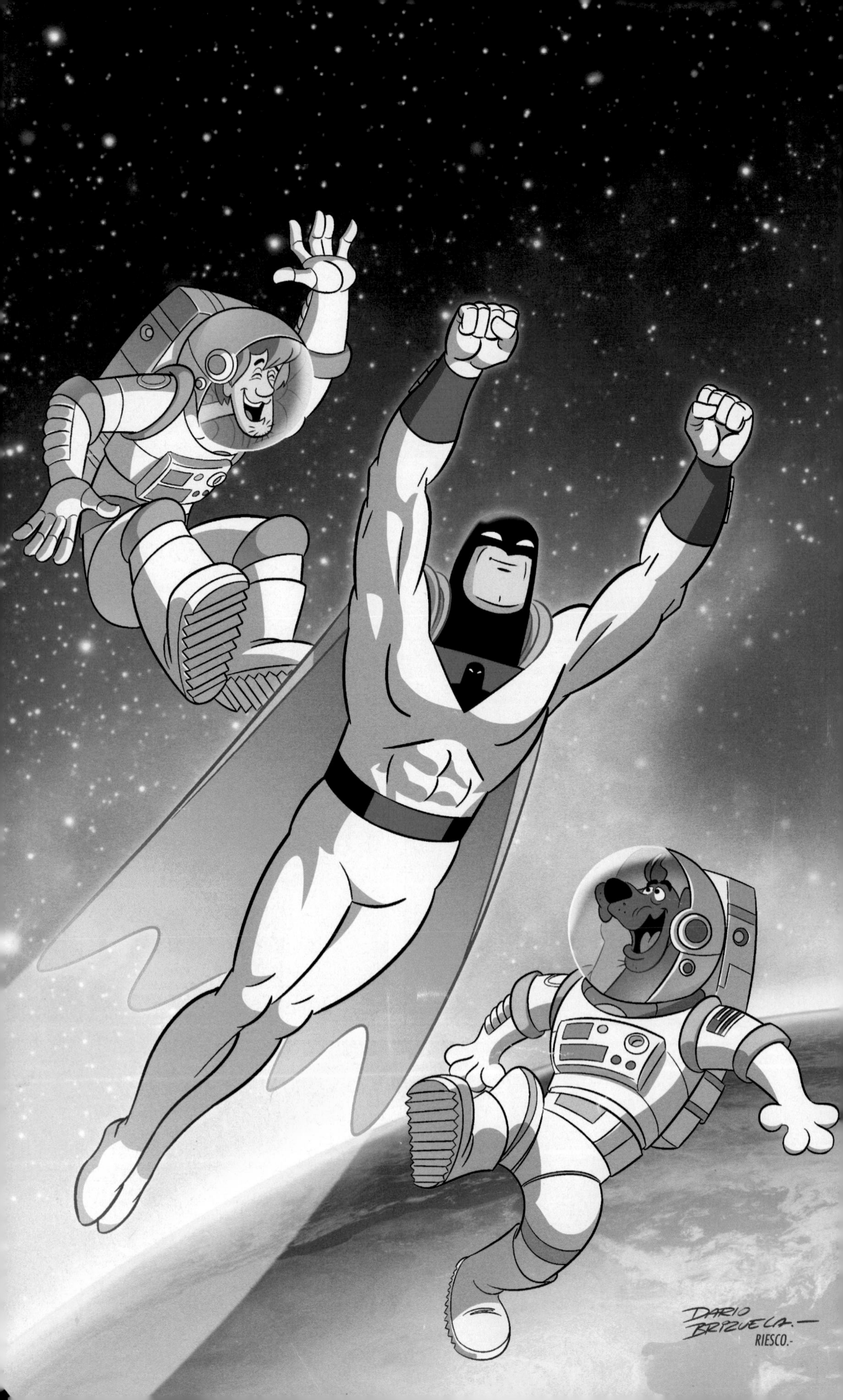
DARIO BRIZUELA
RIESCO.-

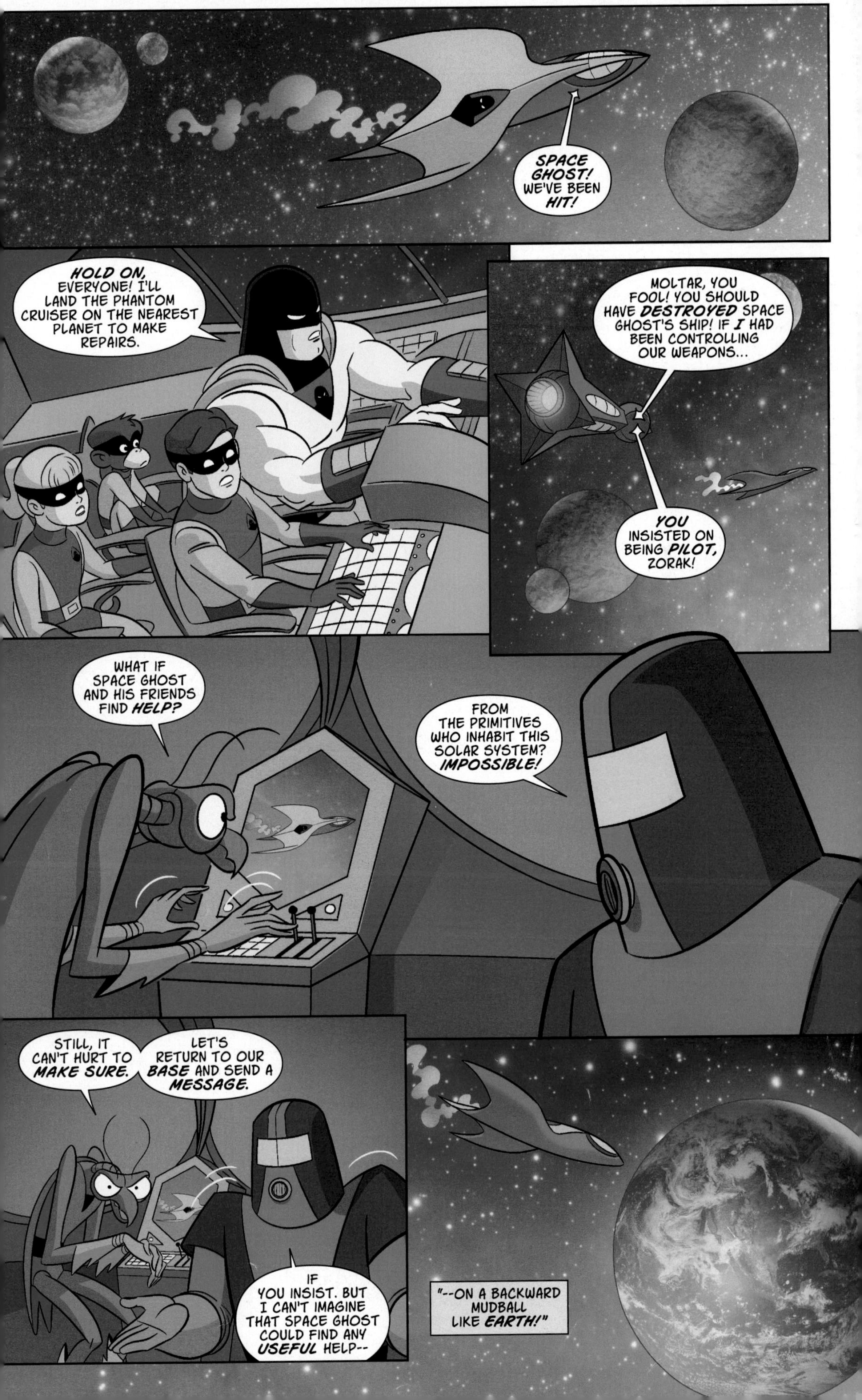

SPACE GHOST! WE'VE BEEN HIT!
HOLD ON, EVERYONE! I'LL LAND THE PHANTOM CRUISER ON THE NEAREST PLANET TO MAKE REPAIRS.
MOLTAR, YOU FOOL! YOU SHOULD HAVE DESTROYED SPACE GHOST'S SHIP! IF I HAD BEEN CONTROLLING OUR WEAPONS...
YOU INSISTED ON BEING PILOT, ZORAK!
WHAT IF SPACE GHOST AND HIS FRIENDS FIND HELP?
FROM THE PRIMITIVES WHO INHABIT THIS SOLAR SYSTEM? IMPOSSIBLE!
STILL, IT CAN'T HURT TO MAKE SURE.
LET'S RETURN TO OUR BASE AND SEND A MESSAGE.
IF YOU INSIST. BUT I CAN'T IMAGINE THAT SPACE GHOST COULD FIND ANY USEFUL HELP--
"--ON A BACKWARD MUDBALL LIKE EARTH!"

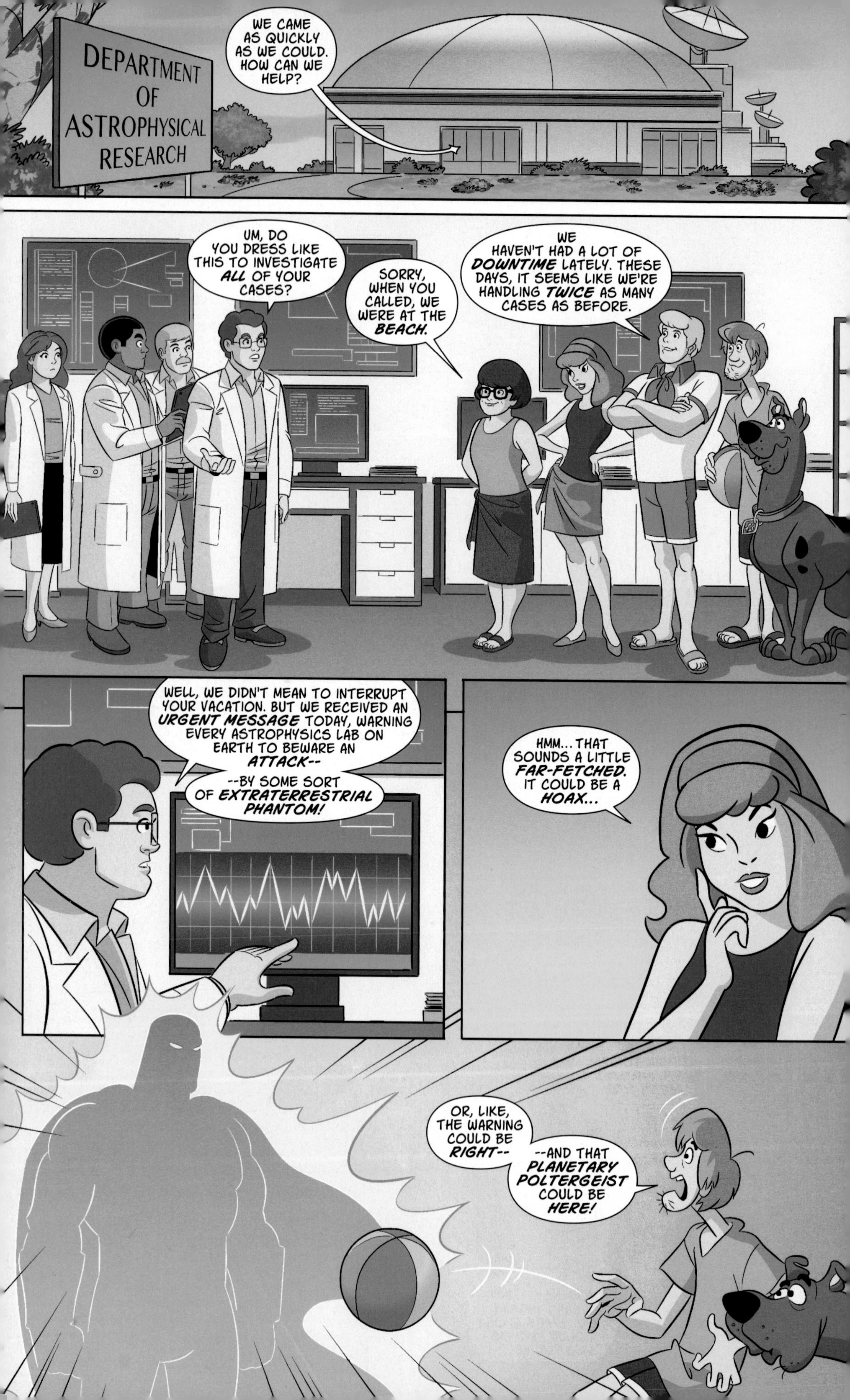
DEPARTMENT OF ASTROPHYSICAL RESEARCH
WE CAME AS QUICKLY AS WE COULD. HOW CAN WE HELP?
UM, DO YOU DRESS LIKE THIS TO INVESTIGATE ALL OF YOUR CASES?
SORRY, WHEN YOU CALLED, WE WERE AT THE BEACH.
WE HAVEN'T HAD A LOT OF DOWNTIME LATELY. THESE DAYS, IT SEEMS LIKE WE'RE HANDLING TWICE AS MANY CASES AS BEFORE.
WELL, WE DIDN'T MEAN TO INTERRUPT YOUR VACATION. BUT WE RECEIVED AN URGENT MESSAGE TODAY, WARNING EVERY ASTROPHYSICS LAB ON EARTH TO BEWARE AN ATTACK--
--BY SOME SORT OF EXTRATERRESTRIAL PHANTOM!
HMM... THAT SOUNDS A LITTLE FAR-FETCHED. IT COULD BE A HOAX...
OR, LIKE, THE WARNING COULD BE RIGHT--
--AND THAT PLANETARY POLTERGEIST COULD BE HERE!

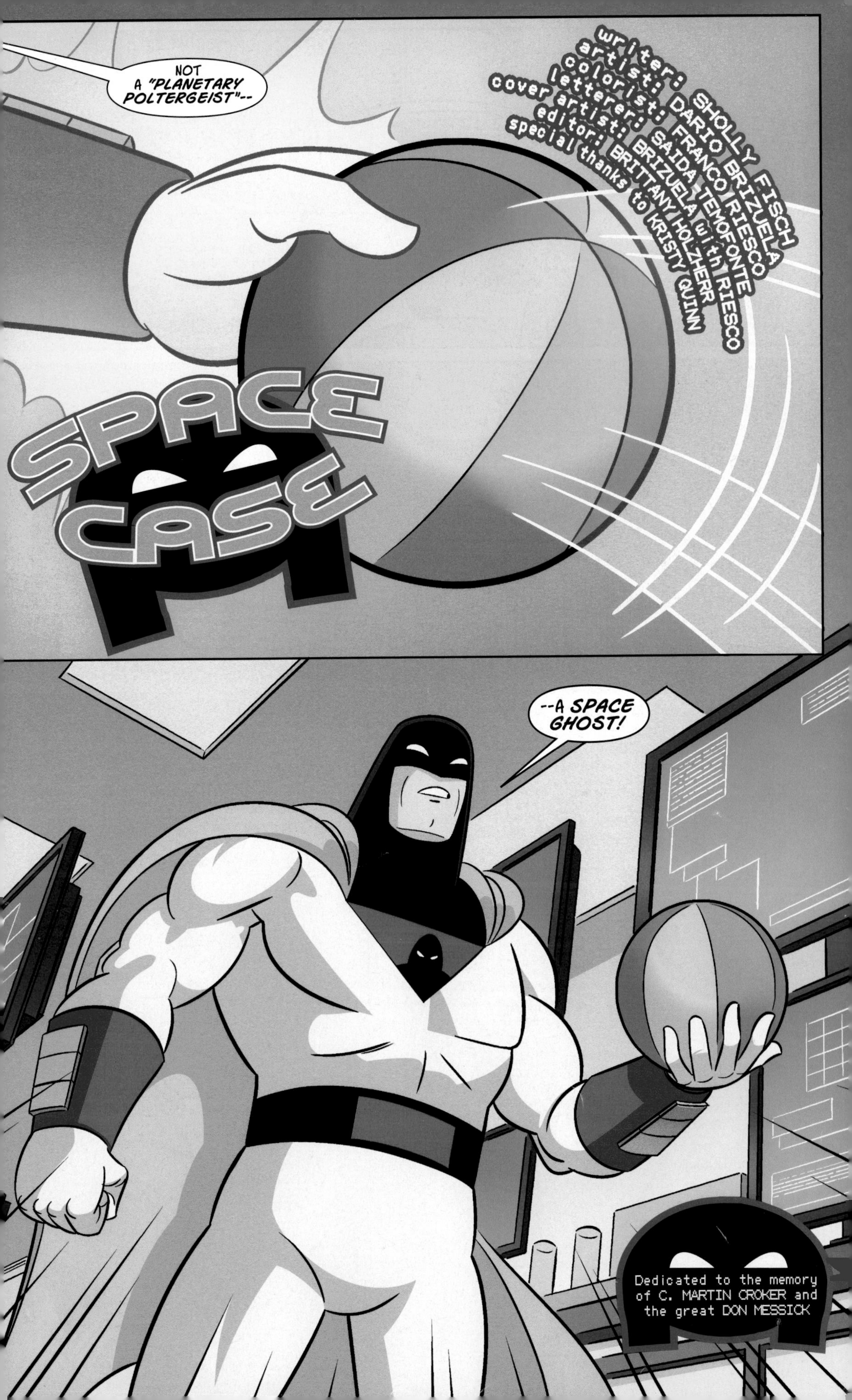
NOT A "PLANETARY POLTERGEIST"--
writer: SHOLLY FISCH
artist: DARIO BRIZUELA
colorist: FRANCO RIESCO
letterer: SAIDA TEMOFONTE
cover artist: BRIZUELA with RIESCO
editor: BRITTANY HOLZHERR
special thanks to KRISTY QUINN
SPACE CASE
--A SPACE GHOST!
Dedicated to the memory of C. MARTIN CROKER and the great DON MESSICK

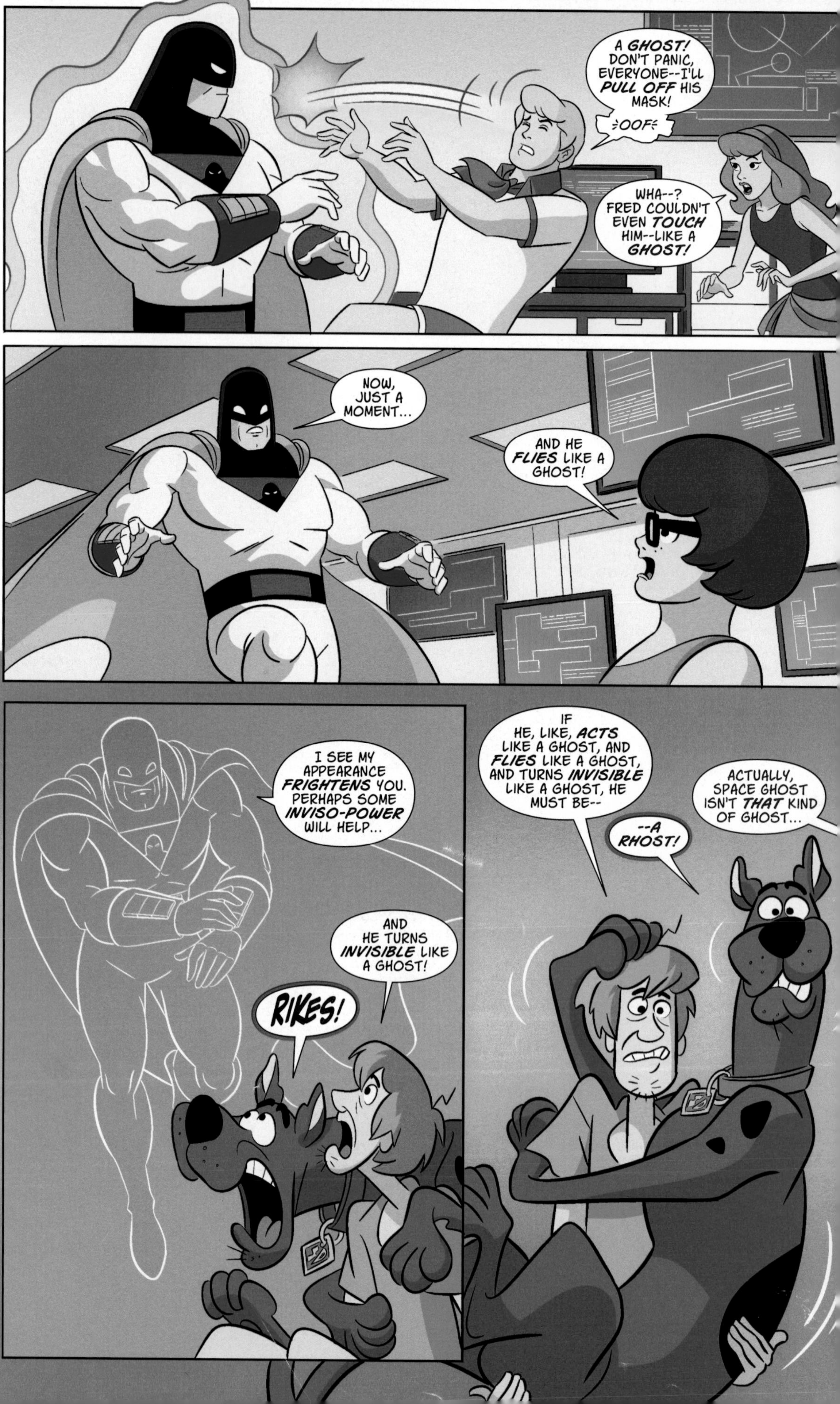
A GHOST! DON'T PANIC, EVERYONE--I'LL PULL OFF HIS MASK!
OOF
WHA--? FRED COULDN'T EVEN TOUCH HIM--LIKE A GHOST!
NOW, JUST A MOMENT...
AND HE FLIES LIKE A GHOST!
I SEE MY APPEARANCE FRIGHTENS YOU. PERHAPS SOME INVISO-POWER WILL HELP...
AND HE TURNS INVISIBLE LIKE A GHOST!
RIKES!
IF HE, LIKE, ACTS LIKE A GHOST, AND FLIES LIKE A GHOST, AND TURNS INVISIBLE LIKE A GHOST, HE MUST BE--
--A RHOST!
ACTUALLY, SPACE GHOST ISN'T THAT KIND OF GHOST...

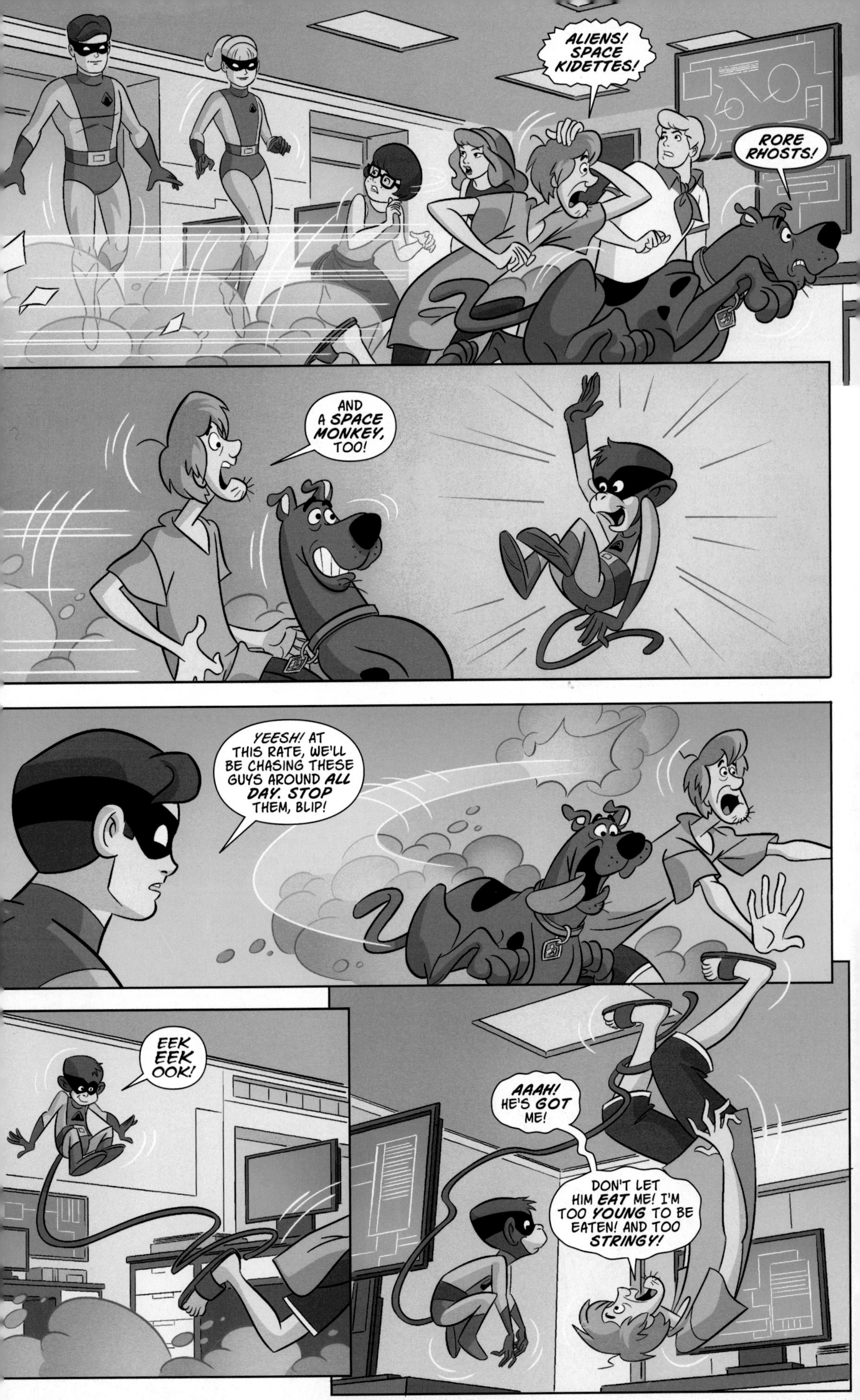

ALIENS! SPACE KIDETTES!
RORE RHOSTS!
AND A SPACE MONKEY, TOO!
YEESH! AT THIS RATE, WE'LL BE CHASING THESE GUYS AROUND ALL DAY. STOP THEM, BLIP!
EEK EEK OOK!
AAAH! HE'S GOT ME!
DON'T LET HIM EAT ME! I'M TOO YOUNG TO BE EATEN! AND TOO STRINGY!

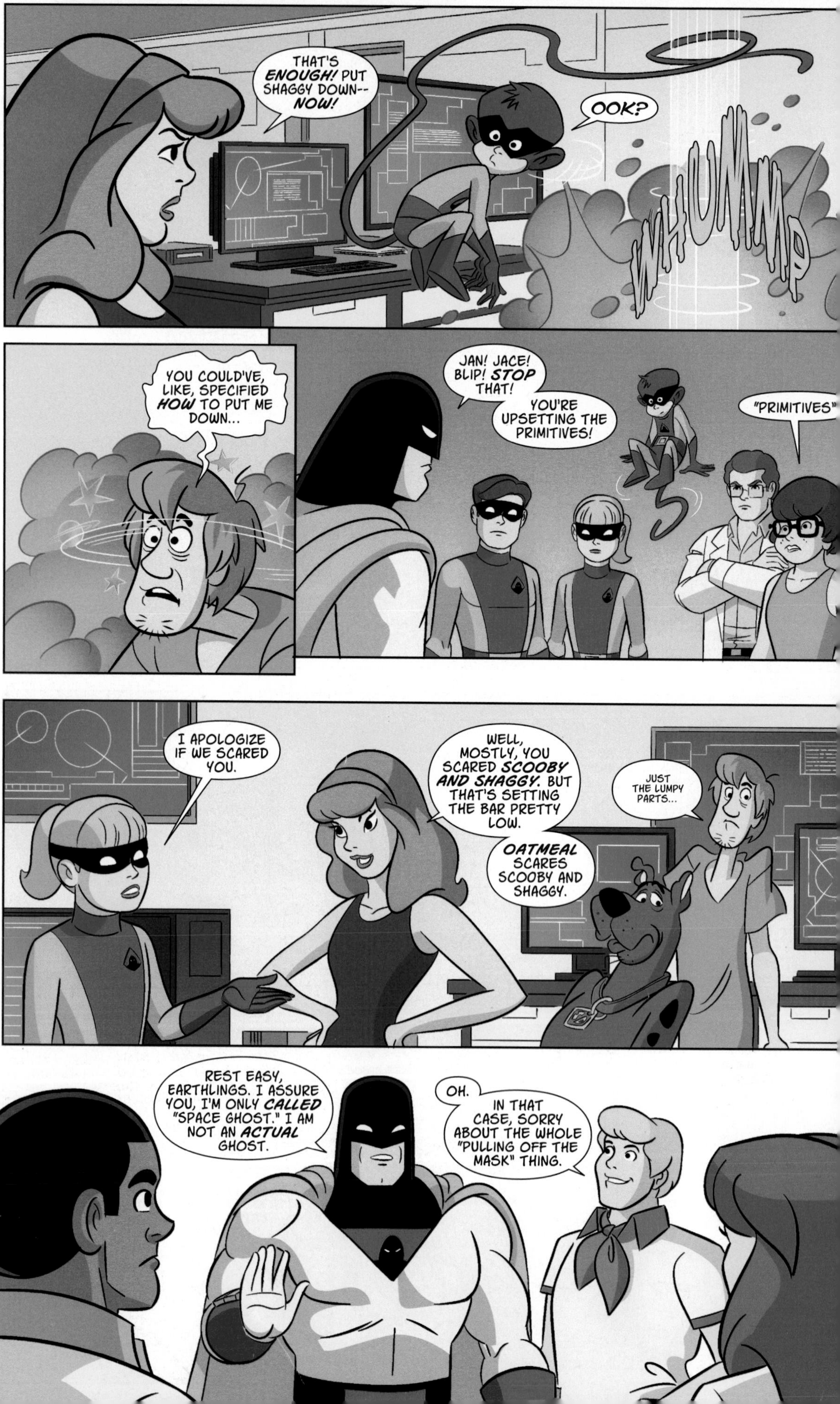
THAT'S ENOUGH! PUT SHAGGY DOWN-- NOW!
OOK?
WHUMMP
YOU COULD'VE, LIKE, SPECIFIED HOW TO PUT ME DOWN...
JAN! JACE! BLIP! STOP THAT!
YOU'RE UPSETTING THE PRIMITIVES!
"PRIMITIVES"
I APOLOGIZE IF WE SCARED YOU.
WELL, MOSTLY, YOU SCARED SCOOBY AND SHAGGY. BUT THAT'S SETTING THE BAR PRETTY LOW.
OATMEAL SCARES SCOOBY AND SHAGGY.
JUST THE LUMPY PARTS...
REST EASY, EARTHLINGS. I ASSURE YOU, I'M ONLY CALLED "SPACE GHOST." I AM NOT AN ACTUAL GHOST.
OH.
IN THAT CASE, SORRY ABOUT THE WHOLE "PULLING OFF THE MASK" THING.

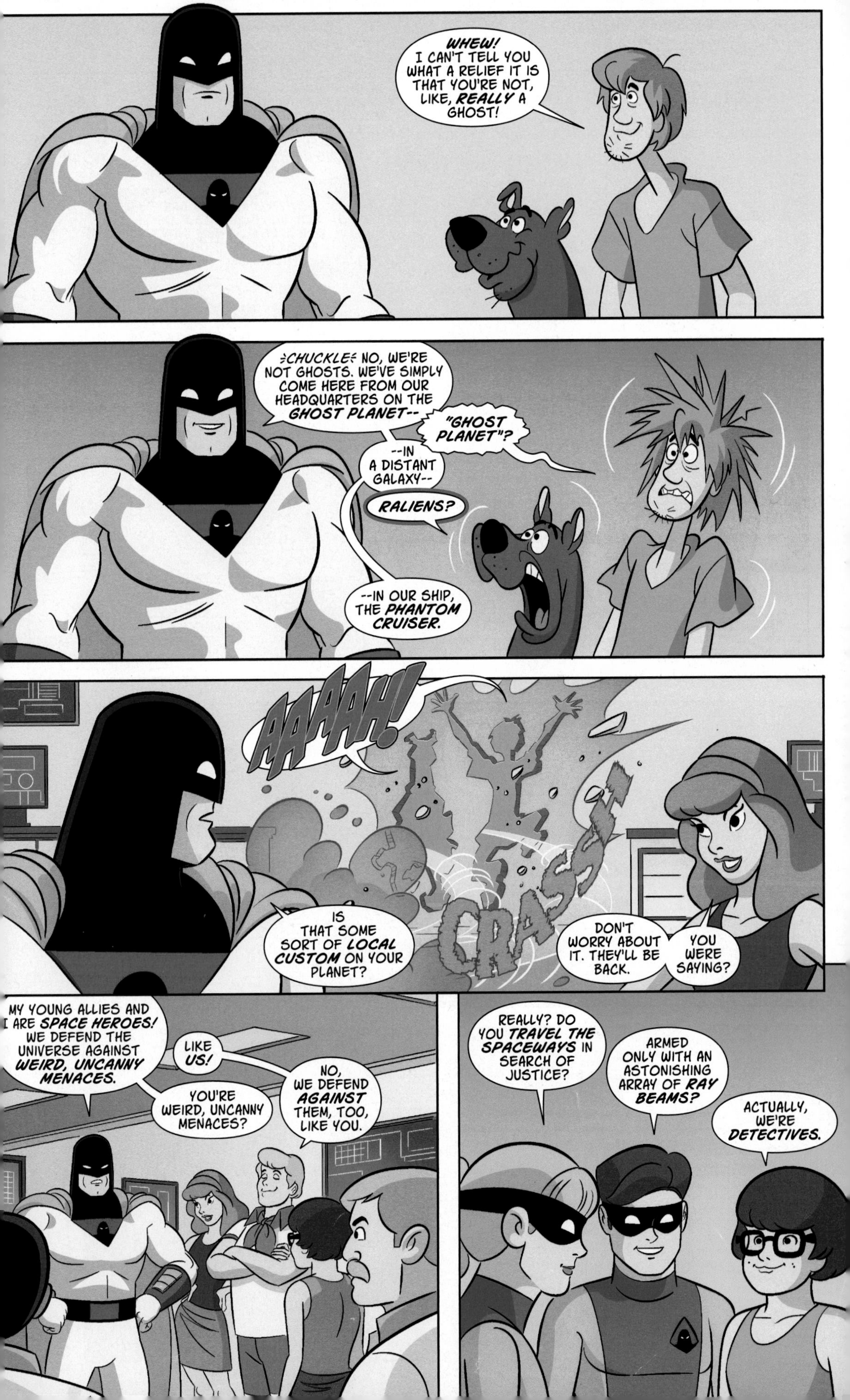
WHEW! I CAN'T TELL YOU WHAT A RELIEF IT IS THAT YOU'RE NOT, LIKE, REALLY A GHOST!
CHUCKLE NO, WE'RE NOT GHOSTS. WE'VE SIMPLY COME HERE FROM OUR HEADQUARTERS ON THE GHOST PLANET--
"GHOST PLANET"?
--IN A DISTANT GALAXY--
RALIENS?
--IN OUR SHIP, THE PHANTOM CRUISER.
AAAAH!
CRASH
IS THAT SOME SORT OF LOCAL CUSTOM ON YOUR PLANET?
DON'T WORRY ABOUT IT. THEY'LL BE BACK.
YOU WERE SAYING?
MY YOUNG ALLIES AND I ARE SPACE HEROES! WE DEFEND THE UNIVERSE AGAINST WEIRD, UNCANNY MENACES.
LIKE US!
YOU'RE WEIRD, UNCANNY MENACES?
NO, WE DEFEND AGAINST THEM, TOO, LIKE YOU.
REALLY? DO YOU TRAVEL THE SPACEWAYS IN SEARCH OF JUSTICE?
ARMED ONLY WITH AN ASTONISHING ARRAY OF RAY BEAMS?
ACTUALLY, WE'RE DETECTIVES.

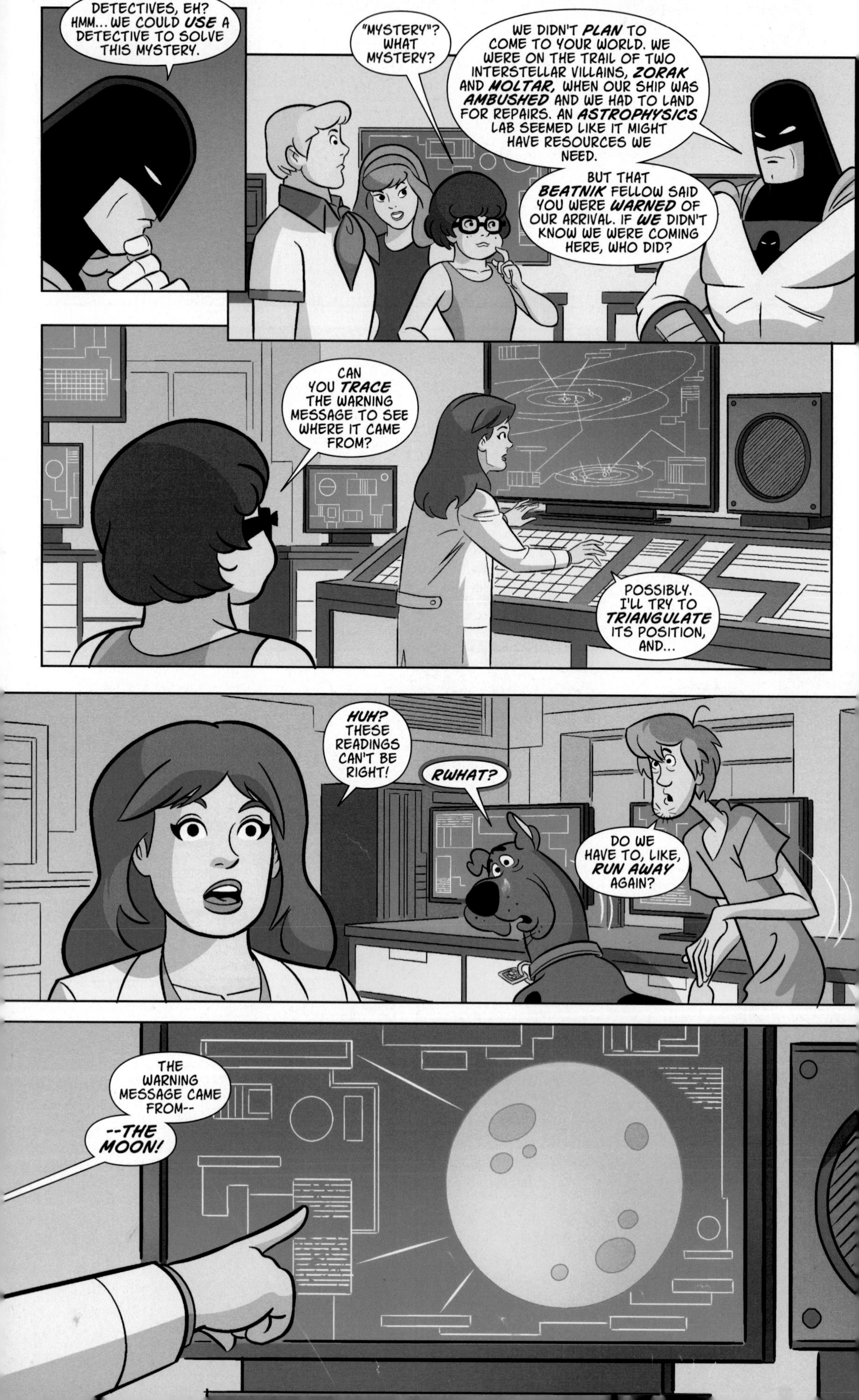
DETECTIVES, EH? HMM... WE COULD USE A DETECTIVE TO SOLVE THIS MYSTERY.
"MYSTERY"? WHAT MYSTERY?
WE DIDN'T PLAN TO COME TO YOUR WORLD. WE WERE ON THE TRAIL OF TWO INTERSTELLAR VILLAINS, ZORAK AND MOLTAR, WHEN OUR SHIP WAS AMBUSHED AND WE HAD TO LAND FOR REPAIRS. AN ASTROPHYSICS LAB SEEMED LIKE IT MIGHT HAVE RESOURCES WE NEED.
BUT THAT BEATNIK FELLOW SAID YOU WERE WARNED OF OUR ARRIVAL. IF WE DIDN'T KNOW WE WERE COMING HERE, WHO DID?
CAN YOU TRACE THE WARNING MESSAGE TO SEE WHERE IT CAME FROM?
POSSIBLY. I'LL TRY TO TRIANGULATE ITS POSITION, AND...
HUH? THESE READINGS CAN'T BE RIGHT!
RWHAT?
DO WE HAVE TO, LIKE, RUN AWAY AGAIN?
THE WARNING MESSAGE CAME FROM--
--THE MOON!

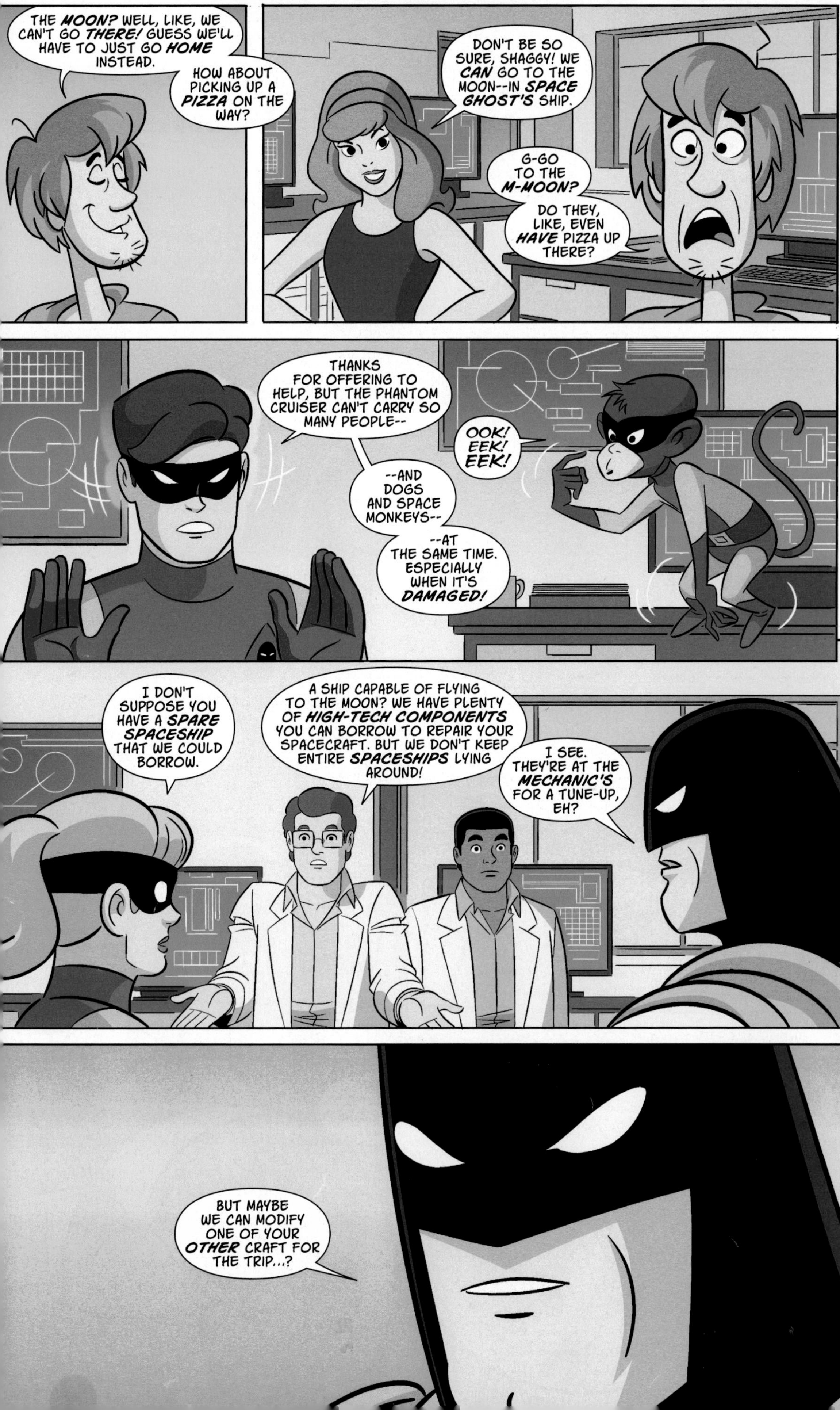
THE MOON? WELL, LIKE, WE CAN'T GO THERE! GUESS WE'LL HAVE TO JUST GO HOME INSTEAD.
HOW ABOUT PICKING UP A PIZZA ON THE WAY?
DON'T BE SO SURE, SHAGGY! WE CAN GO TO THE MOON--IN SPACE GHOST'S SHIP.
G-GO TO THE M-MOON?
DO THEY, LIKE, EVEN HAVE PIZZA UP THERE?
THANKS FOR OFFERING TO HELP, BUT THE PHANTOM CRUISER CAN'T CARRY SO MANY PEOPLE--
OOK! EEK! EEK!
--AND DOGS AND SPACE MONKEYS--
--AT THE SAME TIME. ESPECIALLY WHEN IT'S DAMAGED!
I DON'T SUPPOSE YOU HAVE A SPARE SPACESHIP THAT WE COULD BORROW.
A SHIP CAPABLE OF FLYING TO THE MOON? WE HAVE PLENTY OF HIGH-TECH COMPONENTS YOU CAN BORROW TO REPAIR YOUR SPACECRAFT. BUT WE DON'T KEEP ENTIRE SPACESHIPS LYING AROUND!
I SEE. THEY'RE AT THE MECHANIC'S FOR A TUNE-UP, EH?
BUT MAYBE WE CAN MODIFY ONE OF YOUR OTHER CRAFT FOR THE TRIP...?

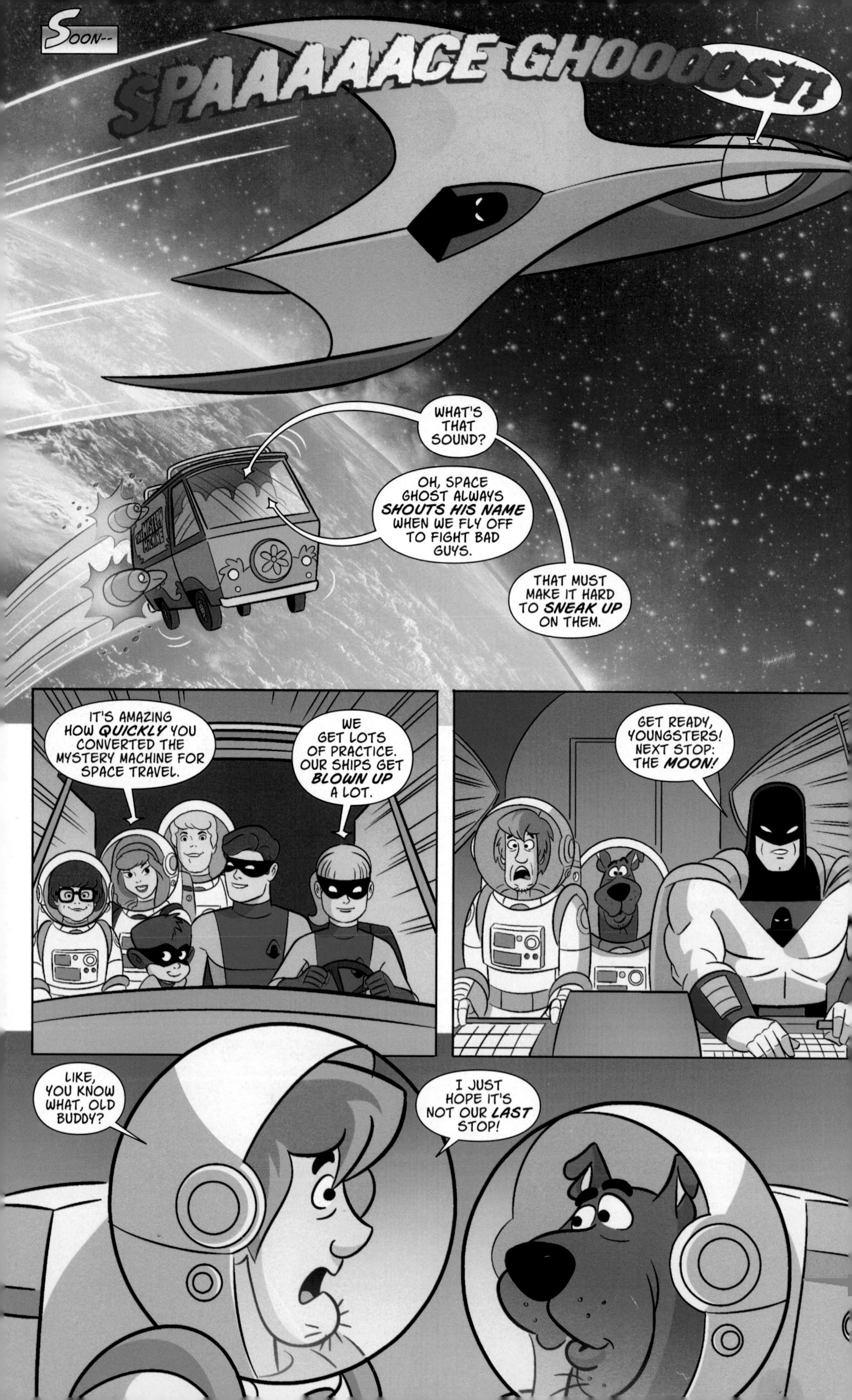
SOON--
SPAAAAAACE GHOOOOOST!
WHAT'S THAT SOUND?
OH, SPACE GHOST ALWAYS SHOUTS HIS NAME WHEN WE FLY OFF TO FIGHT BAD GUYS.
THAT MUST MAKE IT HARD TO SNEAK UP ON THEM.
IT'S AMAZING HOW QUICKLY YOU CONVERTED THE MYSTERY MACHINE FOR SPACE TRAVEL.
WE GET LOTS OF PRACTICE. OUR SHIPS GET BLOWN UP A LOT.
GET READY, YOUNGSTERS! NEXT STOP: THE MOON!
LIKE, YOU KNOW WHAT, OLD BUDDY?
I JUST HOPE IT'S NOT OUR LAST STOP!

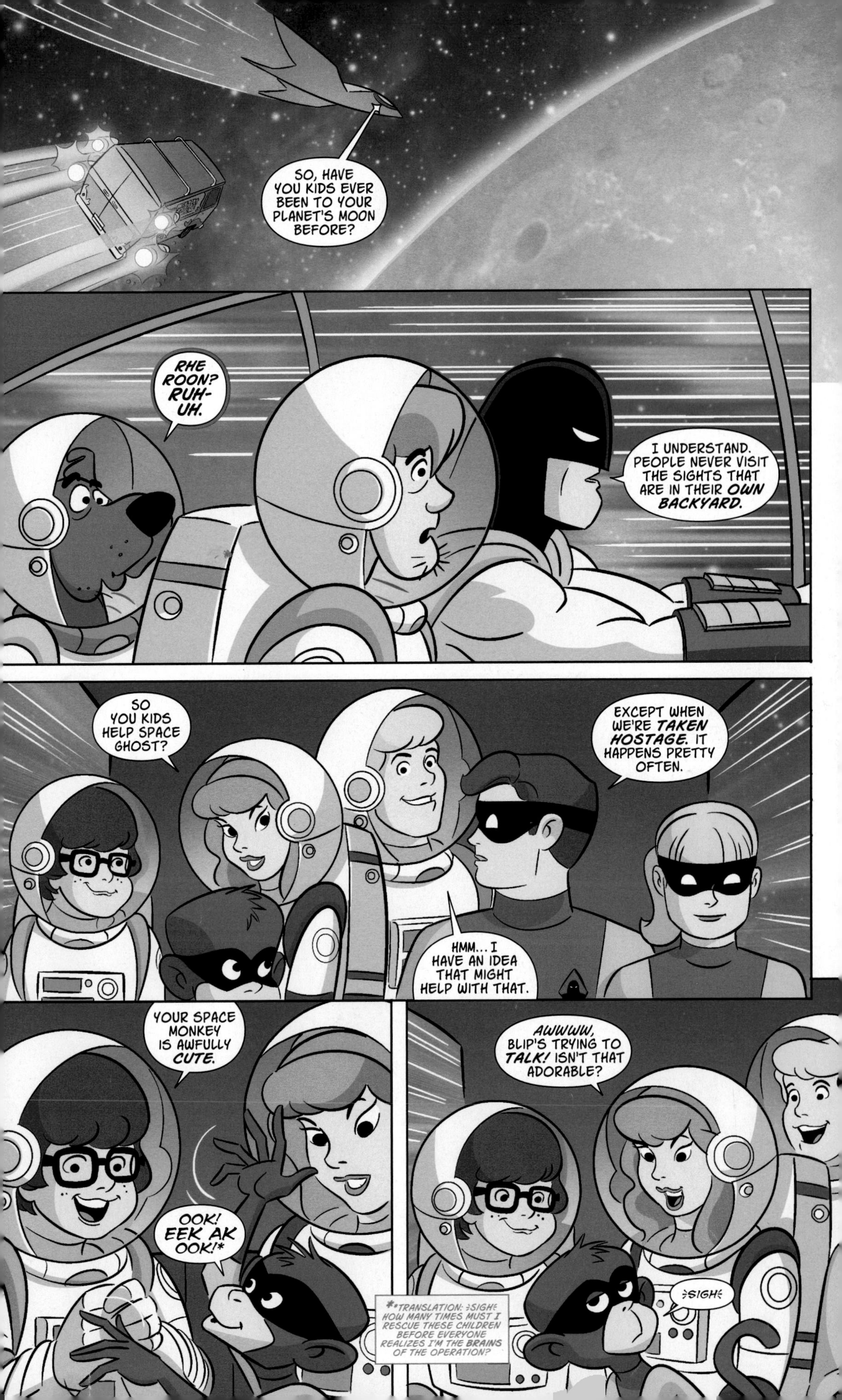
SO, HAVE YOU KIDS EVER BEEN TO YOUR PLANET'S MOON BEFORE?
RHE ROON? RUH-UH.
I UNDERSTAND. PEOPLE NEVER VISIT THE SIGHTS THAT ARE IN THEIR OWN BACKYARD.
SO YOU KIDS HELP SPACE GHOST?
EXCEPT WHEN WE'RE TAKEN HOSTAGE. IT HAPPENS PRETTY OFTEN.
HMM... I HAVE AN IDEA THAT MIGHT HELP WITH THAT.
YOUR SPACE MONKEY IS AWFULLY CUTE.
OOK! EEK AK OOK!*
AWWWW, BLIP'S TRYING TO TALK! ISN'T THAT ADORABLE?
*TRANSLATION: SIGH HOW MANY TIMES MUST I RESCUE THESE CHILDREN BEFORE EVERYONE REALIZES I'M THE BRAINS OF THE OPERATION?
SIGH

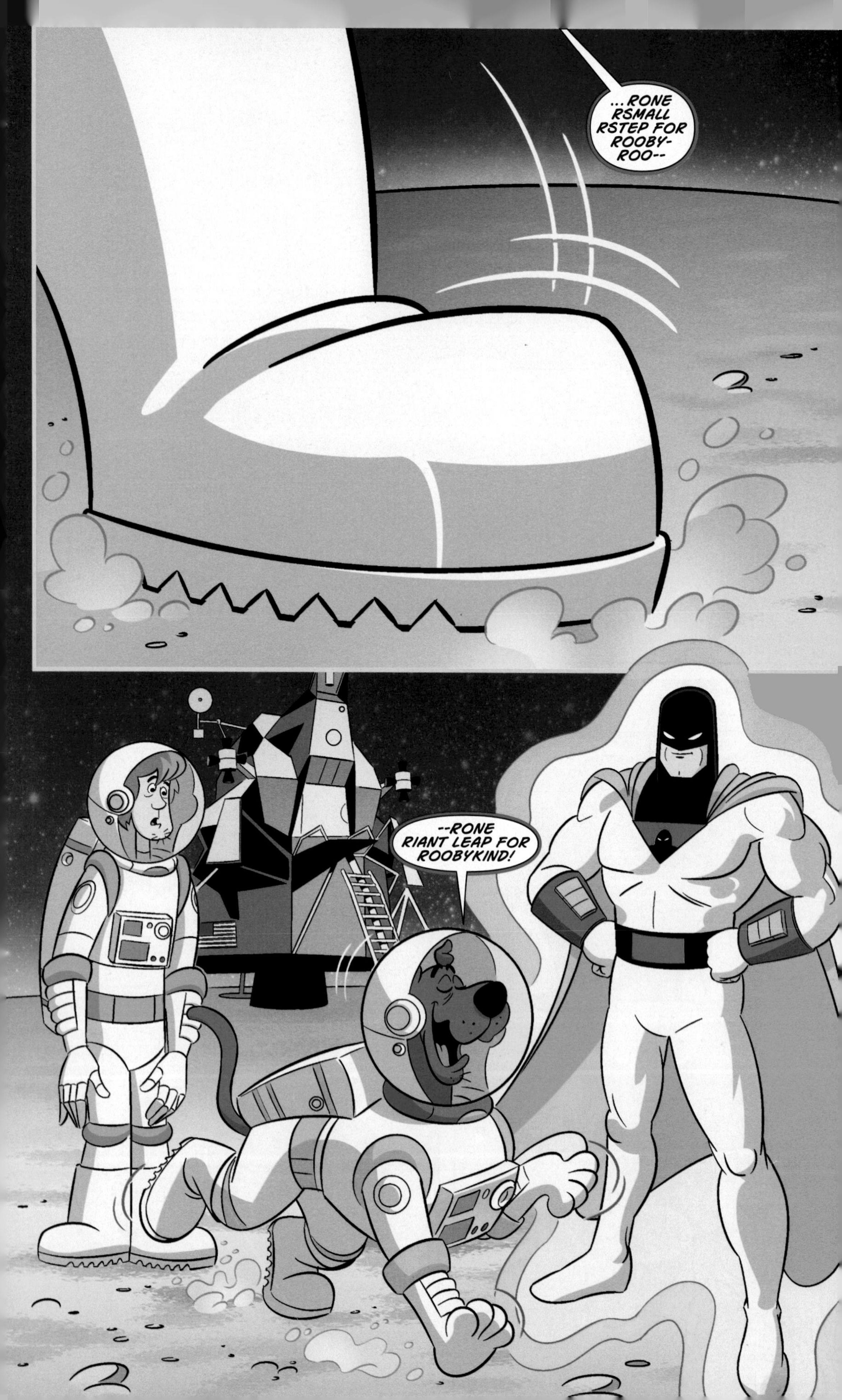
...RONE RSMALL RSTEP FOR ROOBY-ROO--
--RONE RIANT LEAP FOR ROOBYKIND!

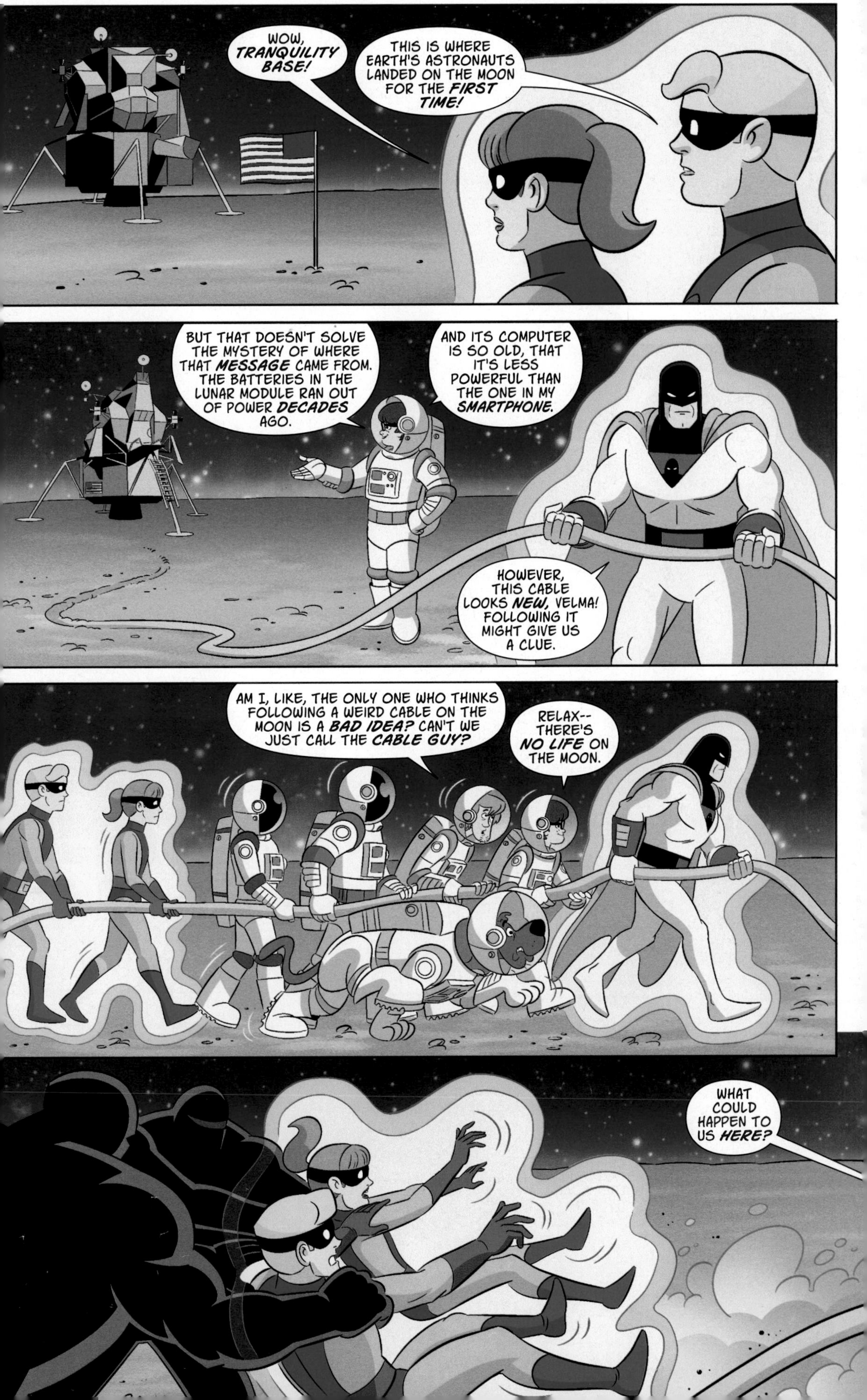
WOW, TRANQUILITY BASE!
THIS IS WHERE EARTH'S ASTRONAUTS LANDED ON THE MOON FOR THE FIRST TIME!
BUT THAT DOESN'T SOLVE THE MYSTERY OF WHERE THAT MESSAGE CAME FROM. THE BATTERIES IN THE LUNAR MODULE RAN OUT OF POWER DECADES AGO.
AND ITS COMPUTER IS SO OLD, THAT IT'S LESS POWERFUL THAN THE ONE IN MY SMARTPHONE.
HOWEVER, THIS CABLE LOOKS NEW, VELMA! FOLLOWING IT MIGHT GIVE US A CLUE.
AM I, LIKE, THE ONLY ONE WHO THINKS FOLLOWING A WEIRD CABLE ON THE MOON IS A BAD IDEA? CAN'T WE JUST CALL THE CABLE GUY?
RELAX-- THERE'S NO LIFE ON THE MOON.
WHAT COULD HAPPEN TO US HERE?

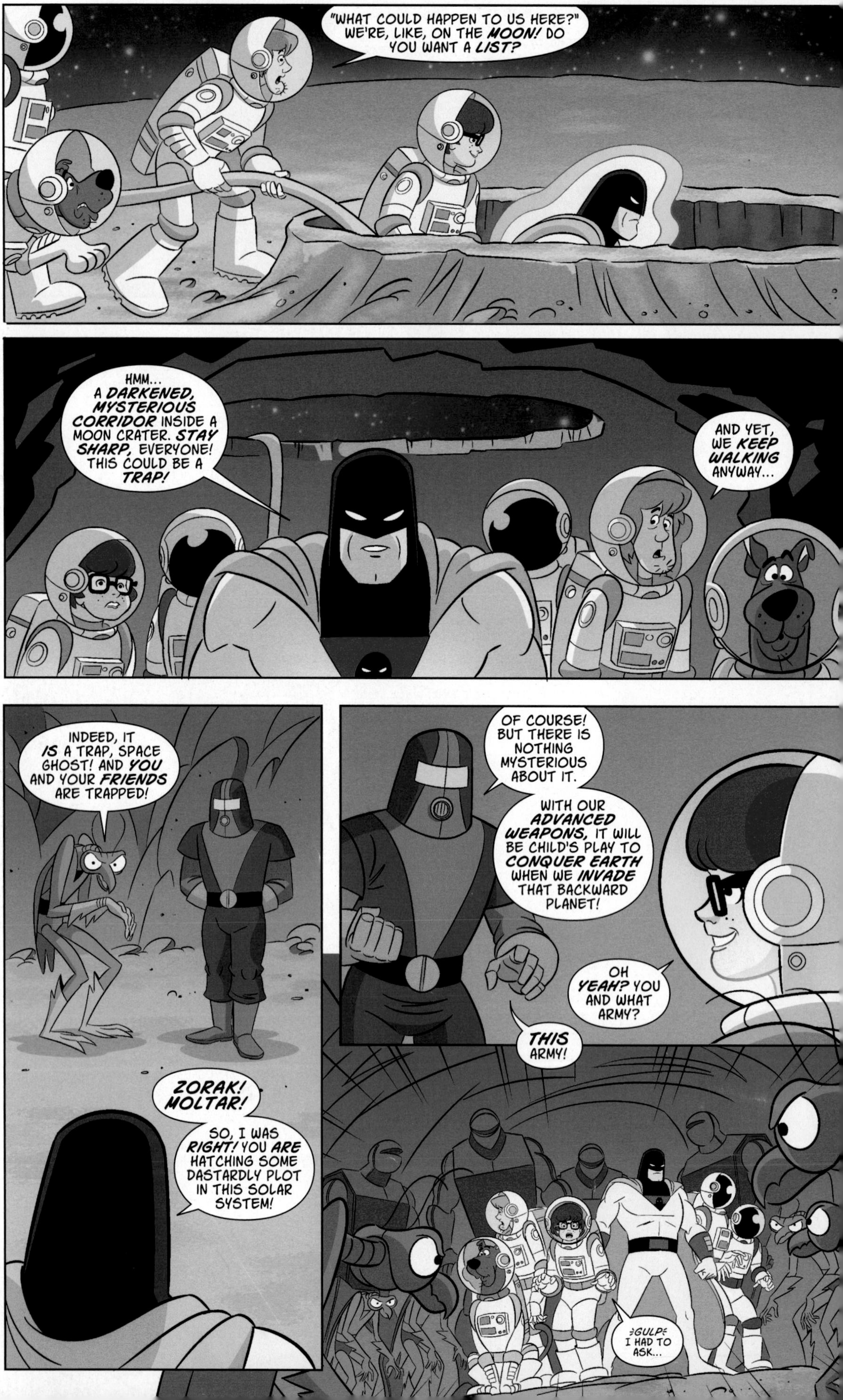
"WHAT COULD HAPPEN TO US HERE?" WE'RE, LIKE, ON THE MOON! DO YOU WANT A LIST?
HMM... A DARKENED, MYSTERIOUS CORRIDOR INSIDE A MOON CRATER. STAY SHARP, EVERYONE! THIS COULD BE A TRAP!
AND YET, WE KEEP WALKING ANYWAY...
INDEED, IT IS A TRAP, SPACE GHOST! AND YOU AND YOUR FRIENDS ARE TRAPPED!
ZORAK! MOLTAR!
SO, I WAS RIGHT! YOU ARE HATCHING SOME DASTARDLY PLOT IN THIS SOLAR SYSTEM!
OF COURSE! BUT THERE IS NOTHING MYSTERIOUS ABOUT IT.
WITH OUR ADVANCED WEAPONS, IT WILL BE CHILD'S PLAY TO CONQUER EARTH WHEN WE INVADE THAT BACKWARD PLANET!
OH YEAH? YOU AND WHAT ARMY?
THIS ARMY!
GULP I HAD TO ASK...

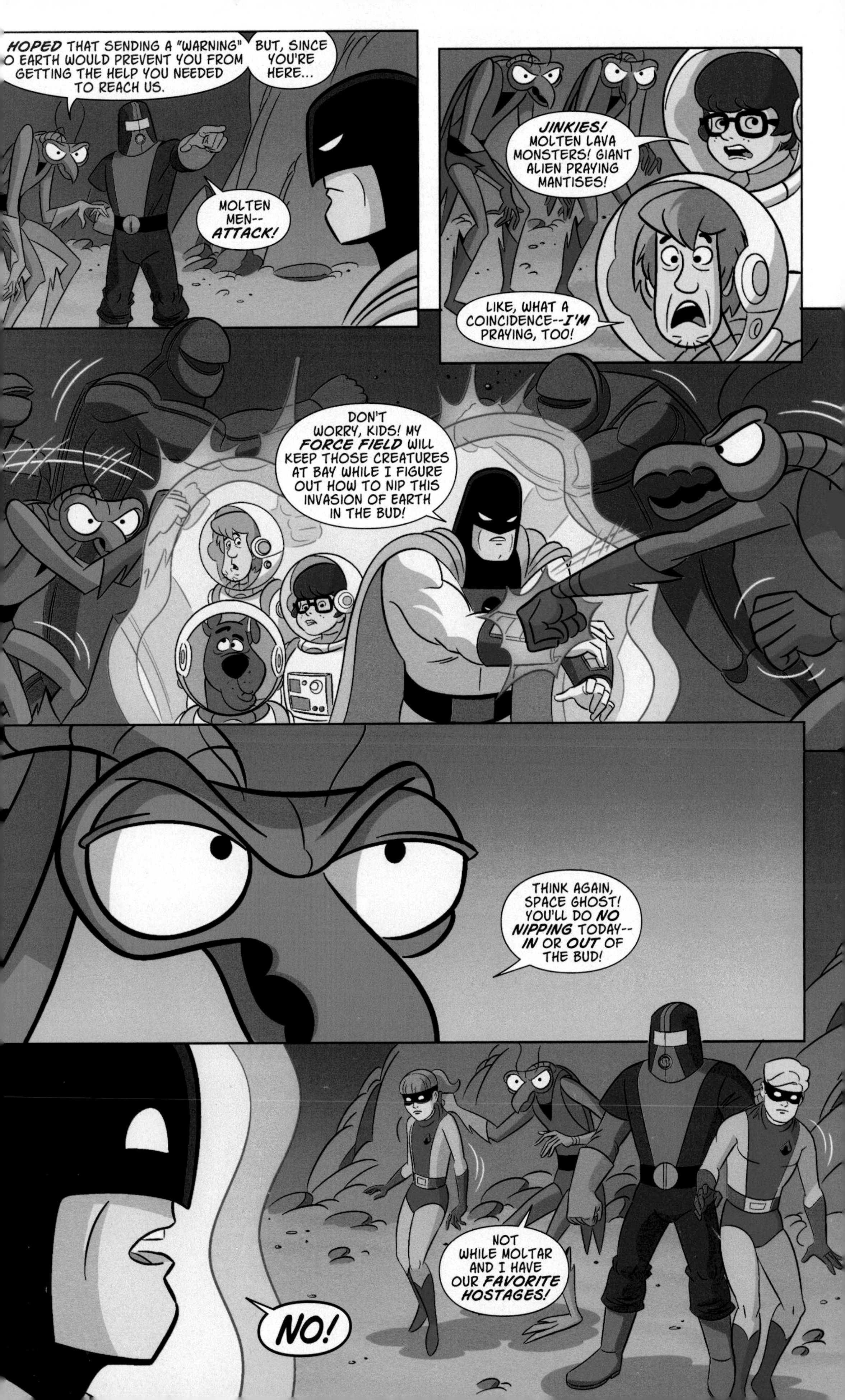
HOPED THAT SENDING A "WARNING" O EARTH WOULD PREVENT YOU FROM GETTING THE HELP YOU NEEDED TO REACH US.
BUT, SINCE YOU'RE HERE...
MOLTEN MEN-- ATTACK!
JINKIES! MOLTEN LAVA MONSTERS! GIANT ALIEN PRAYING MANTISES!
LIKE, WHAT A COINCIDENCE--I'M PRAYING, TOO!
DON'T WORRY, KIDS! MY FORCE FIELD WILL KEEP THOSE CREATURES AT BAY WHILE I FIGURE OUT HOW TO NIP THIS INVASION OF EARTH IN THE BUD!
THINK AGAIN, SPACE GHOST! YOU'LL DO NO NIPPING TODAY-- IN OR OUT OF THE BUD!
NOT WHILE MOLTAR AND I HAVE OUR FAVORITE HOSTAGES!
NO!

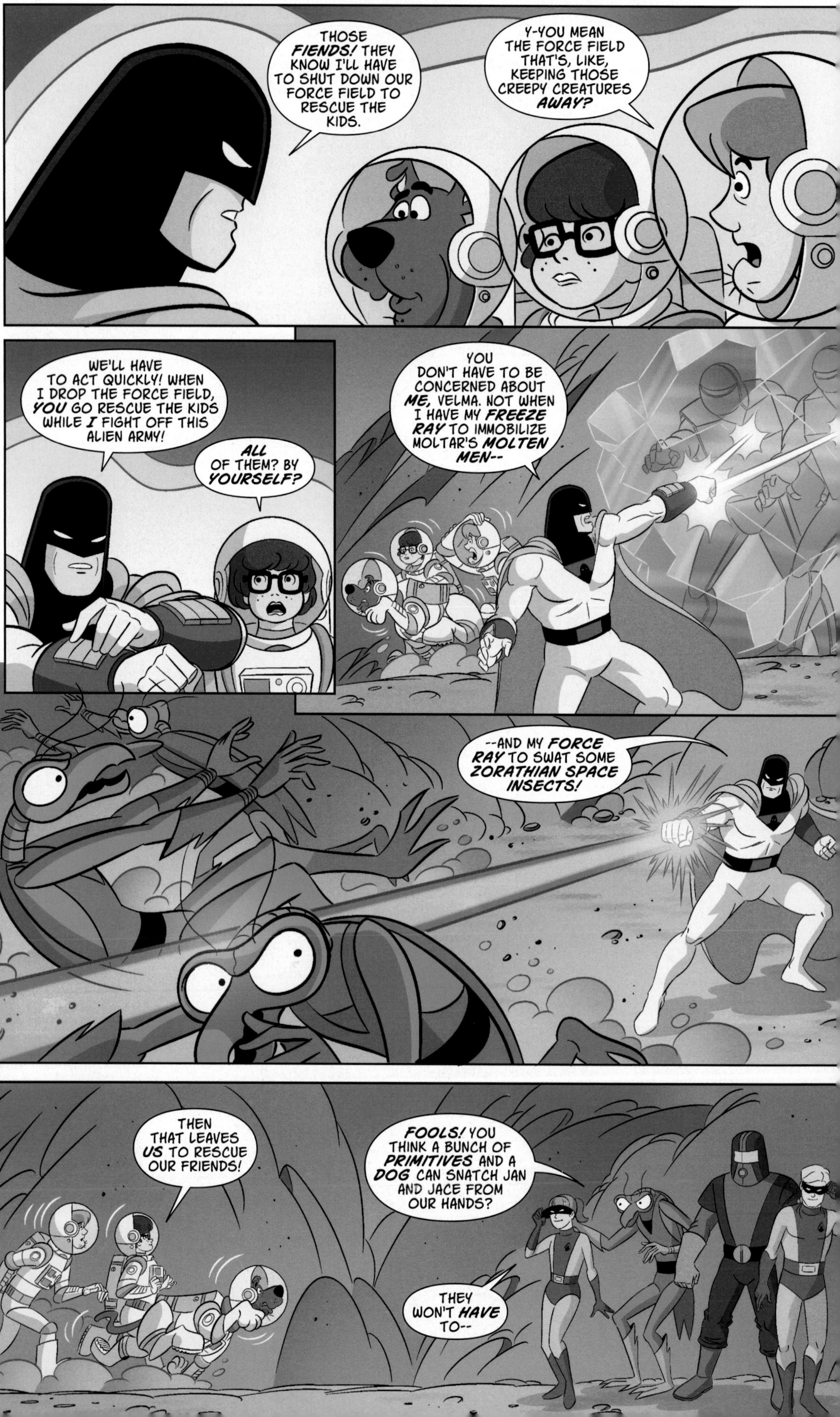
THOSE FIENDS! THEY KNOW I'LL HAVE TO SHUT DOWN OUR FORCE FIELD TO RESCUE THE KIDS.
Y-YOU MEAN THE FORCE FIELD THAT'S, LIKE, KEEPING THOSE CREEPY CREATURES AWAY?
WE'LL HAVE TO ACT QUICKLY! WHEN I DROP THE FORCE FIELD, YOU GO RESCUE THE KIDS WHILE I FIGHT OFF THIS ALIEN ARMY!
ALL OF THEM? BY YOURSELF?
YOU DON'T HAVE TO BE CONCERNED ABOUT ME, VELMA. NOT WHEN I HAVE MY FREEZE RAY TO IMMOBILIZE MOLTAR'S MOLTEN MEN--
--AND MY FORCE RAY TO SWAT SOME ZORATHIAN SPACE INSECTS!
THEN THAT LEAVES US TO RESCUE OUR FRIENDS!
FOOLS! YOU THINK A BUNCH OF PRIMITIVES AND A DOG CAN SNATCH JAN AND JACE FROM OUR HANDS?
THEY WON'T HAVE TO--

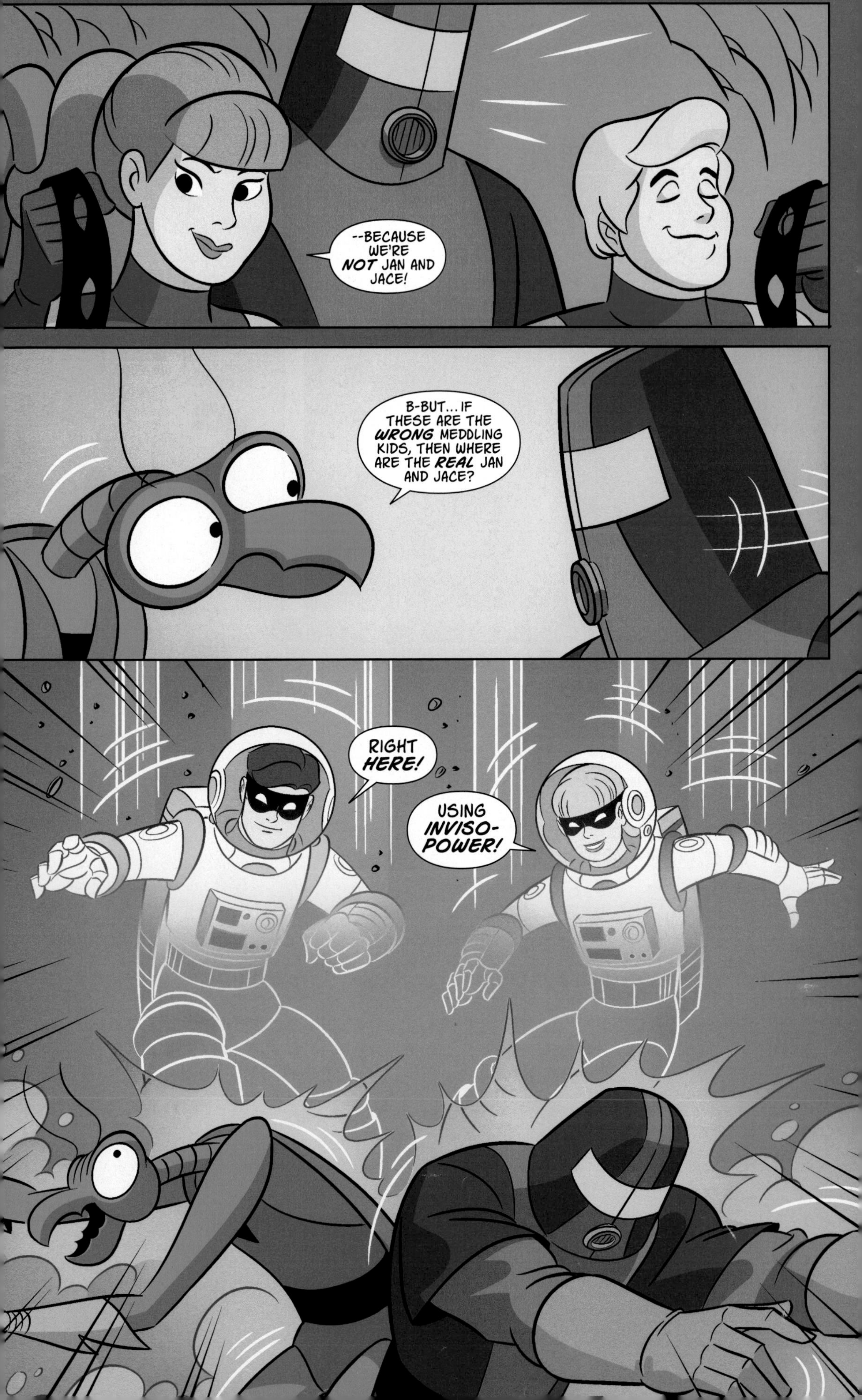
--BECAUSE WE'RE *NOT* JAN AND JACE!
B-BUT... IF THESE ARE THE *WRONG* MEDDLING KIDS, THEN WHERE ARE THE *REAL* JAN AND JACE?
RIGHT *HERE!*
USING *INVISO-POWER!*

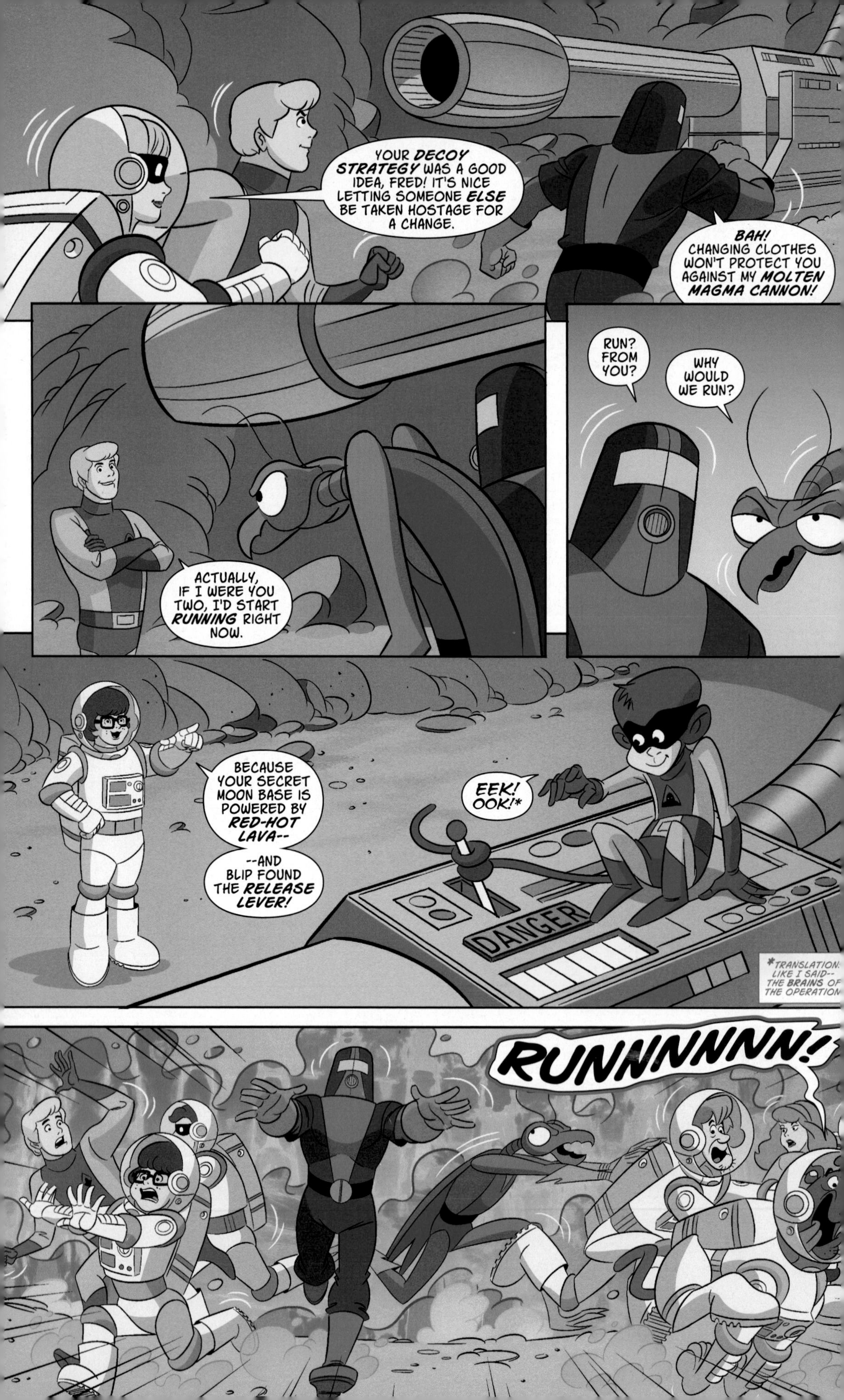
YOUR *DECOY STRATEGY* WAS A GOOD IDEA, FRED! IT'S NICE LETTING SOMEONE *ELSE* BE TAKEN HOSTAGE FOR A CHANGE.
BAH! CHANGING CLOTHES WON'T PROTECT YOU AGAINST MY *MOLTEN MAGMA CANNON!*
ACTUALLY, IF I WERE YOU TWO, I'D START *RUNNING* RIGHT NOW.
RUN? FROM YOU?
WHY WOULD WE RUN?
BECAUSE YOUR SECRET MOON BASE IS POWERED BY *RED-HOT LAVA--*
--AND BLIP FOUND THE *RELEASE LEVER!*
EEK! OOK!*
DANGER
*TRANSLATION: LIKE I SAID-- THE *BRAINS* OF THE OPERATION
RUNNNNNNN!

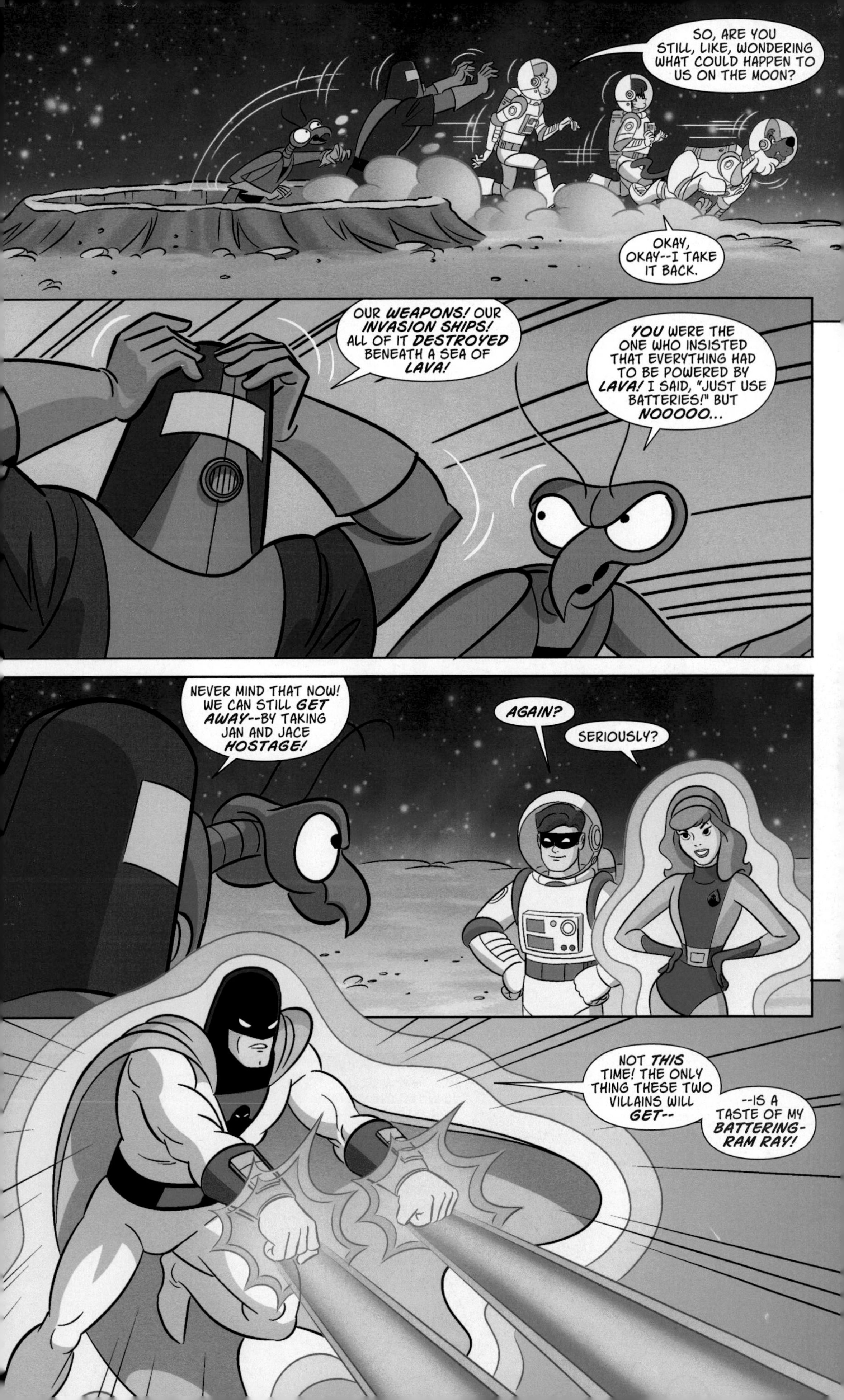

SO, ARE YOU STILL, LIKE, WONDERING WHAT COULD HAPPEN TO US ON THE MOON?
OKAY, OKAY--I TAKE IT BACK.
OUR WEAPONS! OUR INVASION SHIPS! ALL OF IT DESTROYED BENEATH A SEA OF LAVA!
YOU WERE THE ONE WHO INSISTED THAT EVERYTHING HAD TO BE POWERED BY LAVA! I SAID, "JUST USE BATTERIES!" BUT NOOOOO...
NEVER MIND THAT NOW! WE CAN STILL GET AWAY--BY TAKING JAN AND JACE HOSTAGE!
AGAIN?
SERIOUSLY?
NOT THIS TIME! THE ONLY THING THESE TWO VILLAINS WILL GET--
--IS A TASTE OF MY BATTERING-RAM RAY!

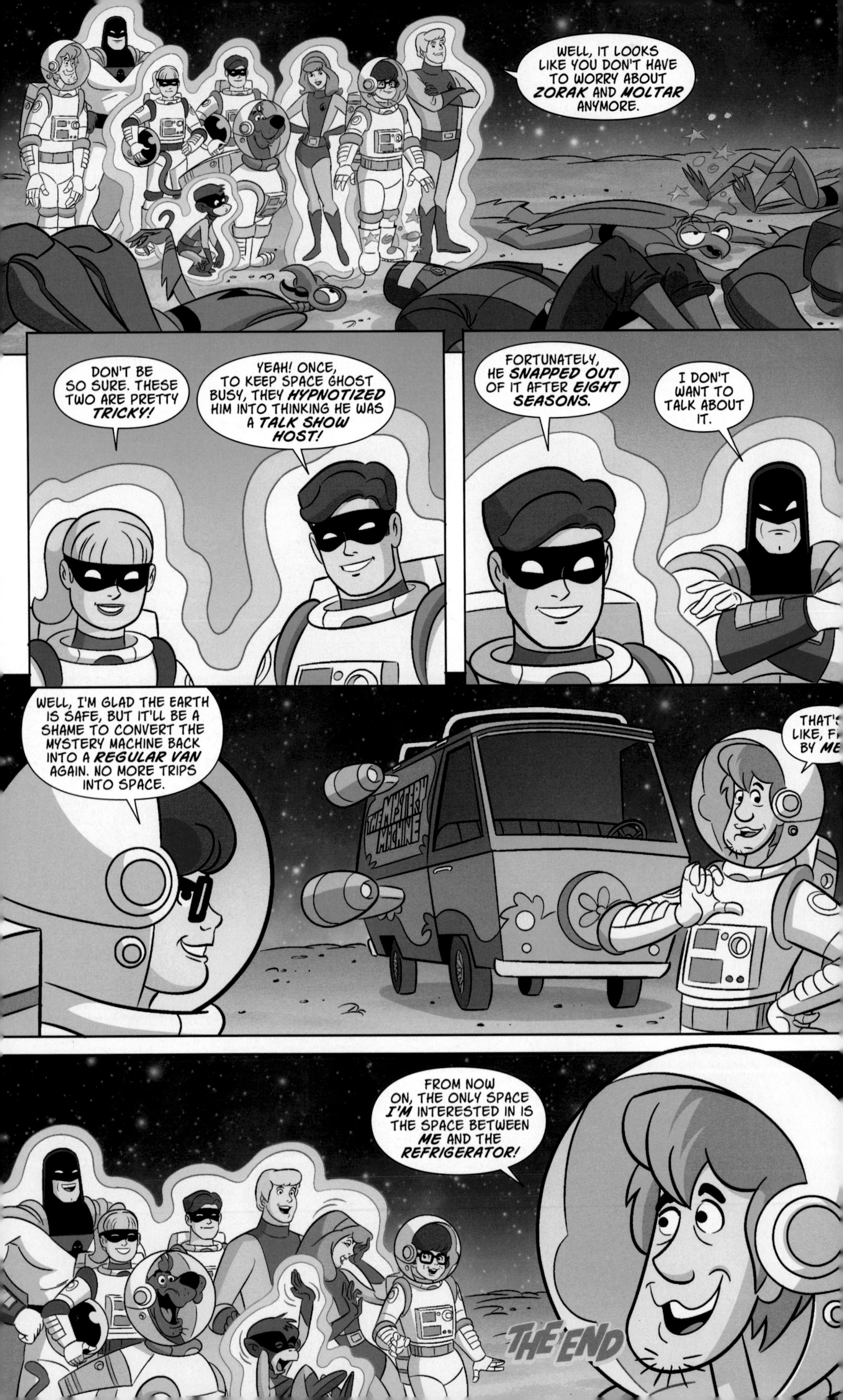
WELL, IT LOOKS LIKE YOU DON'T HAVE TO WORRY ABOUT ZORAK AND MOLTAR ANYMORE.
DON'T BE SO SURE. THESE TWO ARE PRETTY TRICKY!
YEAH! ONCE, TO KEEP SPACE GHOST BUSY, THEY HYPNOTIZED HIM INTO THINKING HE WAS A TALK SHOW HOST!
FORTUNATELY, HE SNAPPED OUT OF IT AFTER EIGHT SEASONS.
I DON'T WANT TO TALK ABOUT IT.
WELL, I'M GLAD THE EARTH IS SAFE, BUT IT'LL BE A SHAME TO CONVERT THE MYSTERY MACHINE BACK INTO A REGULAR VAN AGAIN. NO MORE TRIPS INTO SPACE.
THE MYSTERY MACHINE
FROM NOW ON, THE ONLY SPACE I'M INTERESTED IN IS THE SPACE BETWEEN ME AND THE REFRIGERATOR!
THE END

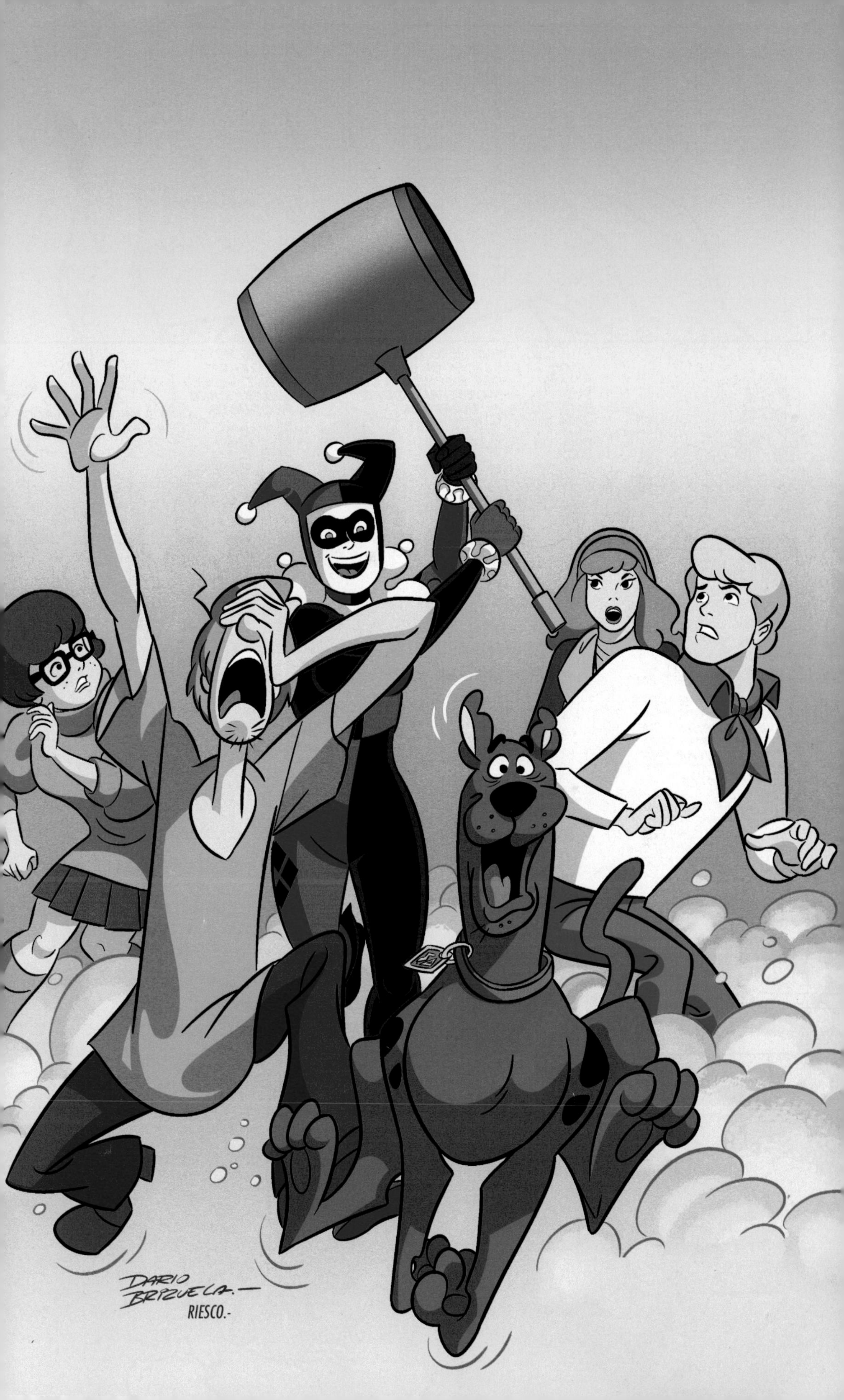
DARIO BRIZUELA.—
RIESCO.-

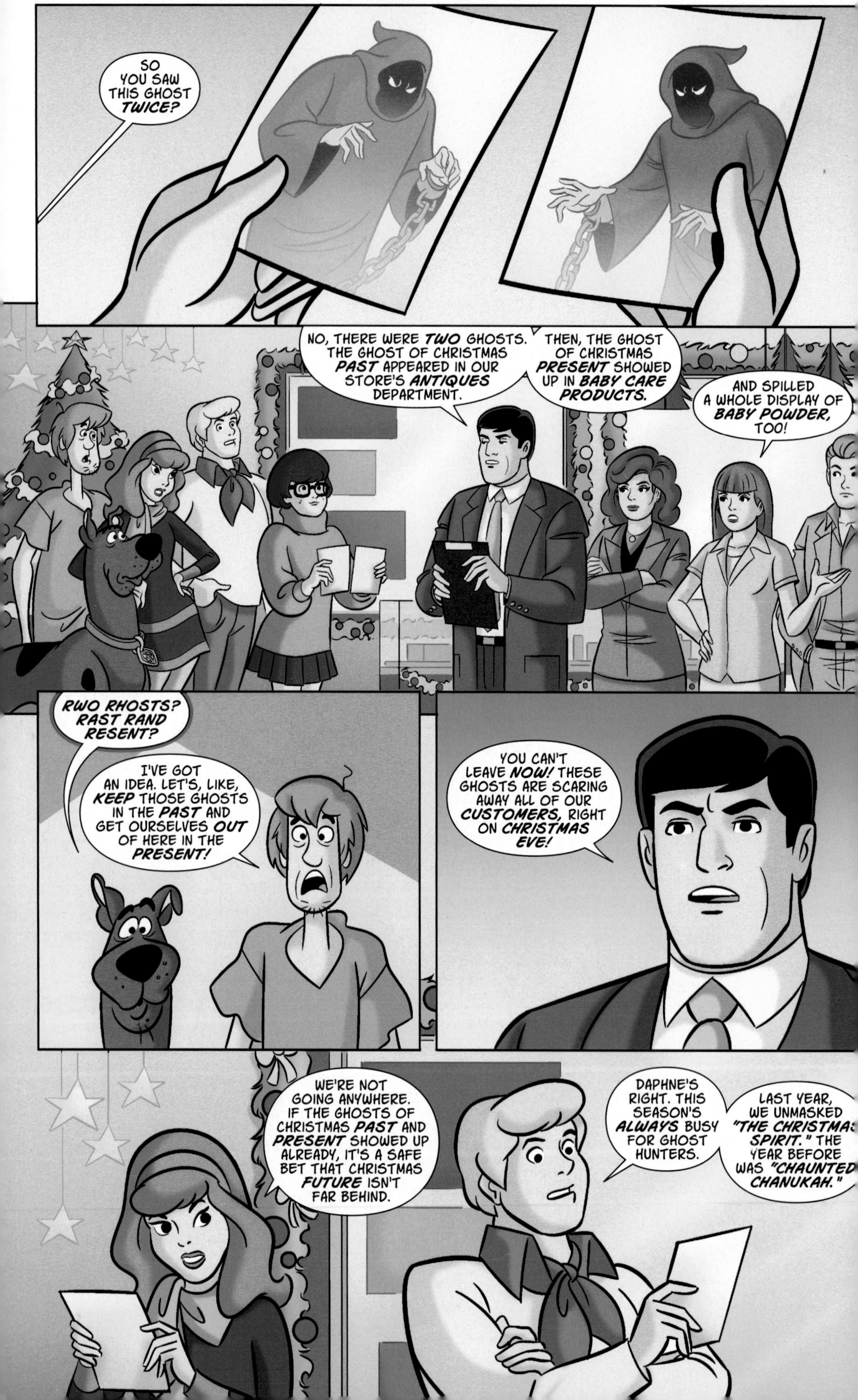

SO YOU SAW THIS GHOST TWICE?
NO, THERE WERE TWO GHOSTS. THE GHOST OF CHRISTMAS PAST APPEARED IN OUR STORE'S ANTIQUES DEPARTMENT.
THEN, THE GHOST OF CHRISTMAS PRESENT SHOWED UP IN BABY CARE PRODUCTS.
AND SPILLED A WHOLE DISPLAY OF BABY POWDER, TOO!
RWO RHOSTS? RAST RAND RESENT?
I'VE GOT AN IDEA. LET'S, LIKE, KEEP THOSE GHOSTS IN THE PAST AND GET OURSELVES OUT OF HERE IN THE PRESENT!
YOU CAN'T LEAVE NOW! THESE GHOSTS ARE SCARING AWAY ALL OF OUR CUSTOMERS, RIGHT ON CHRISTMAS EVE!
WE'RE NOT GOING ANYWHERE. IF THE GHOSTS OF CHRISTMAS PAST AND PRESENT SHOWED UP ALREADY, IT'S A SAFE BET THAT CHRISTMAS FUTURE ISN'T FAR BEHIND.
DAPHNE'S RIGHT. THIS SEASON'S ALWAYS BUSY FOR GHOST HUNTERS.
LAST YEAR, WE UNMASKED "THE CHRISTMAS SPIRIT." THE YEAR BEFORE WAS "CHAUNTED CHANUKAH."

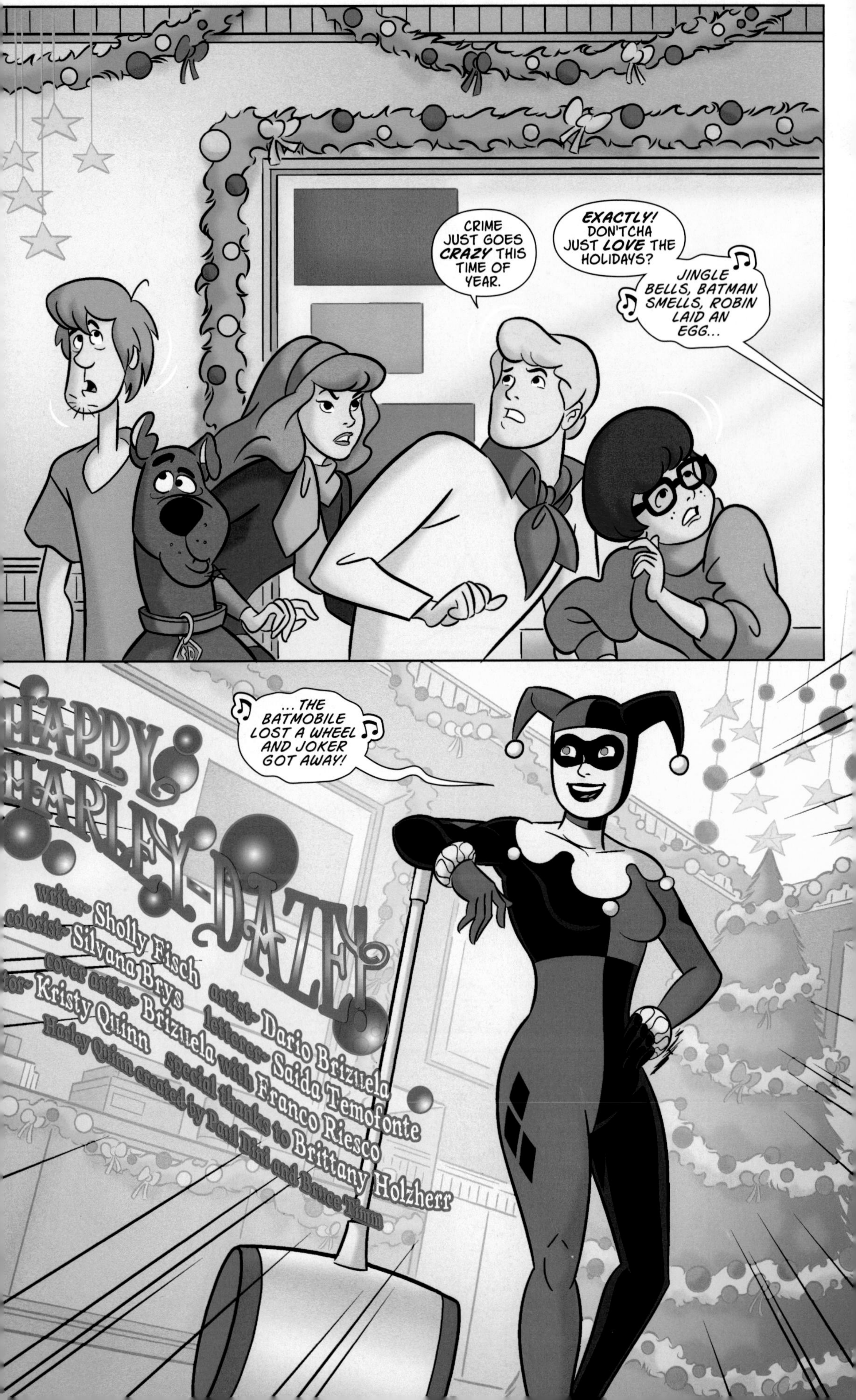
CRIME JUST GOES CRAZY THIS TIME OF YEAR.
EXACTLY! DON'TCHA JUST LOVE THE HOLIDAYS?
JINGLE BELLS, BATMAN SMELLS, ROBIN LAID AN EGG...
...THE BATMOBILE LOST A WHEEL AND JOKER GOT AWAY!
HAPPY HARLEY-DAZE!
writer~ Sholly Fisch
artist~ Dario Brizuela
colorist~ Silvana Brys
letterer~ Saida Temofonte
cover artist~ Brizuela with Franco Riesco
tor~ Kristy Quinn
special thanks to Brittany Holzherr
Harley Quinn created by Paul Dini and Bruce Timm

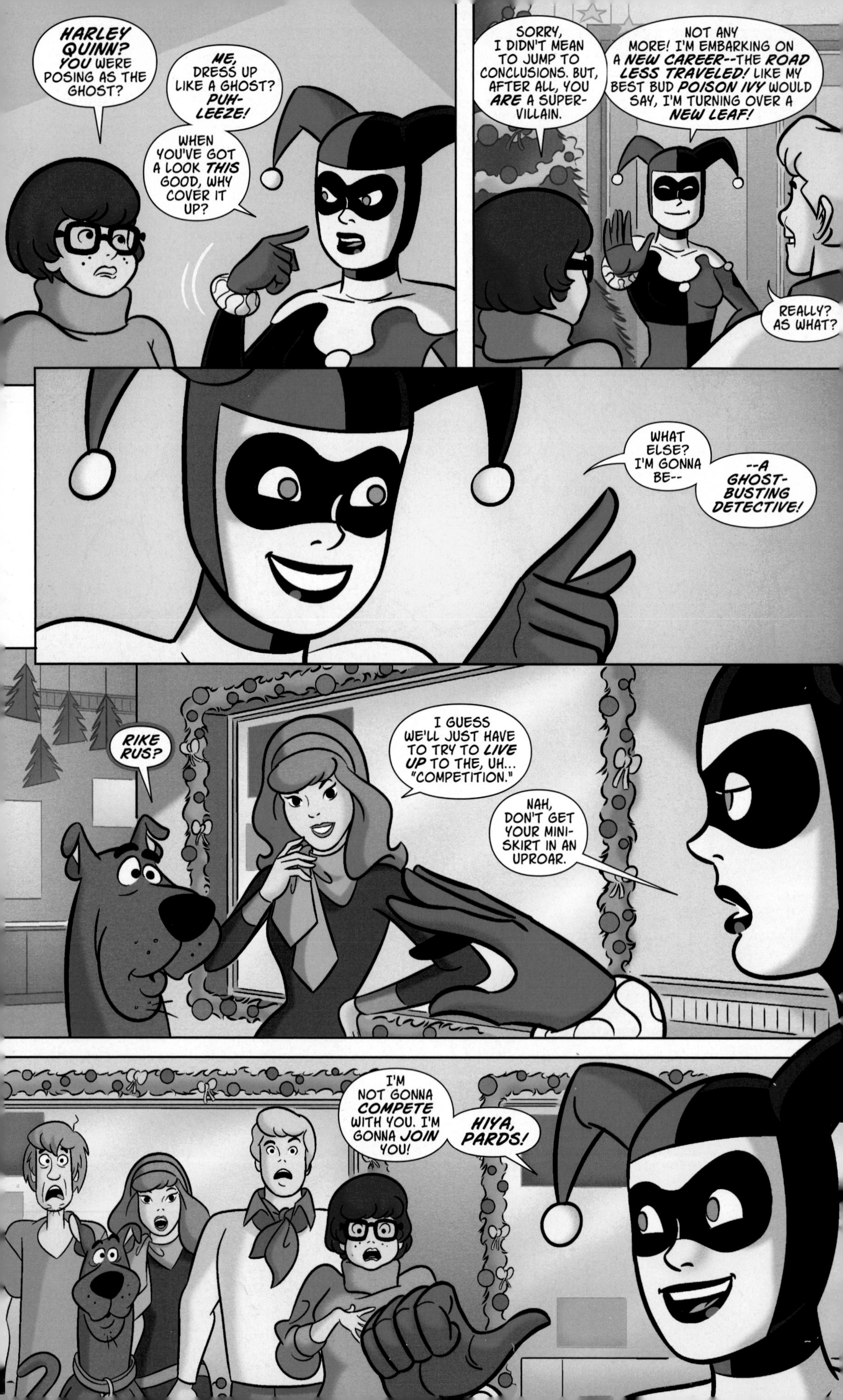
HARLEY QUINN? YOU WERE POSING AS THE GHOST?
ME, DRESS UP LIKE A GHOST? PUH-LEEZE!
WHEN YOU'VE GOT A LOOK THIS GOOD, WHY COVER IT UP?
SORRY, I DIDN'T MEAN TO JUMP TO CONCLUSIONS. BUT, AFTER ALL, YOU ARE A SUPER-VILLAIN.
NOT ANY MORE! I'M EMBARKING ON A NEW CAREER--THE ROAD LESS TRAVELED! LIKE MY BEST BUD POISON IVY WOULD SAY, I'M TURNING OVER A NEW LEAF!
REALLY? AS WHAT?
WHAT ELSE? I'M GONNA BE--
--A GHOST-BUSTING DETECTIVE!
RIKE RUS?
I GUESS WE'LL JUST HAVE TO TRY TO LIVE UP TO THE, UH... "COMPETITION."
NAH, DON'T GET YOUR MINI-SKIRT IN AN UPROAR.
I'M NOT GONNA COMPETE WITH YOU. I'M GONNA JOIN YOU!
HIYA, PARDS!

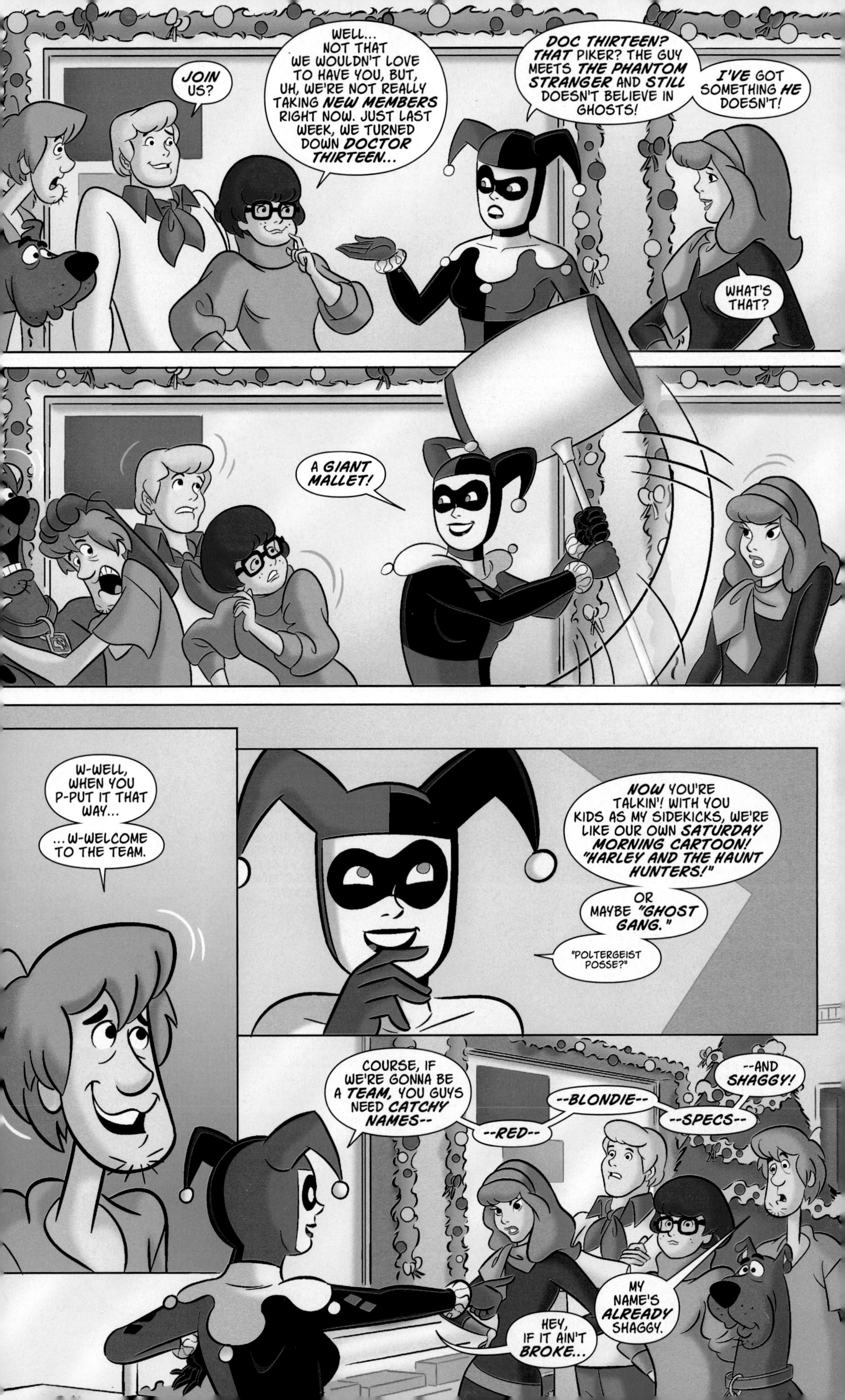
JOIN US?
WELL... NOT THAT WE WOULDN'T LOVE TO HAVE YOU, BUT, UH, WE'RE NOT REALLY TAKING NEW MEMBERS RIGHT NOW. JUST LAST WEEK, WE TURNED DOWN DOCTOR THIRTEEN...
DOC THIRTEEN? THAT PIKER? THE GUY MEETS THE PHANTOM STRANGER AND STILL DOESN'T BELIEVE IN GHOSTS!
I'VE GOT SOMETHING HE DOESN'T!
WHAT'S THAT?
A GIANT MALLET!
W-WELL, WHEN YOU P-PUT IT THAT WAY...
...W-WELCOME TO THE TEAM.
NOW YOU'RE TALKIN'! WITH YOU KIDS AS MY SIDEKICKS, WE'RE LIKE OUR OWN SATURDAY MORNING CARTOON! "HARLEY AND THE HAUNT HUNTERS!"
OR MAYBE "GHOST GANG."
"POLTERGEIST POSSE?"
COURSE, IF WE'RE GONNA BE A TEAM, YOU GUYS NEED CATCHY NAMES--
--RED--
--BLONDIE--
--SPECS--
--AND SHAGGY!
MY NAME'S ALREADY SHAGGY.
HEY, IF IT AIN'T BROKE...

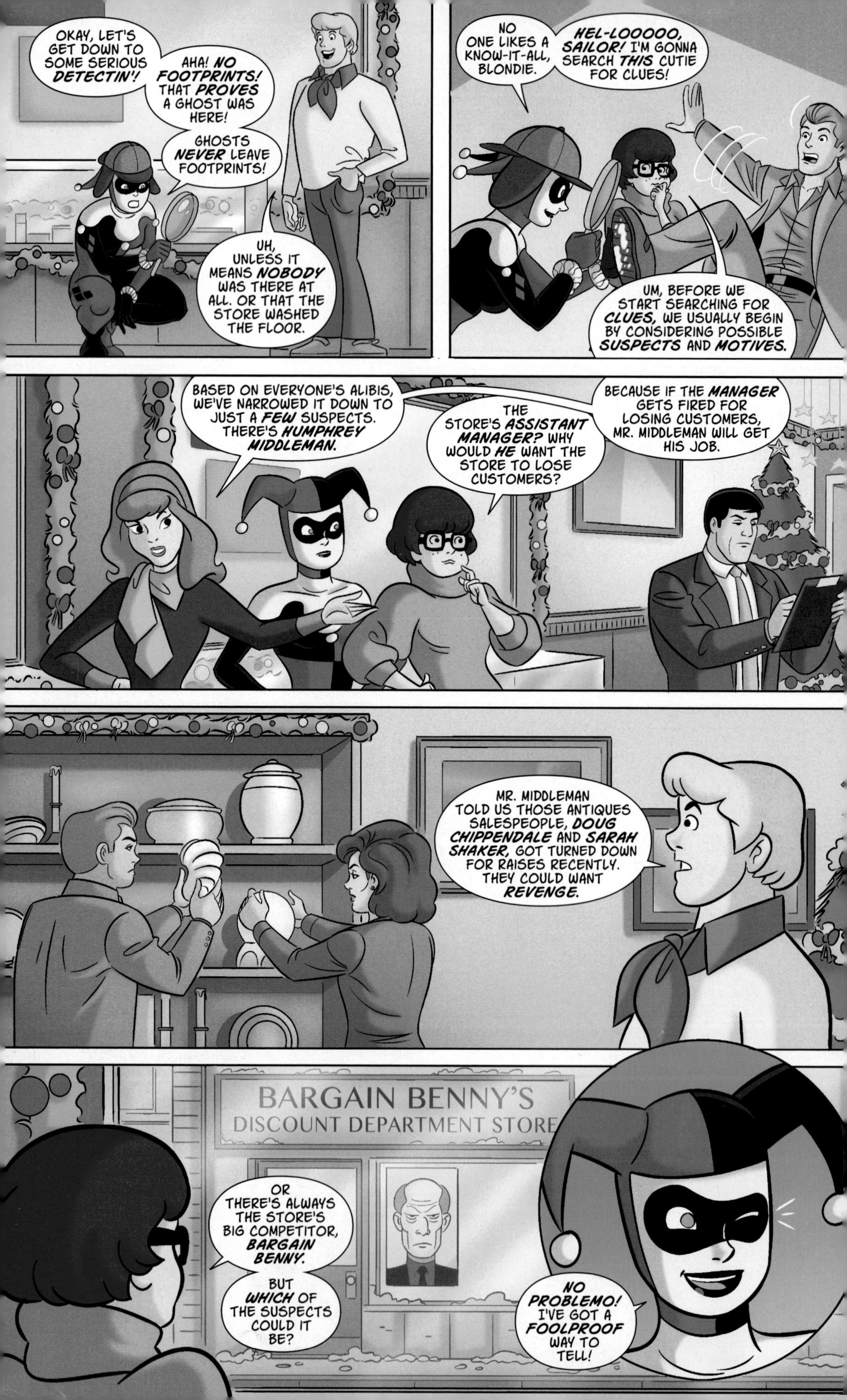
OKAY, LET'S GET DOWN TO SOME SERIOUS DETECTIN'!
AHA! NO FOOTPRINTS! THAT PROVES A GHOST WAS HERE!
GHOSTS NEVER LEAVE FOOTPRINTS!
UH, UNLESS IT MEANS NOBODY WAS THERE AT ALL. OR THAT THE STORE WASHED THE FLOOR.
NO ONE LIKES A KNOW-IT-ALL, BLONDIE.
HEL-LOOOOO, SAILOR! I'M GONNA SEARCH THIS CUTIE FOR CLUES!
UM, BEFORE WE START SEARCHING FOR CLUES, WE USUALLY BEGIN BY CONSIDERING POSSIBLE SUSPECTS AND MOTIVES.
BASED ON EVERYONE'S ALIBIS, WE'VE NARROWED IT DOWN TO JUST A FEW SUSPECTS. THERE'S HUMPHREY MIDDLEMAN.
THE STORE'S ASSISTANT MANAGER? WHY WOULD HE WANT THE STORE TO LOSE CUSTOMERS?
BECAUSE IF THE MANAGER GETS FIRED FOR LOSING CUSTOMERS, MR. MIDDLEMAN WILL GET HIS JOB.
MR. MIDDLEMAN TOLD US THOSE ANTIQUES SALESPEOPLE, DOUG CHIPPENDALE AND SARAH SHAKER, GOT TURNED DOWN FOR RAISES RECENTLY. THEY COULD WANT REVENGE.
BARGAIN BENNY'S
DISCOUNT DEPARTMENT STORE
OR THERE'S ALWAYS THE STORE'S BIG COMPETITOR, BARGAIN BENNY.
BUT WHICH OF THE SUSPECTS COULD IT BE?
NO PROBLEMO! I'VE GOT A FOOLPROOF WAY TO TELL!

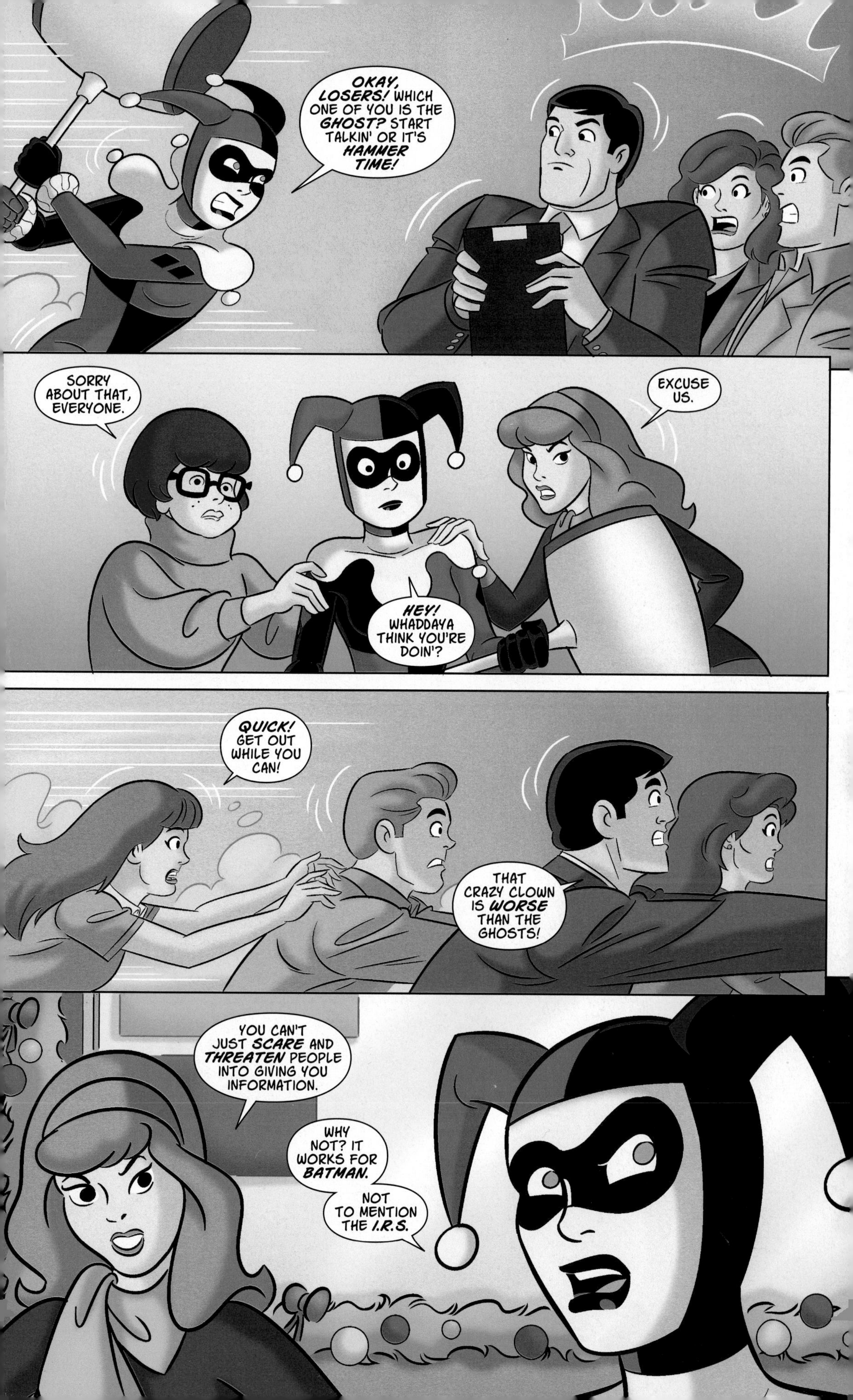
OKAY, LOSERS! WHICH ONE OF YOU IS THE GHOST? START TALKIN' OR IT'S HAMMER TIME!
SORRY ABOUT THAT, EVERYONE.
EXCUSE US.
HEY! WHADDAYA THINK YOU'RE DOIN'?
QUICK! GET OUT WHILE YOU CAN!
THAT CRAZY CLOWN IS WORSE THAN THE GHOSTS!
YOU CAN'T JUST SCARE AND THREATEN PEOPLE INTO GIVING YOU INFORMATION.
WHY NOT? IT WORKS FOR BATMAN.
NOT TO MENTION THE I.R.S.

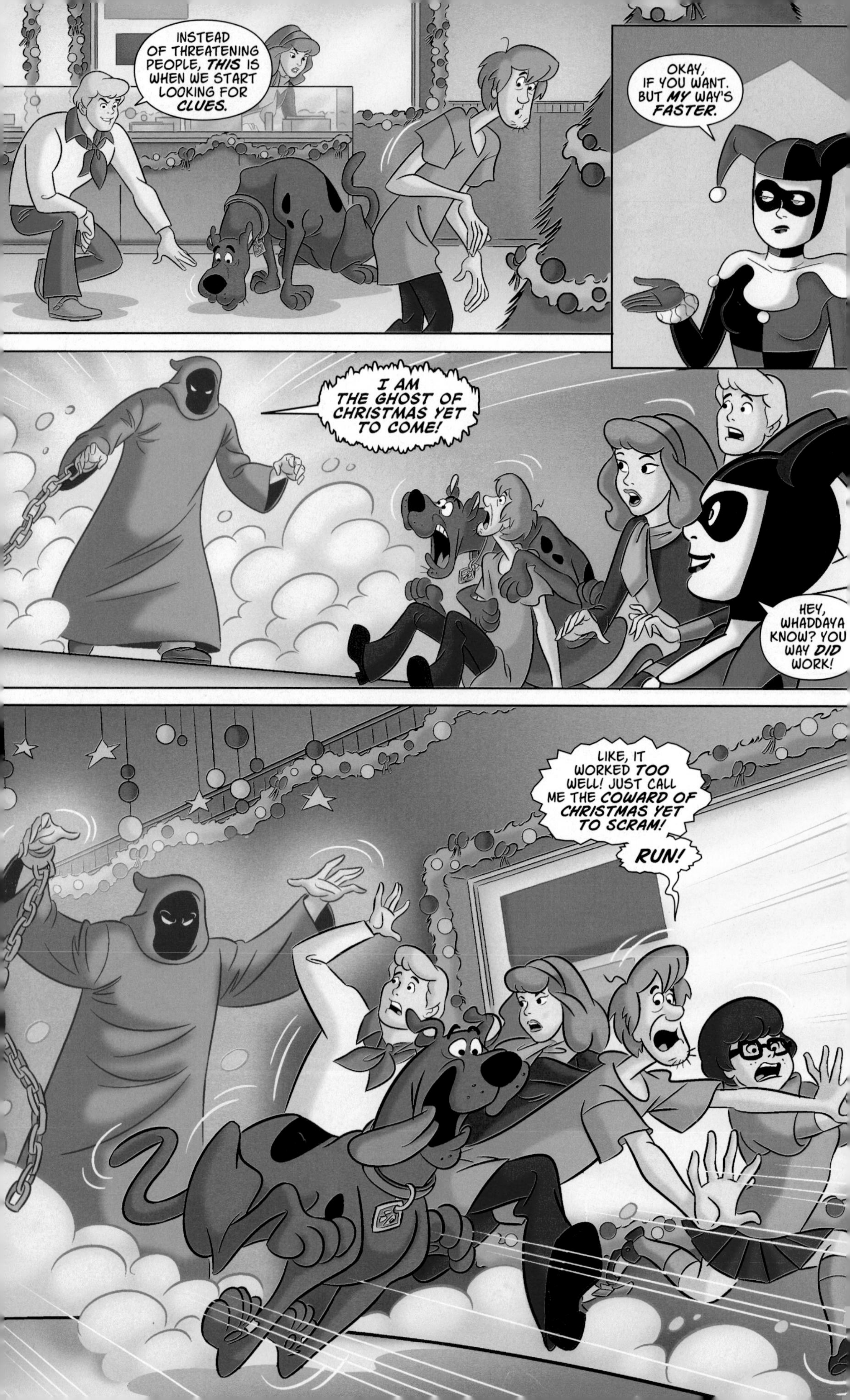
INSTEAD OF THREATENING PEOPLE, THIS IS WHEN WE START LOOKING FOR CLUES.
OKAY, IF YOU WANT. BUT MY WAY'S FASTER.
I AM THE GHOST OF CHRISTMAS YET TO COME!
HEY, WHADDAYA KNOW? YOU WAY DID WORK!
LIKE, IT WORKED TOO WELL! JUST CALL ME THE COWARD OF CHRISTMAS YET TO SCRAM!
RUN!

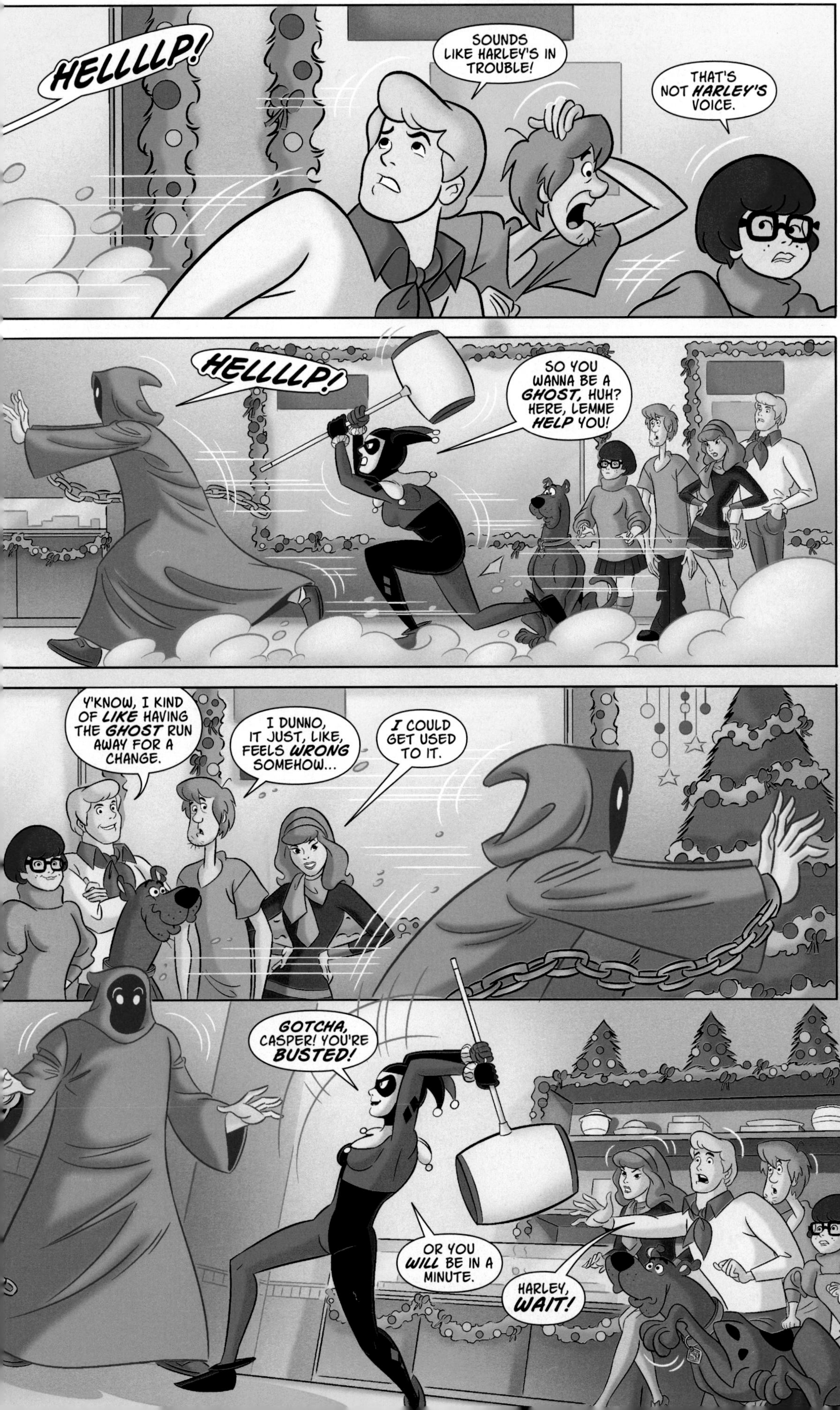
HELLLLP!
SOUNDS LIKE HARLEY'S IN TROUBLE!
THAT'S NOT HARLEY'S VOICE.
HELLLLP!
SO YOU WANNA BE A GHOST, HUH? HERE, LEMME HELP YOU!
Y'KNOW, I KIND OF LIKE HAVING THE GHOST RUN AWAY FOR A CHANGE.
I DUNNO, IT JUST, LIKE, FEELS WRONG SOMEHOW...
I COULD GET USED TO IT.
GOTCHA, CASPER! YOU'RE BUSTED!
OR YOU WILL BE IN A MINUTE.
HARLEY, WAIT!

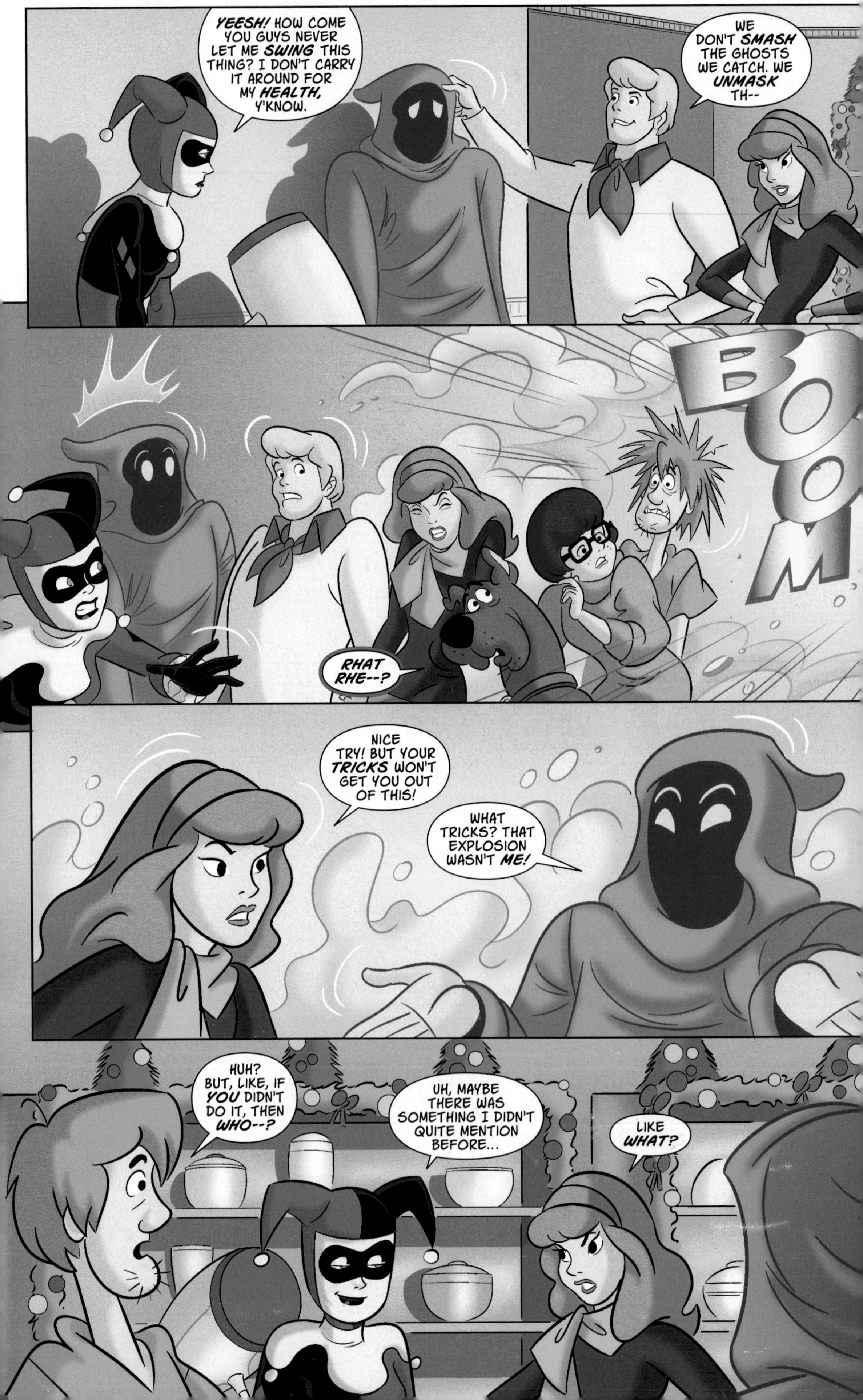
YEESH! HOW COME YOU GUYS NEVER LET ME SWING THIS THING? I DON'T CARRY IT AROUND FOR MY HEALTH, Y'KNOW.
WE DON'T SMASH THE GHOSTS WE CATCH. WE UNMASK TH--
BOOM
RHAT RHE--?
NICE TRY! BUT YOUR TRICKS WON'T GET YOU OUT OF THIS!
WHAT TRICKS? THAT EXPLOSION WASN'T ME!
HUH? BUT, LIKE, IF YOU DIDN'T DO IT, THEN WHO--?
UH, MAYBE THERE WAS SOMETHING I DIDN'T QUITE MENTION BEFORE...
LIKE WHAT?

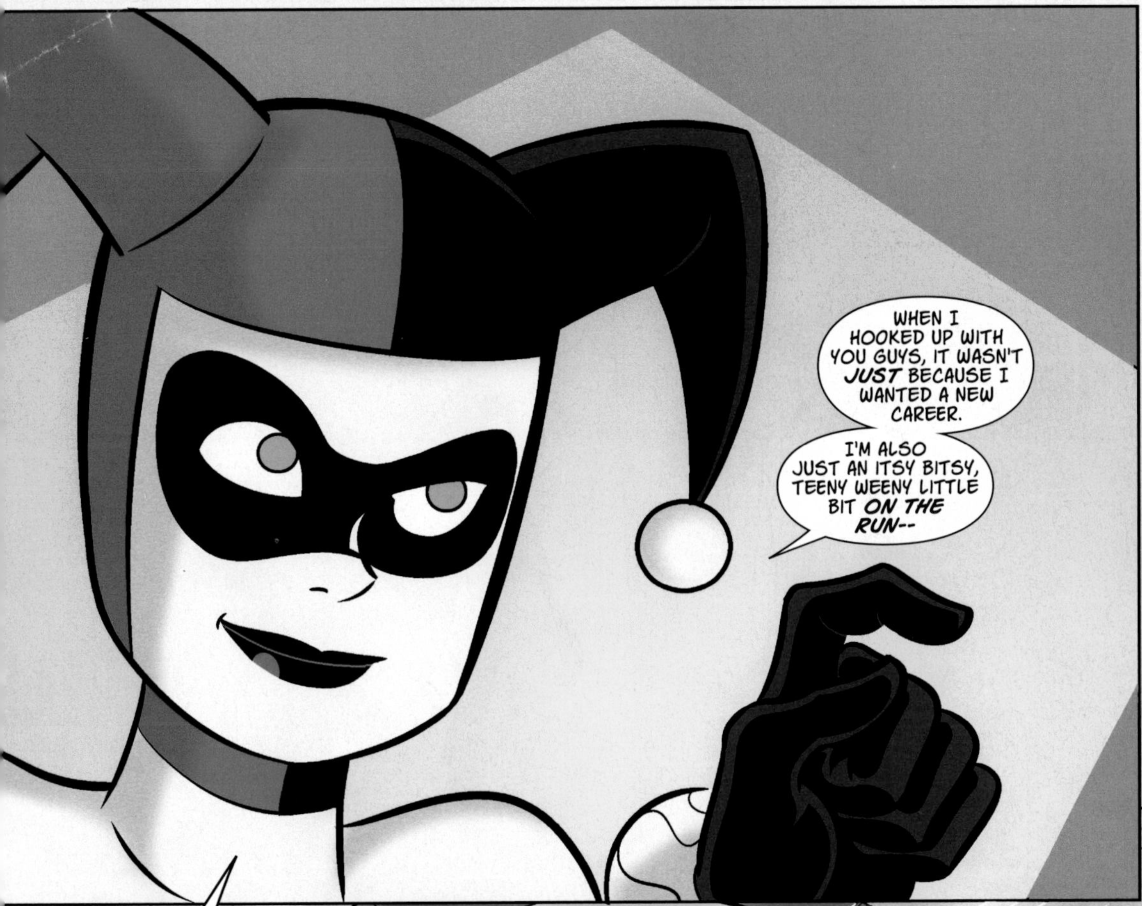
WHEN I HOOKED UP WITH YOU GUYS, IT WASN'T JUST BECAUSE I WANTED A NEW CAREER.
I'M ALSO JUST AN ITSY BITSY, TEENY WEENY LITTLE BIT ON THE RUN--

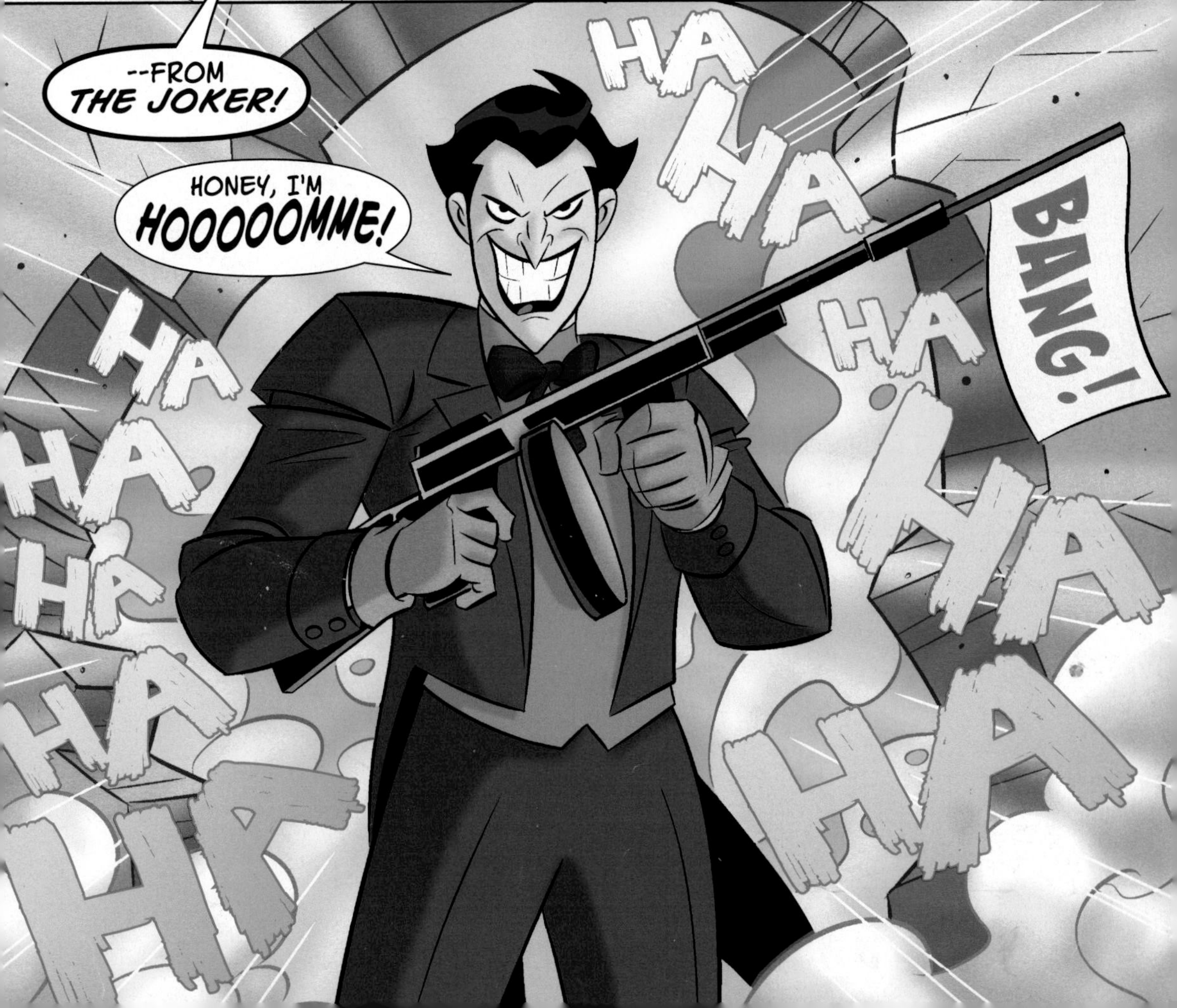
--FROM THE JOKER!
HONEY, I'M HOOOOOMME!
HA HA HA
BANG!
HA HA HA HA
HA HA HA HA HA HA HA

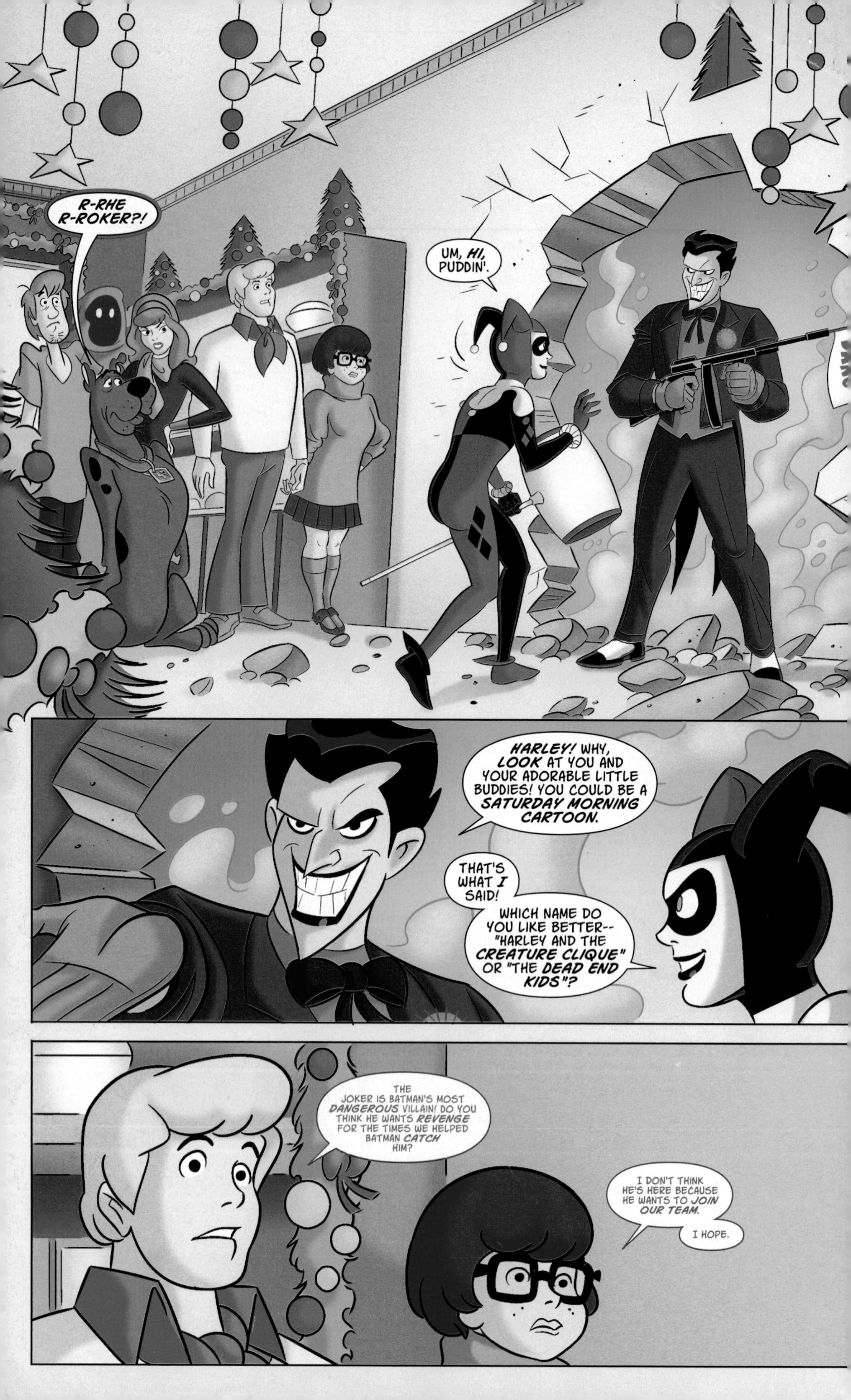
R-RHE R-ROKER?!
UM, HI, PUDDIN'.
HARLEY! WHY, LOOK AT YOU AND YOUR ADORABLE LITTLE BUDDIES! YOU COULD BE A SATURDAY MORNING CARTOON.
THAT'S WHAT I SAID!
WHICH NAME DO YOU LIKE BETTER-- "HARLEY AND THE CREATURE CLIQUE" OR "THE DEAD END KIDS"?
THE JOKER IS BATMAN'S MOST DANGEROUS VILLAIN! DO YOU THINK HE WANTS REVENGE FOR THE TIMES WE HELPED BATMAN CATCH HIM?
I DON'T THINK HE'S HERE BECAUSE HE WANTS TO JOIN OUR TEAM.
I HOPE.

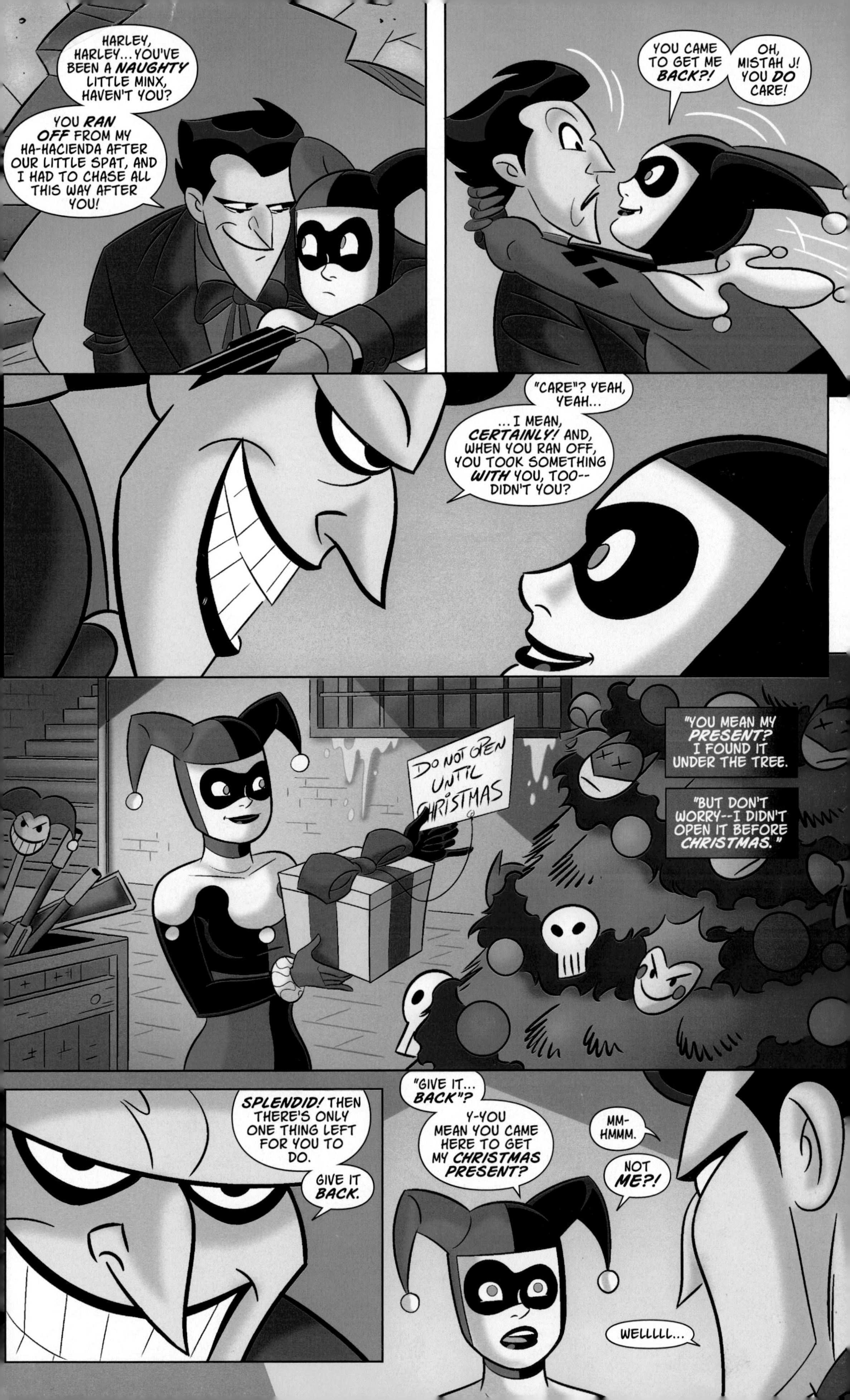
HARLEY, HARLEY... YOU'VE BEEN A NAUGHTY LITTLE MINX, HAVEN'T YOU?
YOU RAN OFF FROM MY HA-HACIENDA AFTER OUR LITTLE SPAT, AND I HAD TO CHASE ALL THIS WAY AFTER YOU!
YOU CAME TO GET ME BACK?!
OH, MISTAH J! YOU DO CARE!
"CARE"? YEAH, YEAH...
...I MEAN, CERTAINLY! AND, WHEN YOU RAN OFF, YOU TOOK SOMETHING WITH YOU, TOO--DIDN'T YOU?
DO NOT OPEN UNTIL CHRISTMAS
"YOU MEAN MY PRESENT? I FOUND IT UNDER THE TREE.
"BUT DON'T WORRY--I DIDN'T OPEN IT BEFORE CHRISTMAS."
SPLENDID! THEN THERE'S ONLY ONE THING LEFT FOR YOU TO DO.
GIVE IT BACK.
"GIVE IT... BACK"?
Y-YOU MEAN YOU CAME HERE TO GET MY CHRISTMAS PRESENT?
MM-HMMM.
NOT ME?!
WELLLLL...

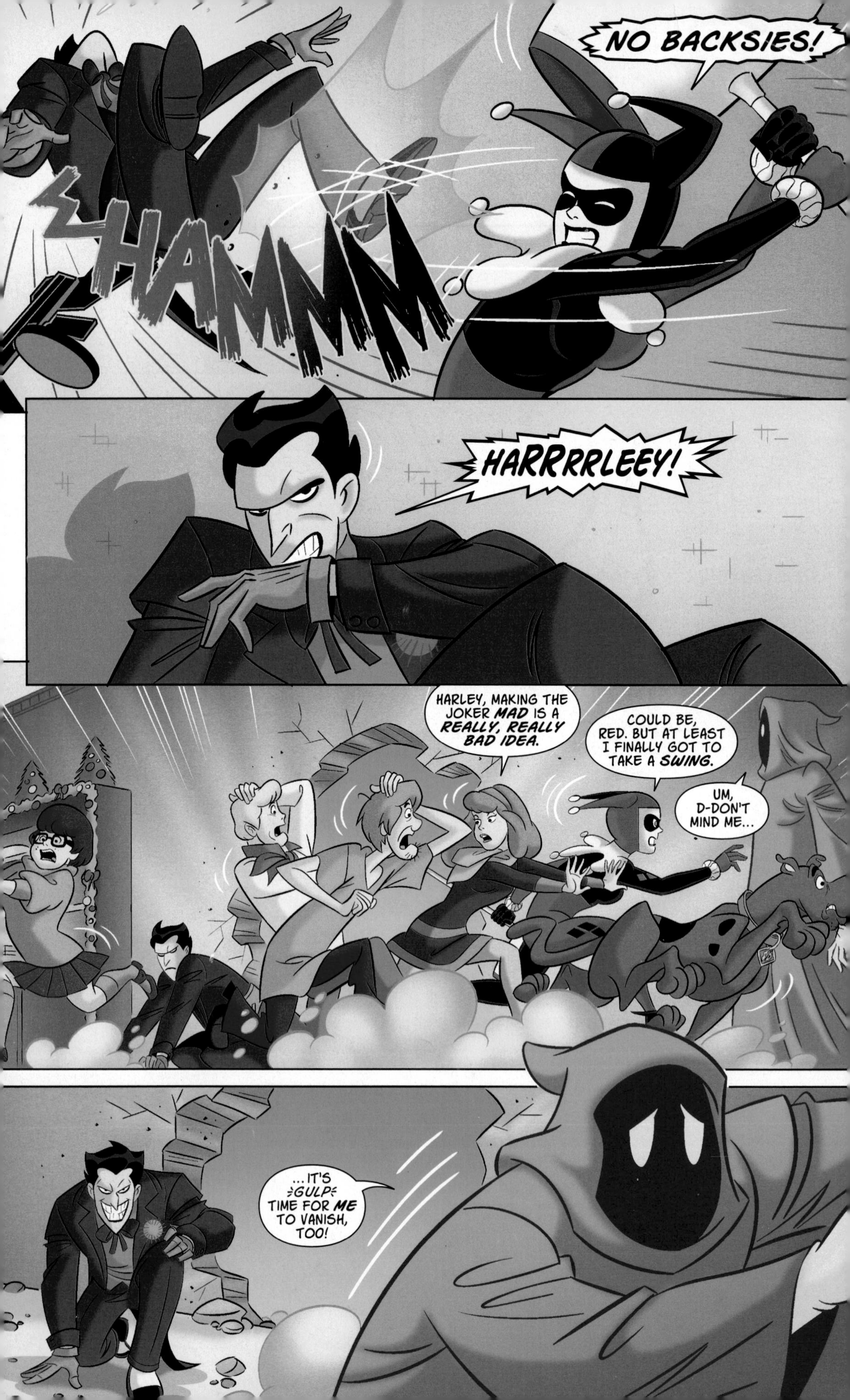
NO BACKSIES!
WHAMMM
HARRRRRLEEY!
HARLEY, MAKING THE JOKER MAD IS A REALLY, REALLY BAD IDEA.
COULD BE, RED. BUT AT LEAST I FINALLY GOT TO TAKE A SWING.
UM, D-DON'T MIND ME...
...IT'S GULP TIME FOR ME TO VANISH, TOO!

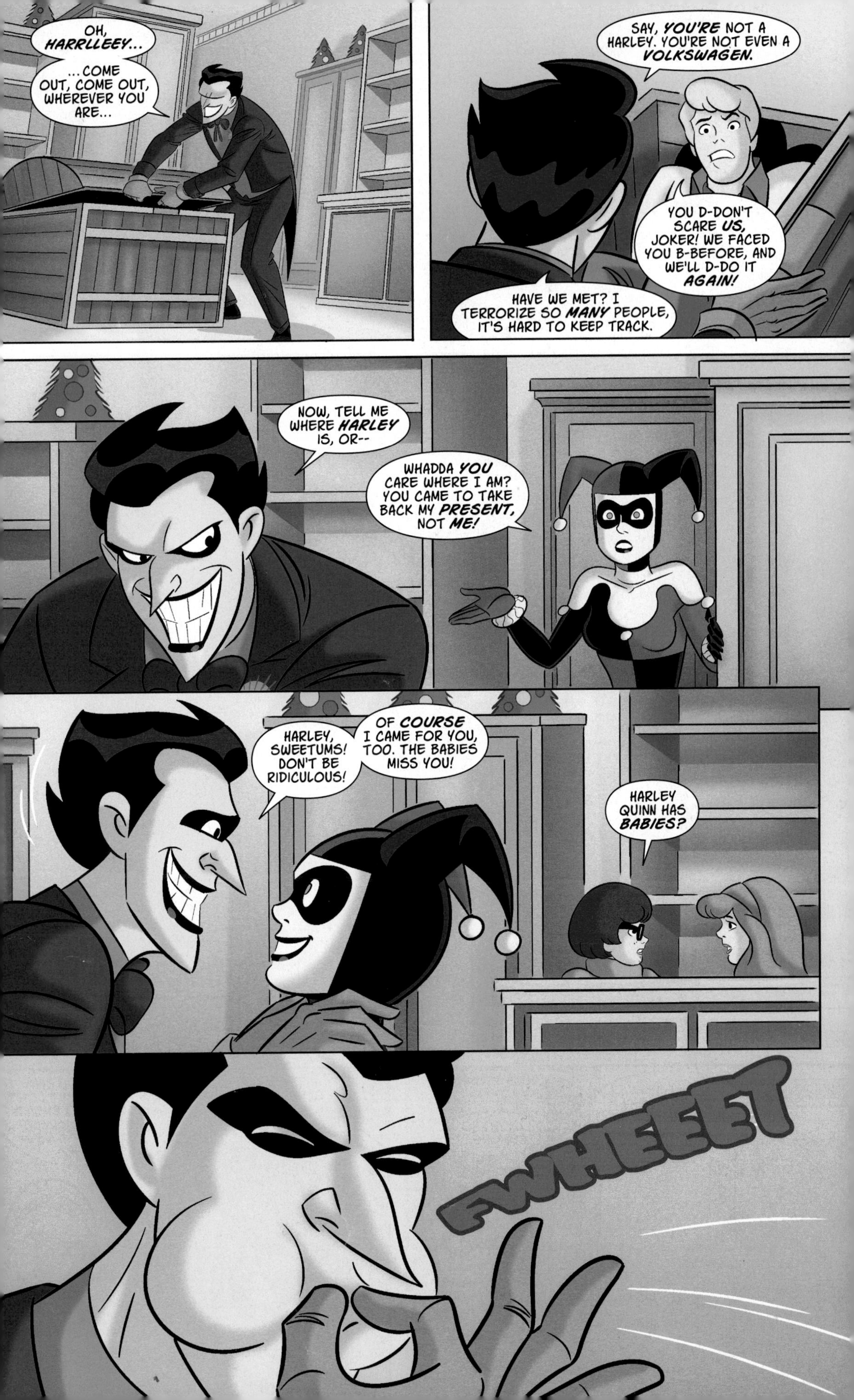

OH, HARRLLEEY...
...COME OUT, COME OUT, WHEREVER YOU ARE...
SAY, YOU'RE NOT A HARLEY. YOU'RE NOT EVEN A VOLKSWAGEN.
YOU D-DON'T SCARE US, JOKER! WE FACED YOU B-BEFORE, AND WE'LL D-DO IT AGAIN!
HAVE WE MET? I TERRORIZE SO MANY PEOPLE, IT'S HARD TO KEEP TRACK.
NOW, TELL ME WHERE HARLEY IS, OR--
WHADDA YOU CARE WHERE I AM? YOU CAME TO TAKE BACK MY PRESENT, NOT ME!
HARLEY, SWEETUMS! DON'T BE RIDICULOUS!
OF COURSE I CAME FOR YOU, TOO. THE BABIES MISS YOU!
HARLEY QUINN HAS BABIES?
FWHEEET

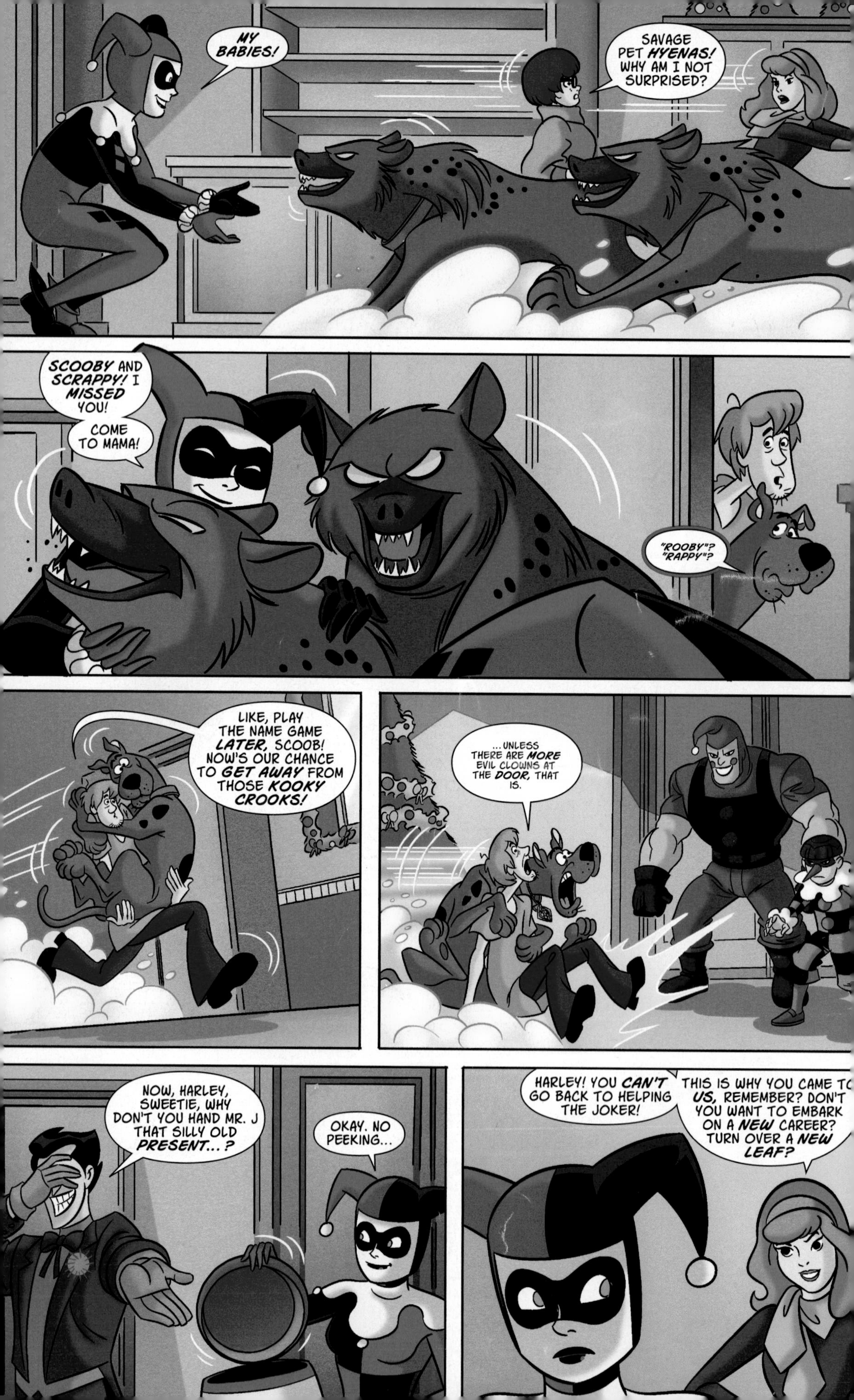
MY BABIES!
SAVAGE PET HYENAS! WHY AM I NOT SURPRISED?
SCOOBY AND SCRAPPY! I MISSED YOU!
COME TO MAMA!
"ROOBY"? "RAPPY"?
LIKE, PLAY THE NAME GAME LATER, SCOOB! NOW'S OUR CHANCE TO GET AWAY FROM THOSE KOOKY CROOKS!
...UNLESS THERE ARE MORE EVIL CLOWNS AT THE DOOR, THAT IS.
NOW, HARLEY, SWEETIE, WHY DON'T YOU HAND MR. J THAT SILLY OLD PRESENT...?
OKAY. NO PEEKING...
HARLEY! YOU CAN'T GO BACK TO HELPING THE JOKER!
THIS IS WHY YOU CAME TO US, REMEMBER? DON'T YOU WANT TO EMBARK ON A NEW CAREER? TURN OVER A NEW LEAF?

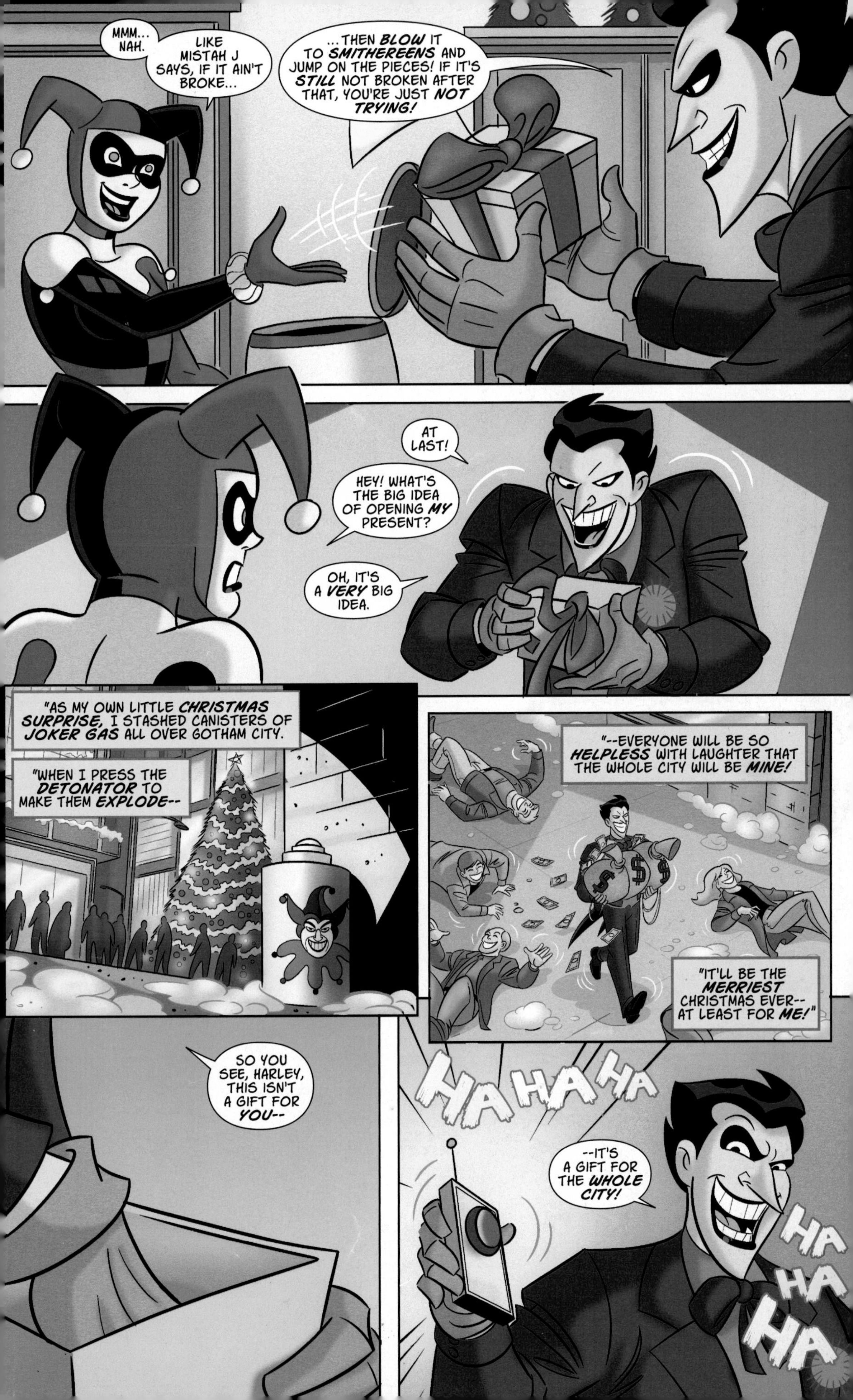

MMM... NAH.
LIKE MISTAH J SAYS, IF IT AIN'T BROKE...
...THEN BLOW IT TO SMITHEREENS AND JUMP ON THE PIECES! IF IT'S STILL NOT BROKEN AFTER THAT, YOU'RE JUST NOT TRYING!
AT LAST!
HEY! WHAT'S THE BIG IDEA OF OPENING MY PRESENT?
OH, IT'S A VERY BIG IDEA.
"AS MY OWN LITTLE CHRISTMAS SURPRISE, I STASHED CANISTERS OF JOKER GAS ALL OVER GOTHAM CITY.
"WHEN I PRESS THE DETONATOR TO MAKE THEM EXPLODE--
"--EVERYONE WILL BE SO HELPLESS WITH LAUGHTER THAT THE WHOLE CITY WILL BE MINE!
"IT'LL BE THE MERRIEST CHRISTMAS EVER--AT LEAST FOR ME!"
SO YOU SEE, HARLEY, THIS ISN'T A GIFT FOR YOU--
HA HA HA HA
--IT'S A GIFT FOR THE WHOLE CITY!
HA HA HA

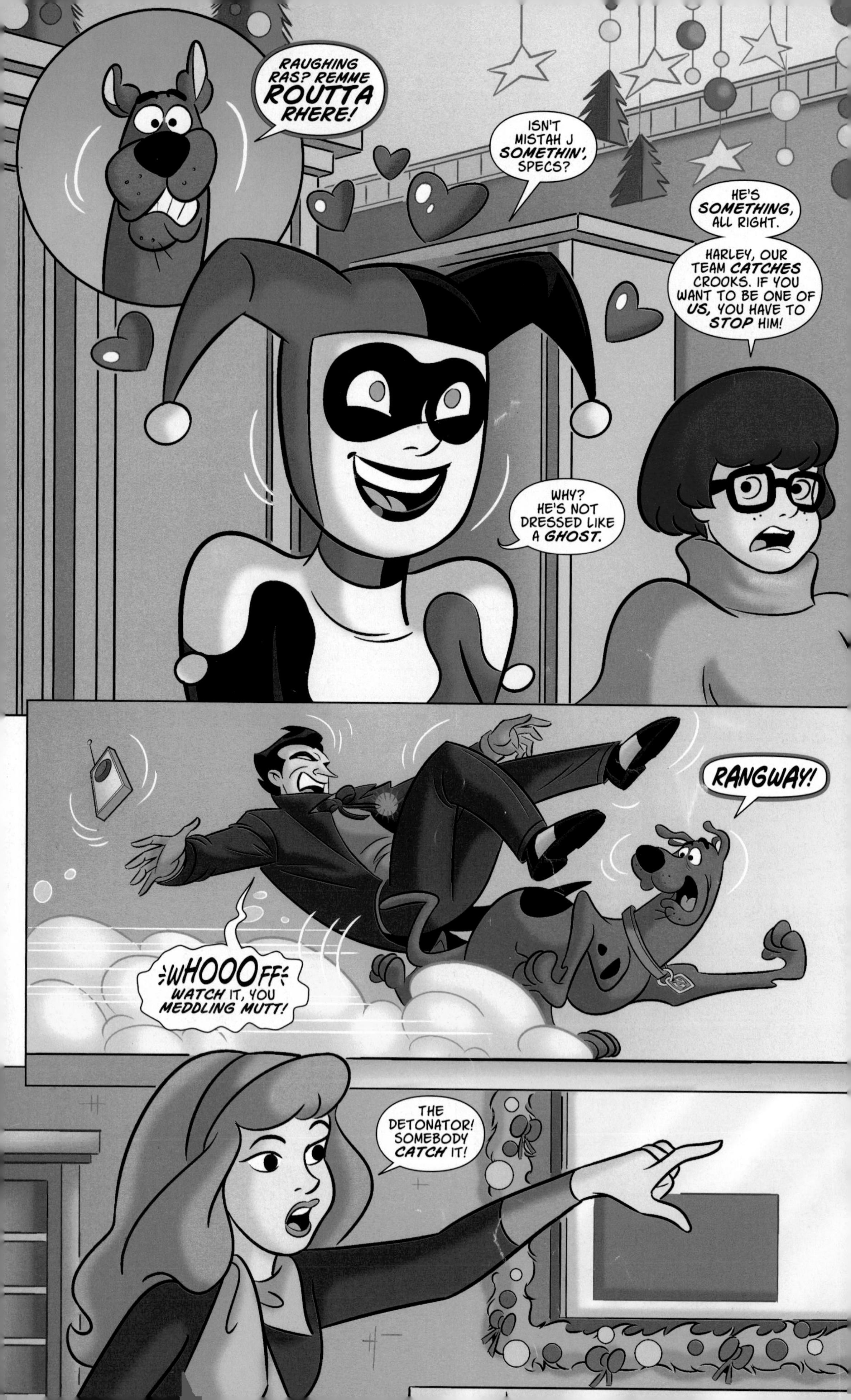
RAUGHING RAS? REMME ROUTTA RHERE!
ISN'T MISTAH J SOMETHIN', SPECS?
HE'S SOMETHING, ALL RIGHT.
HARLEY, OUR TEAM CATCHES CROOKS. IF YOU WANT TO BE ONE OF US, YOU HAVE TO STOP HIM!
WHY? HE'S NOT DRESSED LIKE A GHOST.
RANGWAY!
WHOOOFF
WATCH IT, YOU MEDDLING MUTT!
THE DETONATOR! SOMEBODY CATCH IT!

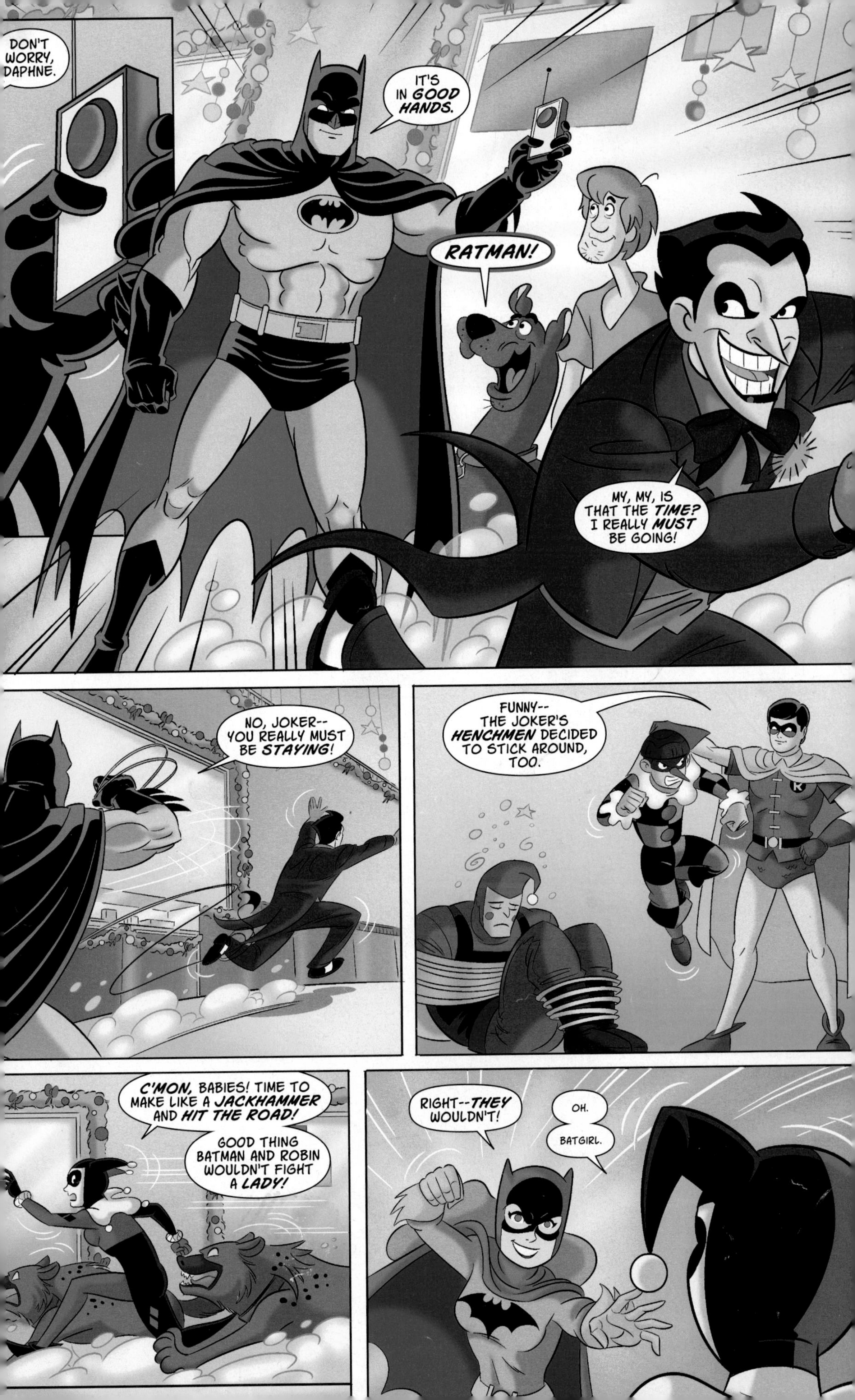

DON'T WORRY, DAPHNE.
IT'S IN GOOD HANDS.
RATMAN!
MY, MY, IS THAT THE TIME? I REALLY MUST BE GOING!
NO, JOKER-- YOU REALLY MUST BE STAYING!
FUNNY-- THE JOKER'S HENCHMEN DECIDED TO STICK AROUND, TOO.
C'MON, BABIES! TIME TO MAKE LIKE A JACKHAMMER AND HIT THE ROAD!
GOOD THING BATMAN AND ROBIN WOULDN'T FIGHT A LADY!
RIGHT--THEY WOULDN'T!
OH.
BATGIRL.

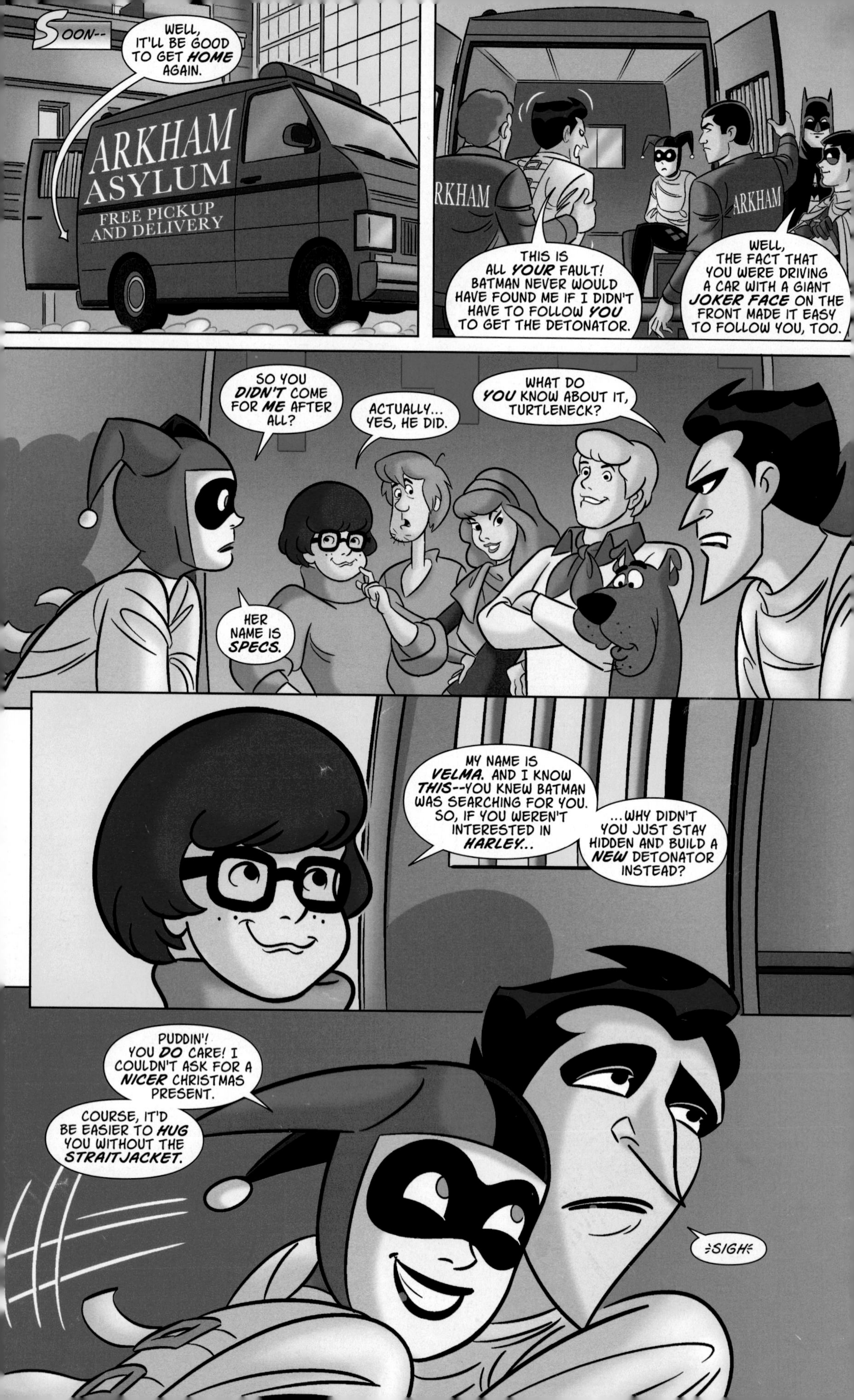
SOON--
WELL, IT'LL BE GOOD TO GET HOME AGAIN.
ARKHAM ASYLUM
FREE PICKUP AND DELIVERY
ARKHAM
ARKHAM
THIS IS ALL YOUR FAULT! BATMAN NEVER WOULD HAVE FOUND ME IF I DIDN'T HAVE TO FOLLOW YOU TO GET THE DETONATOR.
WELL, THE FACT THAT YOU WERE DRIVING A CAR WITH A GIANT JOKER FACE ON THE FRONT MADE IT EASY TO FOLLOW YOU, TOO.
SO YOU DIDN'T COME FOR ME AFTER ALL?
ACTUALLY... YES, HE DID.
WHAT DO YOU KNOW ABOUT IT, TURTLENECK?
HER NAME IS SPECS.
MY NAME IS VELMA. AND I KNOW THIS--YOU KNEW BATMAN WAS SEARCHING FOR YOU. SO, IF YOU WEREN'T INTERESTED IN HARLEY...
...WHY DIDN'T YOU JUST STAY HIDDEN AND BUILD A NEW DETONATOR INSTEAD?
PUDDIN'! YOU DO CARE! I COULDN'T ASK FOR A NICER CHRISTMAS PRESENT.
COURSE, IT'D BE EASIER TO HUG YOU WITHOUT THE STRAITJACKET.
SIGH

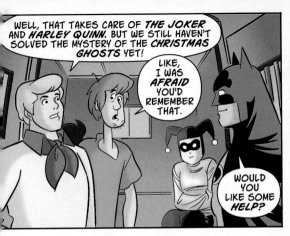

WELL, THAT TAKES CARE OF *THE JOKER* AND *HARLEY QUINN*. BUT WE STILL HAVEN'T SOLVED THE MYSTERY OF THE *CHRISTMAS GHOSTS* YET!

LIKE, I WAS *AFRAID* YOU'D REMEMBER THAT.

WOULD YOU LIKE SOME *HELP?*

AAH, *HARLEY AND THE WRAITH WRANGLERS* DON'T NEED HELP! OBVIOUSLY, IT WAS THAT HUNKY SALES GUY, *CHIPPENDALE!*

WHAT MAKES YOU SAY THAT?

HE AND THE GHOST WERE WEARIN' THE *SAME SHOES.* AND, EVEN THOUGH HE SELLS *ANTIQUES,* HIS SHOES WERE COVERED IN THE *BABY POWDER* THAT THE GHOST KNOCKED OVER.

HEY, I'VE GOT A *Ph.D. IN CLINICAL PSYCHOLOGY.* I'M *CRAZY,* NOT A *DOPE!*

"CRAZY'S" ENOUGH FOR *ME!* LET'S GET THESE LOONS BACK TO THE *ASYLUM,* AND DROP THEIR MUTTS AT ANIMAL *CONTROL.*

WORKS FOR ME! ALL *I* WANT FOR CHRISTMAS IS OUR TEAM BACK TO NORMAL, WITH NO *UNWANTED* ADDITIONS.

ISN'T THAT RIGHT, SCOOB?

SCOOB?!

WAIT! YOU TOOK, LIKE, THE *WRONG* "SCOOBY"!

ARKHAM ASYLUM FREE PICKUP AND DELIVERY

Rappy Rolidays!!

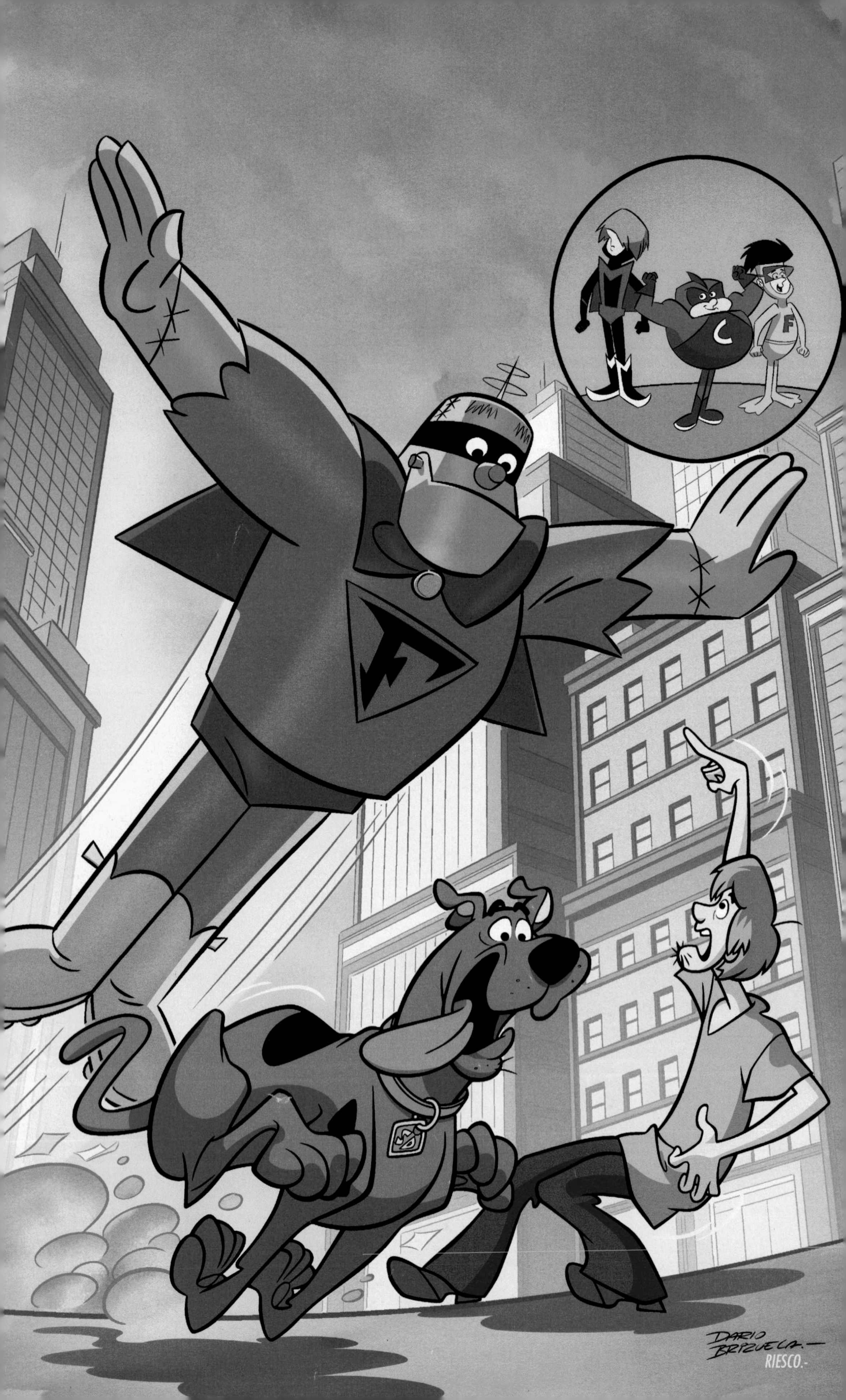
DARIO BRIZUELA
RIESCO.

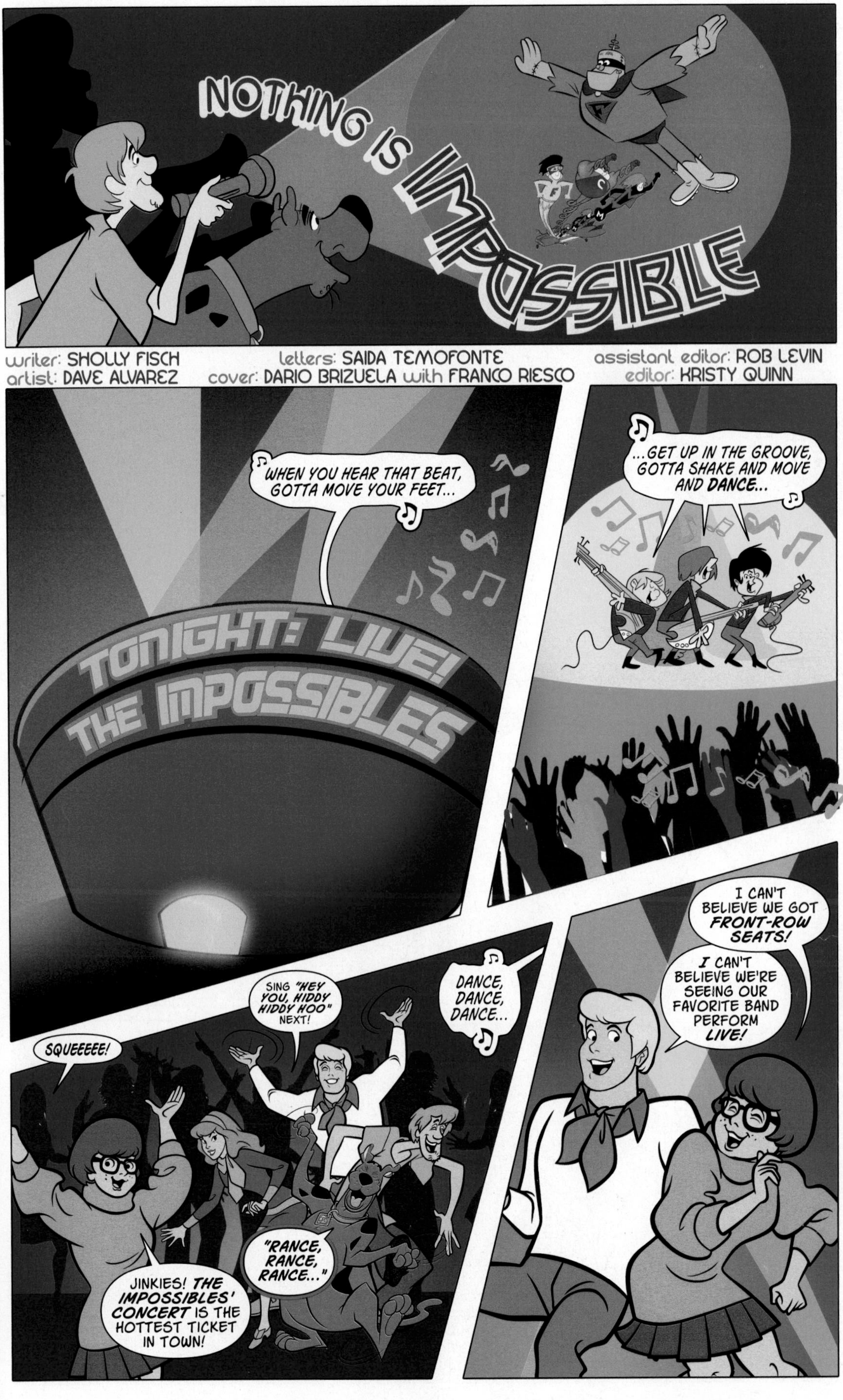
NOTHING IS IMPOSSIBLE
writer: SHOLLY FISCH
artist: DAVE ALVAREZ
letters: SAIDA TEMOFONTE
cover: DARIO BRIZUELA with FRANCO RIESCO
assistant editor: ROB LEVIN
editor: KRISTY QUINN
WHEN YOU HEAR THAT BEAT, GOTTA MOVE YOUR FEET...
TONIGHT: LIVE! THE IMPOSSIBLES
...GET UP IN THE GROOVE, GOTTA SHAKE AND MOVE AND DANCE...
SQUEEEEE!
SING "HEY YOU, HIDDY HIDDY HOO" NEXT!
DANCE, DANCE, DANCE...
JINKIES! THE IMPOSSIBLES' CONCERT IS THE HOTTEST TICKET IN TOWN!
"RANCE, RANCE, RANCE..."
I CAN'T BELIEVE WE GOT FRONT-ROW SEATS!
I CAN'T BELIEVE WE'RE SEEING OUR FAVORITE BAND PERFORM LIVE!

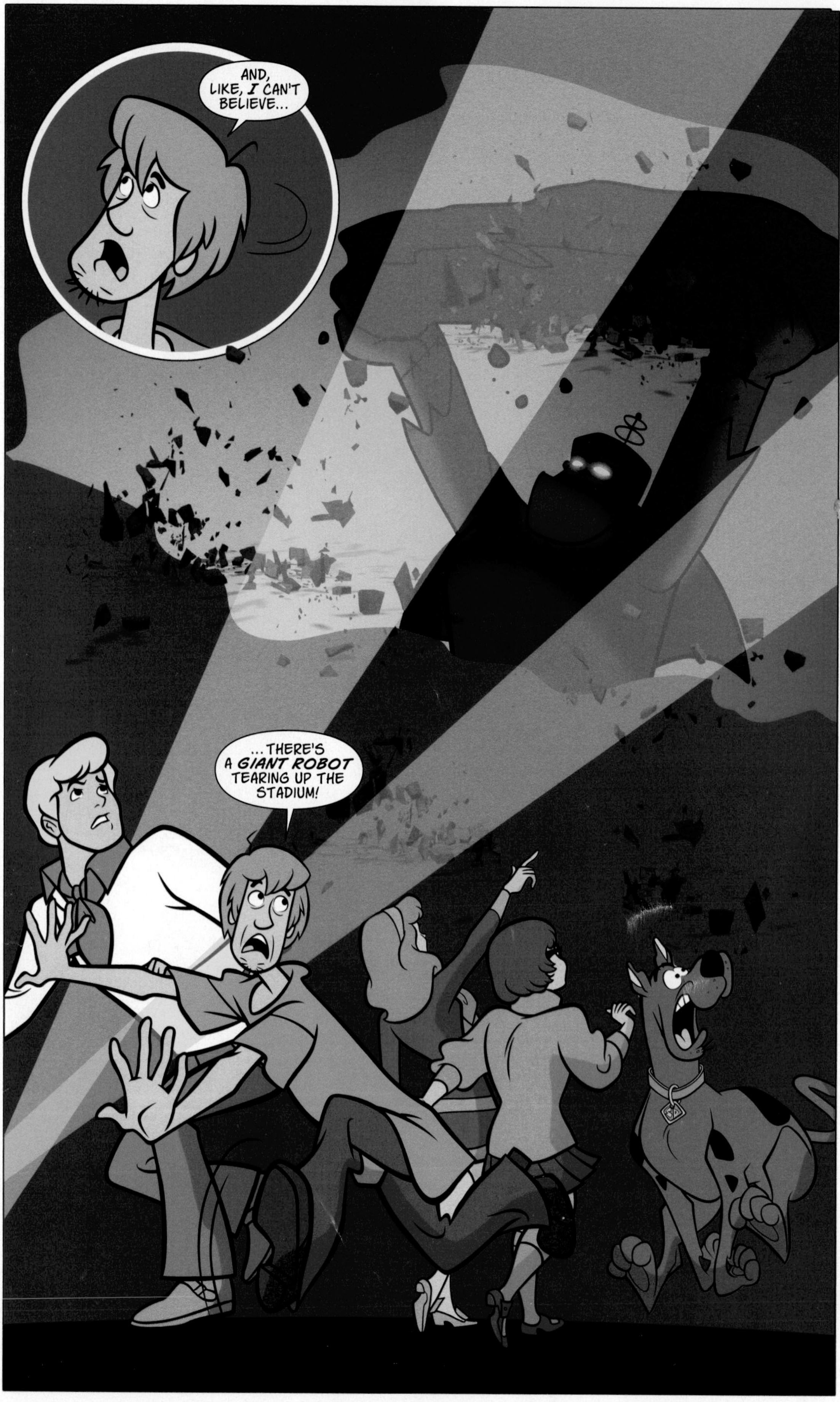
AND, LIKE, I CAN'T BELIEVE...
...THERE'S A GIANT ROBOT TEARING UP THE STADIUM!

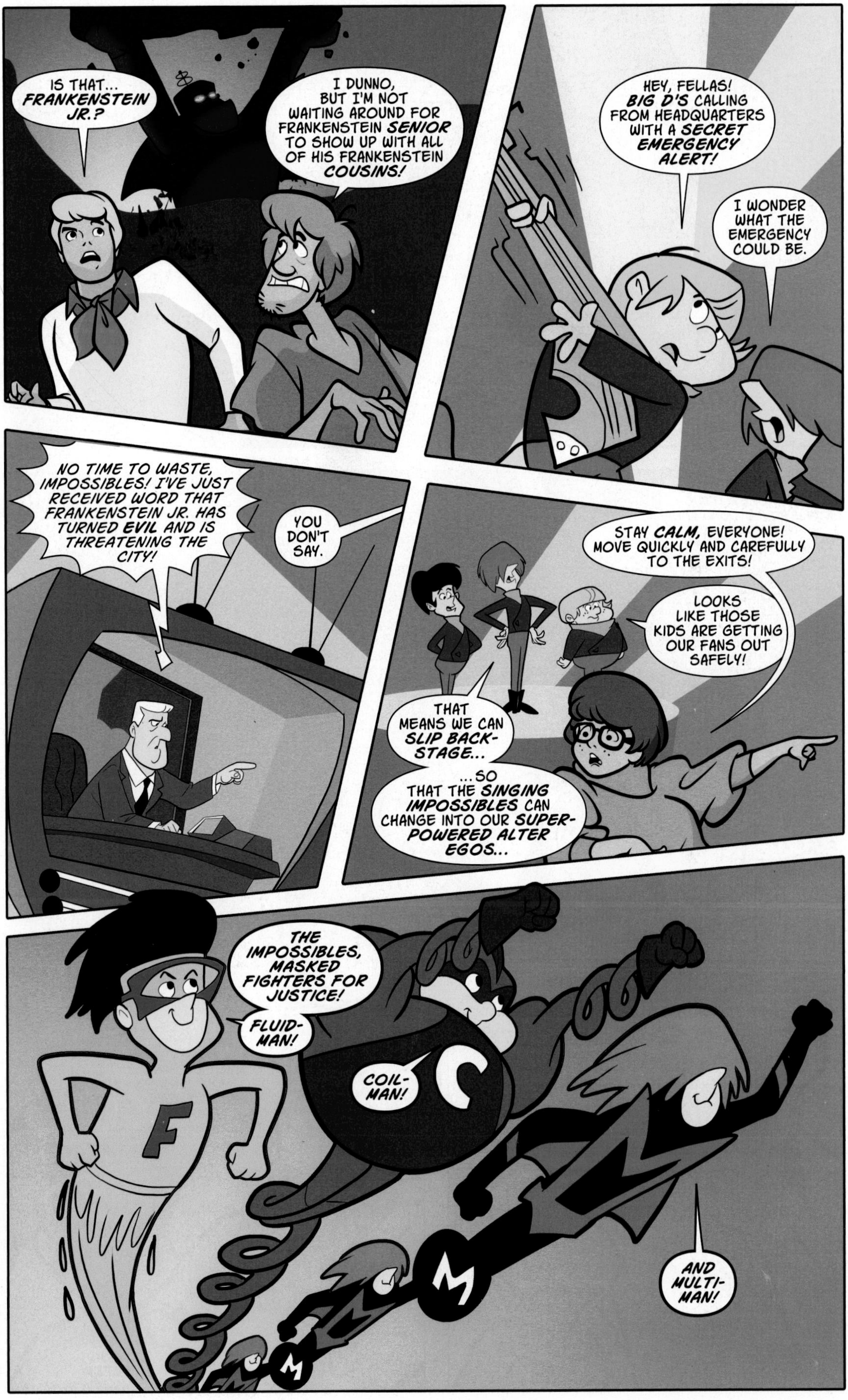
IS THAT... FRANKENSTEIN JR.?
I DUNNO, BUT I'M NOT WAITING AROUND FOR FRANKENSTEIN SENIOR TO SHOW UP WITH ALL OF HIS FRANKENSTEIN COUSINS!
HEY, FELLAS! BIG D'S CALLING FROM HEADQUARTERS WITH A SECRET EMERGENCY ALERT!
I WONDER WHAT THE EMERGENCY COULD BE.
NO TIME TO WASTE, IMPOSSIBLES! I'VE JUST RECEIVED WORD THAT FRANKENSTEIN JR. HAS TURNED EVIL AND IS THREATENING THE CITY!
YOU DON'T SAY.
STAY CALM, EVERYONE! MOVE QUICKLY AND CAREFULLY TO THE EXITS!
LOOKS LIKE THOSE KIDS ARE GETTING OUR FANS OUT SAFELY!
THAT MEANS WE CAN SLIP BACK-STAGE...
...SO THAT THE SINGING IMPOSSIBLES CAN CHANGE INTO OUR SUPER-POWERED ALTER EGOS...
THE IMPOSSIBLES, MASKED FIGHTERS FOR JUSTICE!
FLUID-MAN!
COIL-MAN!
AND MULTI-MAN!

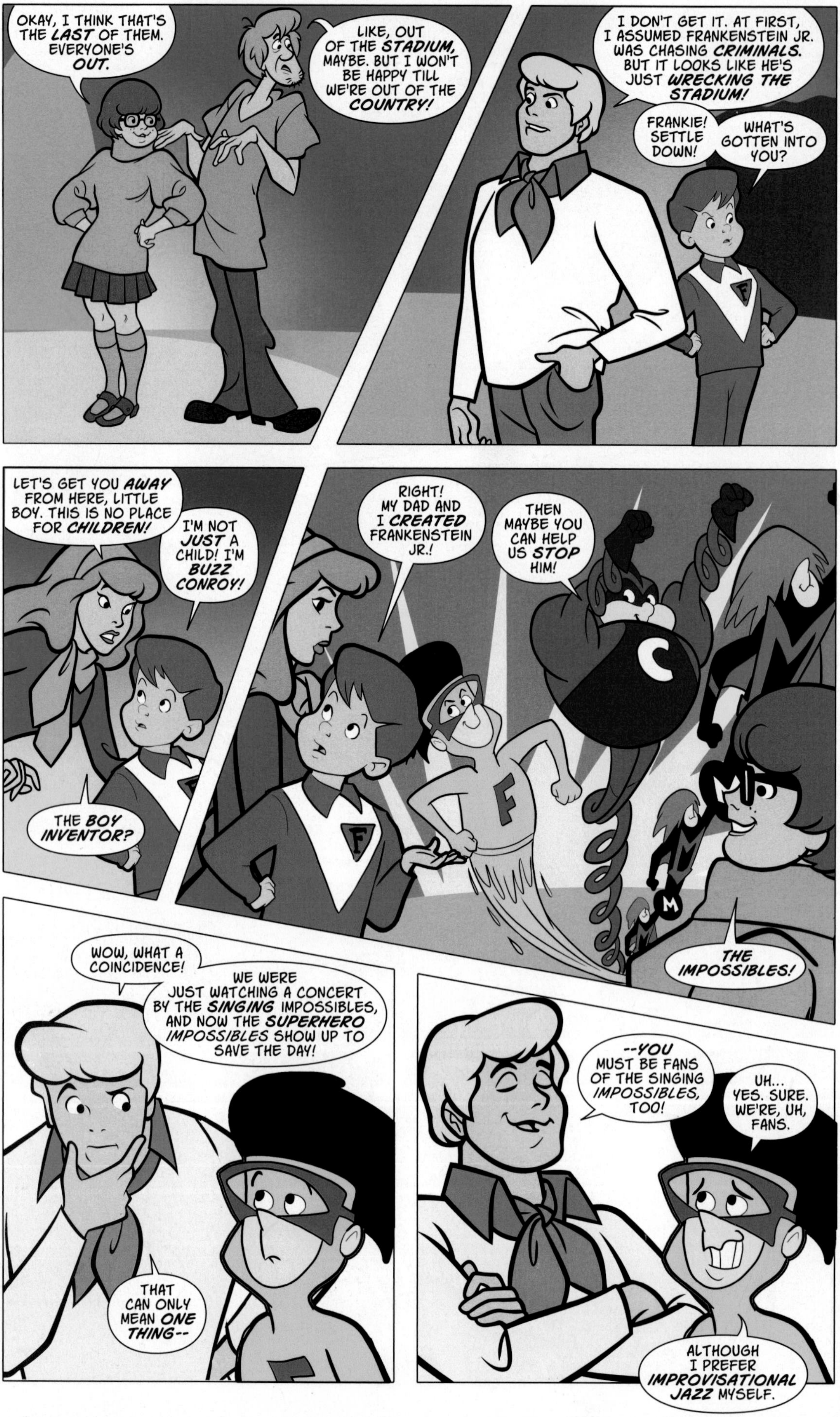
OKAY, I THINK THAT'S THE LAST OF THEM. EVERYONE'S OUT.
LIKE, OUT OF THE STADIUM, MAYBE. BUT I WON'T BE HAPPY TILL WE'RE OUT OF THE COUNTRY!
I DON'T GET IT. AT FIRST, I ASSUMED FRANKENSTEIN JR. WAS CHASING CRIMINALS. BUT IT LOOKS LIKE HE'S JUST WRECKING THE STADIUM!
FRANKIE! SETTLE DOWN!
WHAT'S GOTTEN INTO YOU?
LET'S GET YOU AWAY FROM HERE, LITTLE BOY. THIS IS NO PLACE FOR CHILDREN!
I'M NOT JUST A CHILD! I'M BUZZ CONROY!
THE BOY INVENTOR?
RIGHT! MY DAD AND I CREATED FRANKENSTEIN JR.!
THEN MAYBE YOU CAN HELP US STOP HIM!
THE IMPOSSIBLES!
WOW, WHAT A COINCIDENCE!
WE WERE JUST WATCHING A CONCERT BY THE SINGING IMPOSSIBLES, AND NOW THE SUPERHERO IMPOSSIBLES SHOW UP TO SAVE THE DAY!
THAT CAN ONLY MEAN ONE THING--
--YOU MUST BE FANS OF THE SINGING IMPOSSIBLES, TOO!
UH... YES. SURE. WE'RE, UH, FANS.
ALTHOUGH I PREFER IMPROVISATIONAL JAZZ MYSELF.

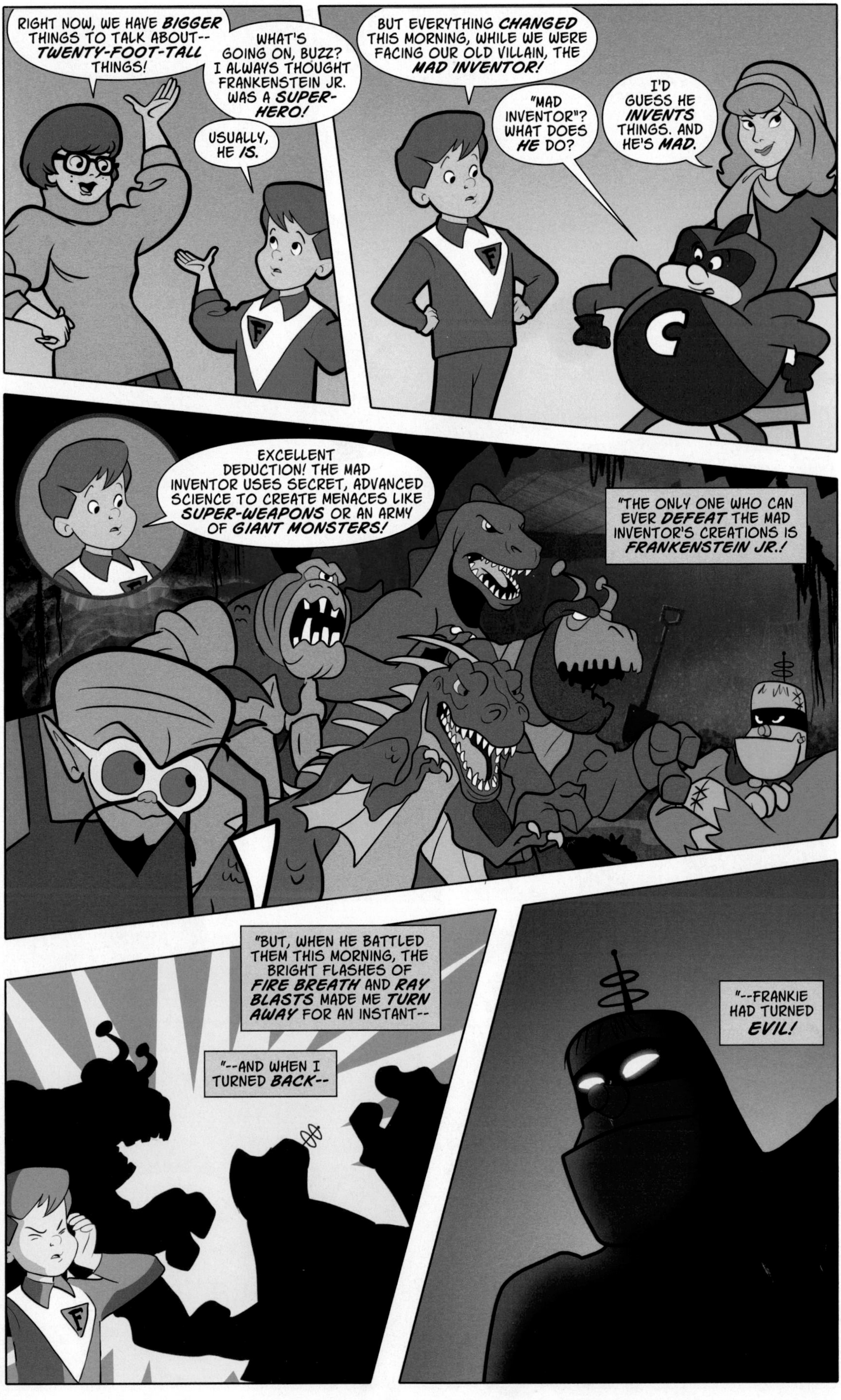
RIGHT NOW, WE HAVE BIGGER THINGS TO TALK ABOUT-- TWENTY-FOOT-TALL THINGS!
WHAT'S GOING ON, BUZZ? I ALWAYS THOUGHT FRANKENSTEIN JR. WAS A SUPER-HERO!
USUALLY, HE IS.
BUT EVERYTHING CHANGED THIS MORNING, WHILE WE WERE FACING OUR OLD VILLAIN, THE MAD INVENTOR!
"MAD INVENTOR"? WHAT DOES HE DO?
I'D GUESS HE INVENTS THINGS. AND HE'S MAD.
EXCELLENT DEDUCTION! THE MAD INVENTOR USES SECRET, ADVANCED SCIENCE TO CREATE MENACES LIKE SUPER-WEAPONS OR AN ARMY OF GIANT MONSTERS!
"THE ONLY ONE WHO CAN EVER DEFEAT THE MAD INVENTOR'S CREATIONS IS FRANKENSTEIN JR.!
"BUT, WHEN HE BATTLED THEM THIS MORNING, THE BRIGHT FLASHES OF FIRE BREATH AND RAY BLASTS MADE ME TURN AWAY FOR AN INSTANT--
"--AND WHEN I TURNED BACK--
"--FRANKIE HAD TURNED EVIL!

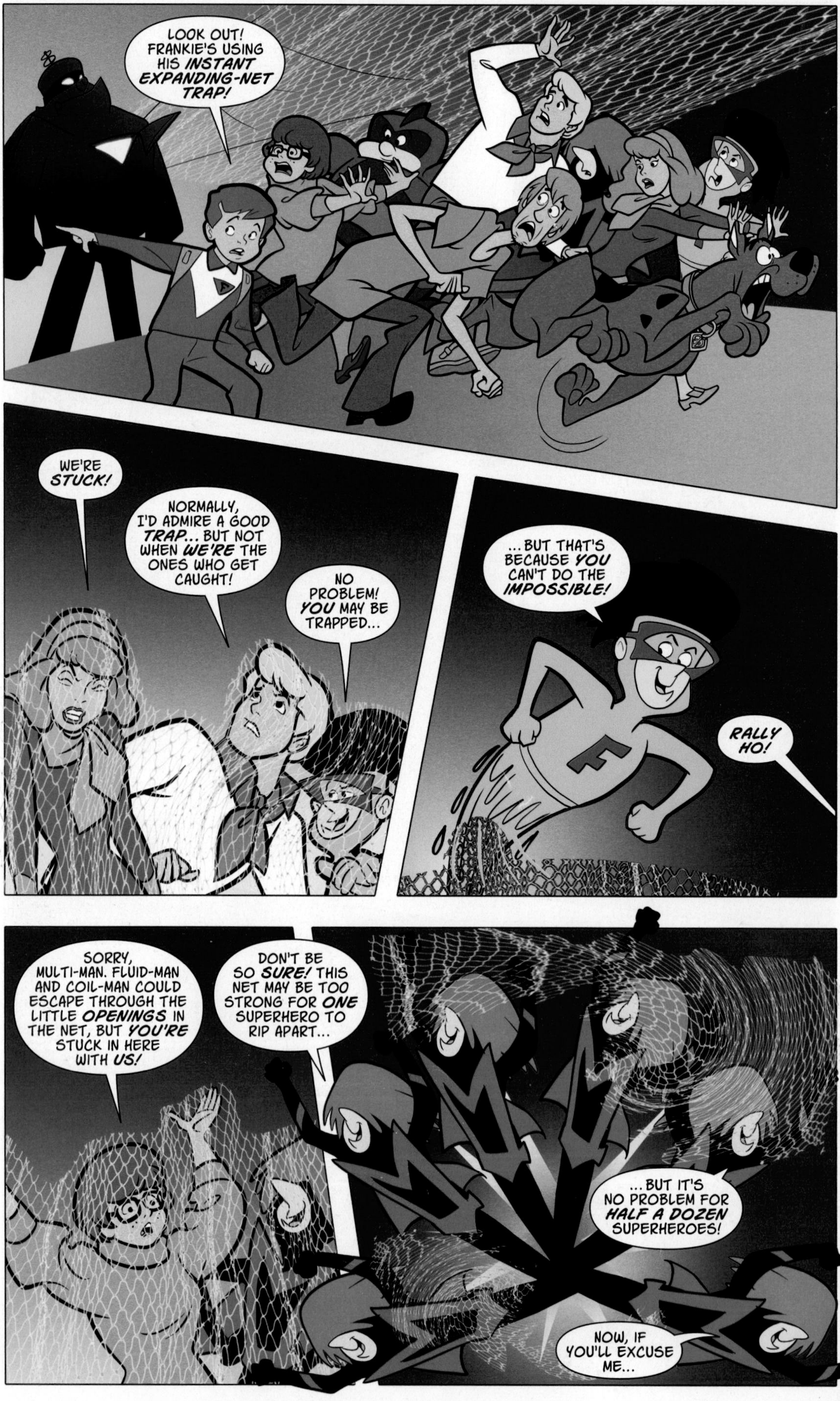
LOOK OUT! FRANKIE'S USING HIS *INSTANT EXPANDING-NET TRAP!*
WE'RE *STUCK!*
NORMALLY, I'D ADMIRE A GOOD *TRAP*... BUT NOT WHEN *WE'RE* THE ONES WHO GET CAUGHT!
NO PROBLEM! *YOU* MAY BE TRAPPED...
...BUT THAT'S BECAUSE *YOU* CAN'T DO THE *IMPOSSIBLE!*
RALLY HO!
SORRY, MULTI-MAN. FLUID-MAN AND COIL-MAN COULD ESCAPE THROUGH THE LITTLE *OPENINGS* IN THE NET, BUT *YOU'RE* STUCK IN HERE WITH *US!*
DON'T BE SO *SURE!* THIS NET MAY BE TOO STRONG FOR *ONE* SUPERHERO TO RIP APART...
...BUT IT'S NO PROBLEM FOR *HALF A DOZEN* SUPERHEROES!
NOW, IF YOU'LL EXCUSE ME...

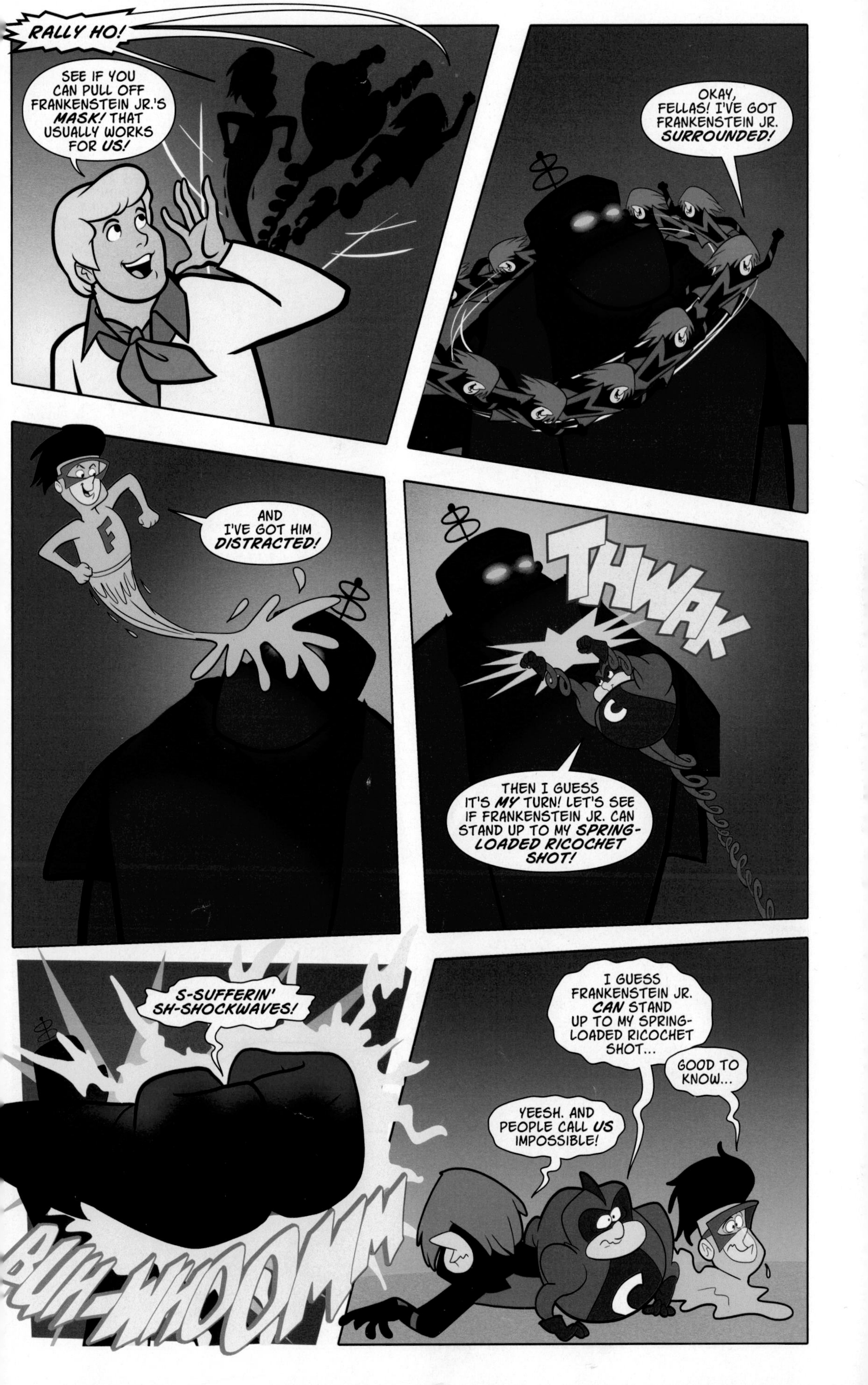
RALLY HO!
SEE IF YOU CAN PULL OFF FRANKENSTEIN JR.'S MASK! THAT USUALLY WORKS FOR US!
OKAY, FELLAS! I'VE GOT FRANKENSTEIN JR. SURROUNDED!
AND I'VE GOT HIM DISTRACTED!
THWAK
THEN I GUESS IT'S MY TURN! LET'S SEE IF FRANKENSTEIN JR. CAN STAND UP TO MY SPRING-LOADED RICOCHET SHOT!
S-SUFFERIN' SH-SHOCKWAVES!
BUH-WHOOMM
I GUESS FRANKENSTEIN JR. CAN STAND UP TO MY SPRING-LOADED RICOCHET SHOT...
GOOD TO KNOW...
YEESH. AND PEOPLE CALL US IMPOSSIBLE!

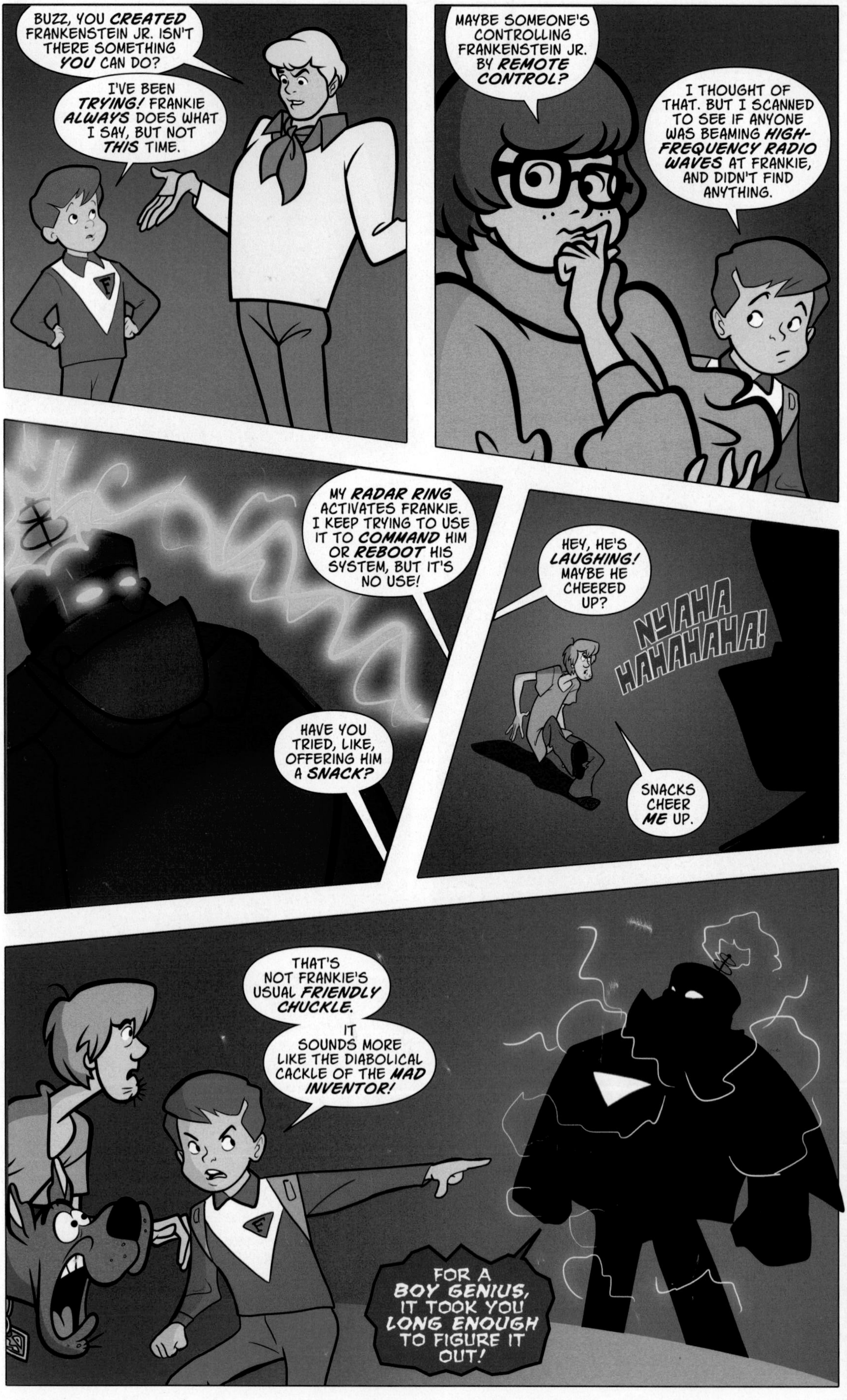
BUZZ, YOU CREATED FRANKENSTEIN JR. ISN'T THERE SOMETHING YOU CAN DO?
I'VE BEEN TRYING! FRANKIE ALWAYS DOES WHAT I SAY, BUT NOT THIS TIME.
MAYBE SOMEONE'S CONTROLLING FRANKENSTEIN JR. BY REMOTE CONTROL?
I THOUGHT OF THAT. BUT I SCANNED TO SEE IF ANYONE WAS BEAMING HIGH-FREQUENCY RADIO WAVES AT FRANKIE, AND DIDN'T FIND ANYTHING.
MY RADAR RING ACTIVATES FRANKIE. I KEEP TRYING TO USE IT TO COMMAND HIM OR REBOOT HIS SYSTEM, BUT IT'S NO USE!
HAVE YOU TRIED, LIKE, OFFERING HIM A SNACK?
HEY, HE'S LAUGHING! MAYBE HE CHEERED UP?
NYAHA HAHAHAHA!
SNACKS CHEER ME UP.
THAT'S NOT FRANKIE'S USUAL FRIENDLY CHUCKLE.
IT SOUNDS MORE LIKE THE DIABOLICAL CACKLE OF THE MAD INVENTOR!
FOR A BOY GENIUS, IT TOOK YOU LONG ENOUGH TO FIGURE IT OUT!

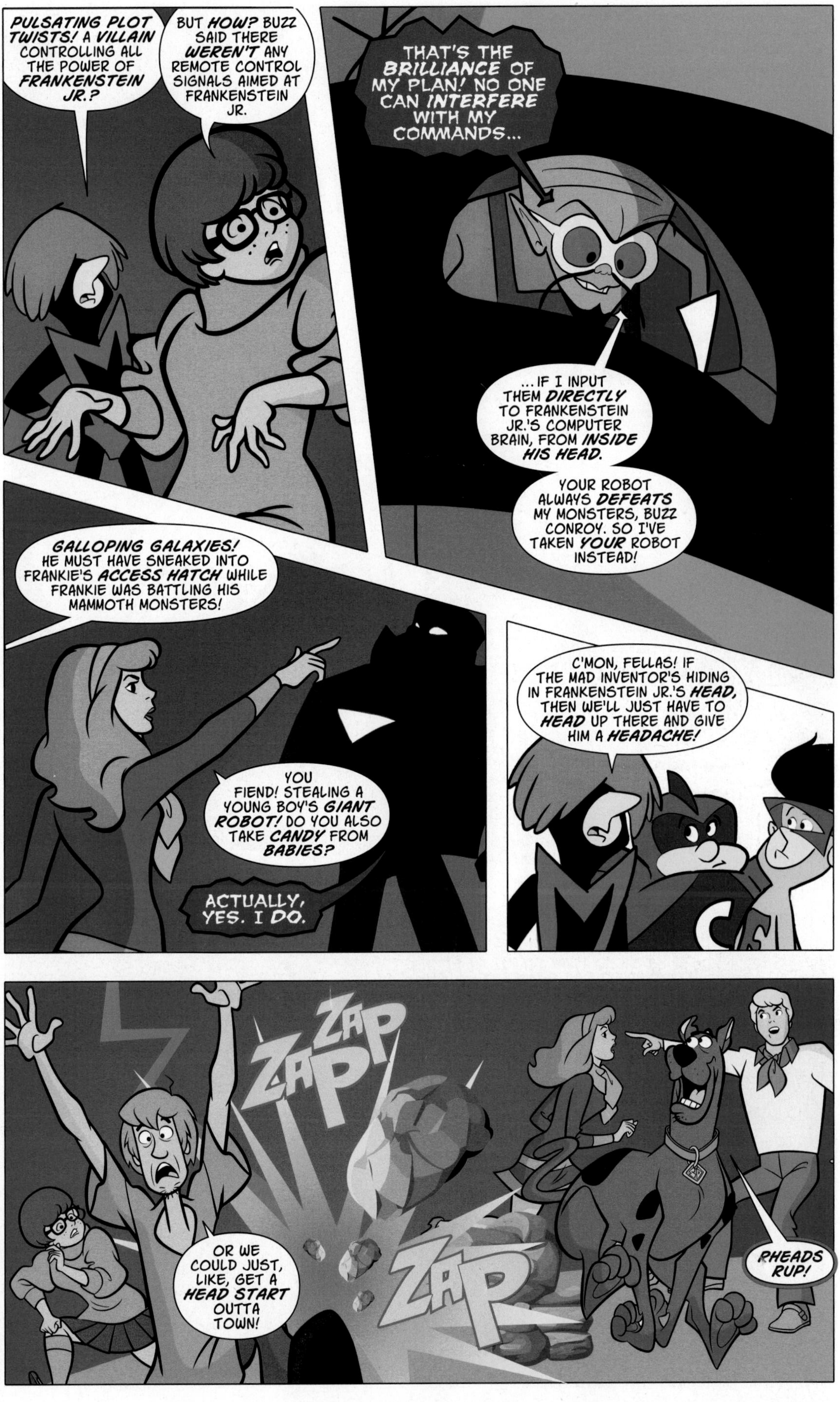
PULSATING PLOT TWISTS! A VILLAIN CONTROLLING ALL THE POWER OF FRANKENSTEIN JR.?
BUT HOW? BUZZ SAID THERE WEREN'T ANY REMOTE CONTROL SIGNALS AIMED AT FRANKENSTEIN JR.
THAT'S THE BRILLIANCE OF MY PLAN! NO ONE CAN INTERFERE WITH MY COMMANDS...
...IF I INPUT THEM DIRECTLY TO FRANKENSTEIN JR.'S COMPUTER BRAIN, FROM INSIDE HIS HEAD.
YOUR ROBOT ALWAYS DEFEATS MY MONSTERS, BUZZ CONROY. SO I'VE TAKEN YOUR ROBOT INSTEAD!
GALLOPING GALAXIES! HE MUST HAVE SNEAKED INTO FRANKIE'S ACCESS HATCH WHILE FRANKIE WAS BATTLING HIS MAMMOTH MONSTERS!
YOU FIEND! STEALING A YOUNG BOY'S GIANT ROBOT! DO YOU ALSO TAKE CANDY FROM BABIES?
ACTUALLY, YES. I DO.
C'MON, FELLAS! IF THE MAD INVENTOR'S HIDING IN FRANKENSTEIN JR.'S HEAD, THEN WE'LL JUST HAVE TO HEAD UP THERE AND GIVE HIM A HEADACHE!
ZAP
ZAP
OR WE COULD JUST, LIKE, GET A HEAD START OUTTA TOWN!
ZAP
RHEADS RUP!

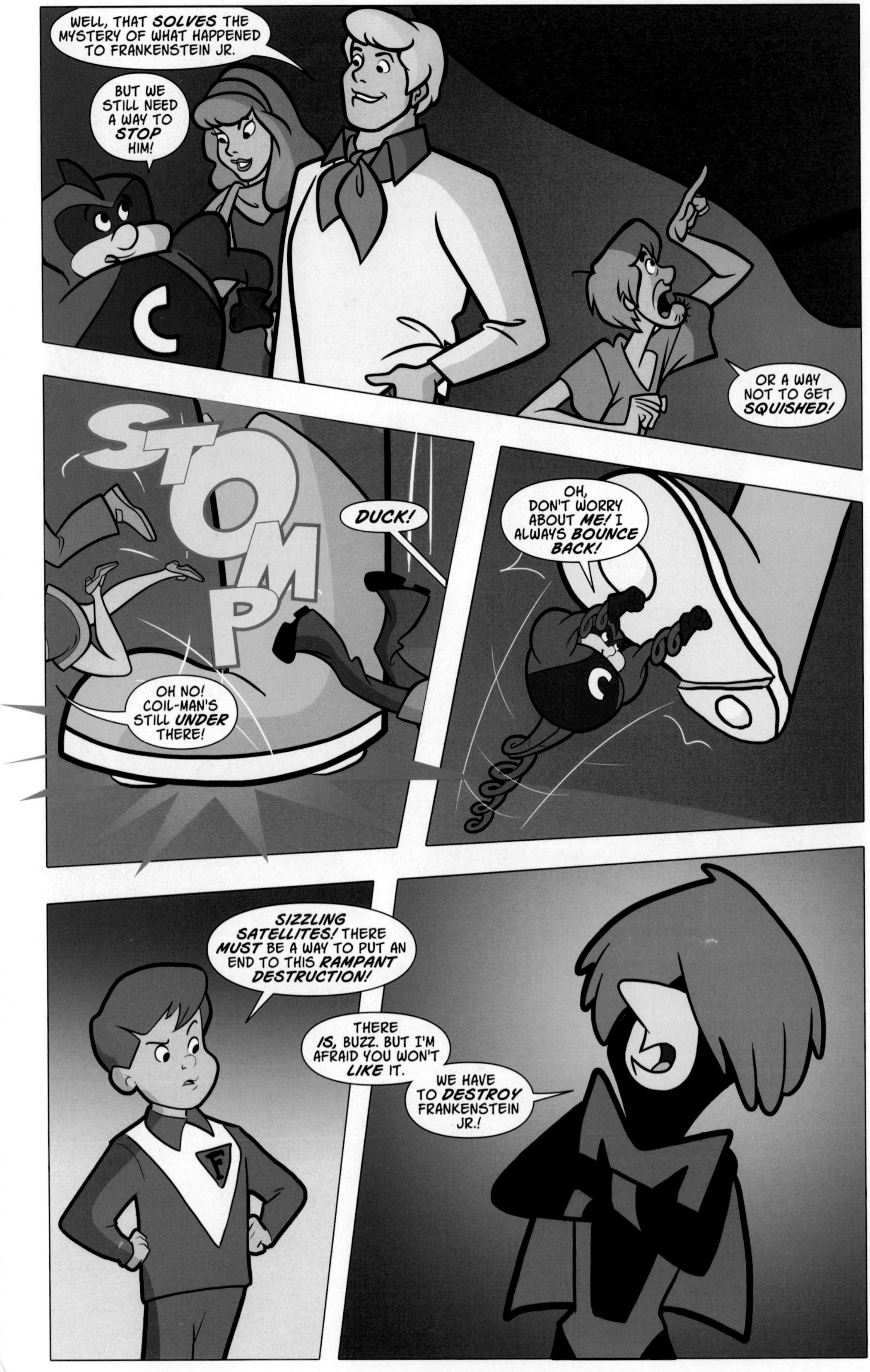
WELL, THAT SOLVES THE MYSTERY OF WHAT HAPPENED TO FRANKENSTEIN JR.
BUT WE STILL NEED A WAY TO STOP HIM!
OR A WAY NOT TO GET SQUISHED!
STOMP
DUCK!
OH NO! COIL-MAN'S STILL UNDER THERE!
OH, DON'T WORRY ABOUT ME! I ALWAYS BOUNCE BACK!
SIZZLING SATELLITES! THERE MUST BE A WAY TO PUT AN END TO THIS RAMPANT DESTRUCTION!
THERE IS, BUZZ. BUT I'M AFRAID YOU WON'T LIKE IT.
WE HAVE TO DESTROY FRANKENSTEIN JR.!

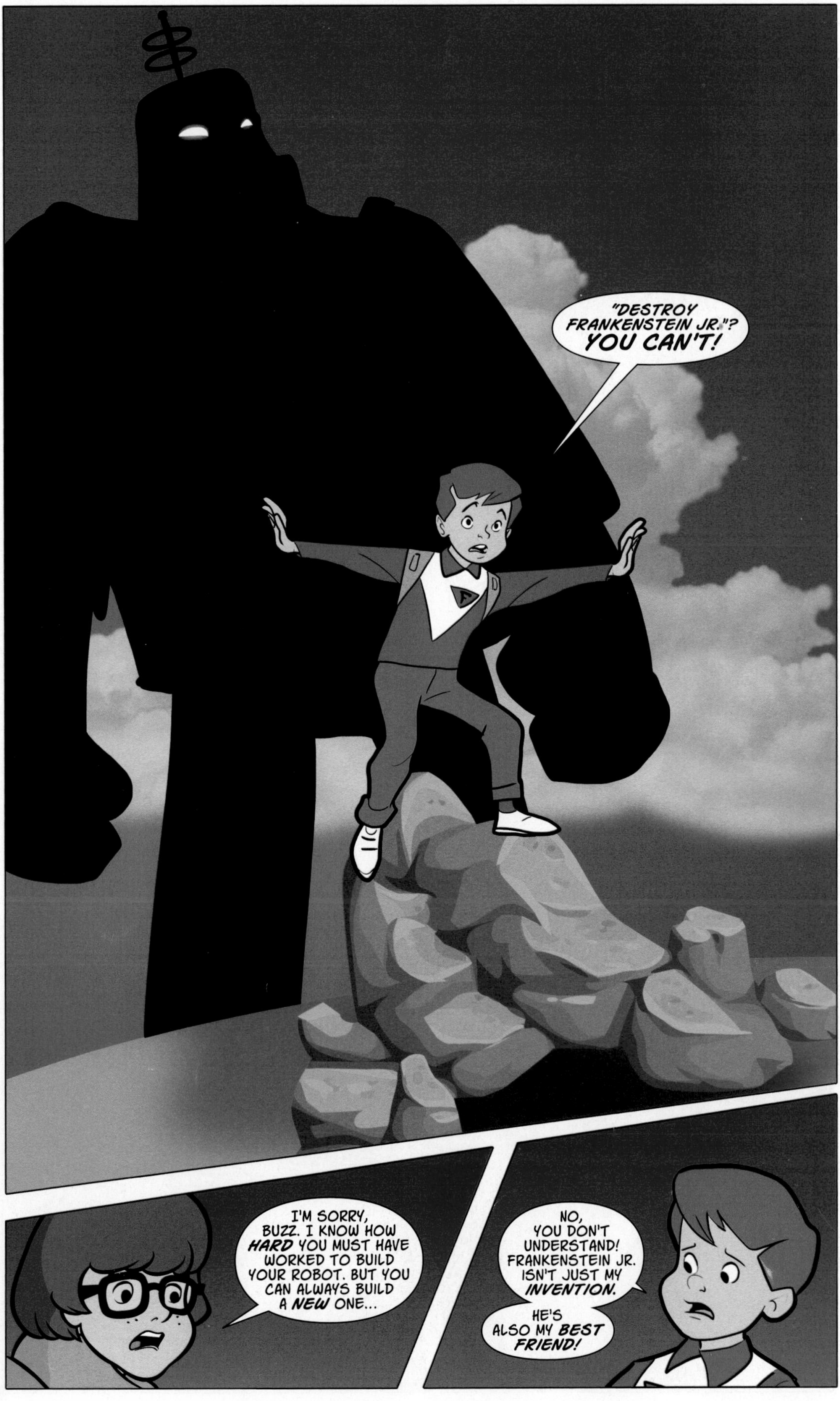
"DESTROY FRANKENSTEIN JR."? YOU CAN'T!
I'M SORRY, BUZZ. I KNOW HOW HARD YOU MUST HAVE WORKED TO BUILD YOUR ROBOT. BUT YOU CAN ALWAYS BUILD A NEW ONE...
NO, YOU DON'T UNDERSTAND! FRANKENSTEIN JR. ISN'T JUST MY INVENTION.
HE'S ALSO MY BEST FRIEND!

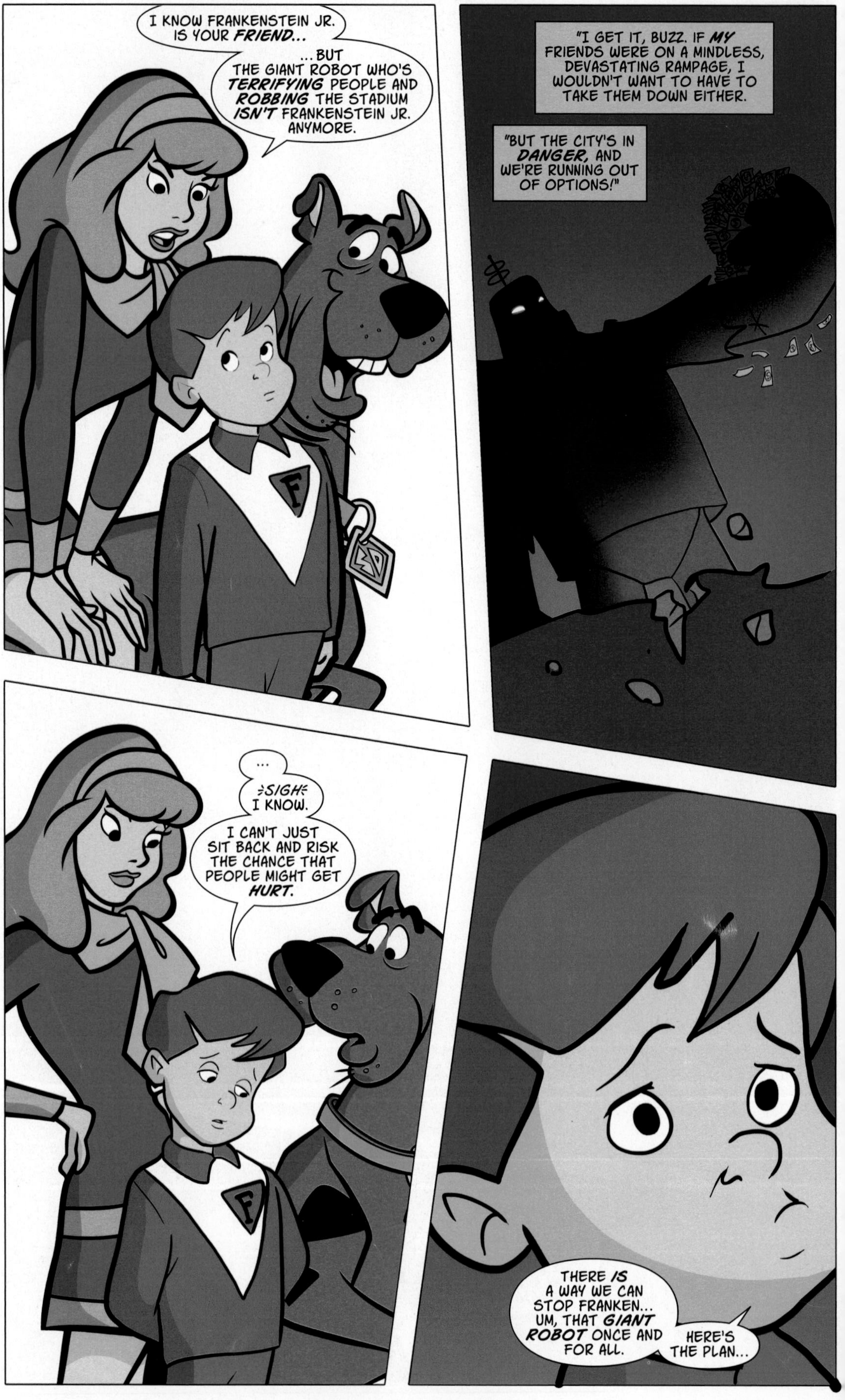
I KNOW FRANKENSTEIN JR. IS YOUR FRIEND...
...BUT THE GIANT ROBOT WHO'S TERRIFYING PEOPLE AND ROBBING THE STADIUM ISN'T FRANKENSTEIN JR. ANYMORE.
"I GET IT, BUZZ. IF MY FRIENDS WERE ON A MINDLESS, DEVASTATING RAMPAGE, I WOULDN'T WANT TO HAVE TO TAKE THEM DOWN EITHER.
"BUT THE CITY'S IN DANGER, AND WE'RE RUNNING OUT OF OPTIONS!"
...
SIGH I KNOW.
I CAN'T JUST SIT BACK AND RISK THE CHANCE THAT PEOPLE MIGHT GET HURT.
THERE IS A WAY WE CAN STOP FRANKEN... UM, THAT GIANT ROBOT ONCE AND FOR ALL.
HERE'S THE PLAN...

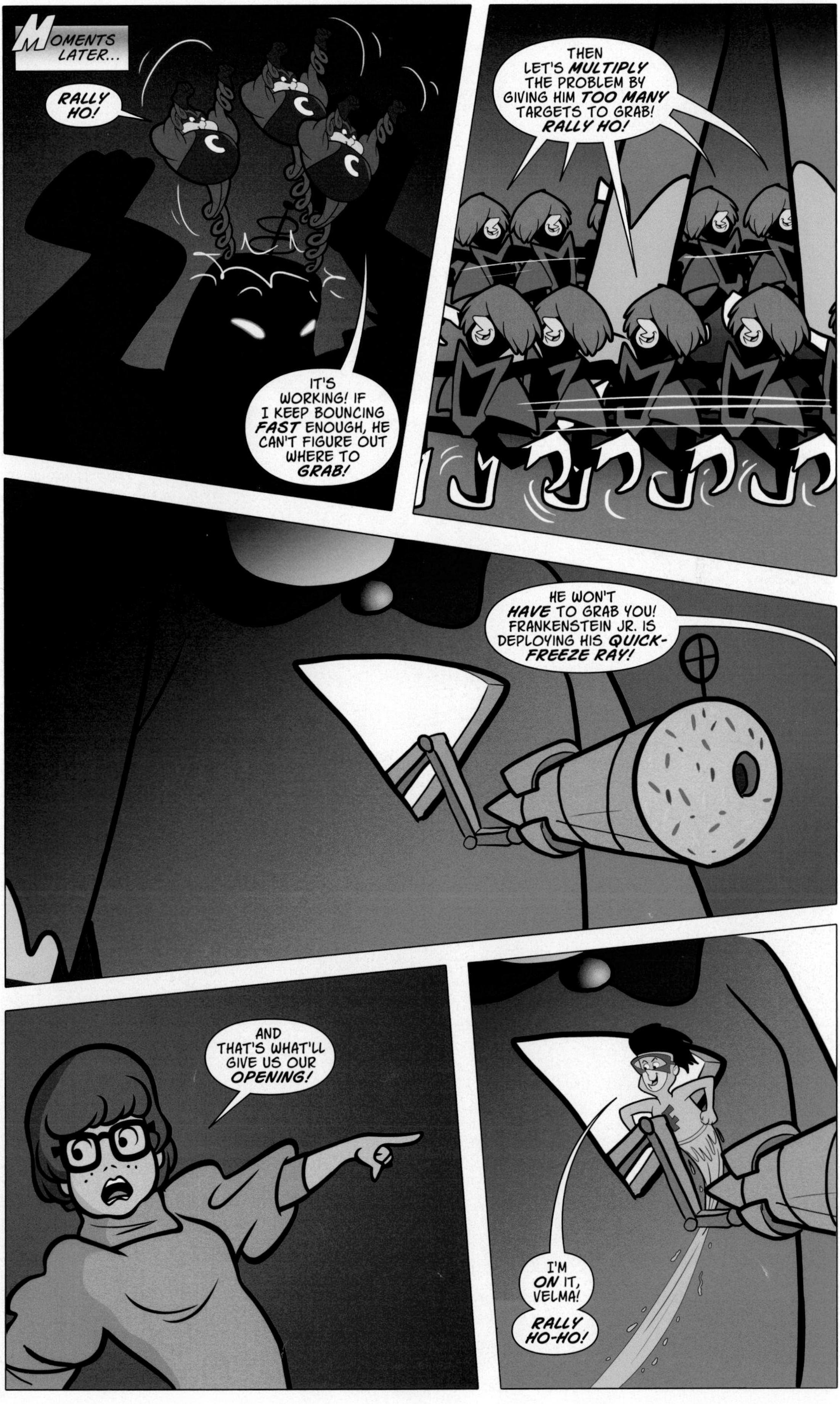
MOMENTS LATER...
RALLY HO!
IT'S WORKING! IF I KEEP BOUNCING FAST ENOUGH, HE CAN'T FIGURE OUT WHERE TO GRAB!
THEN LET'S MULTIPLY THE PROBLEM BY GIVING HIM TOO MANY TARGETS TO GRAB! RALLY HO!
HE WON'T HAVE TO GRAB YOU! FRANKENSTEIN JR. IS DEPLOYING HIS QUICK-FREEZE RAY!
AND THAT'S WHAT'LL GIVE US OUR OPENING!
I'M ON IT, VELMA!
RALLY HO-HO!

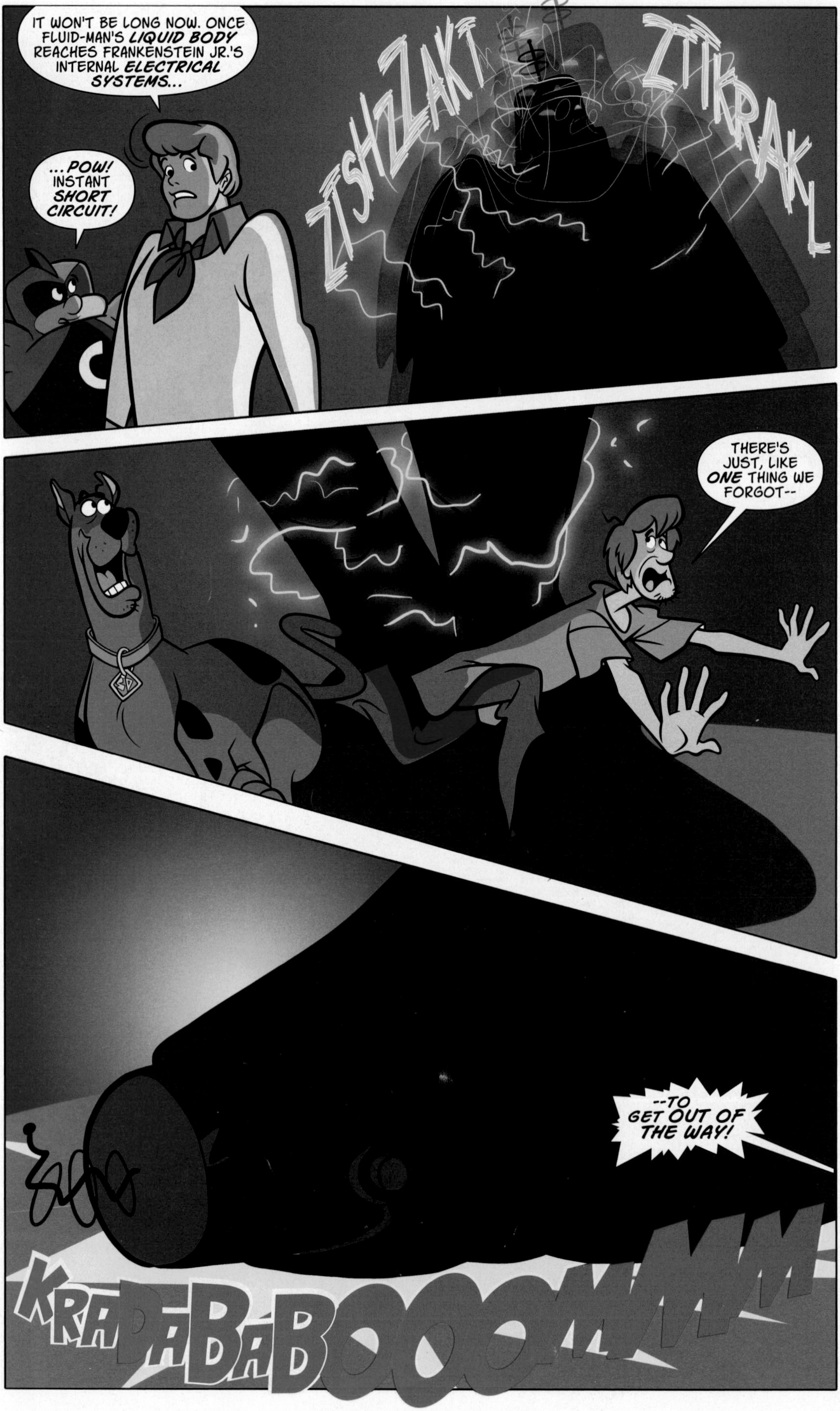
IT WON'T BE LONG NOW. ONCE FLUID-MAN'S LIQUID BODY REACHES FRANKENSTEIN JR.'S INTERNAL ELECTRICAL SYSTEMS...
...POW! INSTANT SHORT CIRCUIT!
ZTSHZZAKT
ZTTKRRAKL
THERE'S JUST, LIKE ONE THING WE FORGOT--
--TO GET OUT OF THE WAY!
KRADABABOOOOMMM

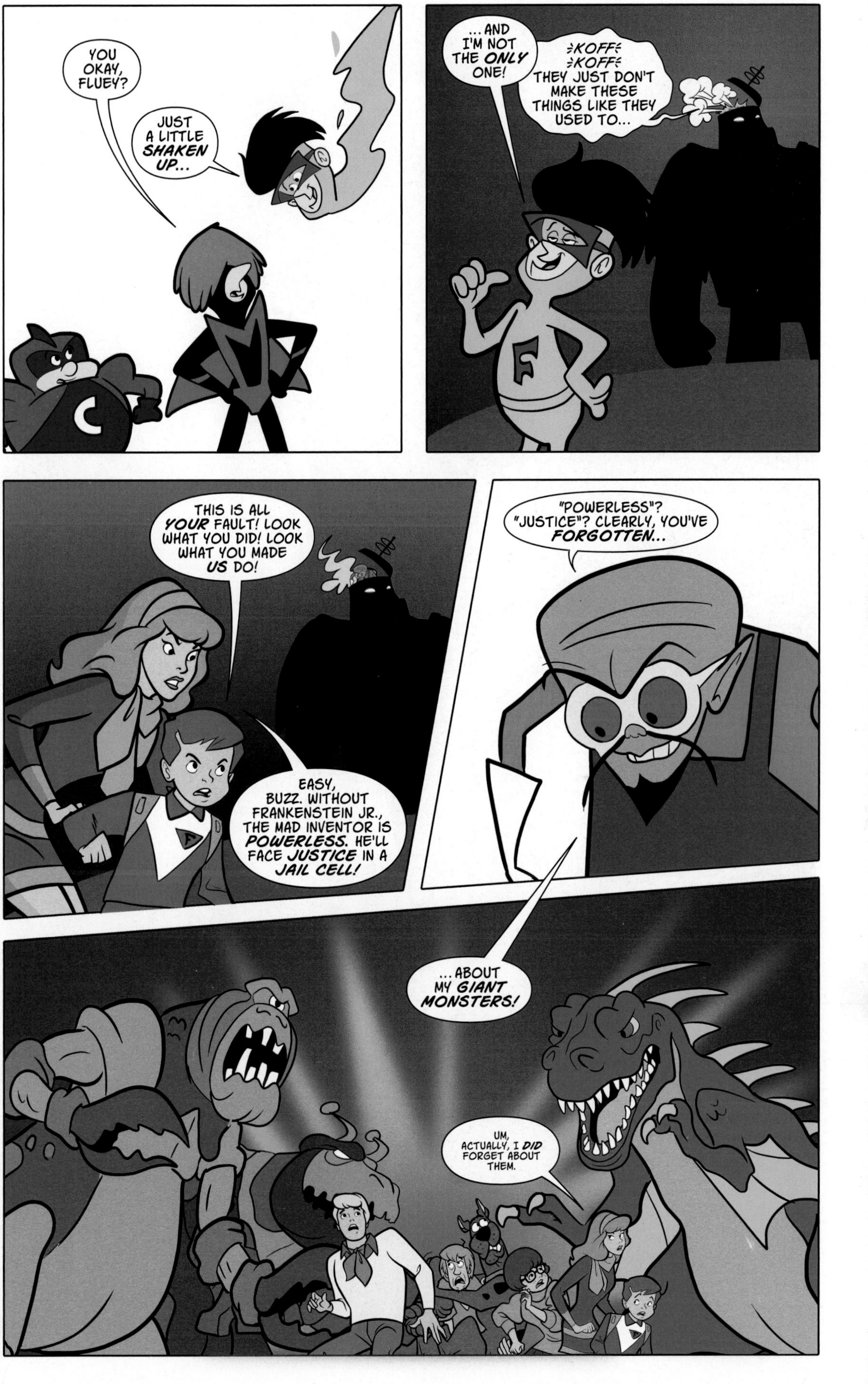
YOU OKAY, FLUEY?
JUST A LITTLE SHAKEN UP...
... AND I'M NOT THE ONLY ONE!
≠KOFF≠ ≠KOFF≠ THEY JUST DON'T MAKE THESE THINGS LIKE THEY USED TO...
THIS IS ALL YOUR FAULT! LOOK WHAT YOU DID! LOOK WHAT YOU MADE US DO!
EASY, BUZZ. WITHOUT FRANKENSTEIN JR., THE MAD INVENTOR IS POWERLESS. HE'LL FACE JUSTICE IN A JAIL CELL!
"POWERLESS"? "JUSTICE"? CLEARLY, YOU'VE FORGOTTEN...
... ABOUT MY GIANT MONSTERS!
UM, ACTUALLY, I DID FORGET ABOUT THEM.

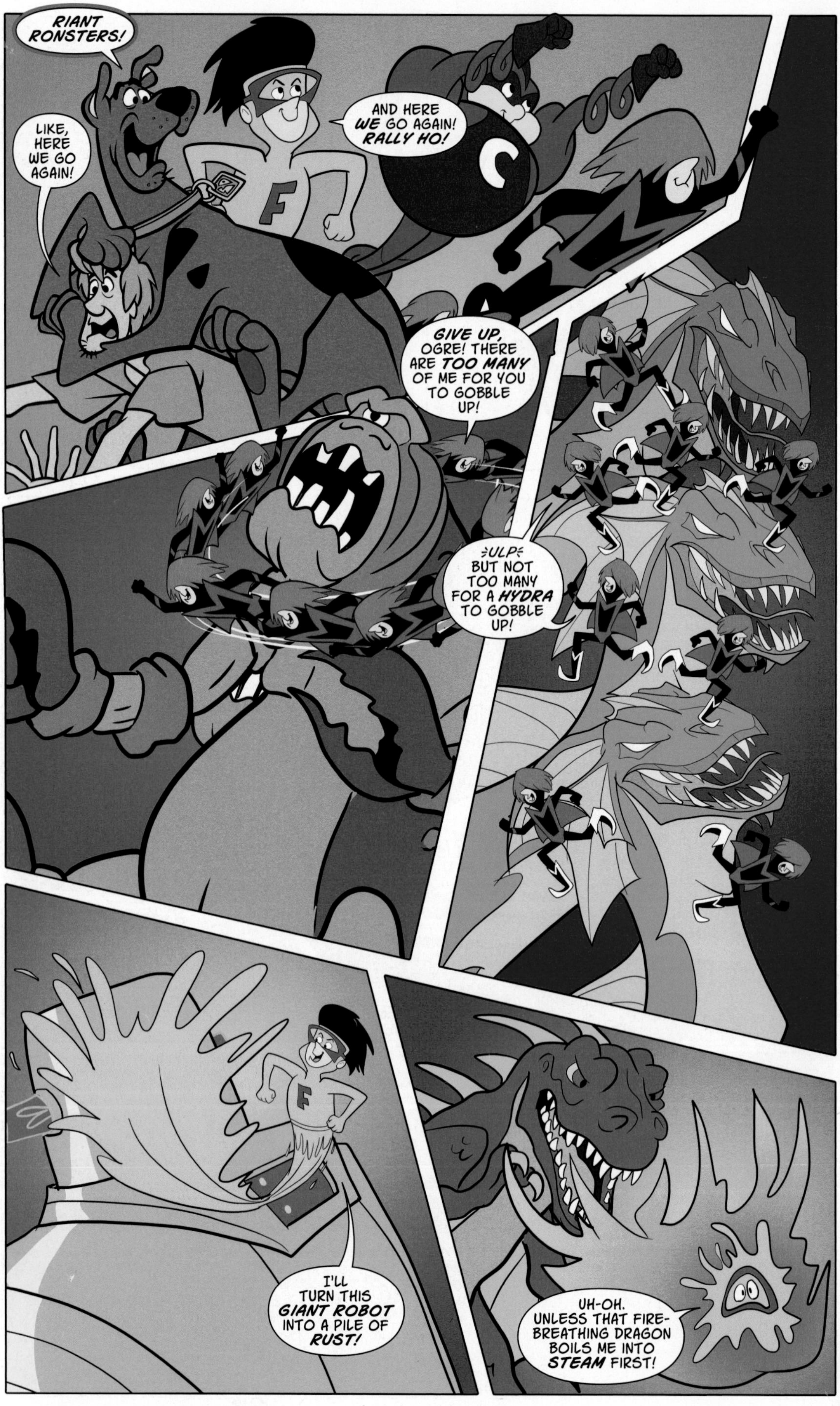
RIANT RONSTERS!
LIKE, HERE WE GO AGAIN!
AND HERE WE GO AGAIN! RALLY HO!
GIVE UP, OGRE! THERE ARE TOO MANY OF ME FOR YOU TO GOBBLE UP!
ULP BUT NOT TOO MANY FOR A HYDRA TO GOBBLE UP!
I'LL TURN THIS GIANT ROBOT INTO A PILE OF RUST!
UH-OH. UNLESS THAT FIRE-BREATHING DRAGON BOILS ME INTO STEAM FIRST!

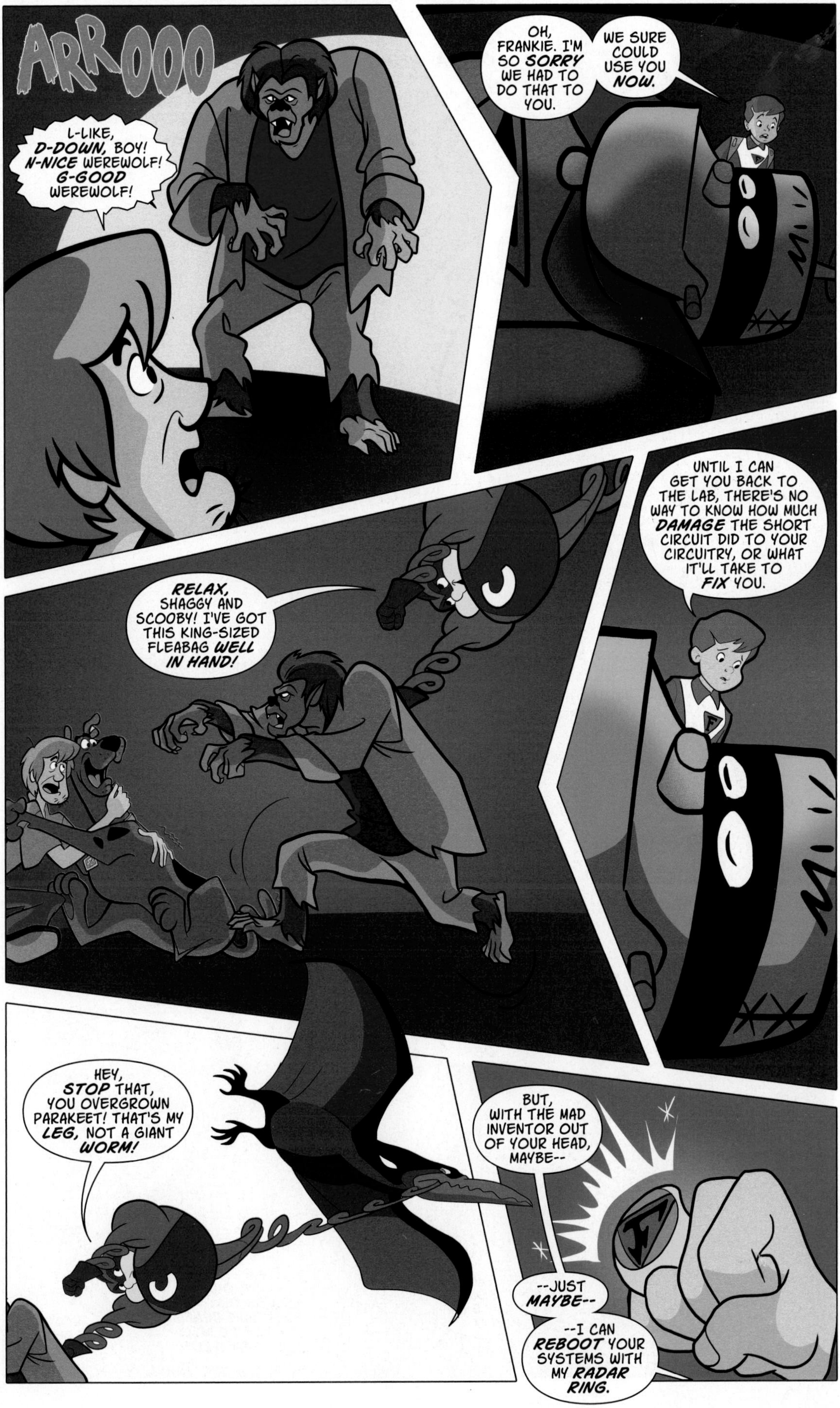

ARROOO
L-LIKE, D-DOWN, BOY! N-NICE WEREWOLF! G-GOOD WEREWOLF!
OH, FRANKIE. I'M SO SORRY WE HAD TO DO THAT TO YOU.
WE SURE COULD USE YOU NOW.
RELAX, SHAGGY AND SCOOBY! I'VE GOT THIS KING-SIZED FLEABAG WELL IN HAND!
UNTIL I CAN GET YOU BACK TO THE LAB, THERE'S NO WAY TO KNOW HOW MUCH DAMAGE THE SHORT CIRCUIT DID TO YOUR CIRCUITRY, OR WHAT IT'LL TAKE TO FIX YOU.
HEY, STOP THAT, YOU OVERGROWN PARAKEET! THAT'S MY LEG, NOT A GIANT WORM!
BUT, WITH THE MAD INVENTOR OUT OF YOUR HEAD, MAYBE--
--JUST MAYBE--
--I CAN REBOOT YOUR SYSTEMS WITH MY RADAR RING.

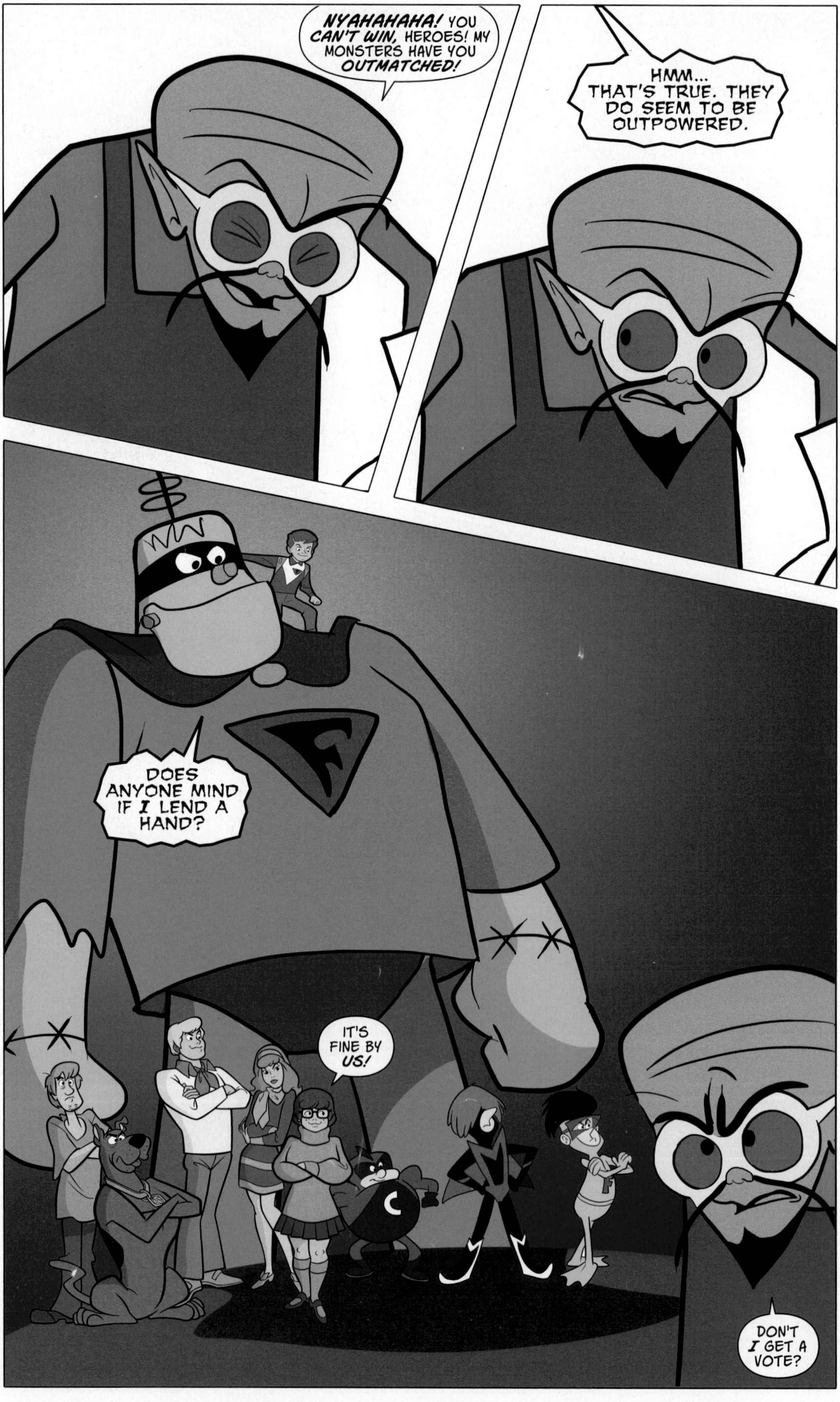
NYAHAHAHA! YOU CAN'T WIN, HEROES! MY MONSTERS HAVE YOU OUTMATCHED!
HMM... THAT'S TRUE. THEY DO SEEM TO BE OUTPOWERED.
DOES ANYONE MIND IF I LEND A HAND?
IT'S FINE BY US!
DON'T I GET A VOTE?

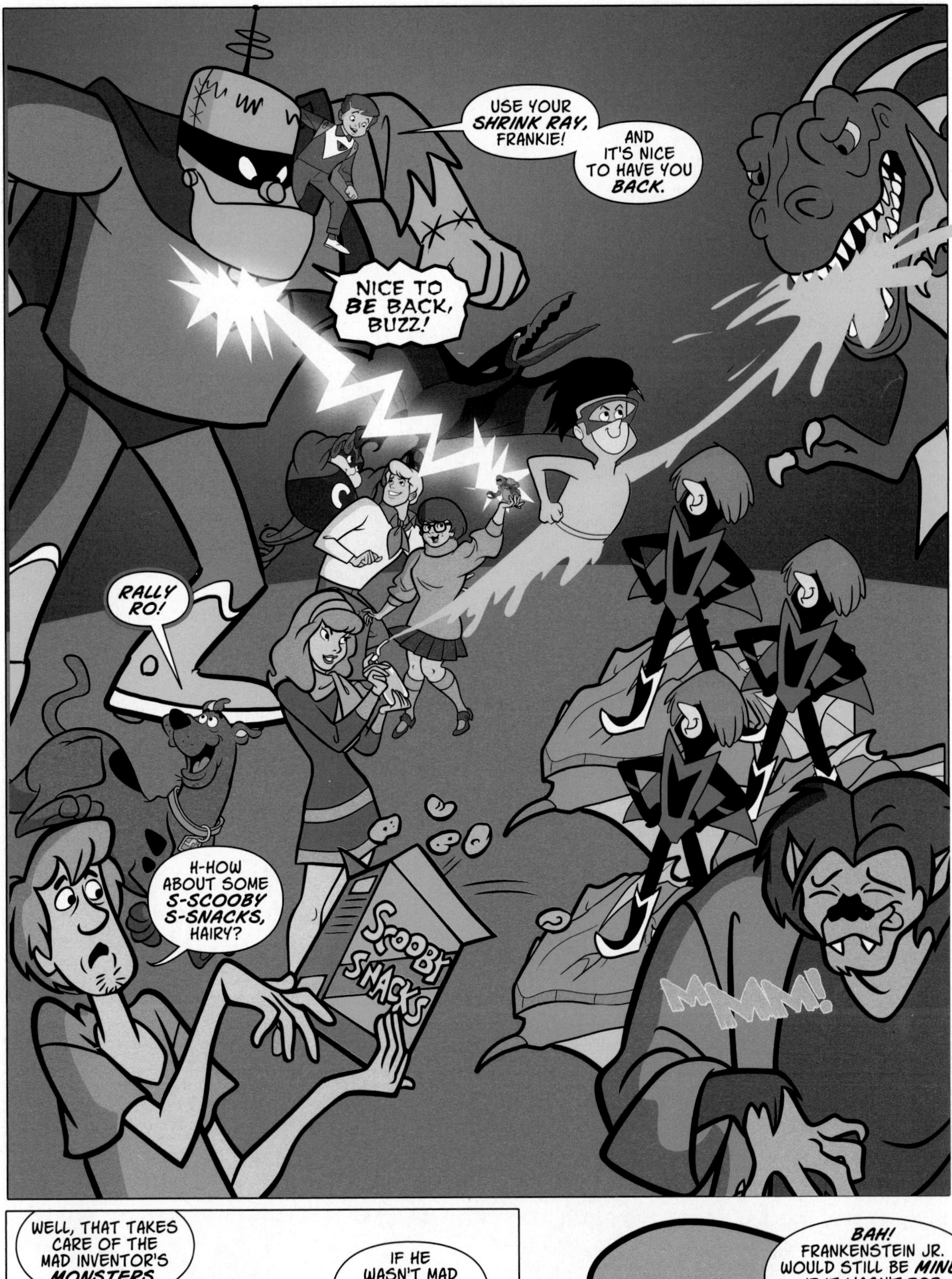
USE YOUR SHRINK RAY, FRANKIE!
AND IT'S NICE TO HAVE YOU BACK.
NICE TO BE BACK, BUZZ!
RALLY RO!
H-HOW ABOUT SOME S-SCOOBY S-SNACKS, HAIRY?
SCOOBY SNACKS
MMM!

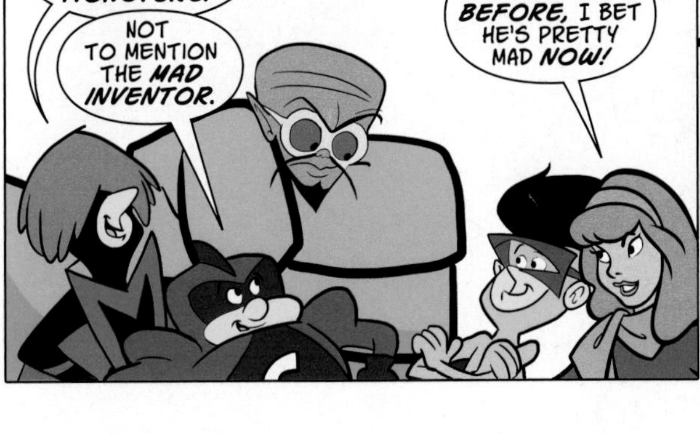
WELL, THAT TAKES CARE OF THE MAD INVENTOR'S MONSTERS.
NOT TO MENTION THE MAD INVENTOR.
IF HE WASN'T MAD BEFORE, I BET HE'S PRETTY MAD NOW!

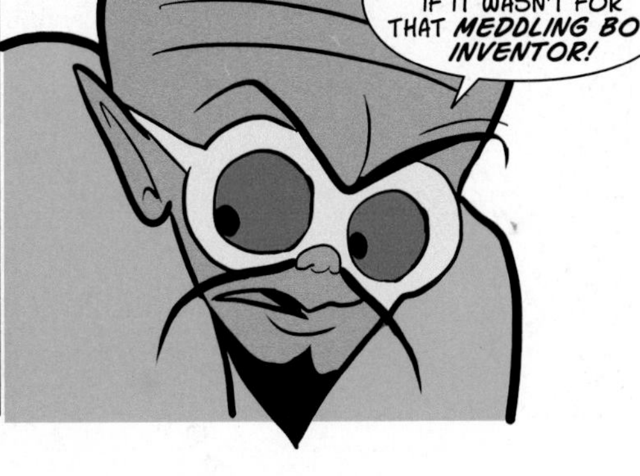
BAH! FRANKENSTEIN JR. WOULD STILL BE MINE, IF IT WASN'T FOR THAT MEDDLING BOY INVENTOR!

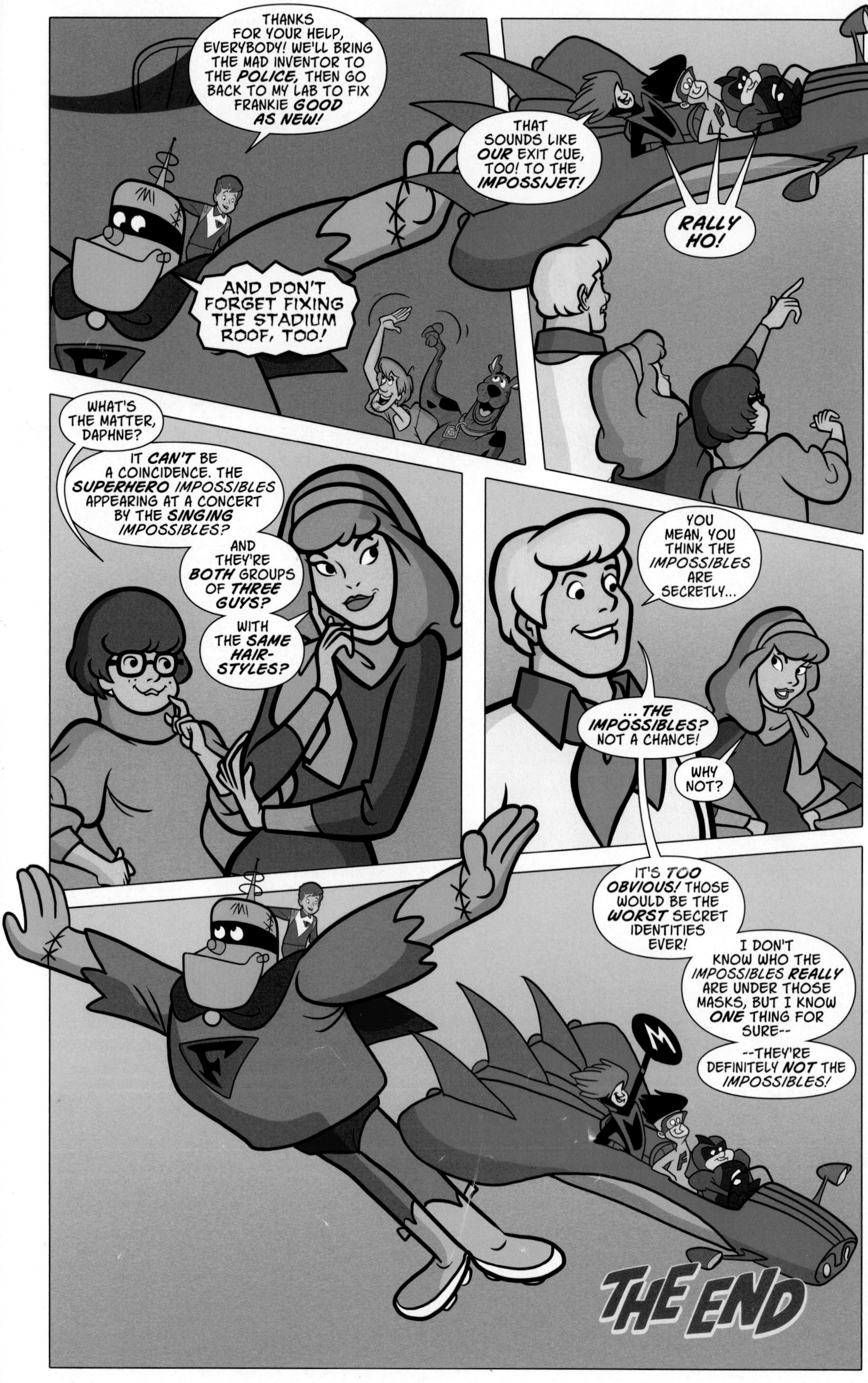
THANKS FOR YOUR HELP, EVERYBODY! WE'LL BRING THE MAD INVENTOR TO THE POLICE, THEN GO BACK TO MY LAB TO FIX FRANKIE GOOD AS NEW!
AND DON'T FORGET FIXING THE STADIUM ROOF, TOO!
THAT SOUNDS LIKE OUR EXIT CUE, TOO! TO THE IMPOSSIJET!
RALLY HO!
WHAT'S THE MATTER, DAPHNE?
IT CAN'T BE A COINCIDENCE. THE SUPERHERO IMPOSSIBLES APPEARING AT A CONCERT BY THE SINGING IMPOSSIBLES?
AND THEY'RE BOTH GROUPS OF THREE GUYS?
WITH THE SAME HAIR-STYLES?
YOU MEAN, YOU THINK THE IMPOSSIBLES ARE SECRETLY...
...THE IMPOSSIBLES? NOT A CHANCE!
WHY NOT?
IT'S TOO OBVIOUS! THOSE WOULD BE THE WORST SECRET IDENTITIES EVER!
I DON'T KNOW WHO THE IMPOSSIBLES REALLY ARE UNDER THOSE MASKS, BUT I KNOW ONE THING FOR SURE--
--THEY'RE DEFINITELY NOT THE IMPOSSIBLES!
THE END

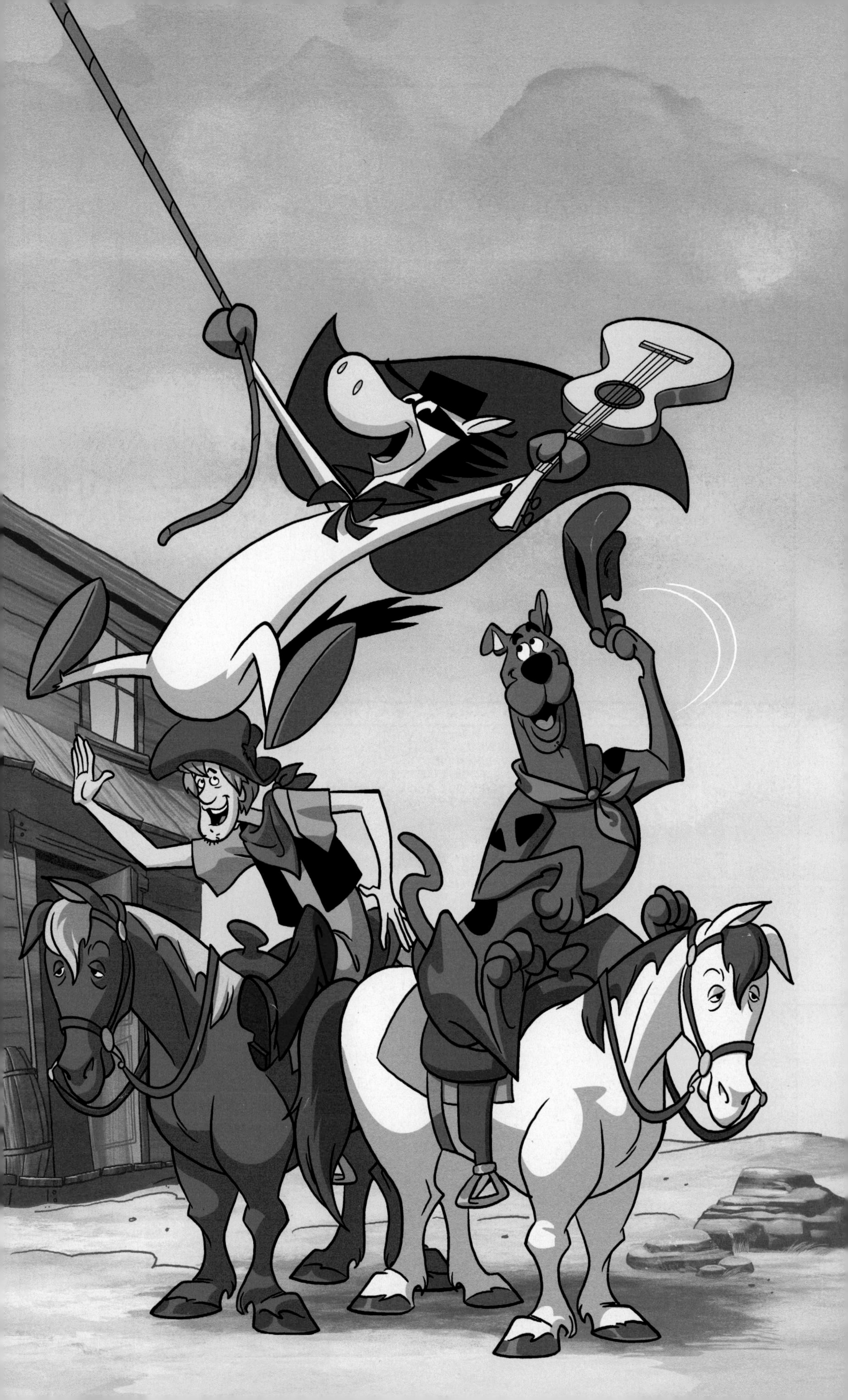

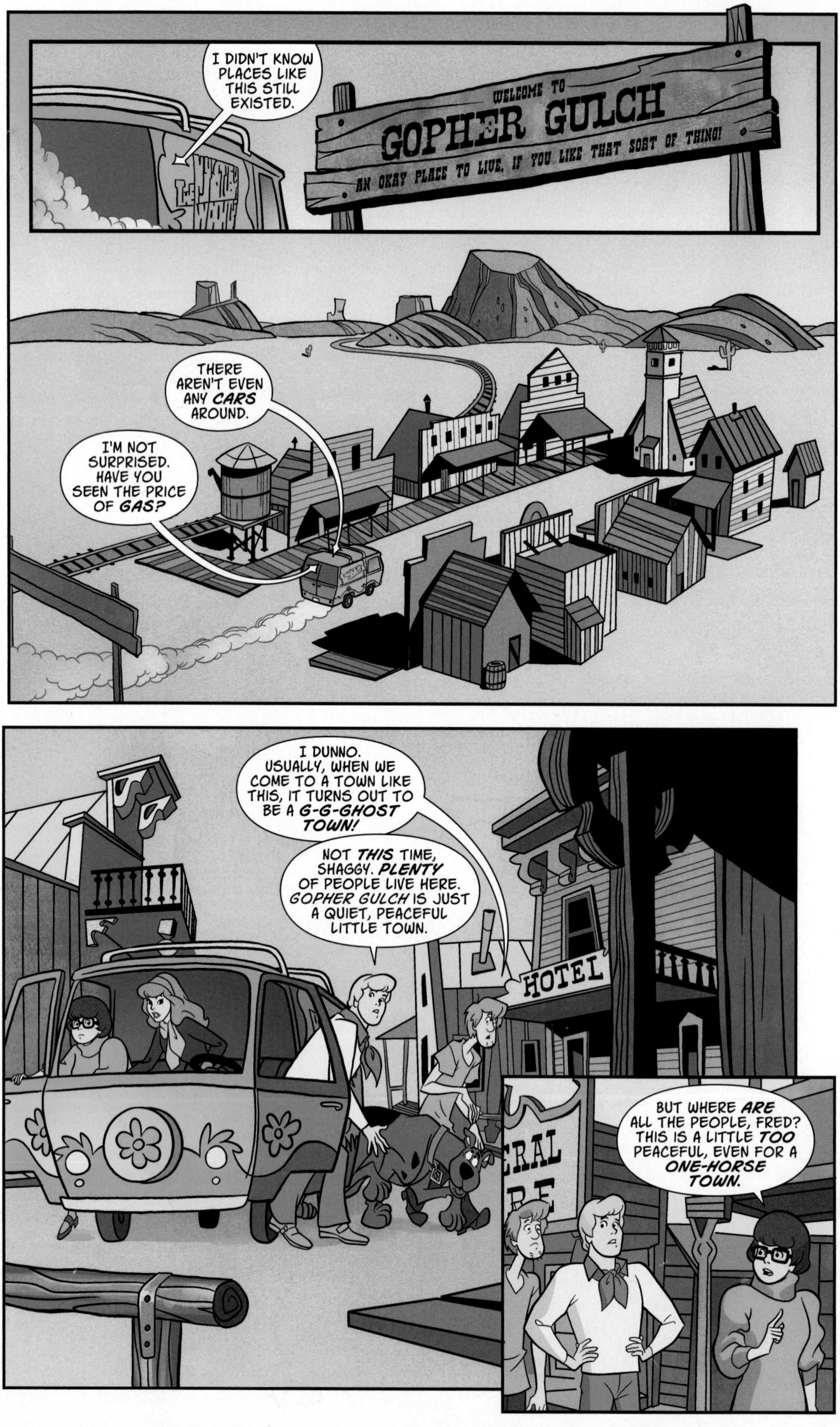
WELCOME TO
GOPHER GULCH
AN OKAY PLACE TO LIVE, IF YOU LIKE THAT SORT OF THING!
I DIDN'T KNOW PLACES LIKE THIS STILL EXISTED.
THERE AREN'T EVEN ANY CARS AROUND.
I'M NOT SURPRISED. HAVE YOU SEEN THE PRICE OF GAS?
I DUNNO. USUALLY, WHEN WE COME TO A TOWN LIKE THIS, IT TURNS OUT TO BE A G-G-GHOST TOWN!
NOT THIS TIME, SHAGGY. PLENTY OF PEOPLE LIVE HERE. GOPHER GULCH IS JUST A QUIET, PEACEFUL LITTLE TOWN.
HOTEL
BUT WHERE ARE ALL THE PEOPLE, FRED? THIS IS A LITTLE TOO PEACEFUL, EVEN FOR A ONE-HORSE TOWN.

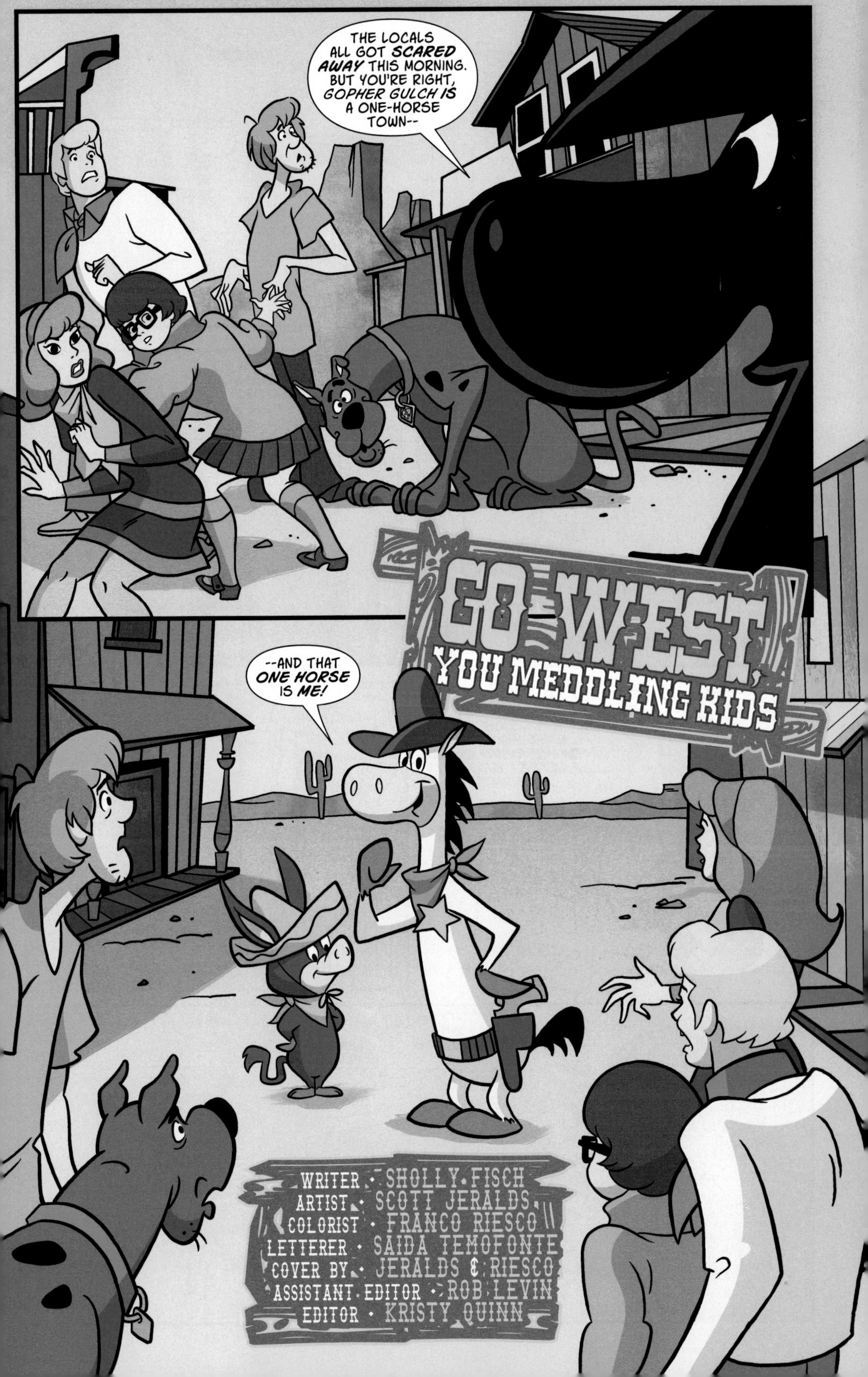
THE LOCALS ALL GOT SCARED AWAY THIS MORNING. BUT YOU'RE RIGHT, GOPHER GULCH IS A ONE-HORSE TOWN--
GO WEST, YOU MEDDLING KIDS
--AND THAT ONE HORSE IS ME!
WRITER • SHOLLY FISCH
ARTIST • SCOTT JERALDS
COLORIST • FRANCO RIESCO
LETTERER • SAIDA TEMOFONTE
COVER BY • JERALDS & RIESCO
ASSISTANT EDITOR • ROB LEVIN
EDITOR • KRISTY QUINN

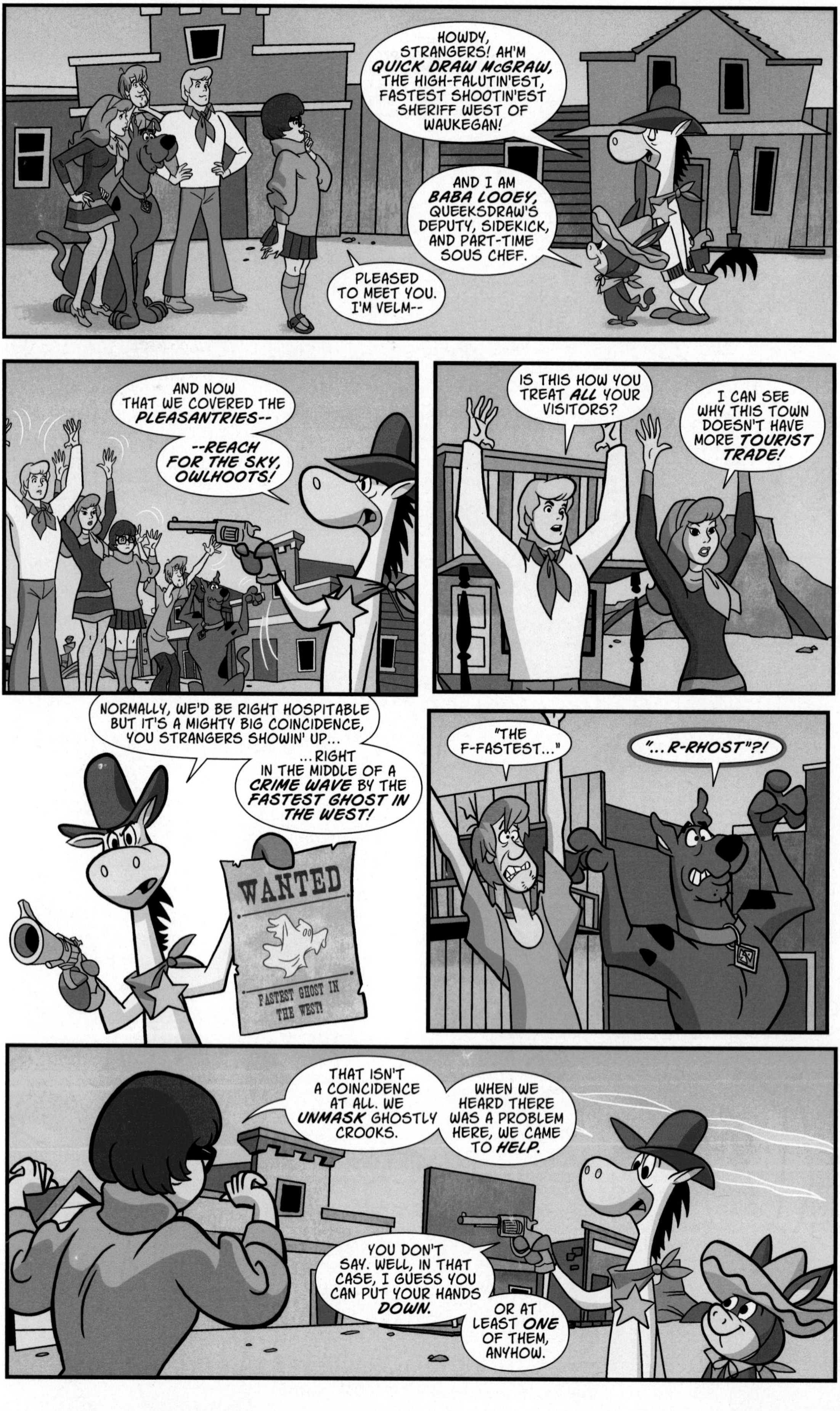
HOWDY, STRANGERS! AH'M QUICK DRAW McGRAW, THE HIGH-FALUTIN'EST, FASTEST SHOOTIN'EST SHERIFF WEST OF WAUKEGAN!
AND I AM BABA LOOEY, QUEEKSDRAW'S DEPUTY, SIDEKICK, AND PART-TIME SOUS CHEF.
PLEASED TO MEET YOU. I'M VELM--
AND NOW THAT WE COVERED THE PLEASANTRIES--
--REACH FOR THE SKY, OWLHOOTS!
IS THIS HOW YOU TREAT ALL YOUR VISITORS?
I CAN SEE WHY THIS TOWN DOESN'T HAVE MORE TOURIST TRADE!
NORMALLY, WE'D BE RIGHT HOSPITABLE BUT IT'S A MIGHTY BIG COINCIDENCE, YOU STRANGERS SHOWIN' UP...
...RIGHT IN THE MIDDLE OF A CRIME WAVE BY THE FASTEST GHOST IN THE WEST!
WANTED
FASTEST GHOST IN THE WEST!
"THE F-FASTEST..."
"...R-RHOST"?!
THAT ISN'T A COINCIDENCE AT ALL. WE UNMASK GHOSTLY CROOKS.
WHEN WE HEARD THERE WAS A PROBLEM HERE, WE CAME TO HELP.
YOU DON'T SAY. WELL, IN THAT CASE, I GUESS YOU CAN PUT YOUR HANDS DOWN.
OR AT LEAST ONE OF THEM, ANYHOW.

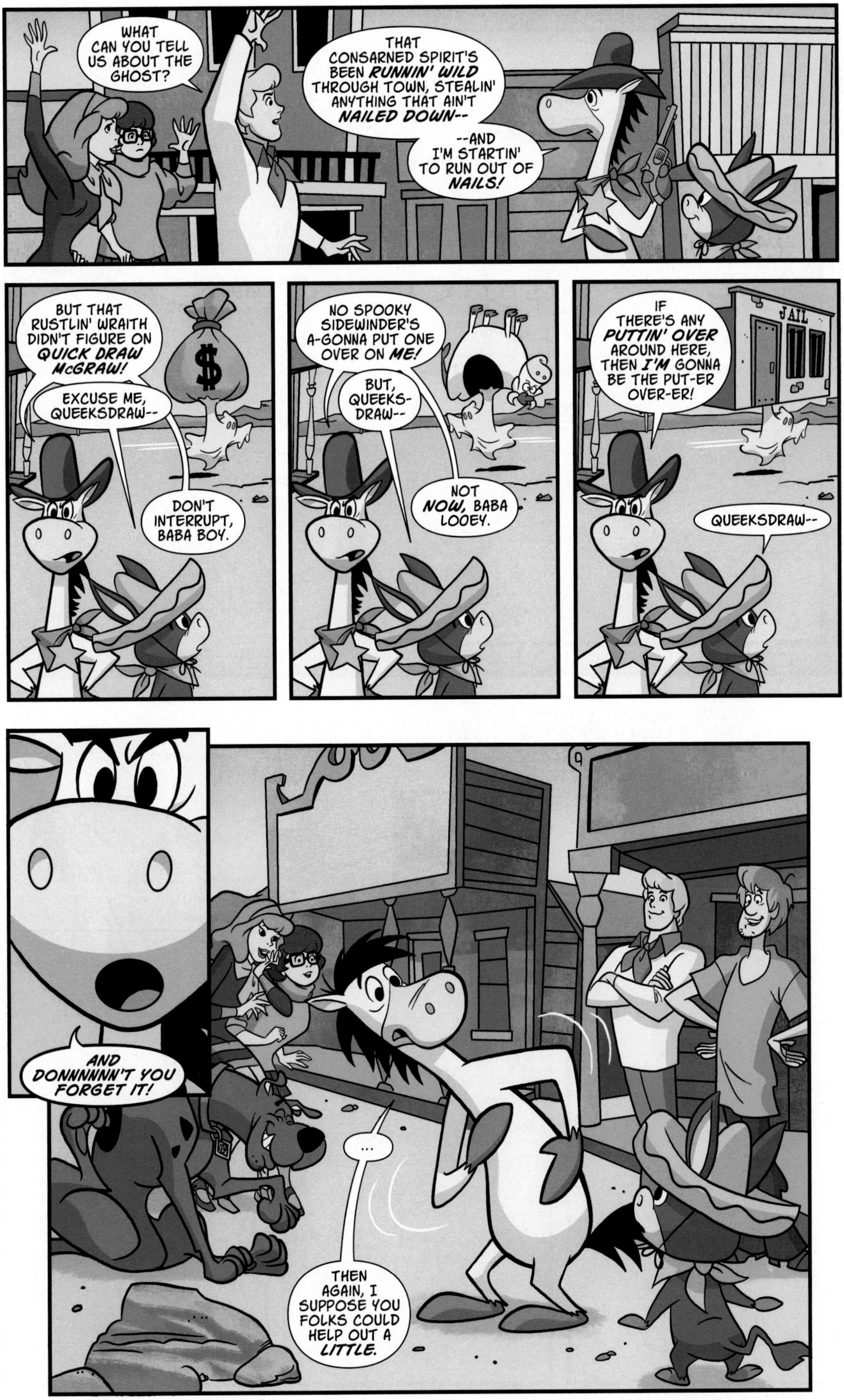
WHAT CAN YOU TELL US ABOUT THE GHOST?
THAT CONSARNED SPIRIT'S BEEN RUNNIN' WILD THROUGH TOWN, STEALIN' ANYTHING THAT AIN'T NAILED DOWN--
--AND I'M STARTIN' TO RUN OUT OF NAILS!
BUT THAT RUSTLIN' WRAITH DIDN'T FIGURE ON QUICK DRAW McGRAW!
EXCUSE ME, QUEEKSDRAW--
DON'T INTERRUPT, BABA BOY.
NO SPOOKY SIDEWINDER'S A-GONNA PUT ONE OVER ON ME!
BUT, QUEEKS-DRAW--
NOT NOW, BABA LOOEY.
JAIL
IF THERE'S ANY PUTTIN' OVER AROUND HERE, THEN I'M GONNA BE THE PUT-ER OVER-ER!
QUEEKSDRAW--
AND DONNNNNN'T YOU FORGET IT!
...
THEN AGAIN, I SUPPOSE YOU FOLKS COULD HELP OUT A LITTLE.

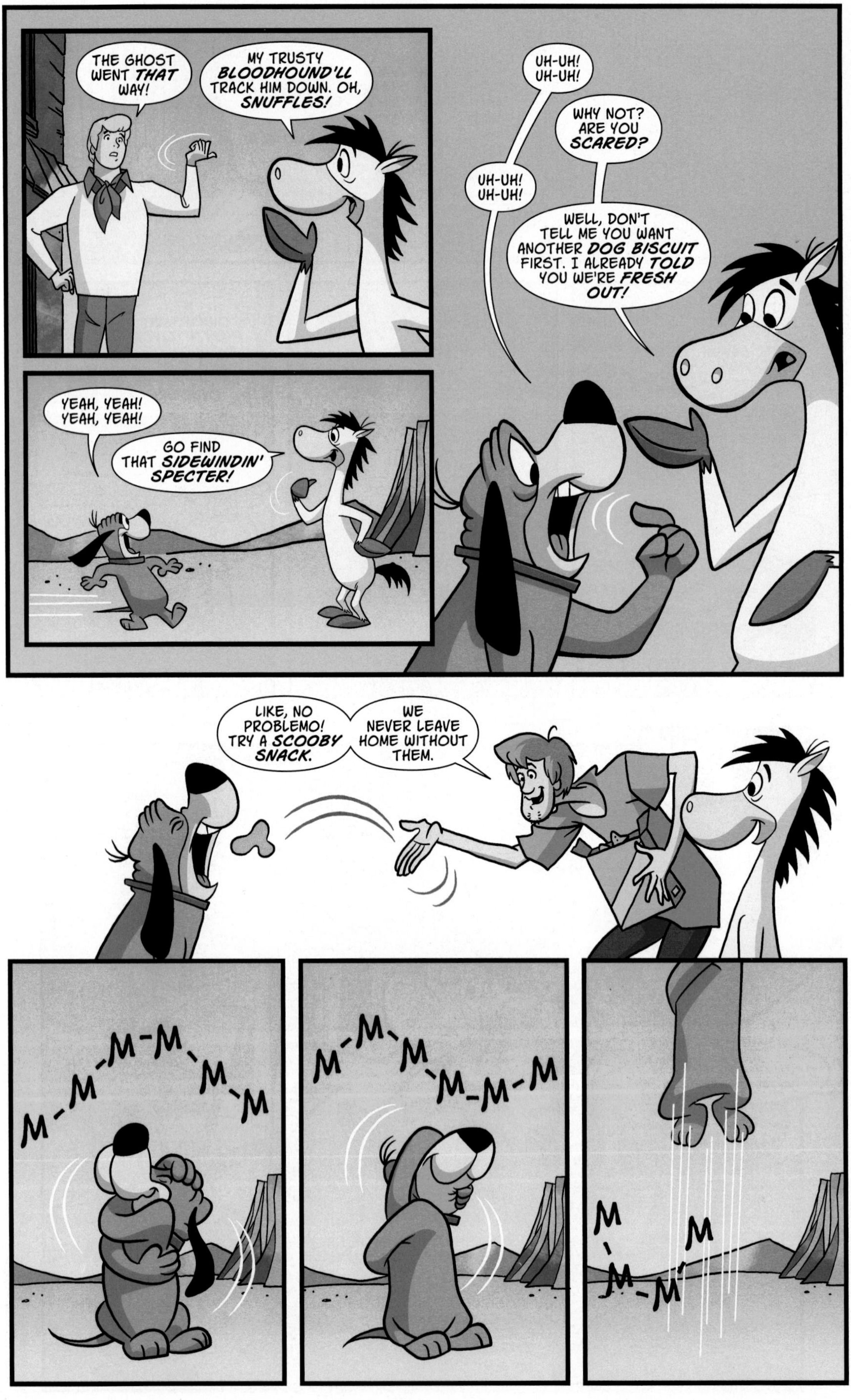
THE GHOST WENT THAT WAY!
MY TRUSTY BLOODHOUND'LL TRACK HIM DOWN. OH, SNUFFLES!
YEAH, YEAH! YEAH, YEAH!
GO FIND THAT SIDEWINDIN' SPECTER!
UH-UH! UH-UH!
WHY NOT? ARE YOU SCARED?
UH-UH! UH-UH!
WELL, DON'T TELL ME YOU WANT ANOTHER DOG BISCUIT FIRST. I ALREADY TOLD YOU WE'RE FRESH OUT!
LIKE, NO PROBLEMO! TRY A SCOOBY SNACK.
WE NEVER LEAVE HOME WITHOUT THEM.
M-M-M-M-M-M
M-M-M-M-M-M
M-M-M-M

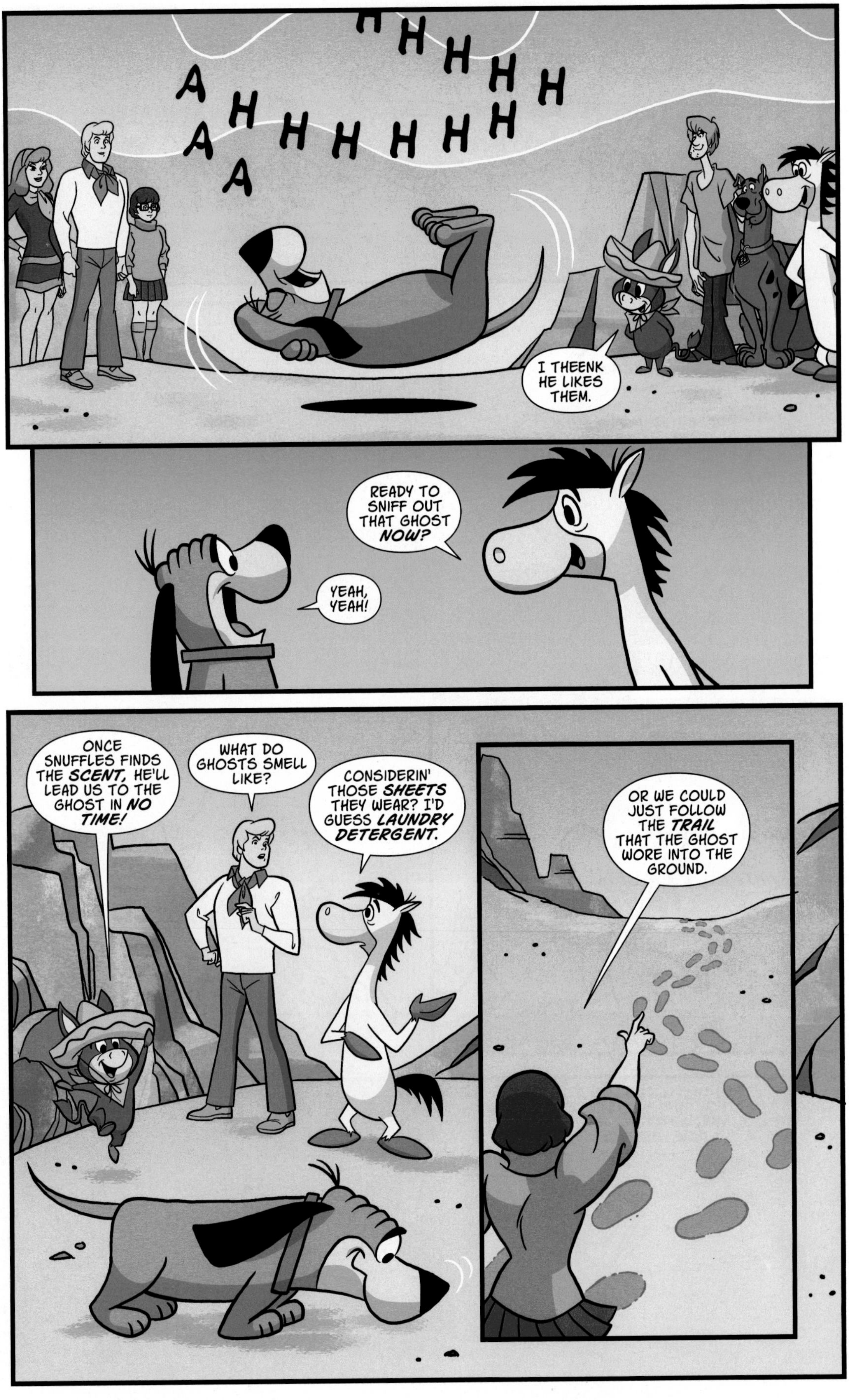
AAAHHHHHHHHHHHHH
I THEENK HE LIKES THEM.
READY TO SNIFF OUT THAT GHOST *NOW?*
YEAH, YEAH!
ONCE SNUFFLES FINDS THE *SCENT,* HE'LL LEAD US TO THE GHOST IN *NO TIME!*
WHAT DO GHOSTS SMELL LIKE?
CONSIDERIN' THOSE *SHEETS* THEY WEAR? I'D GUESS *LAUNDRY DETERGENT*.
OR WE COULD JUST FOLLOW THE *TRAIL* THAT THE GHOST WORE INTO THE GROUND.

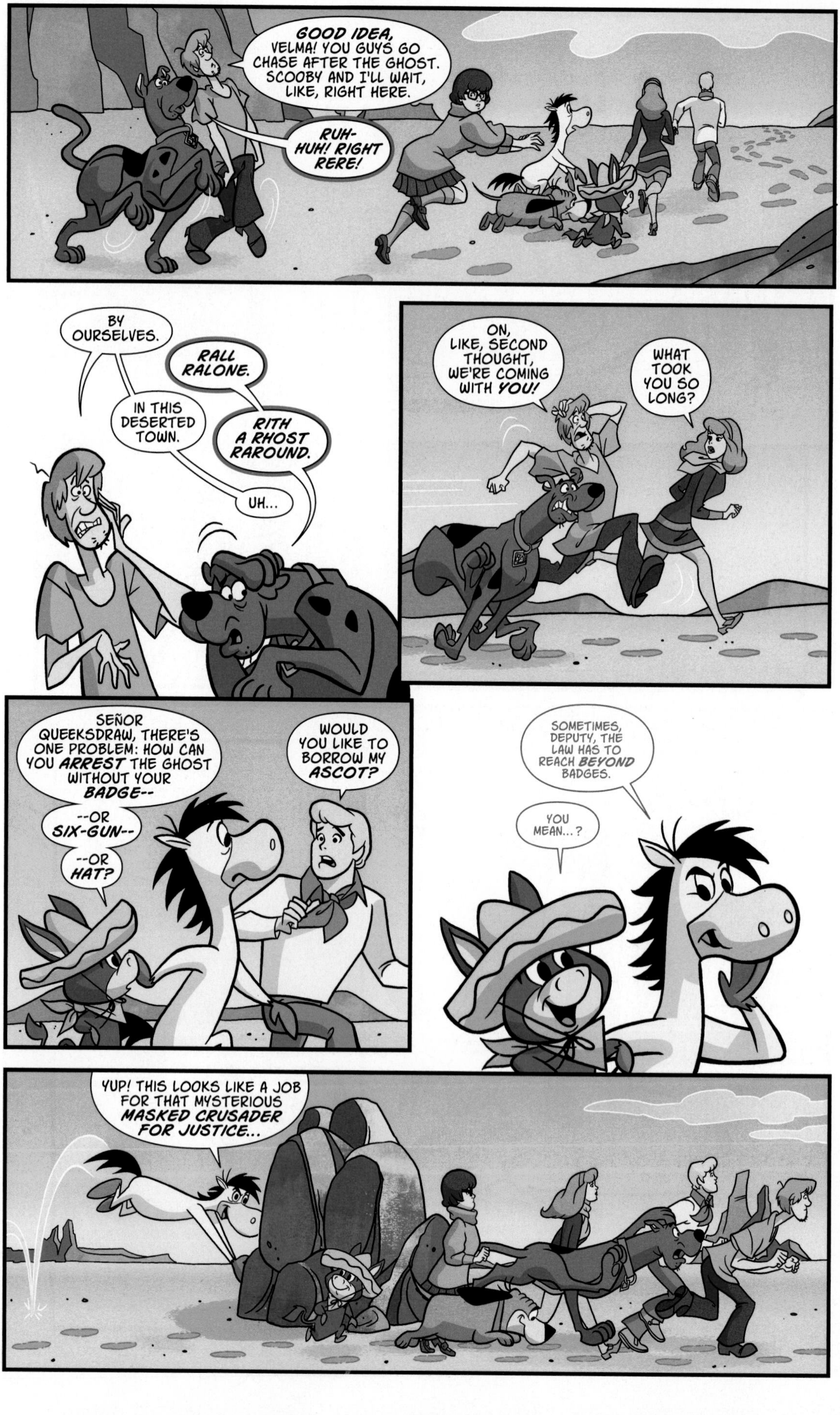

GOOD IDEA, VELMA! YOU GUYS GO CHASE AFTER THE GHOST. SCOOBY AND I'LL WAIT, LIKE, RIGHT HERE.
RUH-HUH! RIGHT RERE!
BY OURSELVES.
RALL RALONE.
IN THIS DESERTED TOWN.
RITH A RHOST RAROUND.
UH...
ON, LIKE, SECOND THOUGHT, WE'RE COMING WITH YOU!
WHAT TOOK YOU SO LONG?
SEÑOR QUEEKSDRAW, THERE'S ONE PROBLEM: HOW CAN YOU ARREST THE GHOST WITHOUT YOUR BADGE--
--OR SIX-GUN--
--OR HAT?
WOULD YOU LIKE TO BORROW MY ASCOT?
SOMETIMES, DEPUTY, THE LAW HAS TO REACH BEYOND BADGES.
YOU MEAN...?
YUP! THIS LOOKS LIKE A JOB FOR THAT MYSTERIOUS MASKED CRUSADER FOR JUSTICE...

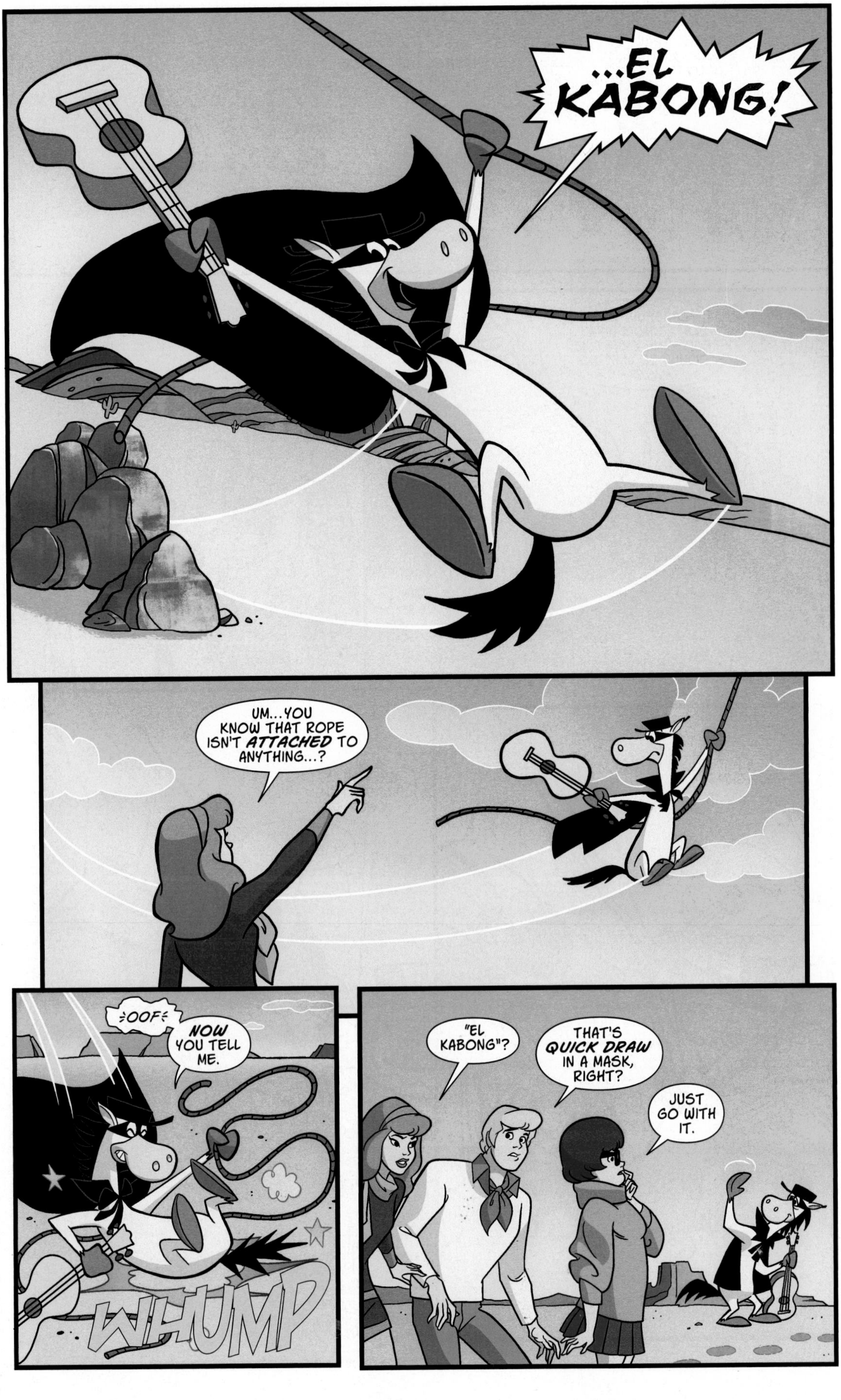
...EL KABONG!
UM...YOU KNOW THAT ROPE ISN'T *ATTACHED* TO ANYTHING...?
OOF
NOW YOU TELL ME.
WHUMP
"EL KABONG"?
THAT'S *QUICK DRAW* IN A MASK, RIGHT?
JUST GO WITH IT.

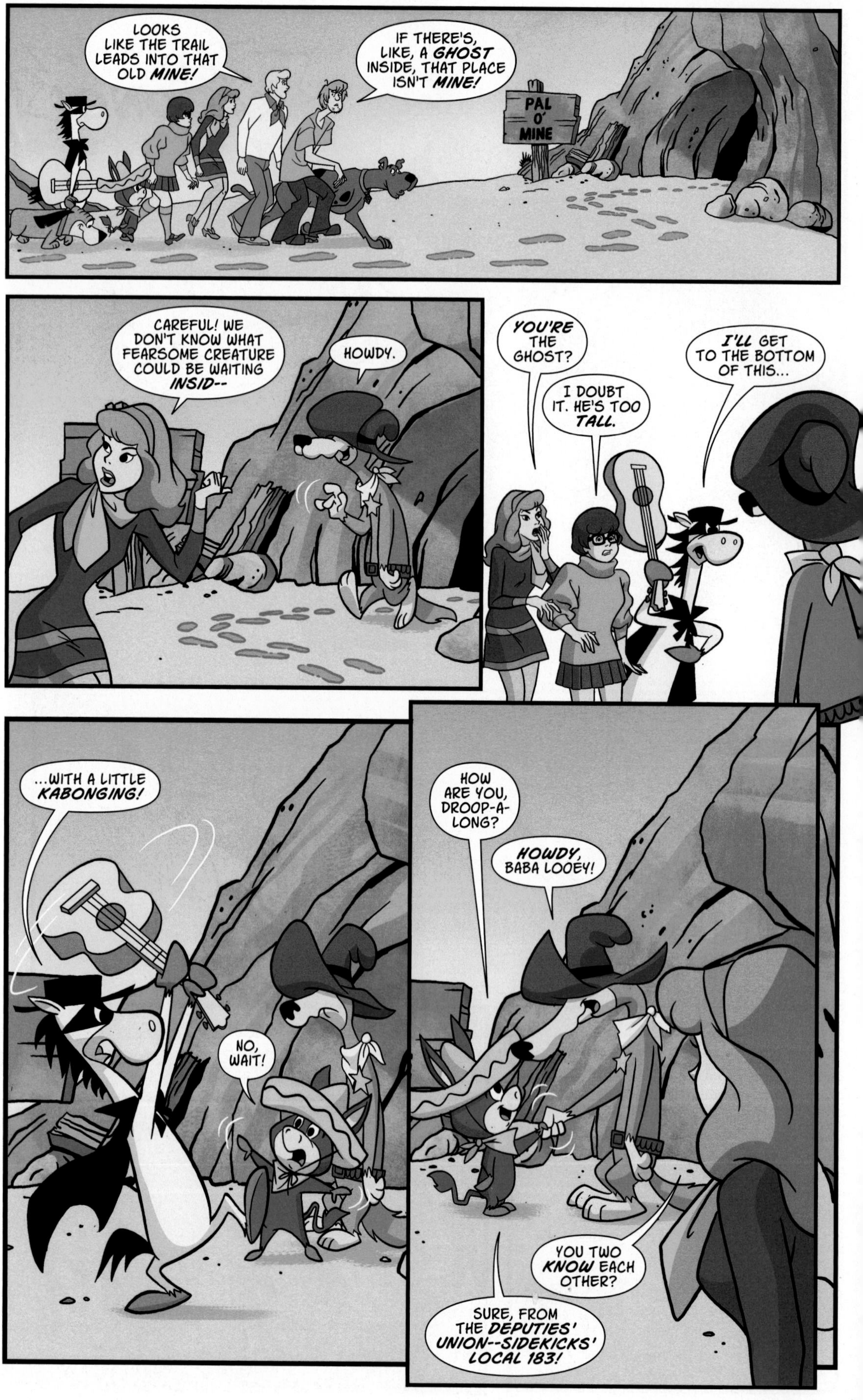
LOOKS LIKE THE TRAIL LEADS INTO THAT OLD MINE!
IF THERE'S, LIKE, A GHOST INSIDE, THAT PLACE ISN'T MINE!
PAL O' MINE
CAREFUL! WE DON'T KNOW WHAT FEARSOME CREATURE COULD BE WAITING INSID--
HOWDY.
YOU'RE THE GHOST?
I DOUBT IT. HE'S TOO TALL.
I'LL GET TO THE BOTTOM OF THIS...
...WITH A LITTLE KABONGING!
NO, WAIT!
HOW ARE YOU, DROOP-A-LONG?
HOWDY, BABA LOOEY!
YOU TWO KNOW EACH OTHER?
SURE, FROM THE DEPUTIES' UNION--SIDEKICKS' LOCAL 183!

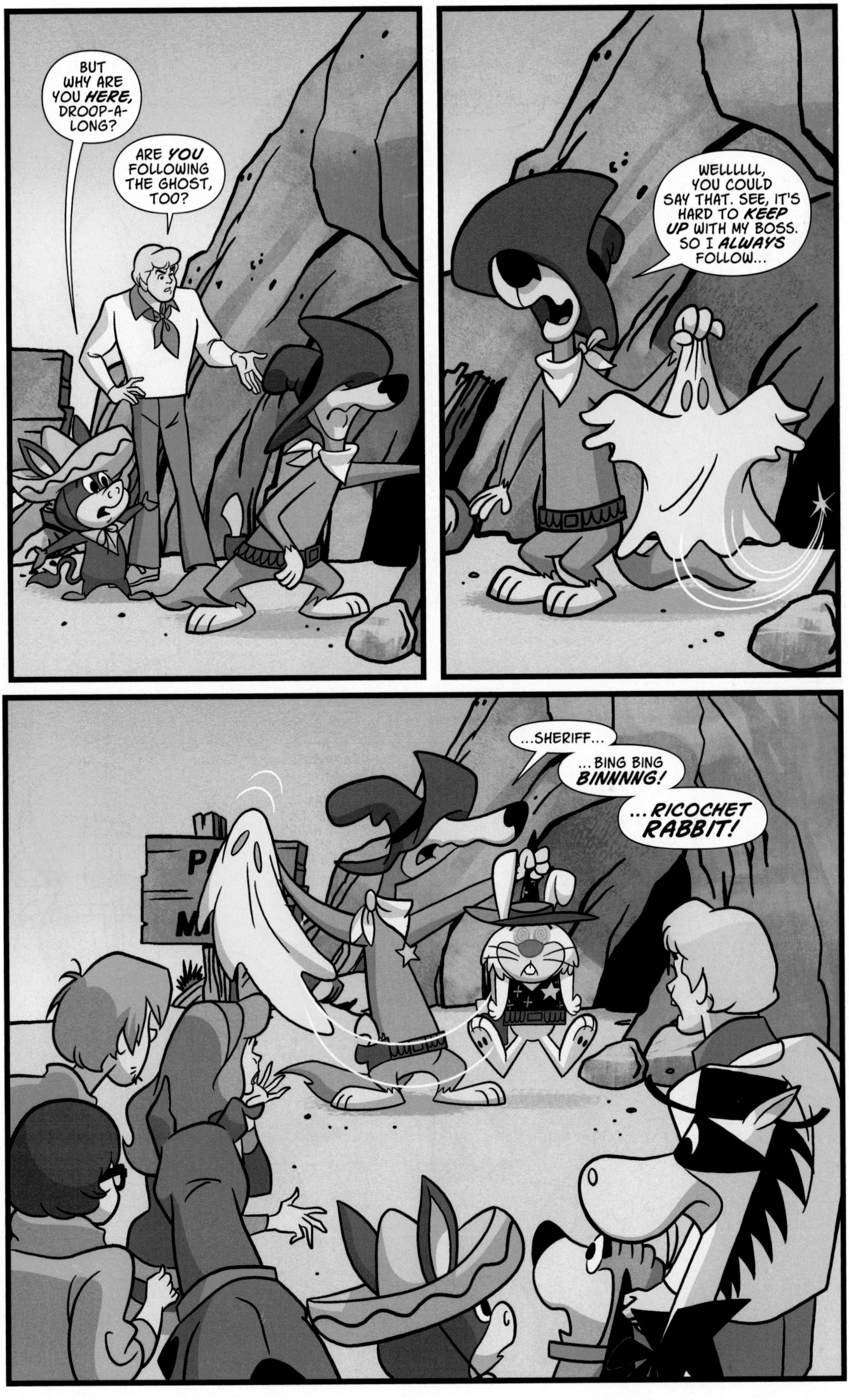
BUT WHY ARE YOU *HERE,* DROOP-A-LONG?
ARE *YOU* FOLLOWING THE GHOST, TOO?
WELLLLLL, YOU COULD SAY THAT. SEE, IT'S HARD TO *KEEP UP* WITH MY BOSS. SO I *ALWAYS* FOLLOW...
...SHERIFF...
...BING BING *BINNNNG!*
...*RICOCHET RABBIT!*

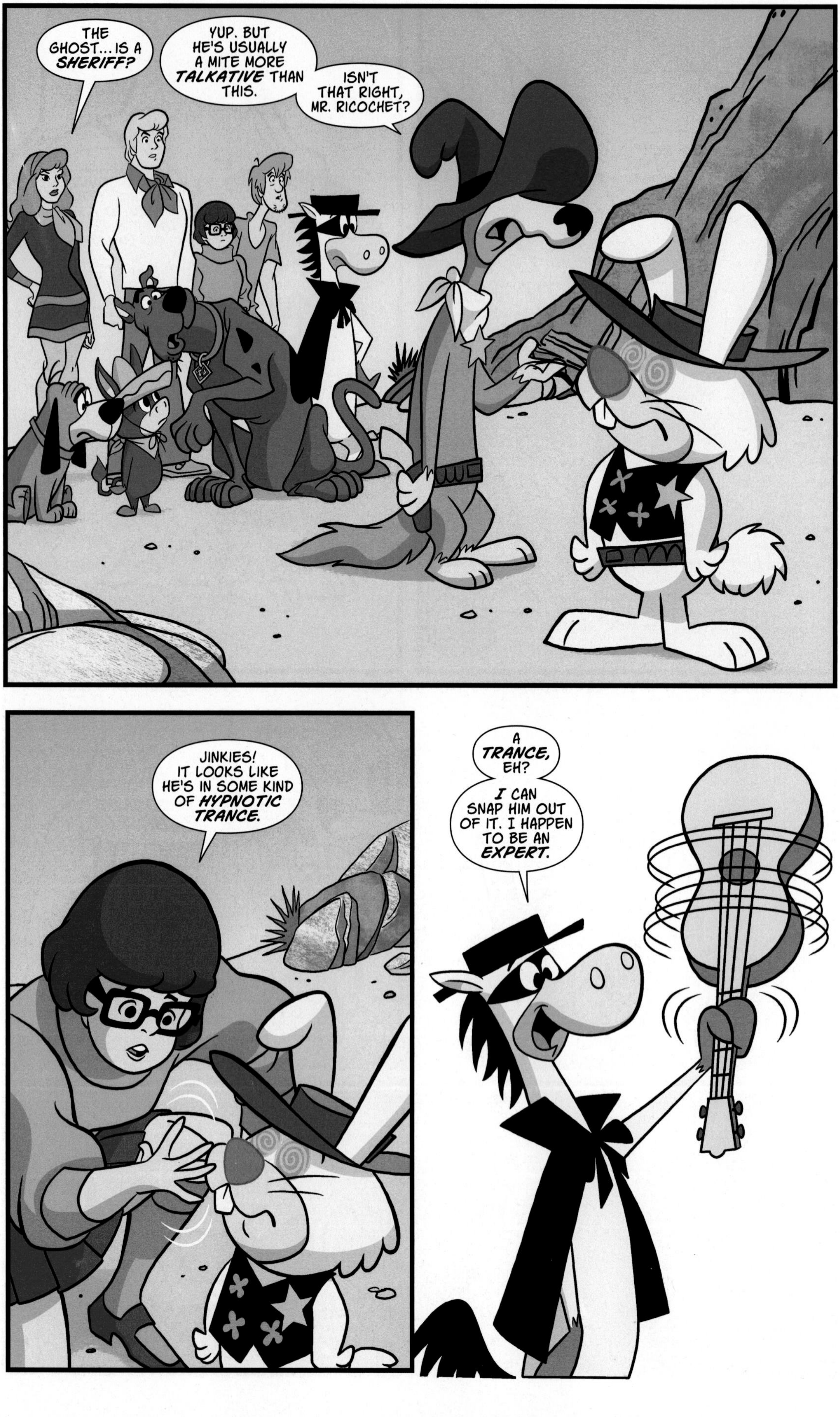
THE GHOST... IS A *SHERIFF?*
YUP. BUT HE'S USUALLY A MITE MORE *TALKATIVE* THAN THIS.
ISN'T THAT RIGHT, MR. RICOCHET?
JINKIES! IT LOOKS LIKE HE'S IN SOME KIND OF *HYPNOTIC TRANCE.*
A *TRANCE,* EH?
I CAN SNAP HIM OUT OF IT. I HAPPEN TO BE AN *EXPERT.*

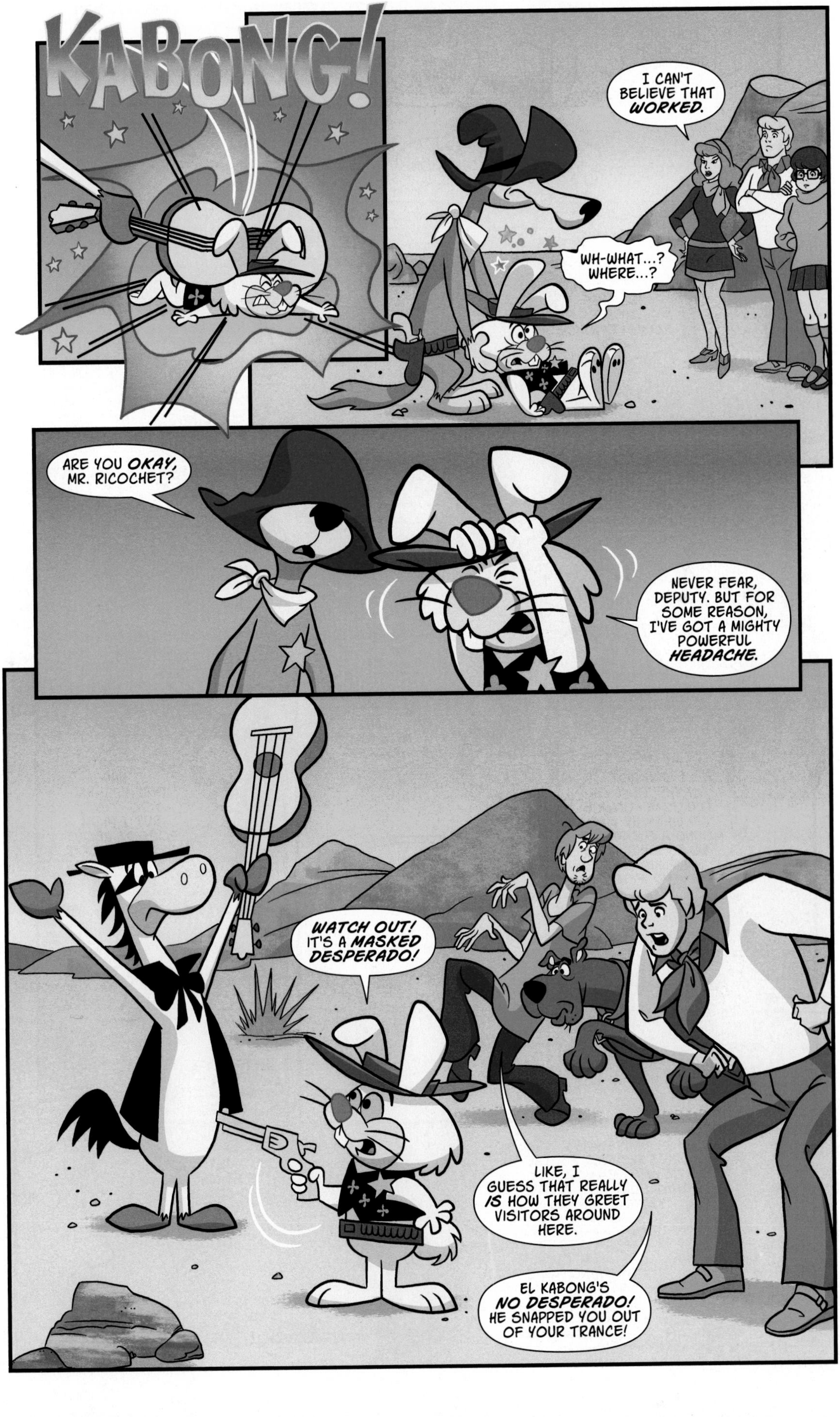
KABONG!
I CAN'T BELIEVE THAT WORKED.
WH-WHAT...? WHERE...?
ARE YOU OKAY, MR. RICOCHET?
NEVER FEAR, DEPUTY. BUT FOR SOME REASON, I'VE GOT A MIGHTY POWERFUL HEADACHE.
WATCH OUT! IT'S A MASKED DESPERADO!
LIKE, I GUESS THAT REALLY IS HOW THEY GREET VISITORS AROUND HERE.
EL KABONG'S NO DESPERADO! HE SNAPPED YOU OUT OF YOUR TRANCE!

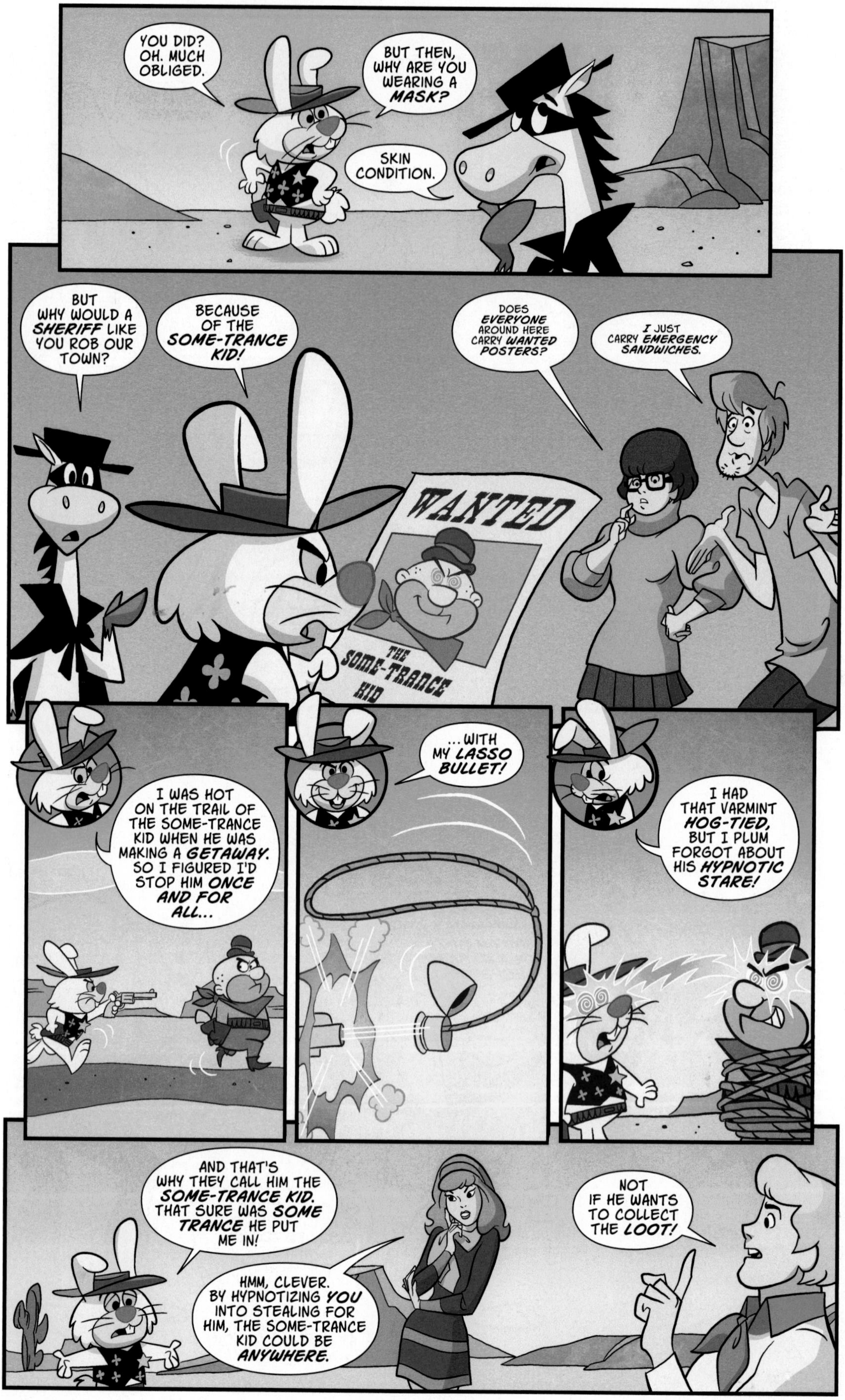

YOU DID? OH. MUCH OBLIGED.
BUT THEN, WHY ARE YOU WEARING A *MASK?*
SKIN CONDITION.
BUT WHY WOULD A *SHERIFF* LIKE YOU ROB OUR TOWN?
BECAUSE OF THE *SOME-TRANCE KID!*
WANTED
THE SOME-TRANCE KID
DOES *EVERYONE* AROUND HERE CARRY *WANTED POSTERS?*
I JUST CARRY *EMERGENCY SANDWICHES.*
I WAS HOT ON THE TRAIL OF THE SOME-TRANCE KID WHEN HE WAS MAKING A *GETAWAY.* SO I FIGURED I'D STOP HIM *ONCE AND FOR ALL...*
...WITH MY *LASSO BULLET!*
I HAD THAT VARMINT *HOG-TIED,* BUT I PLUM FORGOT ABOUT HIS *HYPNOTIC STARE!*
AND THAT'S WHY THEY CALL HIM THE *SOME-TRANCE KID.* THAT SURE WAS *SOME TRANCE* HE PUT ME IN!
HMM, CLEVER. BY HYPNOTIZING *YOU* INTO STEALING FOR HIM, THE SOME-TRANCE KID COULD BE *ANYWHERE.*
NOT IF HE WANTS TO COLLECT THE *LOOT!*

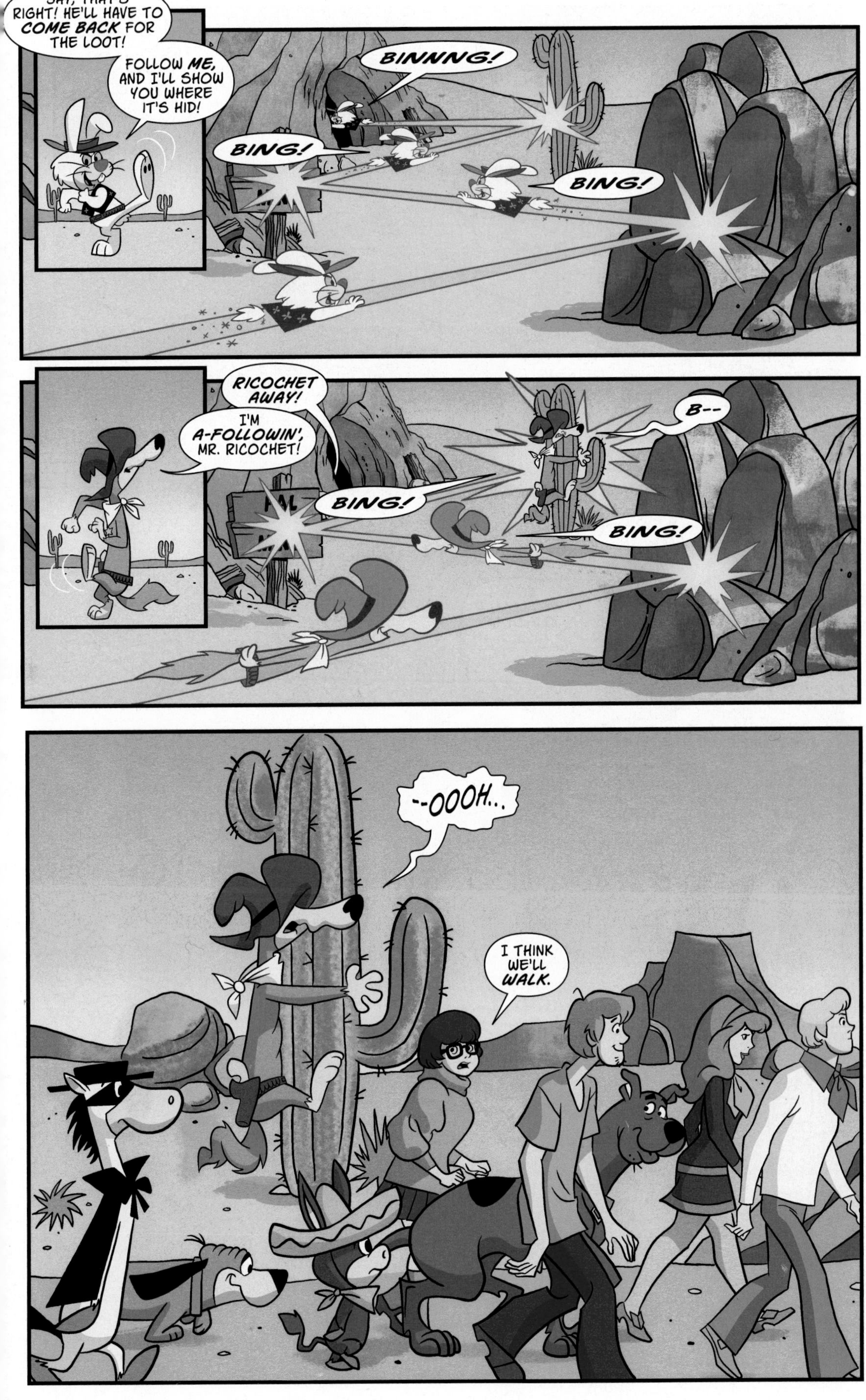
SAY, THAT'S RIGHT! HE'LL HAVE TO COME BACK FOR THE LOOT!
FOLLOW ME, AND I'LL SHOW YOU WHERE IT'S HID!
BINNNG!
BING!
BING!
RICOCHET AWAY!
I'M A-FOLLOWIN', MR. RICOCHET!
B--
BING!
BING!
--OOOH...
I THINK WE'LL WALK.

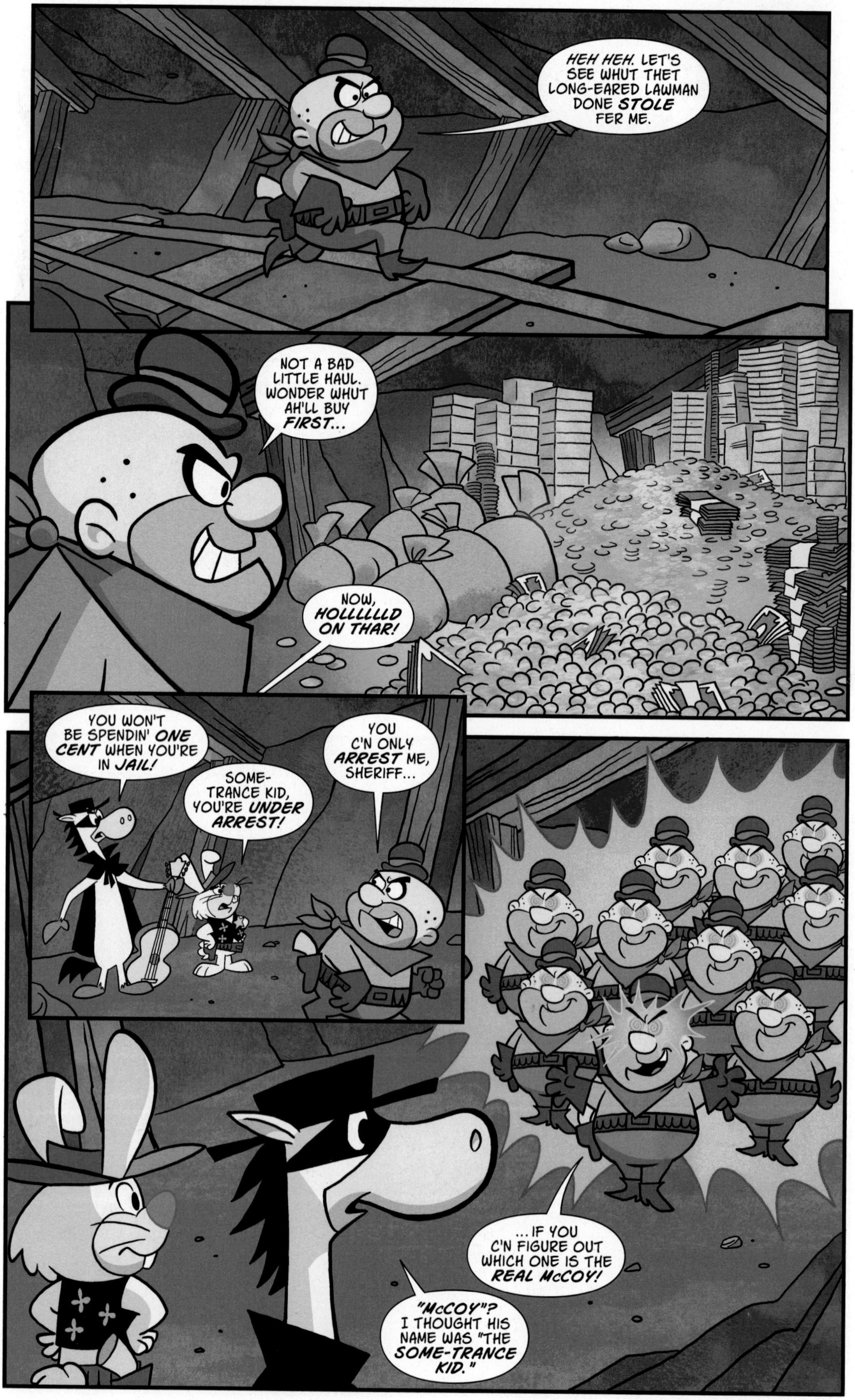
HEH HEH. LET'S SEE WHUT THET LONG-EARED LAWMAN DONE STOLE FER ME.
NOT A BAD LITTLE HAUL. WONDER WHUT AH'LL BUY FIRST...
NOW, HOLLLLLLD ON THAR!
YOU WON'T BE SPENDIN' ONE CENT WHEN YOU'RE IN JAIL!
SOME-TRANCE KID, YOU'RE UNDER ARREST!
YOU C'N ONLY ARREST ME, SHERIFF...
... IF YOU C'N FIGURE OUT WHICH ONE IS THE REAL McCOY!
"McCOY"? I THOUGHT HIS NAME WAS "THE SOME-TRANCE KID."

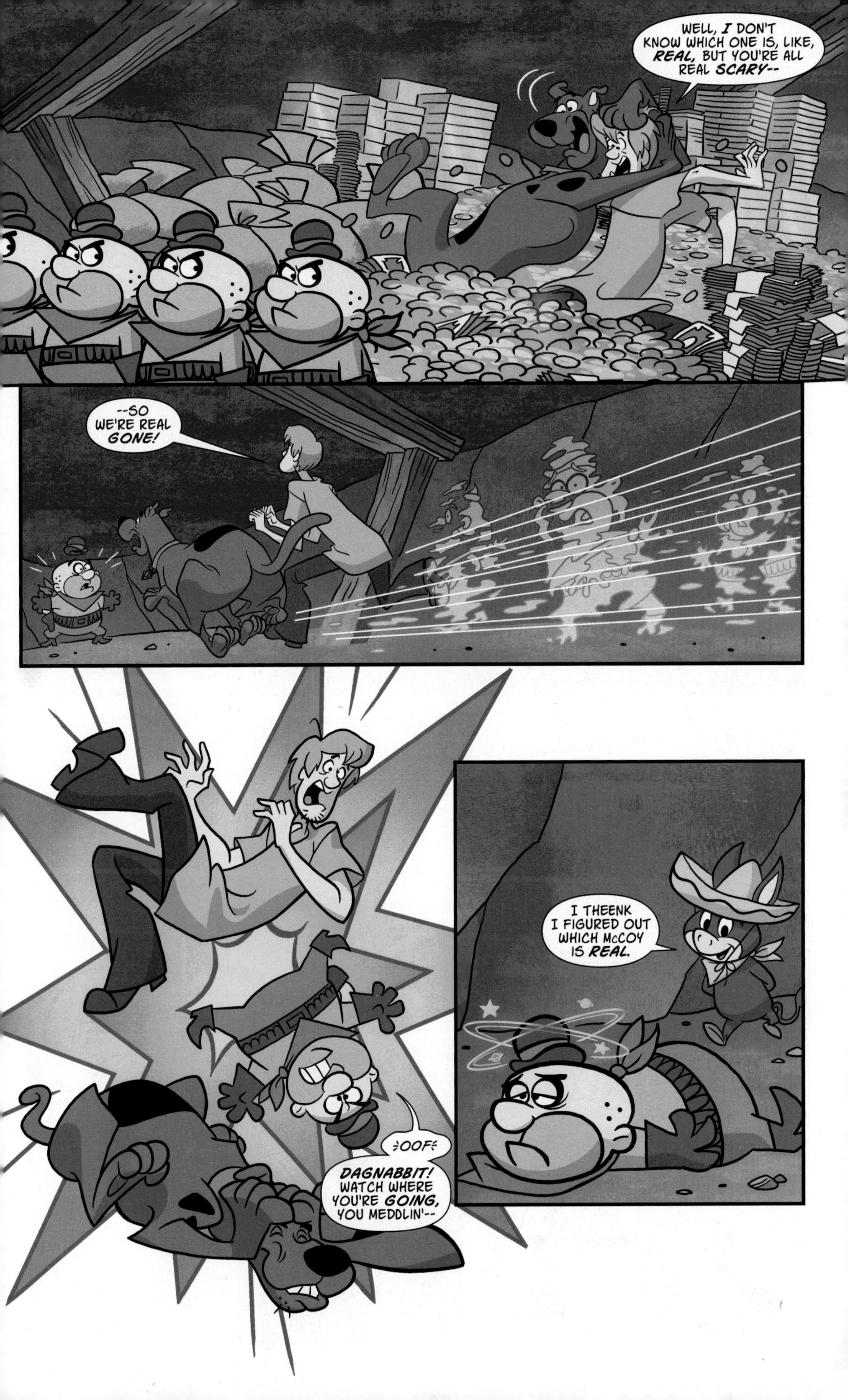
WELL, I DON'T KNOW WHICH ONE IS, LIKE, REAL, BUT YOU'RE ALL REAL SCARY--
--SO WE'RE REAL GONE!
OOF
DAGNABBIT! WATCH WHERE YOU'RE GOING, YOU MEDDLIN'--
I THEENK I FIGURED OUT WHICH McCOY IS REAL.

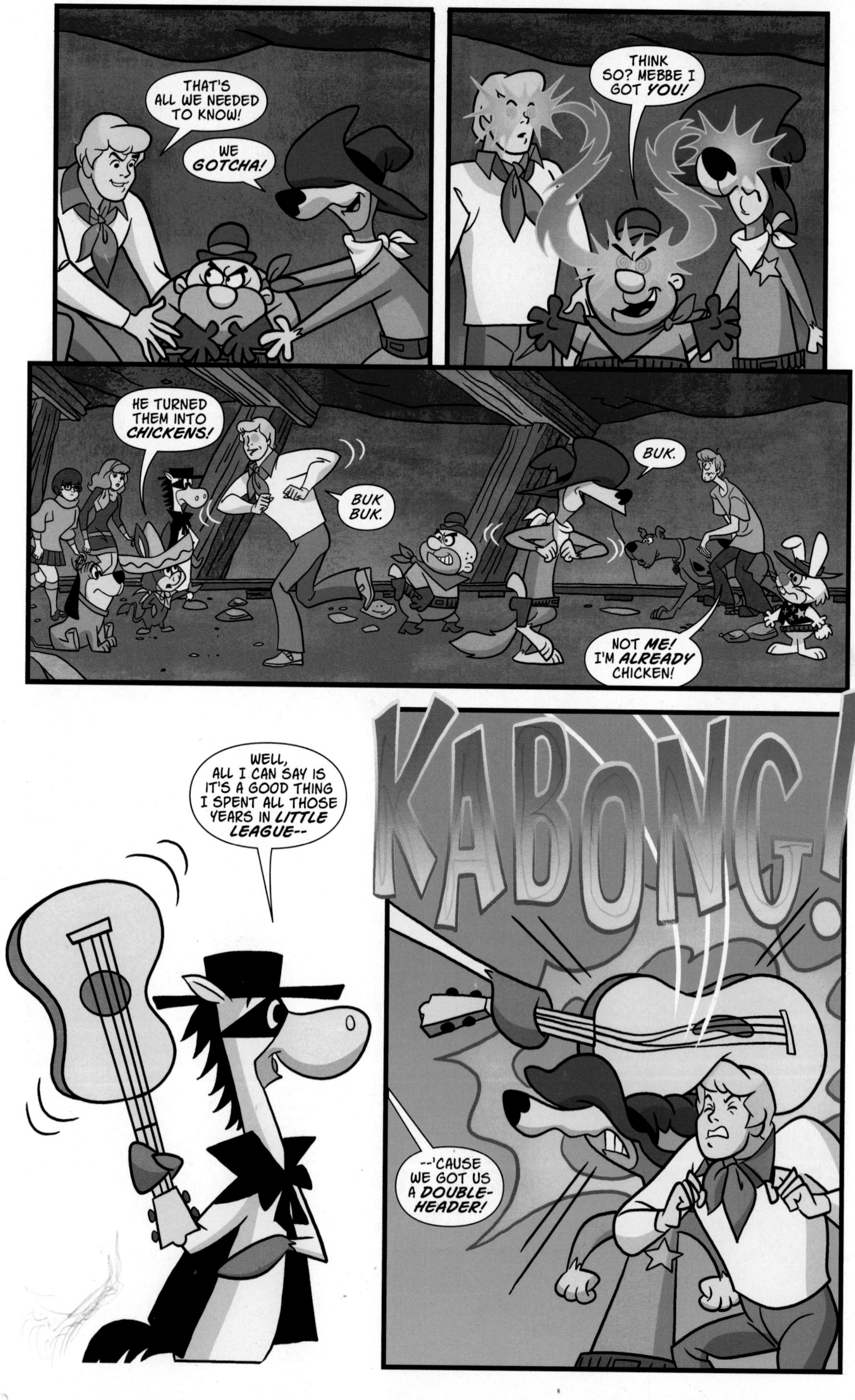

THAT'S ALL WE NEEDED TO KNOW!
WE GOTCHA!
THINK SO? MEBBE I GOT YOU!
HE TURNED THEM INTO CHICKENS!
BUK BUK.
BUK.
NOT ME! I'M ALREADY CHICKEN!
WELL, ALL I CAN SAY IS IT'S A GOOD THING I SPENT ALL THOSE YEARS IN LITTLE LEAGUE--
KABONG!
--'CAUSE WE GOT US A DOUBLE-HEADER!

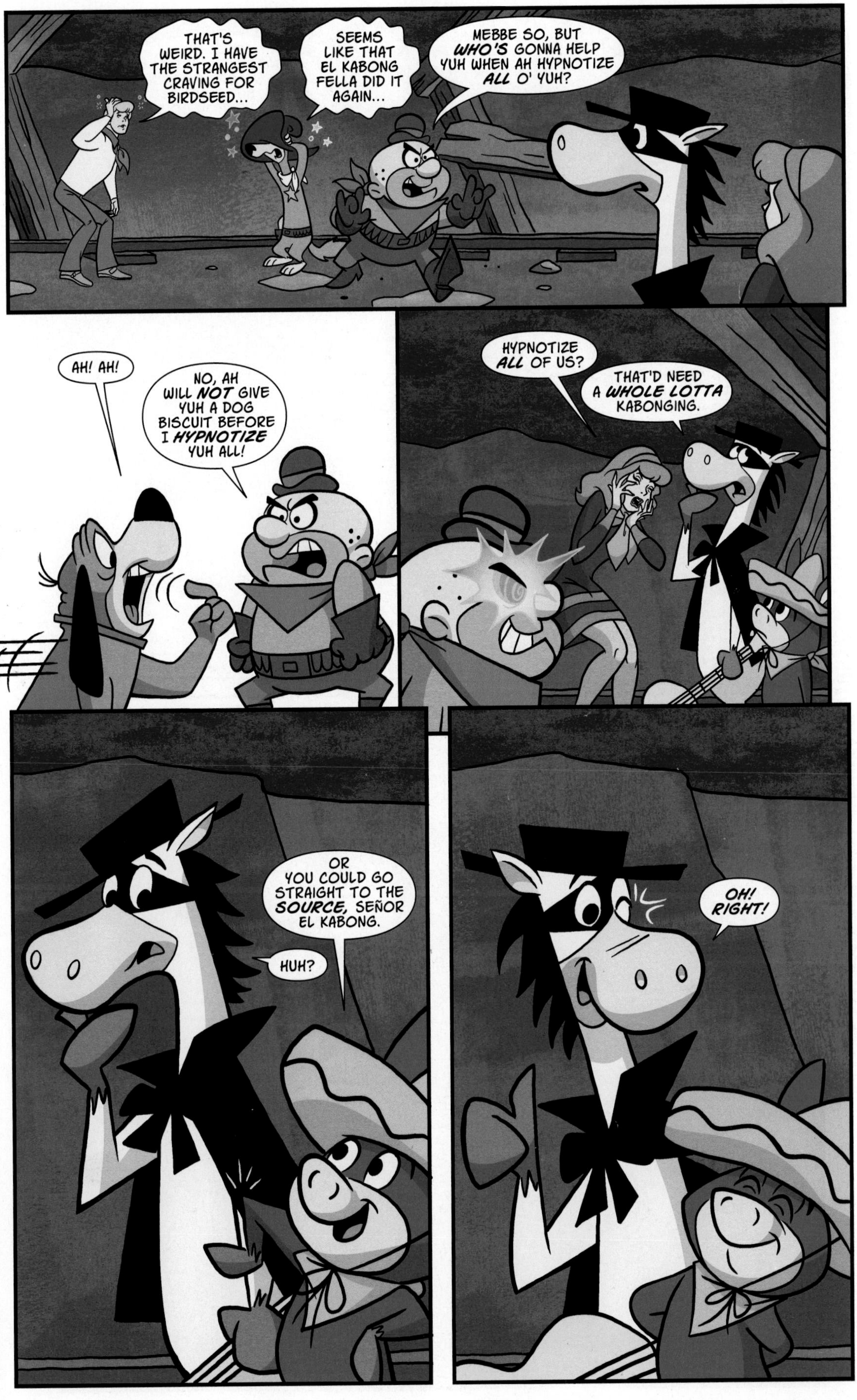
THAT'S WEIRD. I HAVE THE STRANGEST CRAVING FOR BIRDSEED...
SEEMS LIKE THAT EL KABONG FELLA DID IT AGAIN...
MEBBE SO, BUT WHO'S GONNA HELP YUH WHEN AH HYPNOTIZE ALL O' YUH?
AH! AH!
NO, AH WILL NOT GIVE YUH A DOG BISCUIT BEFORE I HYPNOTIZE YUH ALL!
HYPNOTIZE ALL OF US?
THAT'D NEED A WHOLE LOTTA KABONGING.
OR YOU COULD GO STRAIGHT TO THE SOURCE, SEÑOR EL KABONG.
HUH?
OH! RIGHT!

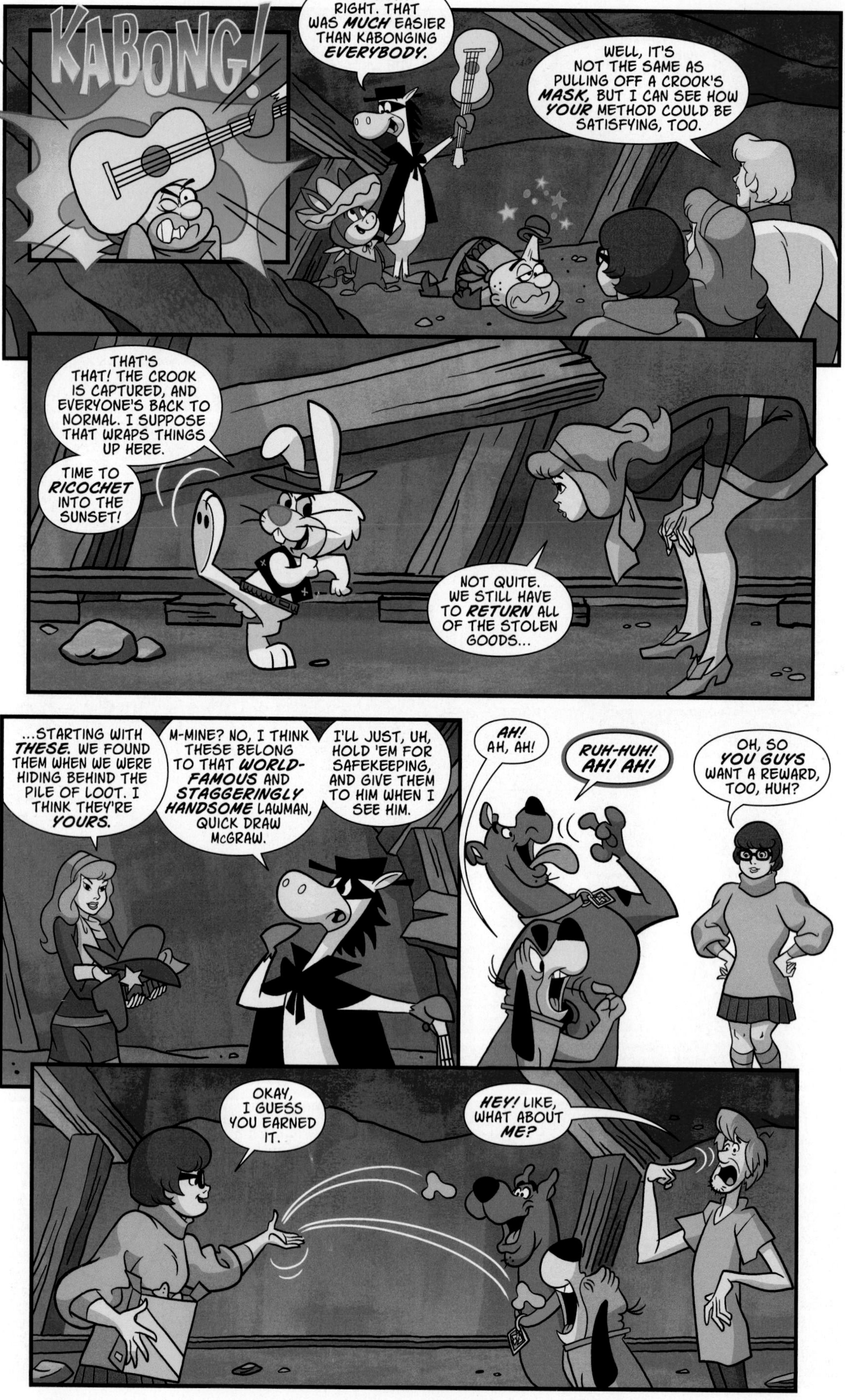
KABONG!
YOU WERE RIGHT. THAT WAS MUCH EASIER THAN KABONGING EVERYBODY.
WELL, IT'S NOT THE SAME AS PULLING OFF A CROOK'S MASK, BUT I CAN SEE HOW YOUR METHOD COULD BE SATISFYING, TOO.
THAT'S THAT! THE CROOK IS CAPTURED, AND EVERYONE'S BACK TO NORMAL. I SUPPOSE THAT WRAPS THINGS UP HERE.
TIME TO RICOCHET INTO THE SUNSET!
NOT QUITE. WE STILL HAVE TO RETURN ALL OF THE STOLEN GOODS...
...STARTING WITH THESE. WE FOUND THEM WHEN WE WERE HIDING BEHIND THE PILE OF LOOT. I THINK THEY'RE YOURS.
M-MINE? NO, I THINK THESE BELONG TO THAT WORLD-FAMOUS AND STAGGERINGLY HANDSOME LAWMAN, QUICK DRAW McGRAW.
I'LL JUST, UH, HOLD 'EM FOR SAFEKEEPING, AND GIVE THEM TO HIM WHEN I SEE HIM.
AH! AH, AH!
RUH-HUH! AH! AH!
OH, SO YOU GUYS WANT A REWARD, TOO, HUH?
OKAY, I GUESS YOU EARNED IT.
HEY! LIKE, WHAT ABOUT ME?

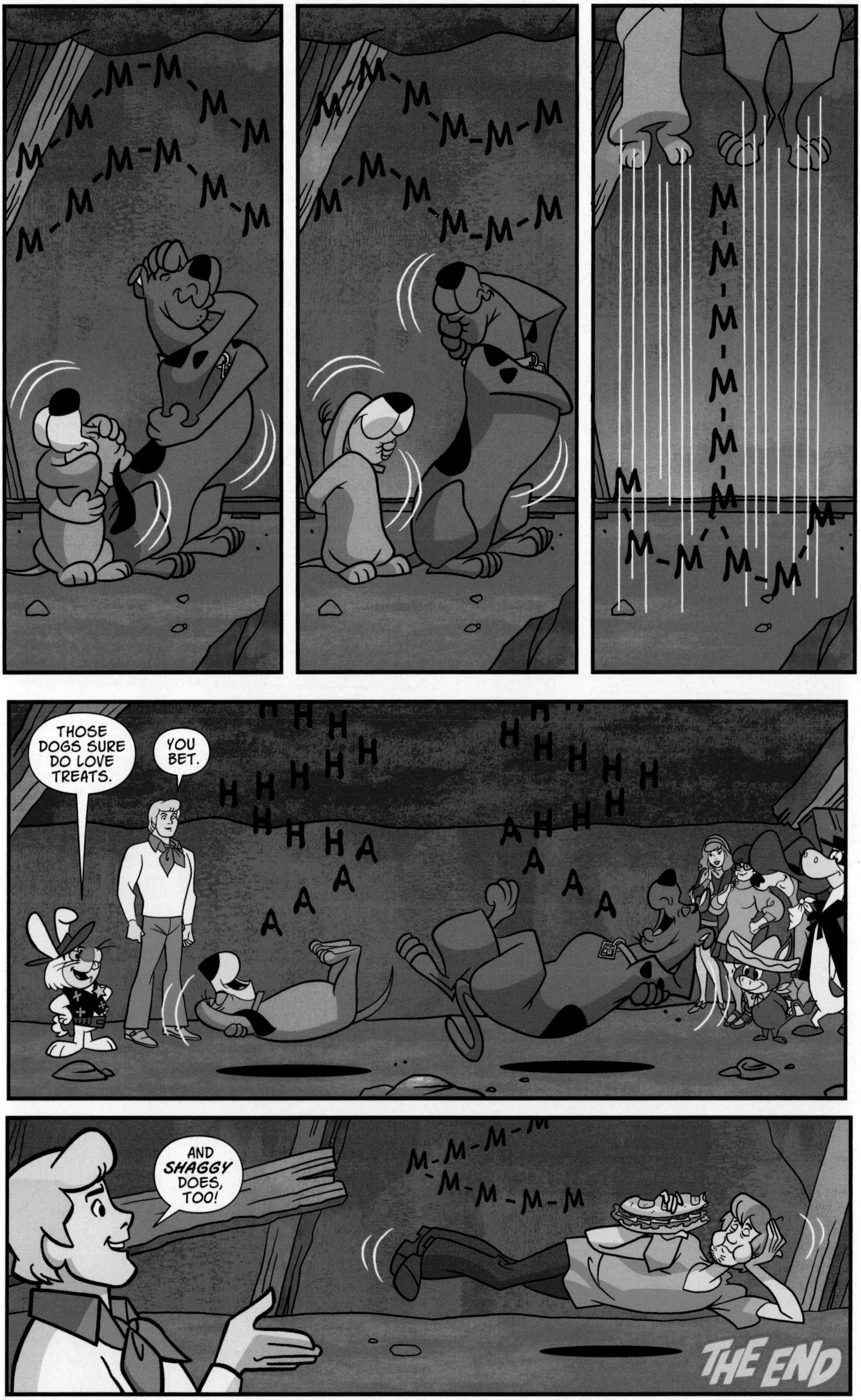
M-M-M-M-M-M-M
M-M-M-M-M-M-M
M-M-M-M-M-M-M
M-M-M-M-M-M-M
M-M-M-M-M-M-M
M-M-M-M-M-M
THOSE DOGS SURE DO LOVE TREATS.
YOU BET.
AND *SHAGGY* DOES, TOO!
M-M-M-M
-M-M-M-M
THE END

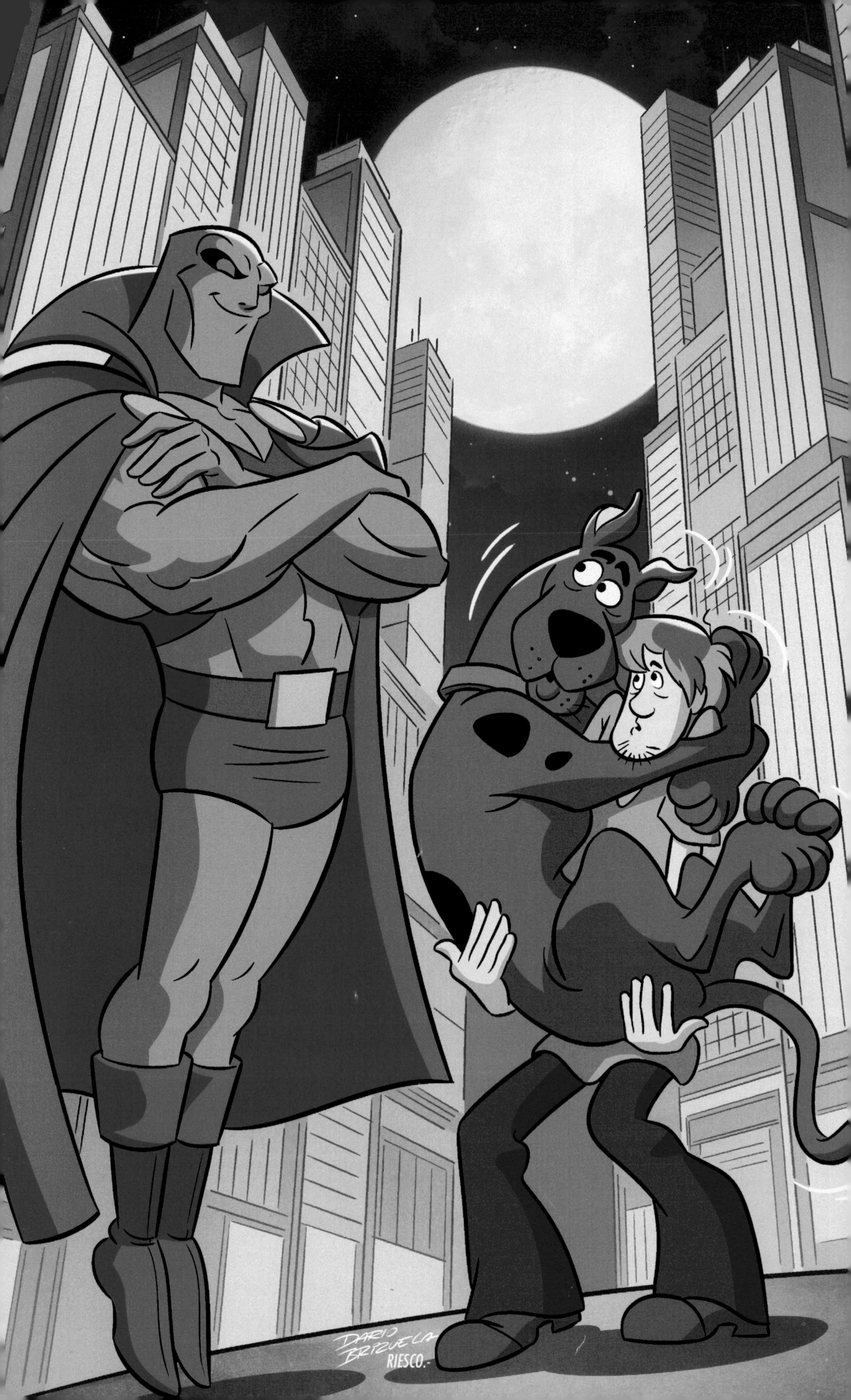
DARIO BRIZUELA
RIESCO.-

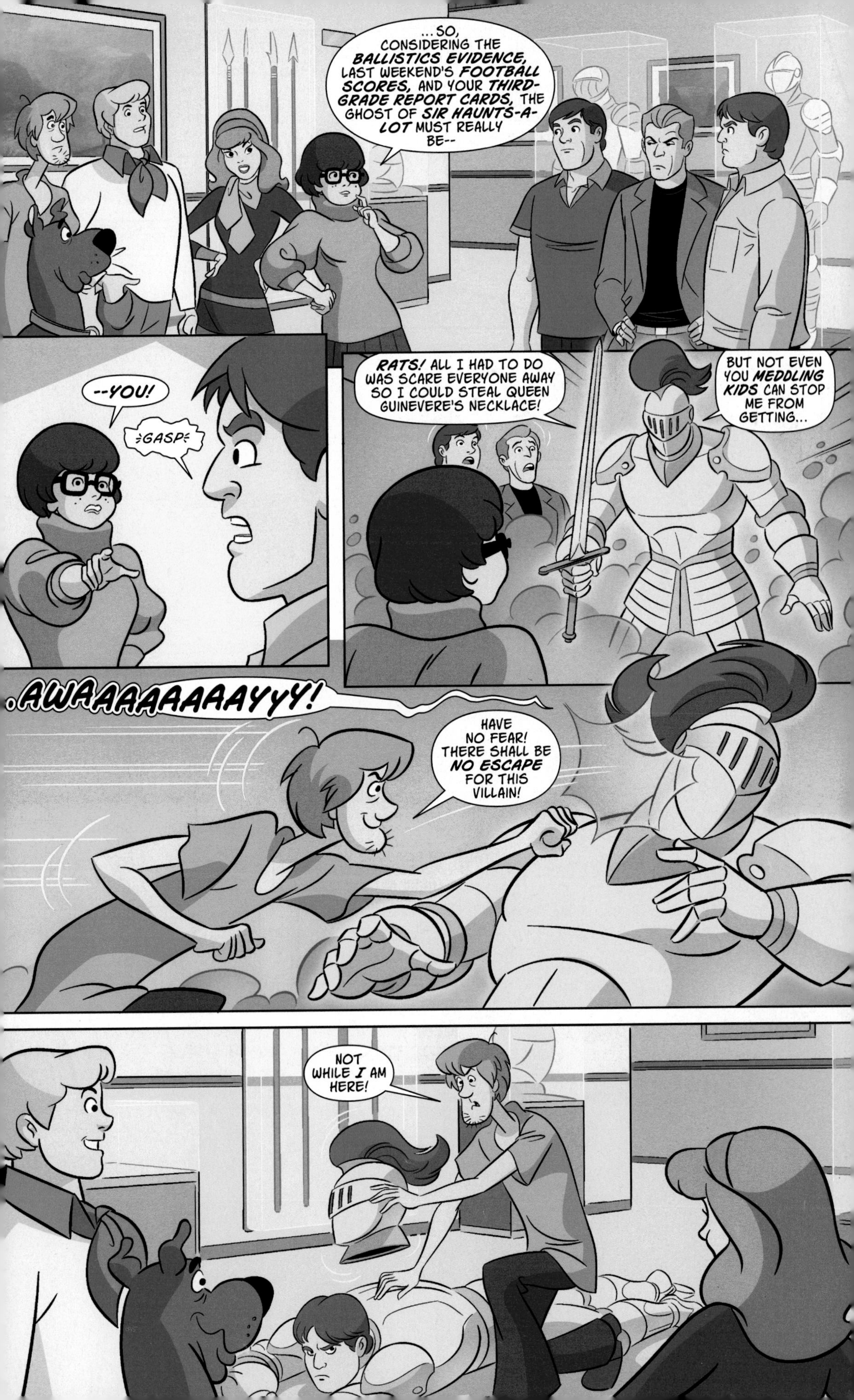
...SO, CONSIDERING THE BALLISTICS EVIDENCE, LAST WEEKEND'S FOOTBALL SCORES, AND YOUR THIRD-GRADE REPORT CARDS, THE GHOST OF SIR HAUNTS-A-LOT MUST REALLY BE--
--YOU!
GASP
RATS! ALL I HAD TO DO WAS SCARE EVERYONE AWAY SO I COULD STEAL QUEEN GUINEVERE'S NECKLACE!
BUT NOT EVEN YOU MEDDLING KIDS CAN STOP ME FROM GETTING...
...AWAAAAAAAAAYYY!
HAVE NO FEAR! THERE SHALL BE NO ESCAPE FOR THIS VILLAIN!
NOT WHILE I AM HERE!

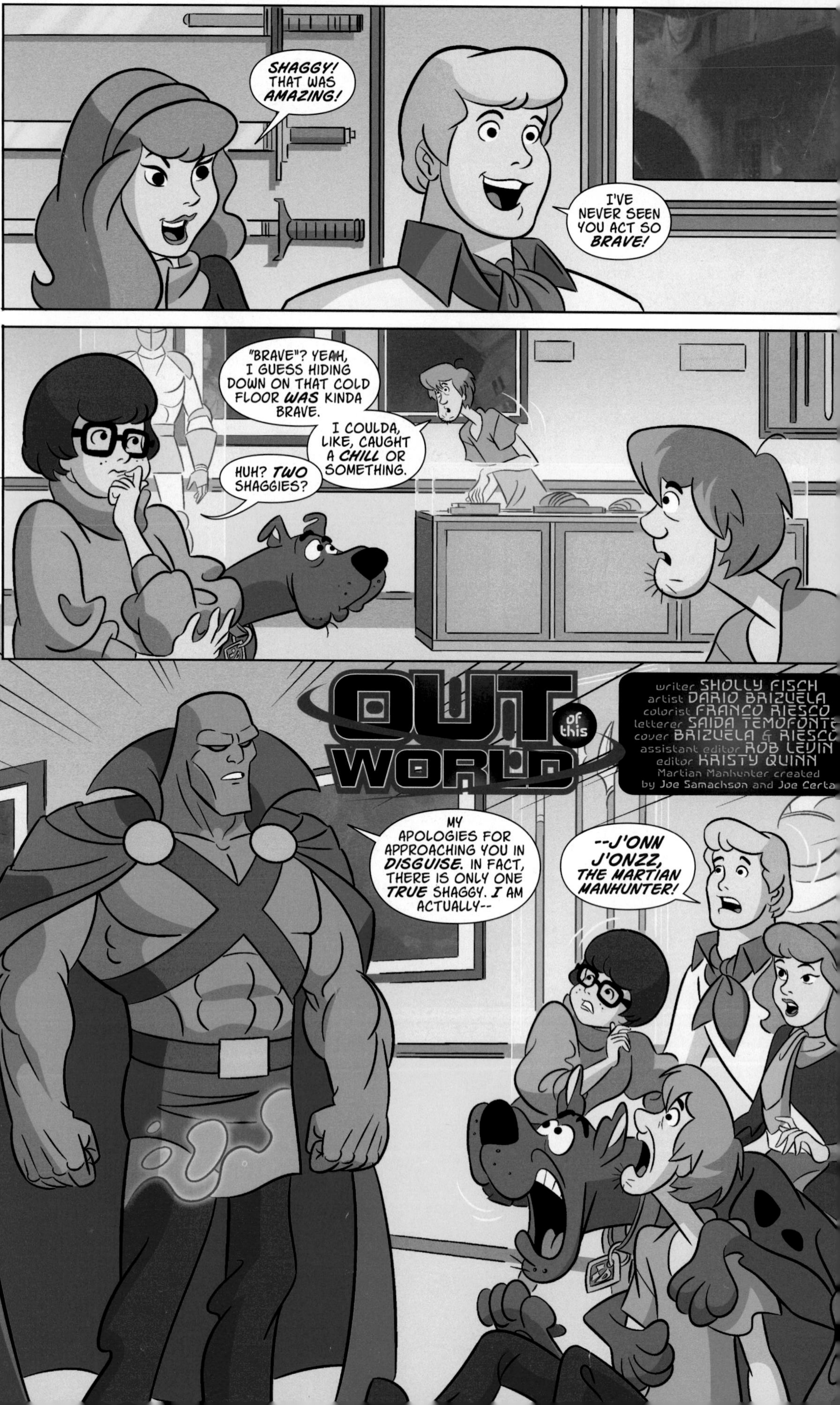
SHAGGY! THAT WAS AMAZING!
I'VE NEVER SEEN YOU ACT SO BRAVE!
"BRAVE"? YEAH, I GUESS HIDING DOWN ON THAT COLD FLOOR WAS KINDA BRAVE.
I COULDA, LIKE, CAUGHT A CHILL OR SOMETHING.
HUH? TWO SHAGGIES?
OUT of this WORLD
writer SHOLLY FISCH
artist DARIO BRIZUELA
colorist FRANCO RIESCO
letterer SAIDA TEMOFONTE
cover BRIZUELA & RIESCO
assistant editor ROB LEVIN
editor KRISTY QUINN
Martian Manhunter created by Joe Samachson and Joe Certa
MY APOLOGIES FOR APPROACHING YOU IN DISGUISE. IN FACT, THERE IS ONLY ONE TRUE SHAGGY. I AM ACTUALLY--
--J'ONN J'ONZZ, THE MARTIAN MANHUNTER!

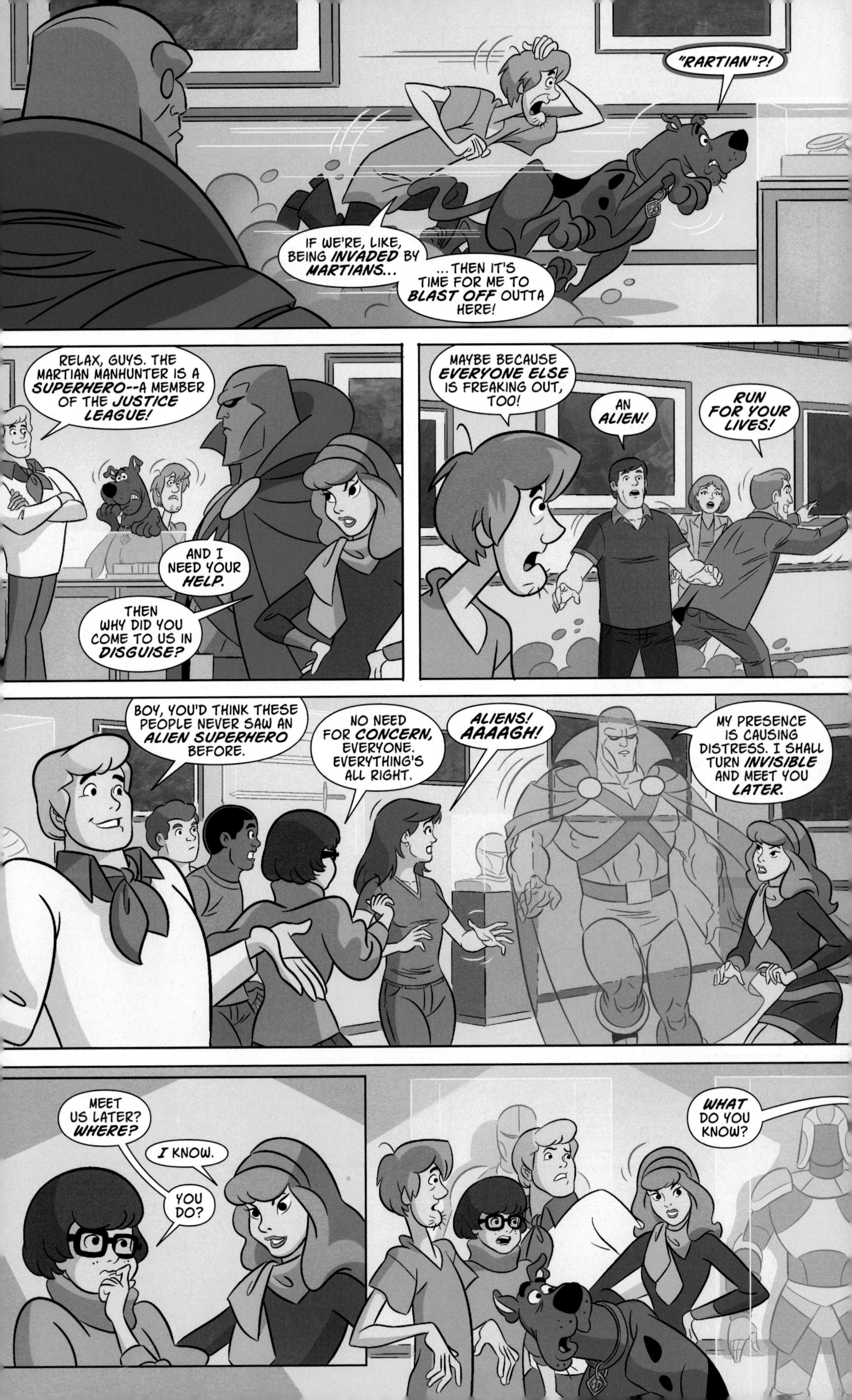

"RARTIAN"?!
IF WE'RE, LIKE, BEING INVADED BY MARTIANS...
...THEN IT'S TIME FOR ME TO BLAST OFF OUTTA HERE!
RELAX, GUYS. THE MARTIAN MANHUNTER IS A SUPERHERO--A MEMBER OF THE JUSTICE LEAGUE!
AND I NEED YOUR HELP.
THEN WHY DID YOU COME TO US IN DISGUISE?
MAYBE BECAUSE EVERYONE ELSE IS FREAKING OUT, TOO!
AN ALIEN!
RUN FOR YOUR LIVES!
BOY, YOU'D THINK THESE PEOPLE NEVER SAW AN ALIEN SUPERHERO BEFORE.
NO NEED FOR CONCERN, EVERYONE. EVERYTHING'S ALL RIGHT.
ALIENS! AAAAGH!
MY PRESENCE IS CAUSING DISTRESS. I SHALL TURN INVISIBLE AND MEET YOU LATER.
MEET US LATER? WHERE?
I KNOW.
YOU DO?
WHAT DO YOU KNOW?

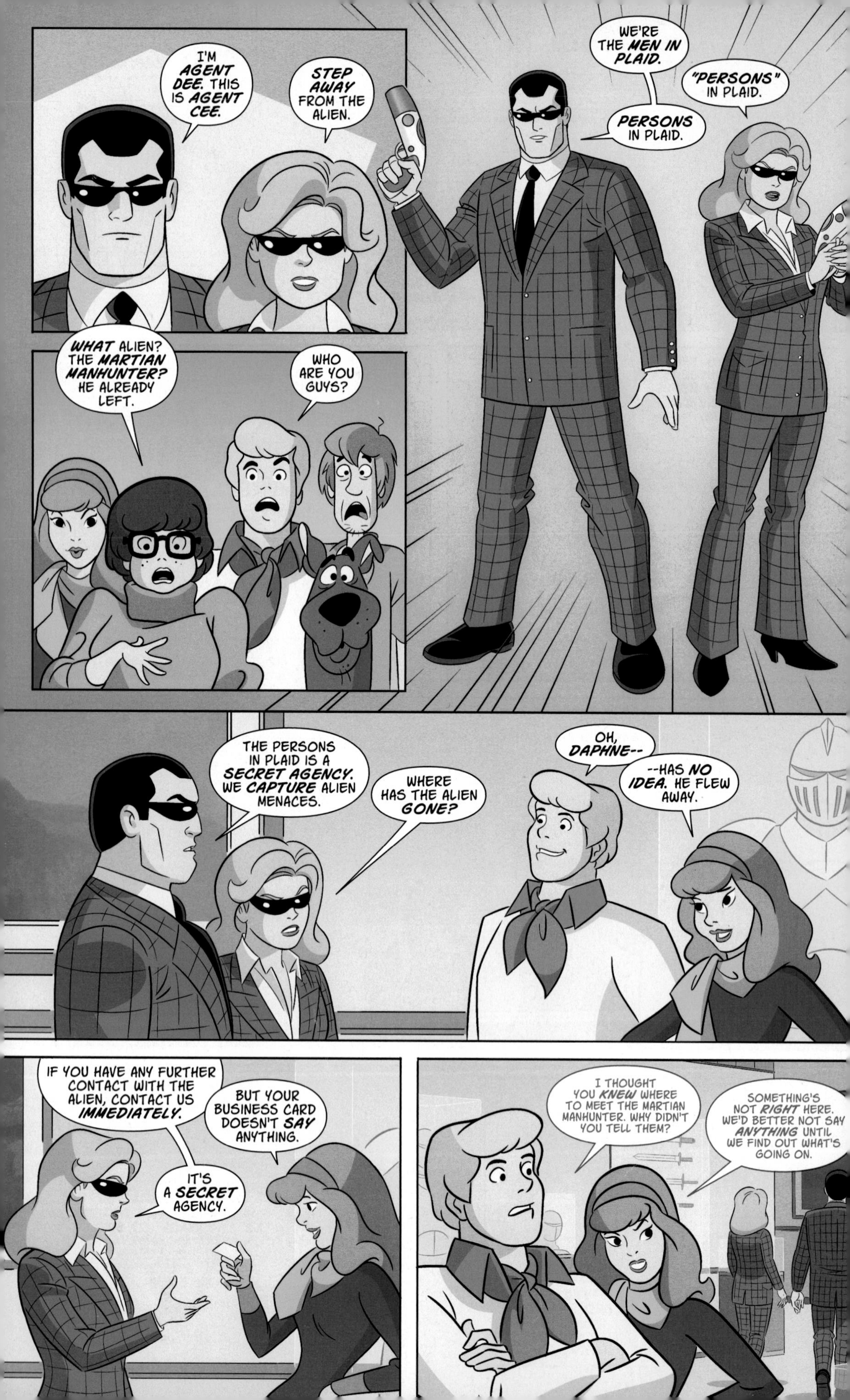
I'M AGENT DEE. THIS IS AGENT CEE.
STEP AWAY FROM THE ALIEN.
WHAT ALIEN? THE MARTIAN MANHUNTER? HE ALREADY LEFT.
WHO ARE YOU GUYS?
WE'RE THE MEN IN PLAID.
PERSONS IN PLAID.
"PERSONS" IN PLAID.
THE PERSONS IN PLAID IS A SECRET AGENCY. WE CAPTURE ALIEN MENACES.
WHERE HAS THE ALIEN GONE?
OH, DAPHNE--
--HAS NO IDEA. HE FLEW AWAY.
IF YOU HAVE ANY FURTHER CONTACT WITH THE ALIEN, CONTACT US IMMEDIATELY.
BUT YOUR BUSINESS CARD DOESN'T SAY ANYTHING.
IT'S A SECRET AGENCY.
I THOUGHT YOU KNEW WHERE TO MEET THE MARTIAN MANHUNTER. WHY DIDN'T YOU TELL THEM?
SOMETHING'S NOT RIGHT HERE. WE'D BETTER NOT SAY ANYTHING UNTIL WE FIND OUT WHAT'S GOING ON.

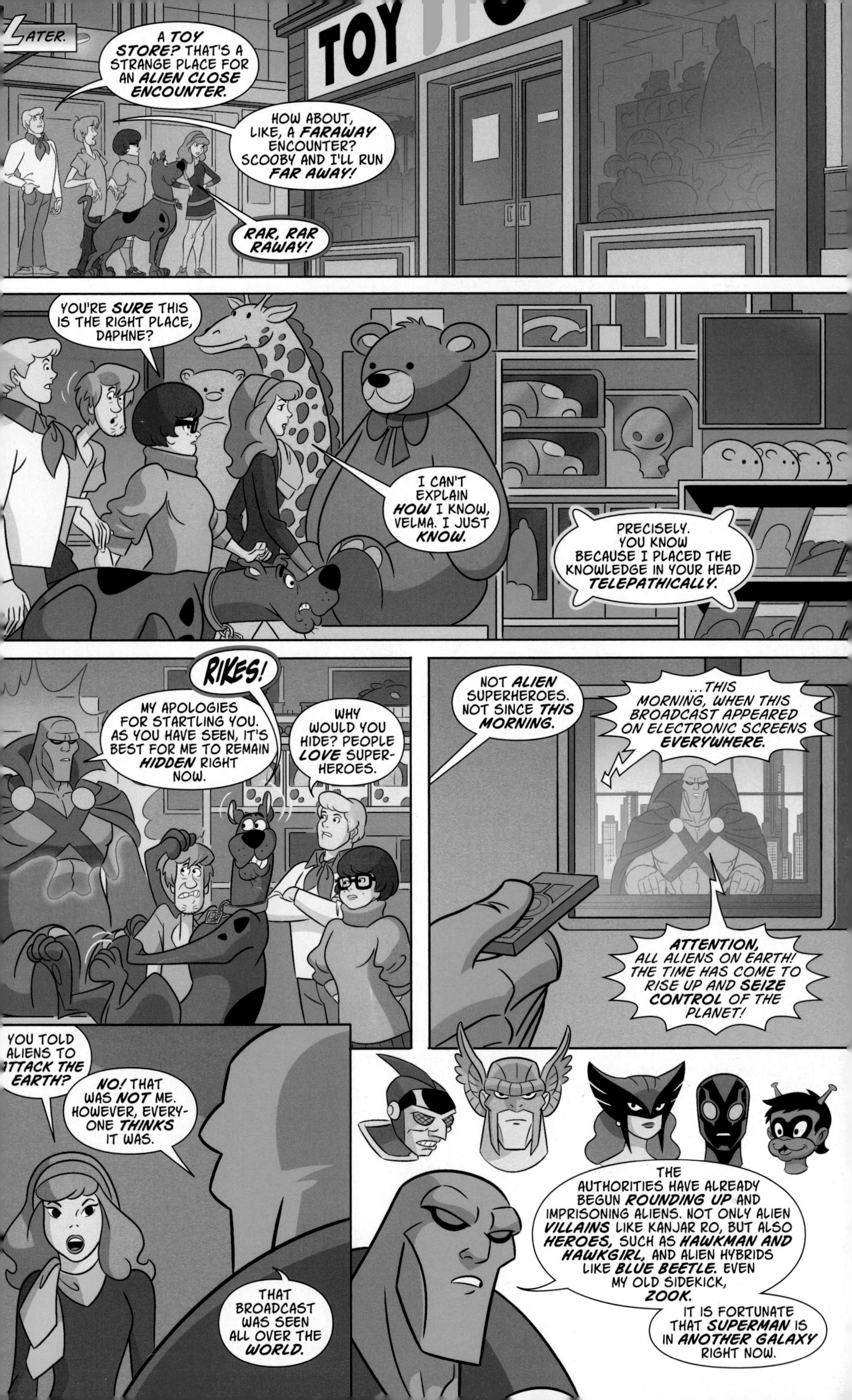
LATER.
A TOY STORE? THAT'S A STRANGE PLACE FOR AN ALIEN CLOSE ENCOUNTER.
HOW ABOUT, LIKE, A FARAWAY ENCOUNTER? SCOOBY AND I'LL RUN FAR AWAY!
RAR, RAR RAWAY!
TOY
YOU'RE SURE THIS IS THE RIGHT PLACE, DAPHNE?
I CAN'T EXPLAIN HOW I KNOW, VELMA. I JUST KNOW.
PRECISELY. YOU KNOW BECAUSE I PLACED THE KNOWLEDGE IN YOUR HEAD TELEPATHICALLY.
RIKES!
MY APOLOGIES FOR STARTLING YOU. AS YOU HAVE SEEN, IT'S BEST FOR ME TO REMAIN HIDDEN RIGHT NOW.
WHY WOULD YOU HIDE? PEOPLE LOVE SUPER-HEROES.
NOT ALIEN SUPERHEROES. NOT SINCE THIS MORNING.
...THIS MORNING, WHEN THIS BROADCAST APPEARED ON ELECTRONIC SCREENS EVERYWHERE.
ATTENTION, ALL ALIENS ON EARTH! THE TIME HAS COME TO RISE UP AND SEIZE CONTROL OF THE PLANET!
YOU TOLD ALIENS TO ATTACK THE EARTH?
NO! THAT WAS NOT ME. HOWEVER, EVERY-ONE THINKS IT WAS.
THAT BROADCAST WAS SEEN ALL OVER THE WORLD.
THE AUTHORITIES HAVE ALREADY BEGUN ROUNDING UP AND IMPRISONING ALIENS. NOT ONLY ALIEN VILLAINS LIKE KANJAR RO, BUT ALSO HEROES, SUCH AS HAWKMAN AND HAWKGIRL, AND ALIEN HYBRIDS LIKE BLUE BEETLE. EVEN MY OLD SIDEKICK, ZOOK.
IT IS FORTUNATE THAT SUPERMAN IS IN ANOTHER GALAXY RIGHT NOW.

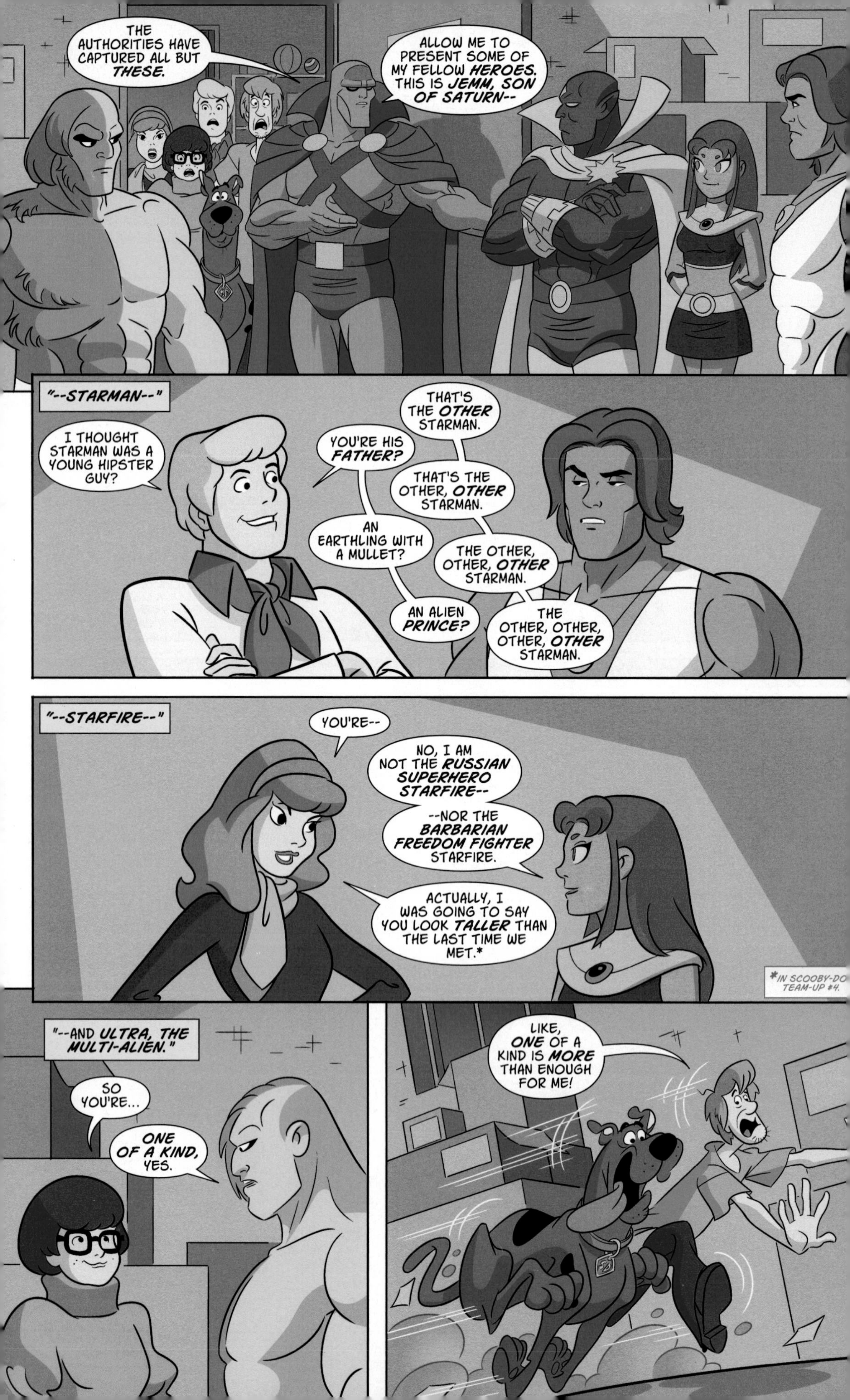
THE AUTHORITIES HAVE CAPTURED ALL BUT *THESE.*
ALLOW ME TO PRESENT SOME OF MY FELLOW *HEROES.* THIS IS *JEMM, SON OF SATURN--*
"--STARMAN--"
I THOUGHT STARMAN WAS A YOUNG HIPSTER GUY?
THAT'S THE *OTHER* STARMAN.
YOU'RE HIS *FATHER?*
THAT'S THE OTHER, *OTHER* STARMAN.
AN EARTHLING WITH A MULLET?
THE OTHER, OTHER, *OTHER* STARMAN.
AN ALIEN *PRINCE?*
THE OTHER, OTHER, OTHER, *OTHER* STARMAN.
"--STARFIRE--"
YOU'RE--
NO, I AM NOT THE *RUSSIAN SUPERHERO STARFIRE--*
--NOR THE *BARBARIAN FREEDOM FIGHTER* STARFIRE.
ACTUALLY, I WAS GOING TO SAY YOU LOOK *TALLER* THAN THE LAST TIME WE MET.*
*IN SCOOBY-DOO TEAM-UP #4.
"--AND *ULTRA, THE MULTI-ALIEN.*"
SO YOU'RE...
ONE OF A KIND, YES.
LIKE, *ONE* OF A KIND IS *MORE* THAN ENOUGH FOR ME!

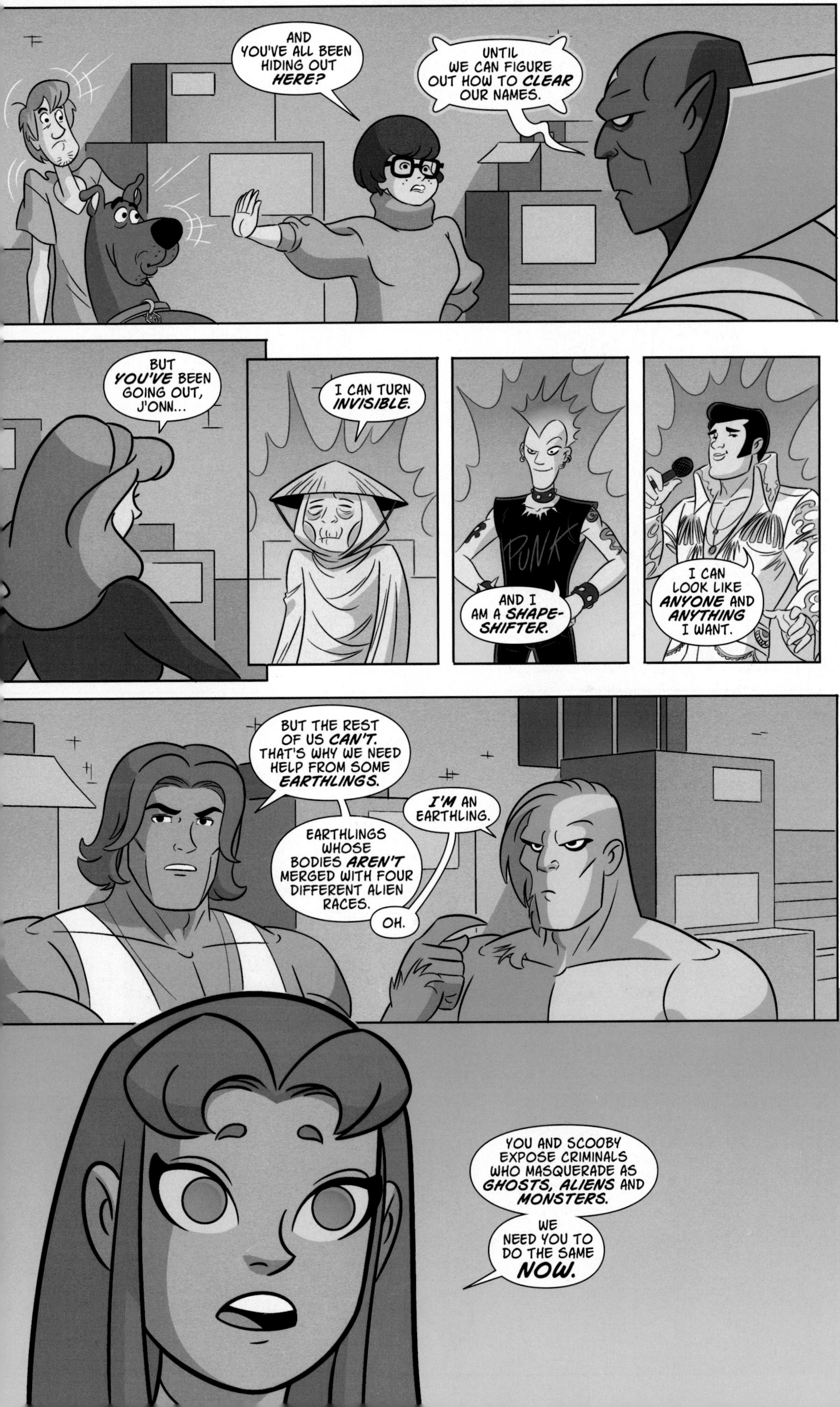
AND YOU'VE ALL BEEN HIDING OUT HERE?
UNTIL WE CAN FIGURE OUT HOW TO CLEAR OUR NAMES.
BUT YOU'VE BEEN GOING OUT, J'ONN...
I CAN TURN INVISIBLE.
AND I AM A SHAPE-SHIFTER.
I CAN LOOK LIKE ANYONE AND ANYTHING I WANT.
BUT THE REST OF US CAN'T. THAT'S WHY WE NEED HELP FROM SOME EARTHLINGS.
I'M AN EARTHLING.
EARTHLINGS WHOSE BODIES AREN'T MERGED WITH FOUR DIFFERENT ALIEN RACES.
OH.
PUNK
YOU AND SCOOBY EXPOSE CRIMINALS WHO MASQUERADE AS GHOSTS, ALIENS AND MONSTERS.
WE NEED YOU TO DO THE SAME NOW.

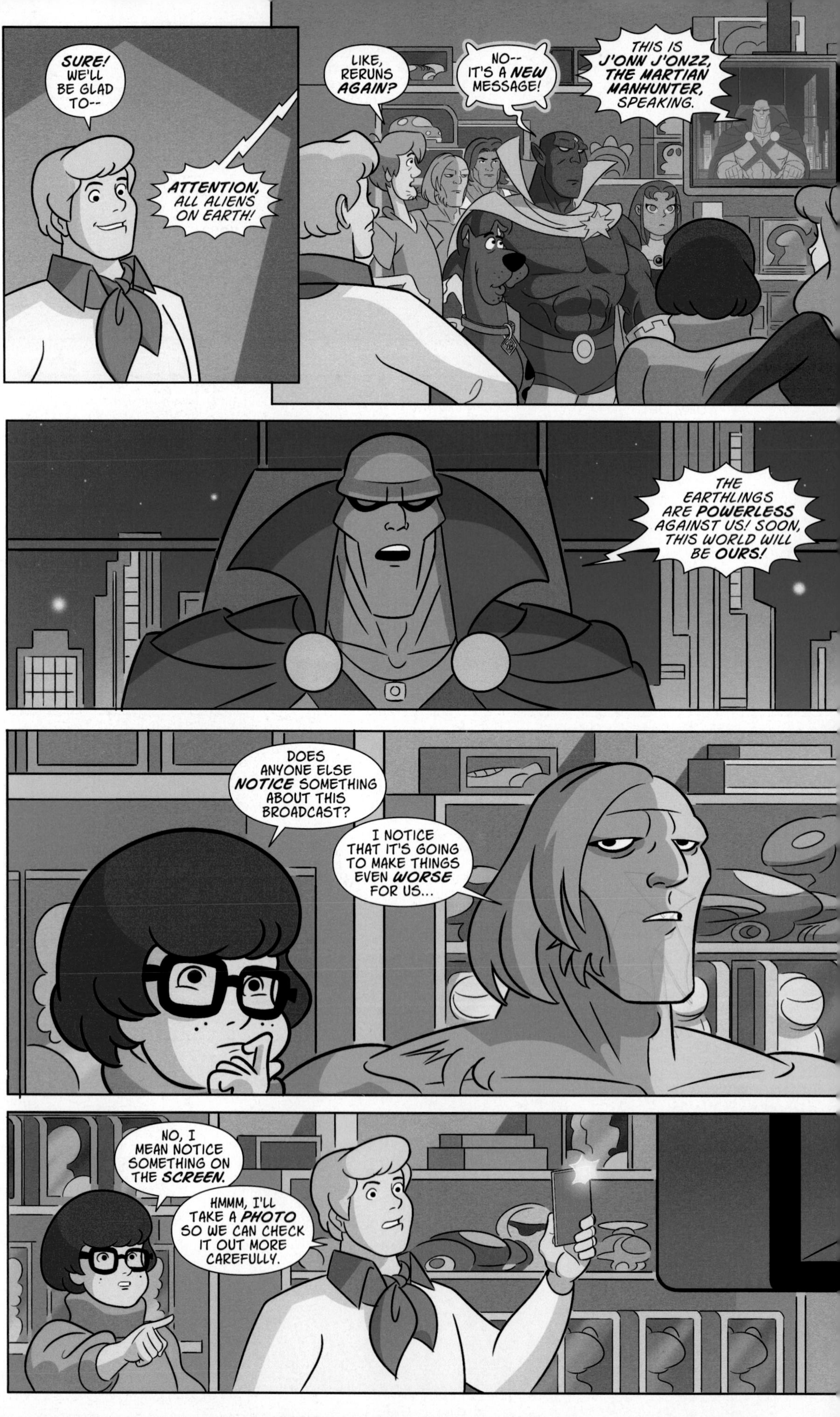
SURE! WE'LL BE GLAD TO--
ATTENTION, ALL ALIENS ON EARTH!
LIKE, RERUNS AGAIN?
NO-- IT'S A NEW MESSAGE!
THIS IS J'ONN J'ONZZ, THE MARTIAN MANHUNTER, SPEAKING.
THE EARTHLINGS ARE POWERLESS AGAINST US! SOON, THIS WORLD WILL BE OURS!
DOES ANYONE ELSE NOTICE SOMETHING ABOUT THIS BROADCAST?
I NOTICE THAT IT'S GOING TO MAKE THINGS EVEN WORSE FOR US...
NO, I MEAN NOTICE SOMETHING ON THE SCREEN.
HMMM, I'LL TAKE A PHOTO SO WE CAN CHECK IT OUT MORE CAREFULLY.

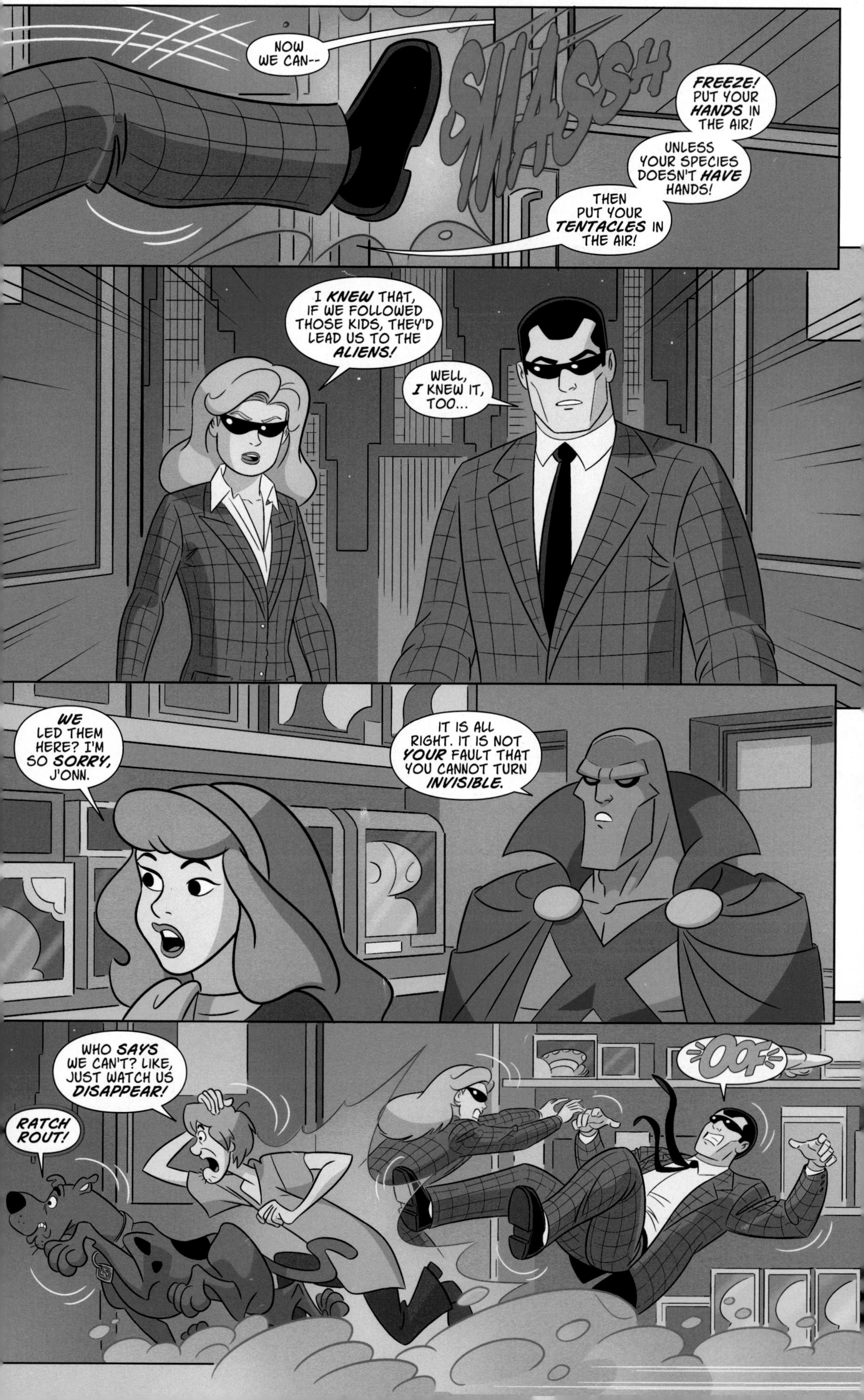
NOW WE CAN--
SMASSH
FREEZE! PUT YOUR HANDS IN THE AIR!
UNLESS YOUR SPECIES DOESN'T HAVE HANDS!
THEN PUT YOUR TENTACLES IN THE AIR!
I KNEW THAT, IF WE FOLLOWED THOSE KIDS, THEY'D LEAD US TO THE ALIENS!
WELL, I KNEW IT, TOO...
WE LED THEM HERE? I'M SO SORRY, J'ONN.
IT IS ALL RIGHT. IT IS NOT YOUR FAULT THAT YOU CANNOT TURN INVISIBLE.
WHO SAYS WE CAN'T? LIKE, JUST WATCH US DISAPPEAR!
RATCH ROUT!
OOF

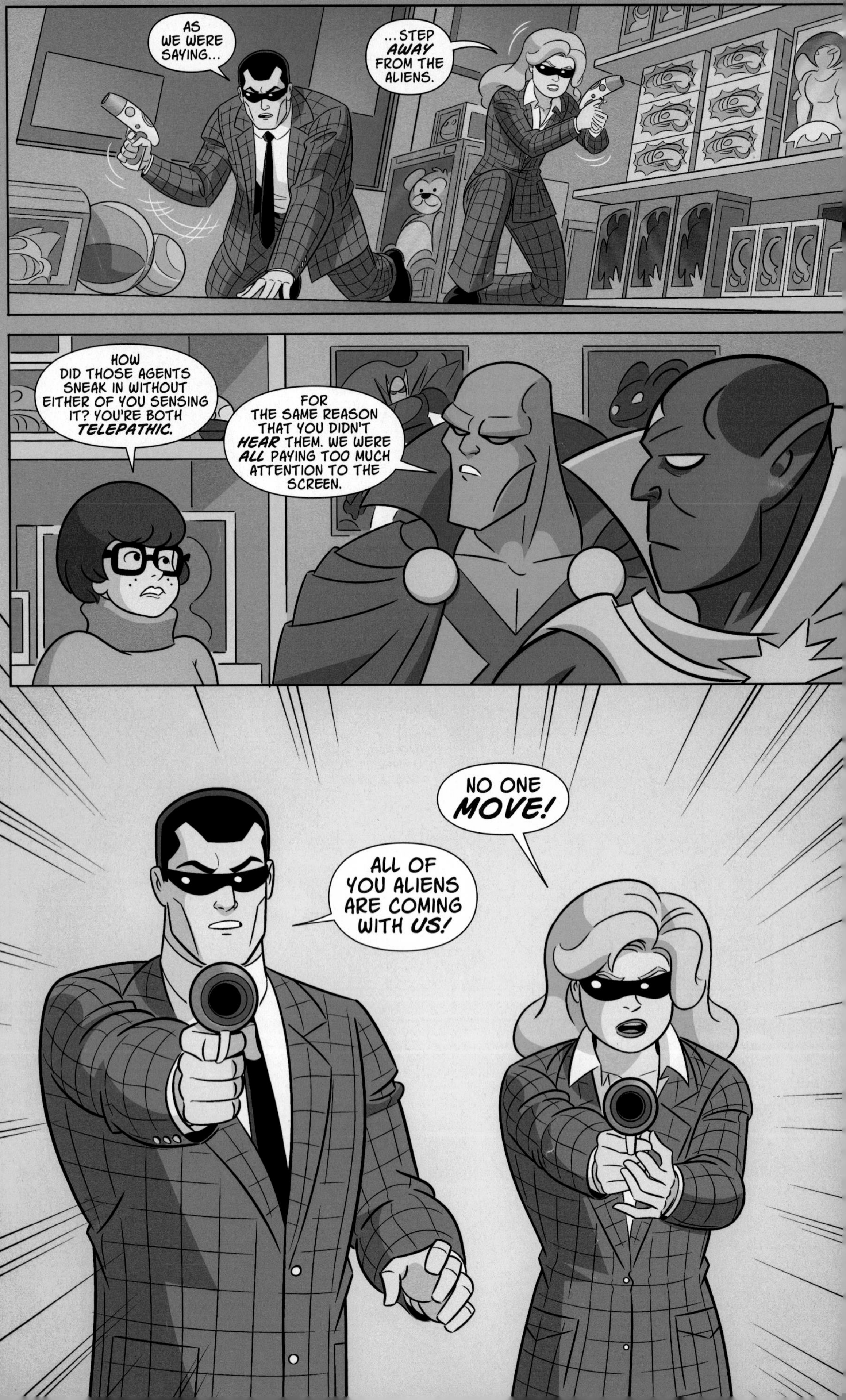
AS WE WERE SAYING...
...STEP AWAY FROM THE ALIENS.
HOW DID THOSE AGENTS SNEAK IN WITHOUT EITHER OF YOU SENSING IT? YOU'RE BOTH TELEPATHIC.
FOR THE SAME REASON THAT YOU DIDN'T HEAR THEM. WE WERE ALL PAYING TOO MUCH ATTENTION TO THE SCREEN.
NO ONE MOVE!
ALL OF YOU ALIENS ARE COMING WITH US!

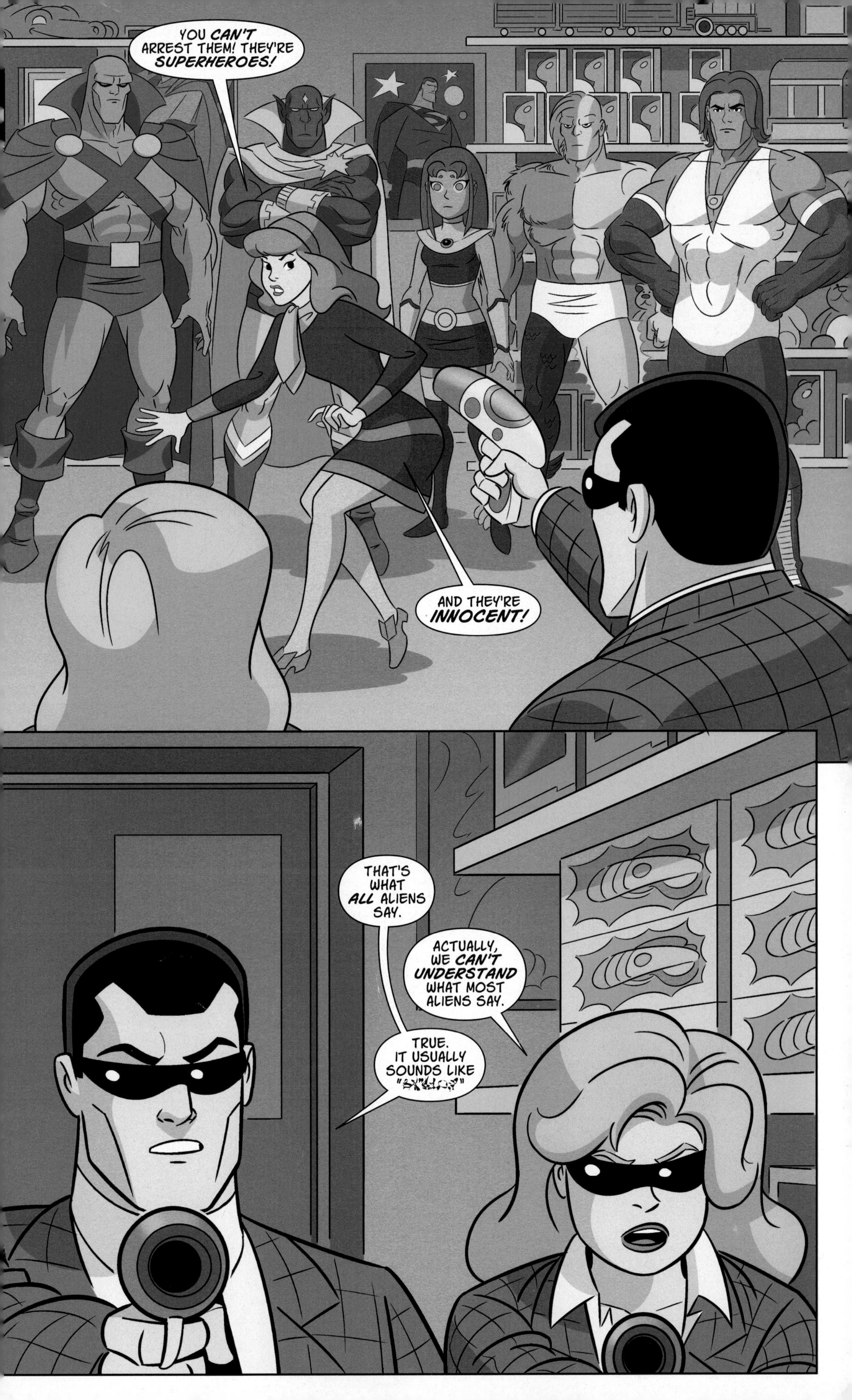
YOU CAN'T ARREST THEM! THEY'RE SUPERHEROES!
AND THEY'RE INNOCENT!
THAT'S WHAT ALL ALIENS SAY.
ACTUALLY, WE CAN'T UNDERSTAND WHAT MOST ALIENS SAY.
TRUE. IT USUALLY SOUNDS LIKE

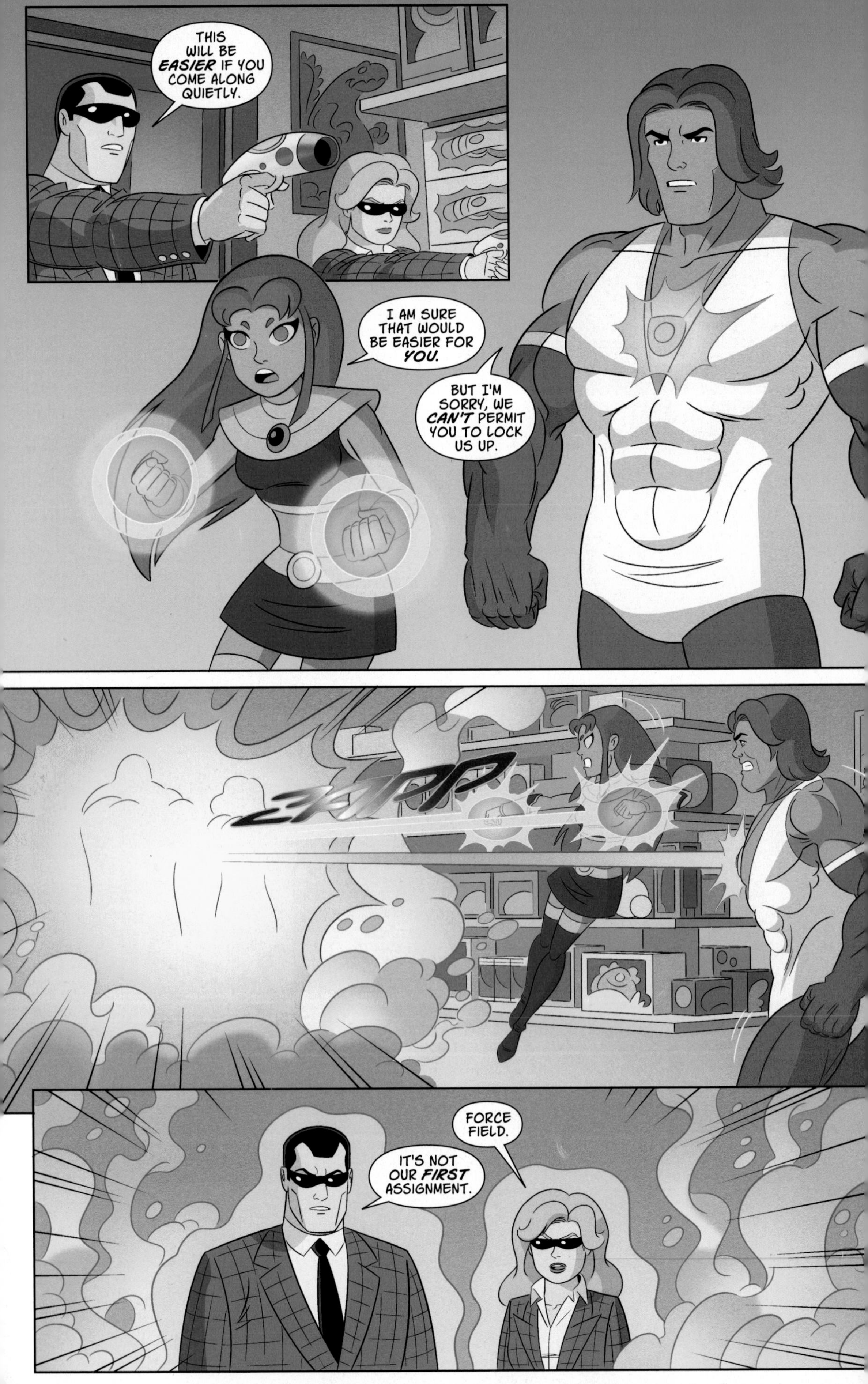
THIS WILL BE EASIER IF YOU COME ALONG QUIETLY.
I AM SURE THAT WOULD BE EASIER FOR YOU.
BUT I'M SORRY, WE CAN'T PERMIT YOU TO LOCK US UP.
ZAPP
FORCE FIELD.
IT'S NOT OUR FIRST ASSIGNMENT.

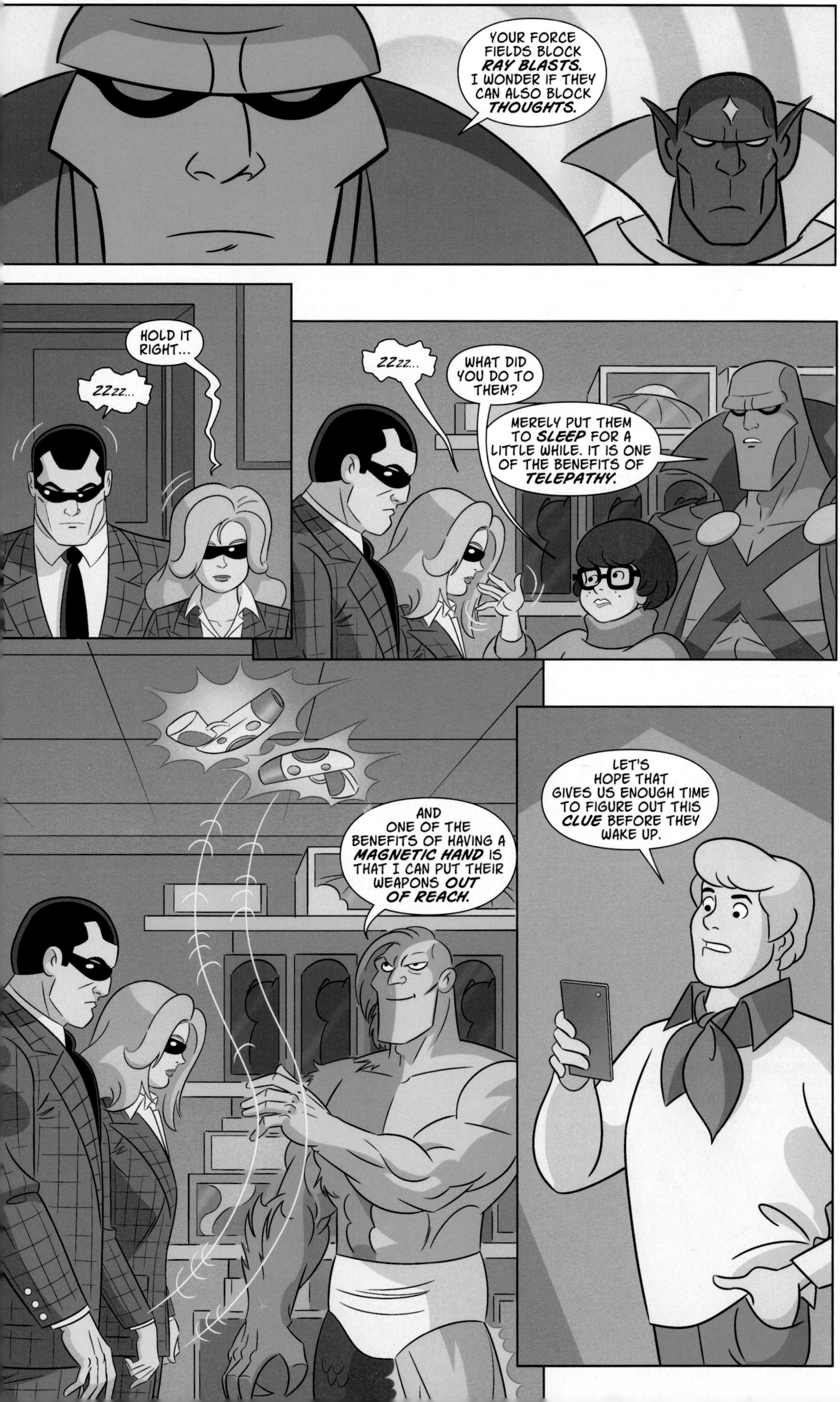
YOUR FORCE FIELDS BLOCK RAY BLASTS. I WONDER IF THEY CAN ALSO BLOCK THOUGHTS.
HOLD IT RIGHT...
ZZzz...
ZZzz...
WHAT DID YOU DO TO THEM?
MERELY PUT THEM TO SLEEP FOR A LITTLE WHILE. IT IS ONE OF THE BENEFITS OF TELEPATHY.
AND ONE OF THE BENEFITS OF HAVING A MAGNETIC HAND IS THAT I CAN PUT THEIR WEAPONS OUT OF REACH.
LET'S HOPE THAT GIVES US ENOUGH TIME TO FIGURE OUT THIS CLUE BEFORE THEY WAKE UP.

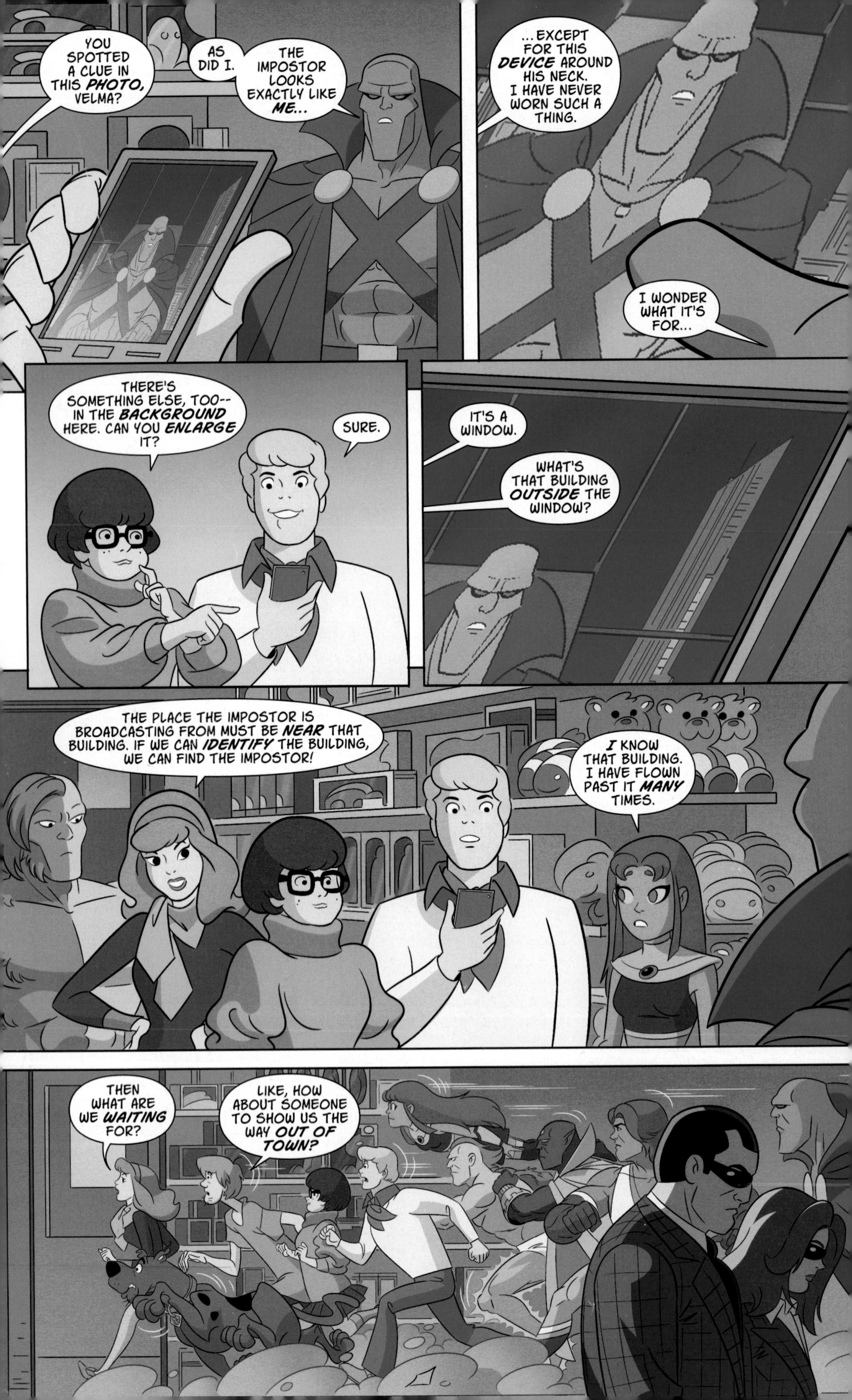
YOU SPOTTED A CLUE IN THIS PHOTO, VELMA?
AS DID I.
THE IMPOSTOR LOOKS EXACTLY LIKE ME...
...EXCEPT FOR THIS DEVICE AROUND HIS NECK. I HAVE NEVER WORN SUCH A THING.
I WONDER WHAT IT'S FOR...
THERE'S SOMETHING ELSE, TOO-- IN THE BACKGROUND HERE. CAN YOU ENLARGE IT?
SURE.
IT'S A WINDOW.
WHAT'S THAT BUILDING OUTSIDE THE WINDOW?
THE PLACE THE IMPOSTOR IS BROADCASTING FROM MUST BE NEAR THAT BUILDING. IF WE CAN IDENTIFY THE BUILDING, WE CAN FIND THE IMPOSTOR!
I KNOW THAT BUILDING. I HAVE FLOWN PAST IT MANY TIMES.
THEN WHAT ARE WE WAITING FOR?
LIKE, HOW ABOUT SOMEONE TO SHOW US THE WAY OUT OF TOWN?

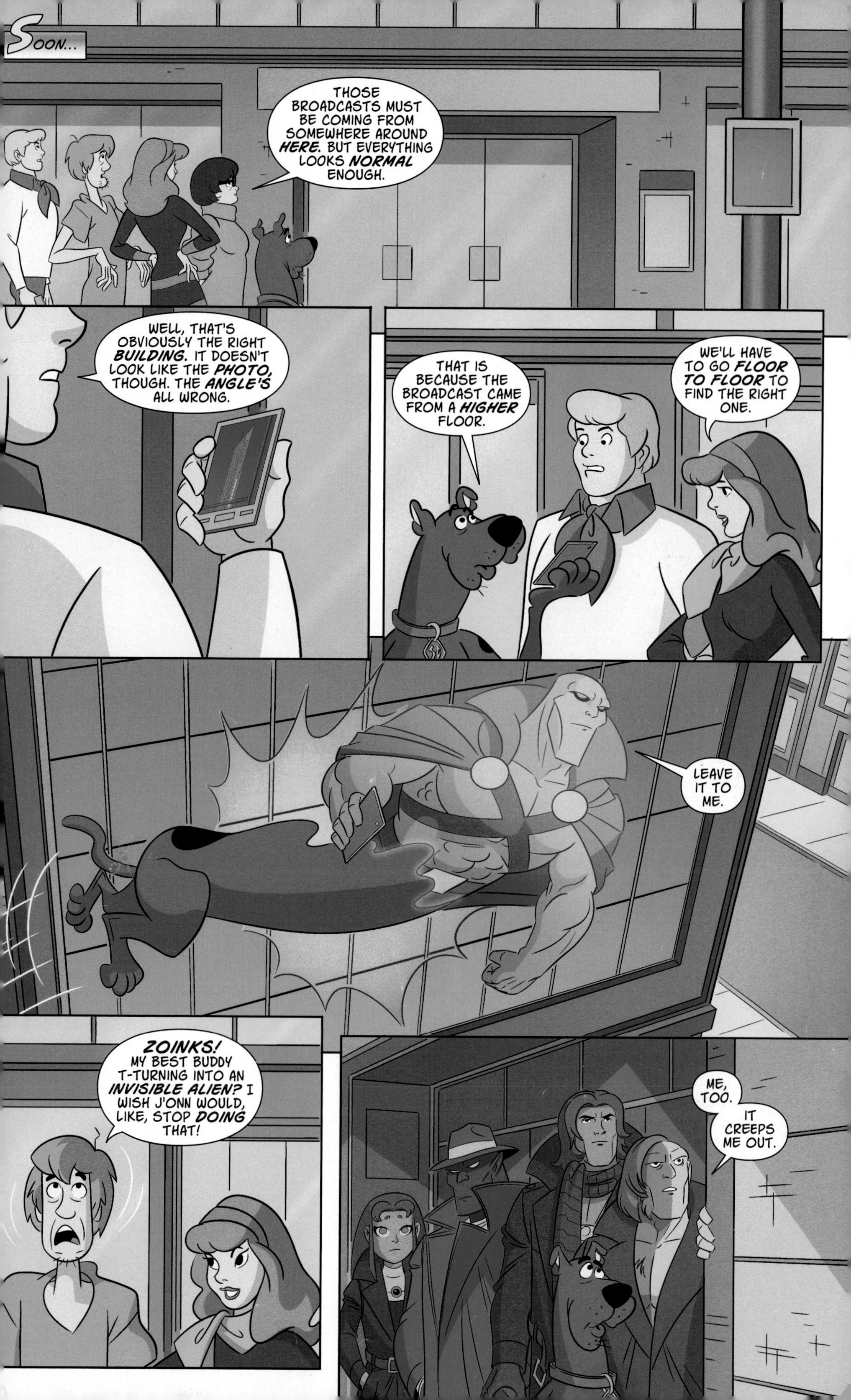
SOON...
THOSE BROADCASTS MUST BE COMING FROM SOMEWHERE AROUND HERE. BUT EVERYTHING LOOKS NORMAL ENOUGH.
WELL, THAT'S OBVIOUSLY THE RIGHT BUILDING. IT DOESN'T LOOK LIKE THE PHOTO, THOUGH. THE ANGLE'S ALL WRONG.
THAT IS BECAUSE THE BROADCAST CAME FROM A HIGHER FLOOR.
WE'LL HAVE TO GO FLOOR TO FLOOR TO FIND THE RIGHT ONE.
LEAVE IT TO ME.
ZOINKS! MY BEST BUDDY T-TURNING INTO AN INVISIBLE ALIEN? I WISH J'ONN WOULD, LIKE, STOP DOING THAT!
ME, TOO.
IT CREEPS ME OUT.

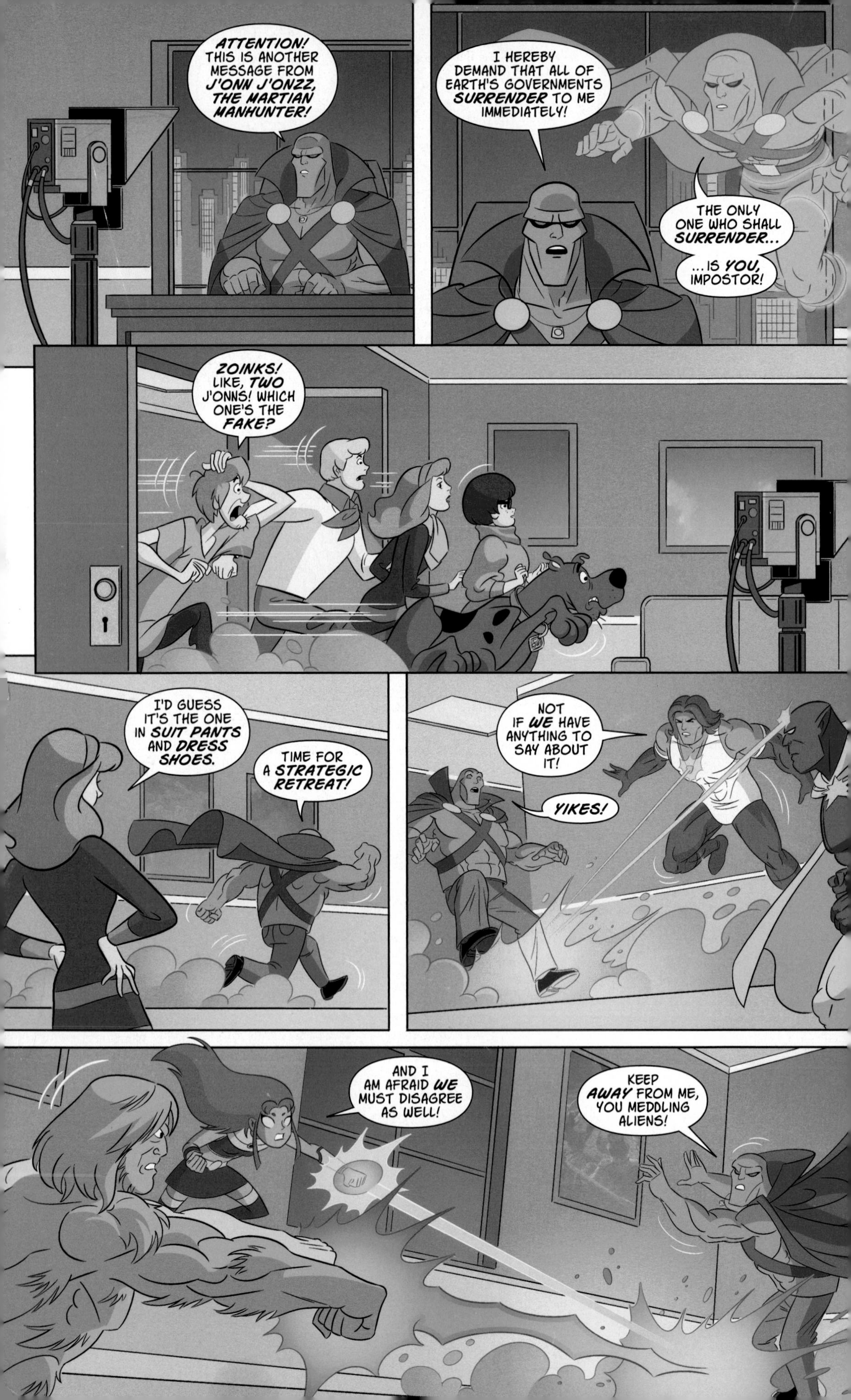
ATTENTION! THIS IS ANOTHER MESSAGE FROM J'ONN J'ONZZ, THE MARTIAN MANHUNTER!
I HEREBY DEMAND THAT ALL OF EARTH'S GOVERNMENTS SURRENDER TO ME IMMEDIATELY!
THE ONLY ONE WHO SHALL SURRENDER...
...IS YOU, IMPOSTOR!
ZOINKS! LIKE, TWO J'ONNS! WHICH ONE'S THE FAKE?
I'D GUESS IT'S THE ONE IN SUIT PANTS AND DRESS SHOES.
TIME FOR A STRATEGIC RETREAT!
NOT IF WE HAVE ANYTHING TO SAY ABOUT IT!
YIKES!
AND I AM AFRAID WE MUST DISAGREE AS WELL!
KEEP AWAY FROM ME, YOU MEDDLING ALIENS!

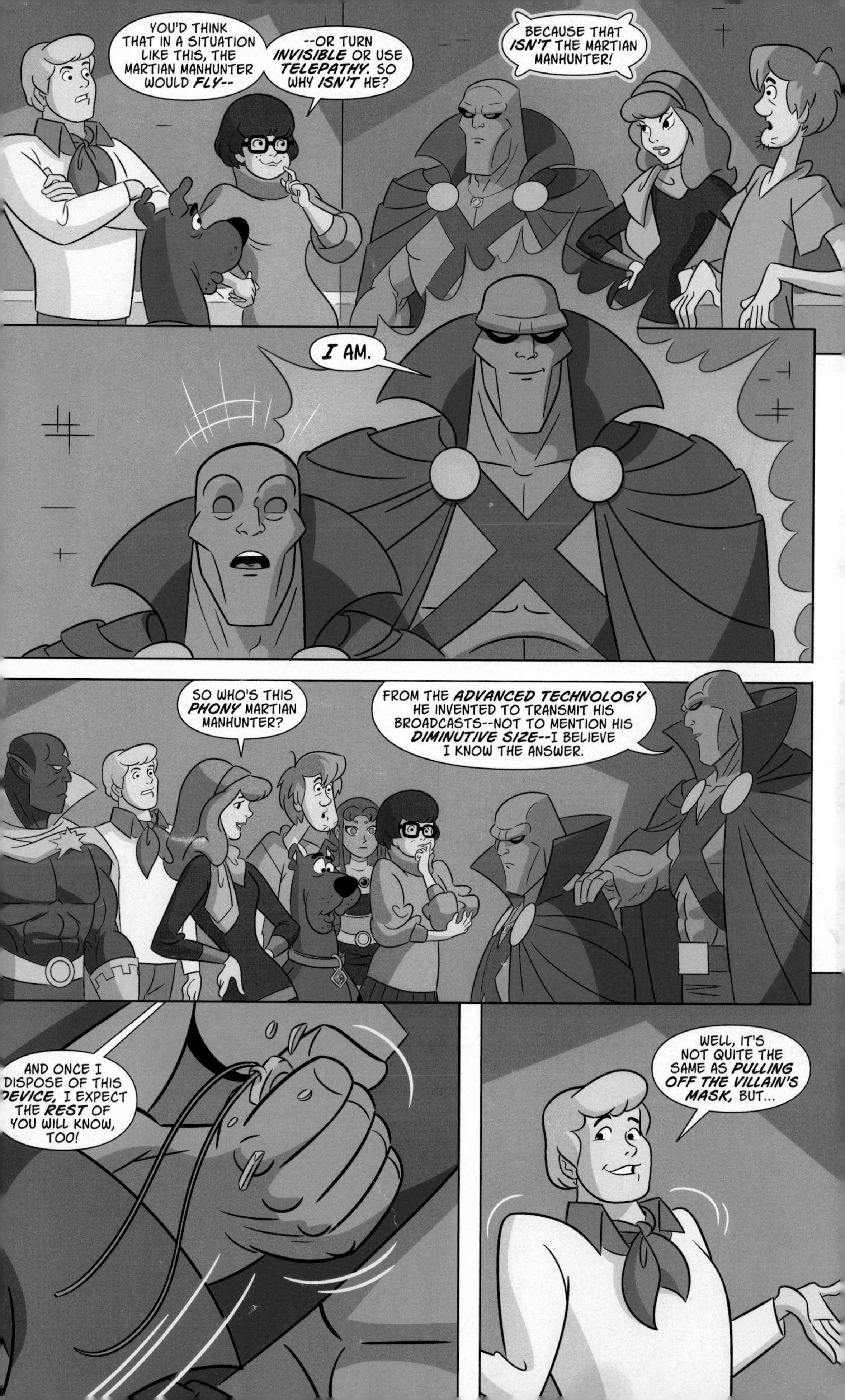

YOU'D THINK THAT IN A SITUATION LIKE THIS, THE MARTIAN MANHUNTER WOULD FLY--
--OR TURN INVISIBLE OR USE TELEPATHY. SO WHY ISN'T HE?
BECAUSE THAT ISN'T THE MARTIAN MANHUNTER!
I AM.
SO WHO'S THIS PHONY MARTIAN MANHUNTER?
FROM THE ADVANCED TECHNOLOGY HE INVENTED TO TRANSMIT HIS BROADCASTS--NOT TO MENTION HIS DIMINUTIVE SIZE--I BELIEVE I KNOW THE ANSWER.
AND ONCE I DISPOSE OF THIS DEVICE, I EXPECT THE REST OF YOU WILL KNOW, TOO!
WELL, IT'S NOT QUITE THE SAME AS PULLING OFF THE VILLAIN'S MASK, BUT...

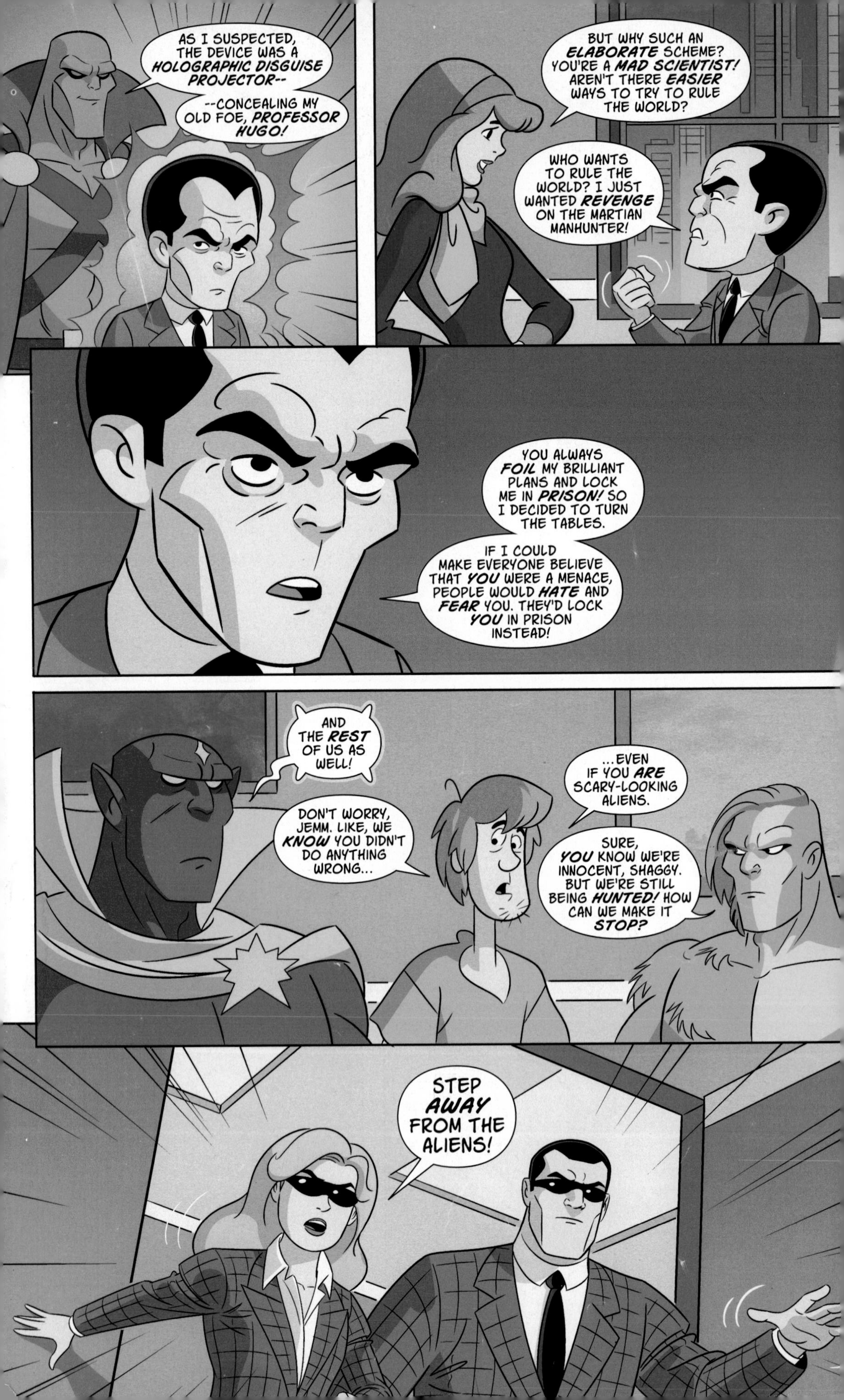
AS I SUSPECTED, THE DEVICE WAS A HOLOGRAPHIC DISGUISE PROJECTOR--
--CONCEALING MY OLD FOE, PROFESSOR HUGO!
BUT WHY SUCH AN ELABORATE SCHEME? YOU'RE A MAD SCIENTIST! AREN'T THERE EASIER WAYS TO TRY TO RULE THE WORLD?
WHO WANTS TO RULE THE WORLD? I JUST WANTED REVENGE ON THE MARTIAN MANHUNTER!
YOU ALWAYS FOIL MY BRILLIANT PLANS AND LOCK ME IN PRISON! SO I DECIDED TO TURN THE TABLES.
IF I COULD MAKE EVERYONE BELIEVE THAT YOU WERE A MENACE, PEOPLE WOULD HATE AND FEAR YOU. THEY'D LOCK YOU IN PRISON INSTEAD!
AND THE REST OF US AS WELL!
DON'T WORRY, JEMM. LIKE, WE KNOW YOU DIDN'T DO ANYTHING WRONG...
...EVEN IF YOU ARE SCARY-LOOKING ALIENS.
SURE, YOU KNOW WE'RE INNOCENT, SHAGGY. BUT WE'RE STILL BEING HUNTED! HOW CAN WE MAKE IT STOP?
STEP AWAY FROM THE ALIENS!

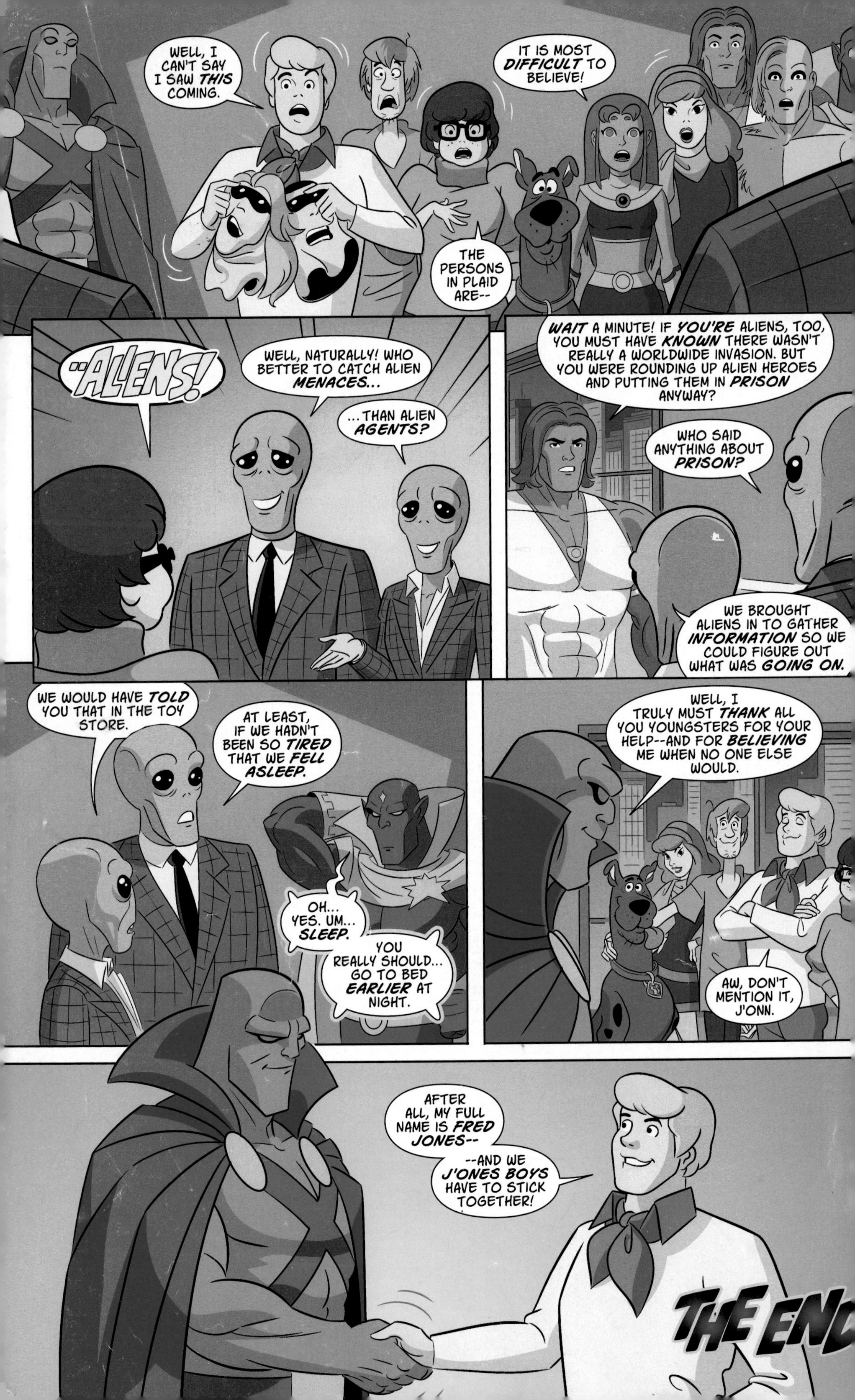
WELL, I CAN'T SAY I SAW THIS COMING.
IT IS MOST DIFFICULT TO BELIEVE!
THE PERSONS IN PLAID ARE--
--ALIENS!
WELL, NATURALLY! WHO BETTER TO CATCH ALIEN MENACES...
...THAN ALIEN AGENTS?
WAIT A MINUTE! IF YOU'RE ALIENS, TOO, YOU MUST HAVE KNOWN THERE WASN'T REALLY A WORLDWIDE INVASION. BUT YOU WERE ROUNDING UP ALIEN HEROES AND PUTTING THEM IN PRISON ANYWAY?
WHO SAID ANYTHING ABOUT PRISON?
WE BROUGHT ALIENS IN TO GATHER INFORMATION SO WE COULD FIGURE OUT WHAT WAS GOING ON.
WE WOULD HAVE TOLD YOU THAT IN THE TOY STORE.
AT LEAST, IF WE HADN'T BEEN SO TIRED THAT WE FELL ASLEEP.
OH... YES. UM... SLEEP.
YOU REALLY SHOULD... GO TO BED EARLIER AT NIGHT.
WELL, I TRULY MUST THANK ALL YOU YOUNGSTERS FOR YOUR HELP--AND FOR BELIEVING ME WHEN NO ONE ELSE WOULD.
AW, DON'T MENTION IT, J'ONN.
AFTER ALL, MY FULL NAME IS FRED JONES--
--AND WE J'ONES BOYS HAVE TO STICK TOGETHER!
THE END

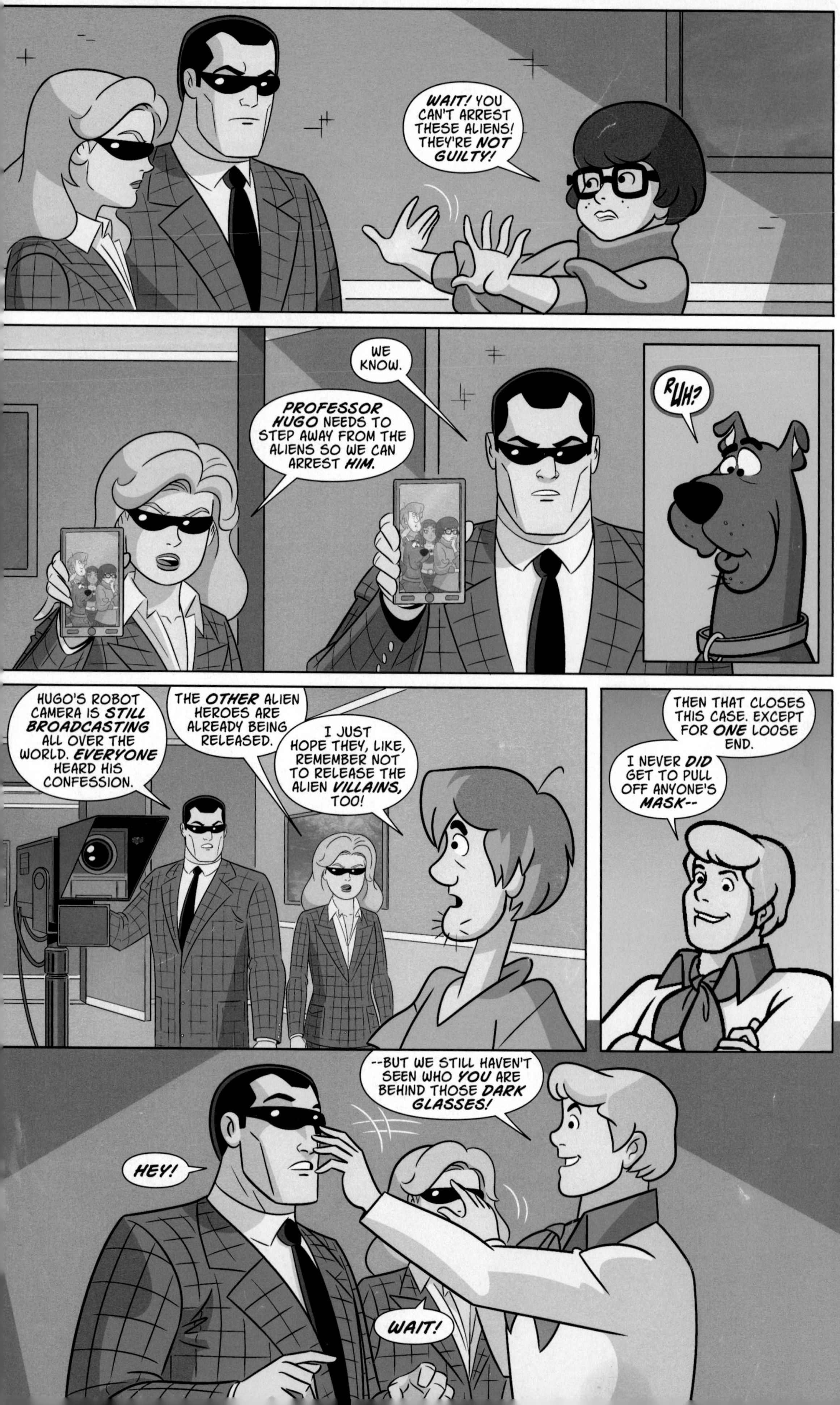
WAIT! YOU CAN'T ARREST THESE ALIENS! THEY'RE NOT GUILTY!
WE KNOW.
PROFESSOR HUGO NEEDS TO STEP AWAY FROM THE ALIENS SO WE CAN ARREST HIM.
RUH?
HUGO'S ROBOT CAMERA IS STILL BROADCASTING ALL OVER THE WORLD. EVERYONE HEARD HIS CONFESSION.
THE OTHER ALIEN HEROES ARE ALREADY BEING RELEASED.
I JUST HOPE THEY, LIKE, REMEMBER NOT TO RELEASE THE ALIEN VILLAINS, TOO!
THEN THAT CLOSES THIS CASE. EXCEPT FOR ONE LOOSE END.
I NEVER DID GET TO PULL OFF ANYONE'S MASK--
--BUT WE STILL HAVEN'T SEEN WHO YOU ARE BEHIND THOSE DARK GLASSES!
HEY!
WAIT!